EMPIRE'S RIFT

The Baedecker Invasion

A Takamo Universe Novel

STEVE RZASA

Kgruppe LLC, 2016, 2025

EMPIRE'S RIFT: THE
BAEDECKER INVASION

A Takamo Universe Novel

Copyright 2016, 2025 Kgruppe, LLC

ISBN 978-1-64709-014-2

Cover Design by Dmitry Borodin

Original Cover Artwork Image by BA Sparks

Randall Ritnour, Art Director

Published by
Takamo Universe, an imprint of
Kgruppe, LLC
Lincoln, Nebraska, USA
Takamo Universe Trade Paperback 2nd Edition April 2025

www.takamo.com

TAKAMO

What Is It?

TA'KA'MO (High Radnian, Radnia—Central continent from TAI (Universe) and KHA'MO (ebb and flow) 1. Gestalt, the wholeness of the universe. 2. History. 3. Conflict.

- VOL. 234, FILE 451 – SEPAL'S UNABRIDGED GALACTIC DICTIONARY

Takamo started as a massive multiplayer science fiction play-by-mail game in the early 1980s. It had a newsletter where players and staff published descriptions and stories about their interstellar empires. That generated spin off publications for fan fiction and stories rooted in Takamo lore. Over the years, the worldbuilding took on a life of its own and became a library of four decades of collected works .

In 2014, Kevin J. Anderson and Wordfire Press published the first Takamo novel, Empire's Rift, by Steve Rzasa. Takamo is now a science fiction imprint with over twenty titles by various authors, all based in the shared Takamo universe.

I like to say that Takamo is the ancient language of space. Any moment in the Takamo timeline is one part of the whole – a single point of light in a complex, limitless, gestalt universe. Takamo stories are set in a historical timeline spanning half a million years. They are penned by different authors in a shared universe with a collective destiny. This book is a part of that universe.

Want to know more? Visit www.takamo.com

THE ENCROACHING CONFLICT...

In the Senarias Spiral Arm lies a region beyond the Great Desert Rift called the Rimward Reaches. This vast area is where the great empires of the Imperial Union, led by the Naplian Empire, fought a series of wars against the Grand Alliance, led by the Audro-Dresch Empire, and the Briddarri Kingdom, for the possession of millions of star systems.

By the late 27th Century, the fighting had spilled over into the coreward territories of this region. A series of devastating Briddarri strikes on Imperial fuel reserves in the Eission star system forced the Naplians to invade the Terran Republic in 2678 to secure vital fuel resources. Their target was the Terran provincial capital at the Baedecker star system.

That region was quiet five years after the two brutal Consular Wars had introduced a new form of cybernetic soldier. The rebellious Northern Alliance had employed a force of cybernetic troopers developed through the use of volunteers who signed on to have their brains and nervous system surgically harvested and fitted to a human shaped cybernetic chassis. They were designated "Truppen" by the Northern Alliance. They were formidable adversaries and practically immortal. Unless the headpiece was compromised, a Truppen could continue indefinitely.

The Northern Alliance suffered its final defeat at the Baedecker star system, ending the Second Consular War. The victorious Terrans and their Reittian allies combed the killing fields of Baedecker Four and destroyed every Truppen head they could find. But they did not discover them all. Thousands of living casualties were left buried in forgotten trenches, sunken into muddy river bottoms, or lay unseen amongst the detritus of the battlefields.

Minds trapped in headpieces, they waited.

With the arrival of the Naplians, and the return of a Northern Alliance scion, Baedecker became the pivotal point in time for the galaxy. Its fourth planet, the exact middle point of destiny for countless species and empires.

The firestorm of war that engulfed the Estra galaxy began there.

PART ONE

CHAPTER ONE

Staging Sector 311-58

June 2765, Terran Calendar

Admiral Tir Ad'Andra Daviont stood before the broad oval of his ready room's viewport, watching the graceful, curved forms of the Naplian Fleet's III Corps cruise in close formation. Behind him, the holographic message from the Admiralty played a second time, flickering images lighting up the dim space.

"The Eission raid has potentially crippled us. Our fuel reserves are badly depleted. Without additional serjaum sources, half the expeditionary forces won't be able to continue our expansion throughout Estra, let alone return to the empire."

Call off the expansion? Daviont shook his head. He caught his reflection glowering in the viewport—a single large eye, on a long neck that topped a tall, lean body wearing the black and burnished orange of a Naplian Fleet officer. How could a true Ffawe and loyal servant of the Shoffets allow such a disaster? It was his duty to bring the rest of the galaxy into Naplia's embrace.

It was the duty of *all* Ffawe.

"There is a possible solution. Included with this transmission are the encrypted contents of a report filed by our Denic agents. They have uncovered the location of a serjaum source within Terran space. The III Corps is hereby tasked with subduing the target system and the fuel. Take heed. The Terrans are not as trustworthy as our Denic servants, nor are they as docile. They have more in common with the treacherous Briddarri than any other race. Your mission orders are clear. Do not fail. All hail their Glories, Bonate and Benaltep."

There was a soft click as the holoprojector shut down. "All hail," Daviont murmured.

"If by 'all hail' you mean 'ruinous novas!' then yes, I concur."

Daviont turned. The only other occupants of the ready room were Vice Admirals Gol Yi'Andra Hilder and Kiv Sa'Andra Bouchtok. Both wore the same uniforms as Daviont, lacking only the twin silver suns on either shoulder. Hilder had pale gray skin with a yellowish tinge, several shades lighter than Daviont and Bouchtok, and his iris an iridescent pearl. Bouchtok was a few centimeters shorter than both Daviont and Hilder, though his eye bore a similar shade of blue to Daviont's.

"Steady, Gol. I do not need your critique of imperial decisions. I need your assessment. Can we do this?"

Hilder exhaled a burst of air from his nostrils in a long sigh. He held up his hand, showing both fingers and its opposing thumb, and counted off. "One, we have a full squadron of battlecruisers in need of serious repair. Two, our fuel supplies range from middling to low. Can I guarantee we can get an entire flying column to our target and back? No. Which brings me to Three: I do not trust Denic spies, no matter how much our superiors do."

"Denics have proven useful in the current campaign," Bouchtok said.

"They are humans," Hilder said.

"They are sentient beings with the dual redeeming qualities of being very accurate in their intelligence gathering, and having an appearance similar to not just our Briddarri opponents. They can come and go from practically any human territory as they please." Bouchtok steeped his fingers before his face. "The wisdom of the Ascended Masters will guide us."

Hilder's eye rolled from left to right, the lid half-shut. Daviont had seen the Denics roll both their eyes, which he found disturbing. "Yes, fine, we can all sing the praises our glorious Masters at the prescribed time. Meanwhile, I will be content with staying alive."

"You did not answer, Gol," Daviont said.

"We can do it, Tir, but I cannot promise we will not pay a heavy price. After all, everyone thought Eission was secure, and left it at our backsides without a single eye on it as we spread out through the region. Look where that got us."

Daviont touched a panel on his desk. The holographic message transferred into his private files, and decrypted the intelligence provided by the Denic agents. An image of swirling stars burst from the projector.

"Our Corps is located here." Daviont indicated a flashing blue star ringed in gold. "The Denic report this star system as the objective."

Hilder shook his head with a slight bobbing motion. "Did you not read the scale? The estimated transit time is 1,072 days to this—Baedecker? I have never heard of it."

"A Terran backwater, most recently the site of one of their most brutal and final battles in their civil war. Five years have passed but the Denics who compiled this report indicate their defenses have not returned to their peak." Daviont glanced back at his desk, where a long list of data pooled in three clusters. "At most there are the equivalent of two squadrons of warships, six vessels apiece, plus attendant reserve vessels and fighters."

"There is a great difference one squadron could make."

"Surely not against the III Corps," Bouchtok said. "Tir, my Fourth Naval Division alone would be enough to handle them."

"Laudable sentiment, Kiv, but I think it best if the entire Corps were to share the glory." Daviont smiled. "Baedecker's sole redeeming quality is the massive reserves of serjaum that the Terrans have only just begun to tap."

"But the distance!" Hilder stood, encompassing the holographic stars with outstretched arms. "A long jump through Audrian space is bad enough, but crossing the Great Rift? We will be blessed by those Masters if we do not find ourselves riding down a black hole instead of a wormhole. We will be vulnerable to interception by the Audrian fleets—and who knows what the cursed Briddarri have lurking about. This is an operation that will take nearly three years, by the Denic's accounting. There have to be better options on this side of the Rift."

"There are not. You know this as well as I, Gol. Our scouts come up empty. The fuel depots that do have enough are still in possession of our enemies, and with our reserves as low as they are we cannot risk broadening the offensive against the Briddarri and their Grand alliance. This flying column will, as the Denics say, make or break us."

Hilder grumbled something in *ffawe-kresh* that Daviont knew would be the highest insult if spoken in the *ffawe-aul* technical dialect they had been using for this briefing.

"Vice Admiral Bouchtok and I hear your concerns, and we will take them into consideration. But this operation is ordered; it will be done. We will secure the serjaum fuel supplies at Baedecker for the glory of Naplia, so that our people may continue their reach throughout the Estra galaxy." Daviont put both his hands together, and held them out before him with his eye closed. The

Ffawe gesture of friendship mimicked the surrender of an armed opponent to the mercy of his captor; it signified total trust in the Naplian to whom it was offered.

Hilder sighed. Daviont opened his eye, and saw Hilder return the gesture. "Very well, Tir. I consent to the mission."

"We will keep your concerns from the official mission log, of course," Bouchtok said.

"So I may avoid investigation by the Druwei?" Hilder made the long snort of derision again. "My clan friends are ever too kind."

Daviont returned to his place by the window. "Prepare your forces, my clansmen. I will issue commands to the rest of III Corps; they will subdue the surrounding systems of the Baedecker system. Gol, attach the bombard *Napliae* to your division; Kiv, do likewise with *Solon*. I will choose four more bombards and four troopships to accompany my flagship."

Both Hilder and Bouchtok got to one knee and bowed. "Your will for our victory, Admiral."

Daviont returned the bow. "Your service is honored."

Once they had departed, he replaced the data circles on his desk with a diagram of *Narsa*, his flagship. The man-of-war, with its long, arcing main hull and sweeping jump sails extended, dwarfed even the battlecruisers of Hilder's 2nd Naval Division. They had more than enough firepower among 70 ships plus *Narsa* to subdue and hold a single Terran backwater.

Almost three Terran years. Daviont knew it would be a long slog. That long away from his family, his mates, his children and grandchildren, would stretch what was tolerable, even for a veteran of this great war. How many would reach their Age of Combat Rites without Daviont's guidance? How many would he see enter Ffawe service without his blessing? But that was a small price to pay for a species whose lifespan could easily top three centuries. There would be time enough to make up for long absences, when the conquest of Audrian space was accomplished.

More to the point, he knew the III Corps would be entirely on its own. What choice did they have? Without a new, secure source of fuel, the entire Naplian expansion would halt and have to withdraw from Audrian space, losing every gain they had made in this long campaign. It would be humiliating, and no amount of honors gathered in battle would save Daviont or his fellow admirals from summary execution. He doubted any of his clan or indebted pensioners would submit to substitutionary punishment to save Daviont from that end.

Yet.

Daviont inclined his eye to the stars and began the Litany of Request to the Ascended Masters, in hopes they would look upon his service to the empire and grant him victory.

He could leave nothing to chance.

***

Two and a Half Months Later

Admiral Sett San Ergen, commander of the Ninth Stellar Fleet, scowled at the reports flowing down three monitors arrayed on the bridge of his battleship, *Winter Scourge*. Ergen was balding, with graying black hair where it remained and a bushy moustache that hid almost his whole mouth. His uniform was the same slate gray as the rest of his crew, though with five gold braids on each shoulder and twin white cuffs on each sleeve, there'd be no mistaking him for an Engineering tech. Like all Briddarri, he looked human, except for the greenish tinge to his skin. Unlike most Briddarri, he was two meters tall and massed 135 kilos, making him tower over the rest.

The young lieutenant waiting before his station was quite a bit shorter, much more fit and trim. Ergen despised that.

"There's no mistaking this. They've sent an entire Corps?"

"Yes, sir," the lieutenant said. "We have confirmation from two pickets stationed along the Western Front in contested Audrian space: the III Corps, under Admiral Daviont, moved out seventy-six days ago. We've lost their exact location, but a scout ship spotted them near Castillo Prime before they jumped again."

Ergen didn't like that trajectory one bit. "What's Analysis say? They give any good reason the One-Eyes are headed for the Great Desert Rift?"

"No, sir, but we have a man following up on the Denic infiltrators among the Terrans."

"Everett Lind."

"Yes, Admiral."

"The man's a snake."

The lieutenant stayed prudently silent.

"Go on, then, what's the snake been whispering?"

The lieutenant handed over a scroll. It was a cylinder ten centimeters long, glowing blue, with a silver top-cap and black end-cap. Ergen snatched it away, and pressed the top-cap. The scroll unrolled into a sheet as long as his forearm, and when he touched the edge, it stiffened into a screen that spilled a new report. Still images of men among crowds, taken at a distance, glowed bright with captions indicating their activities.

"Denic operatives among the Terrans, sir. Lind isn't certain of their identities, yet, but he was able to decrypt a communique they slipped off Baedecker Four. Seems the Naplians have found themselves a new source of serjaum."

"Hmph. Eission made them desperate. Good." Ergen smiled. "Desperate means their leadership will make mistakes. Even Daviont's been known to slip up."

"Yes, sir."

Ergen read the report, and compared it with the data on Naplian fleet movements. "Right. What units do we have available for an intercept?"

"Ah…" The lieutenant consulted his own scroll. "The Sixth Fleet is spread along the front with the Dresch Kingdom, and down into Audrian space. Things have quieted down there—Analysis suspects it's due to the Eission success. But they're quite a distance away."

"Should hope so. Hmph. Sixth Fleet? That'd be Admiral Frid Fol Josimin. He'd never agree to anything so crazed. Anyone else?"

"No, sir. We are the closest to the Baedecker System."

Ergen grumbled. "We'll have to detach whatever ships we can scrounge up—can't be any more than a few squadrons, but that'll have to do. I'll inform the High Command of our plans. Have to let the Audrians in on it, too, I suppose, so they don't panic when we slough off some battleships from the front."

"Our plans, sir?"

"To muck up whatever the Naplians have going on, by the Galaxy!"

"What about the Terrans, sir?"

"They've sat this mess out for too long. Be that as it may, I'm not about to let the Naplians run roughshod over a bunch of humans who've barely picked themselves back up from a civil war. If we're lucky, we might pick up a new set of allies. If we're *extremely* lucky, we'll catch the One-Eyes with their lids shut. You follow?"

"Yes, sir!" The lieutenant snapped off a salute and hurried to the Comms station.

Ergen swiveled his chair, and swept his gaze around the dozen bridge consoles arrayed in a semi-circle. It'd be close, sending units from the Ninth. They might be able to get to Baedecker ahead of the Naplians. It was dozens of months away for them, but they were the nearest Briddarri units. The timing had to be precise.

Everything was made far too complex with the Naplians clocking in at more than 300 years old, for their maximum lifespans. Briddarri reached 100 on average, maybe 120, without extended measures.

Ergen drummed his fingers on his console. Even if they couldn't drive the One-Eyes away from a heap of serjaum, maybe they could come out with some other advantage. Like he'd told the lieutenant, the Terrans could be useful additions to the Grand Alliance.

He switched his third monitor over to the report from the battle at Aeshon-Brid. The casualty list was long.

They could use a change of luck.

CHAPTER TWO

Baedecker Four
May 2768, Terran Calendar

1st Lieutenant Taggart "Tag" Wester banked through a scudding row of cumulus clouds, shredding them with the wing-mounted engines of his fighter. Though the AF-32G "Raider" fighter-bomber was equally at home in the vacuum of space as it was in the atmosphere of a planet, using a pair of sublight ionic fusion engines, Tag was convinced she flew better with air streaming against her fuselage.

Engines roared as his craft dropped low over the broad Luran Plains, a desert plateau stretching for dozens of kilometers between the spire-studded capital city of Vossberg and the jagged gray peaks of the Koth mountains. It was as barren an expanse as any, devoid of all but the hardiest scrub plants and made all the more desolate by the detritus of the late Second Consular War. Craters gouged otherwise smooth hills. Battered remnants of ships and armor were manmade landforms half covered by dirt and sand.

Tag descended below a thousand meters. His fighter-bomber whipped up dust devils in its wake, scouring the ochre and sienna sands along with the deteriorating wreckage.

"I don't think that's what the wing commander had in mind when she assigned us refit testing, Tag." The voice echoing in his helmet's intercom belonged to Ichiro "Scrape" Sakawa, his radar intercept officer seated just behind him.

"Seriously? I remember something in her orders about 'stress tolerance.' Like this." Tag dropped the fighter-bomber with a suddenness that made his stomach lurch, and tipped her on her port wing. The plains below were a yellow and brown blur, interspersed with the shadows of bone dry gullies.

Proximity alerts flashed red and screeched throughout the cockpit. "I think we're good. That should do," Scrape said.

"Targeting sensors happy?"

"Of course. I've calibrated them three times since we left base."

Tag put the nose up and powered skyward at full thrust. There were few clouds, save for the one he'd just cut through; the rest of the view above was a rich blue with tinges of violet. Nothing like the home sky. "Three? You're a heck of a lot more efficient on this run."

"Not really, Tag, when you consider we've been out here half an hour on what was supposed to be a fifteen-minute test run."

Tag shook his head. "That's the problem with bureaucracies and the chain of command, Scrape. There's always somebody holding on to the other end of the chain. What's the last thing up on our checklist?"

"We dry-fired the bomb mounts and ran through the simulated missile launches. That just leaves the railguns."

Tag grinned. "I thought so. Line me up something nice to shatter."

"Hang on... here you go. There's a sandstone cairn, two klicks south by southeast, on that ridge you used to tear our belly paint off."

"Come on, it wasn't *that* close." A map of their immediate surroundings ghosted over the inside of Tag's helmet visor. The heads-up display showed the fighter-bomber as a green star at the center. Scrape's target rock formation was bracketed with a red diamond with a double outline.

"We'll let the maintenance techs back at the hangar decide that. Okay. Range is one point four klicks and closing. Railgun charge is green."

"Standby." In atmospheric flight mode, the Raider's primary controls were mounted on a simple joystick. Tag flipped the cover off the top, and poised his thumb over the red circle. Funny how over centuries of human diaspora from ancient Earth, some things about aerial combat had never changed. "Firing."

The railgun rattled the Raider, sending a shimmy through its starboard side that Tag, through countless hours of practice, compensated. White flashes of light erupted from the starboard fuselage, just under the canard wings on the nose cone. The electromagnets lining the barrel of the railgun accelerated tungsten projectiles coated with artificial diamond at hypervelocity. Tag's shots pummeled the stone cairn. It exploded a ball of dust and rock. Tag swept by, and the Raider's exhaust blew the cloud of debris left over onto the wind.

Tag whooped and spun the Raider twice before steadying onto an eastward course. The Baedecker suns, one a small orange-yellow disc and the other a red circle half its size, shone brilliant above, and the Raider's green and gray fuselage gleamed in the light.

"Target eliminated," Scrape said.

"That's it? We won!"

"Hardly a fair fight, Tag."

"Doesn't matter to me if it's fair. If we win, it's all good. You think we beat the rebels five years ago by fighting fair? We fought better. That's it."

"I'll leave that for the historians." An incessant beep echoed in the cockpit. "Meantime, Lieutenant, there's an urgent signal from Base. Wing Commander Dillon."

Tag groaned.

"You really think she'd let us get this far off?"

"Being the governor's son has to have some perks." Tag switched over to receive the signal and put a fake cheer into his voice. "Deedee! Is there a problem, Commander?"

"The problem, Wester, is that the only thing keeping me from slapping you in restraints and turning you over to the MPs is your training scores." Diana "Deedee" Dillon sounded as if she'd gargled with the rock shards Tag had just blown off the Luran Plains. "Get back to base on the double. You're way outside our planetside operational range and you know it."

"Yes, Ma'am, but you see, my dear sister's getting married soon, and she'd be absolutely heartbroken if I didn't swing by for a visit." Tag had already lined up the Raider on a new course that took it over the Iwa Valley to the east, and curved sharply over the mountain peaks back toward the only spot of color between there and Vossberg—the Baedecker governor's compound. From his current position it was a tiny patch of brilliant green speckled with whites. Beyond that, another 20 klicks out, was Vossberg City itself.

"Wester! Get your carcass back here before I pull you from the flight roster!"

"Relax, Deedee. My duty shift is up in three hours. I'll touch down on the tarmac with whole seconds to spare, I promise." Tag killed the signal, cutting of a screech of protest from Dillon.

Scrape chuckled. "Got to say, I wouldn't mind being able to fly around wherever and whenever I wanted without fear of repercussions."

"Oh, there'll be repercussions. Deedee will add another tart reprimand to my profile, and send Fighter Command a copy, which will no doubt get to Father." Tag glanced out the canopy. Far below, the Guralve River wound through the Koth Mountains like a cobalt snake. Pale green hills formed a boundary between the slate peaks and the twisting water. Other shapes, too—tiny black and white ones. Possibly machinery. The monks, no doubt, with their fanatical excavations. He shifted the Raider's course and shed altitude.

"Oh, no. You leave them be this time."

Tag made a face but heeded the advice of his RIO. The Raider climbed up and turned back toward the plains. "What's the deal with them, anyway? You deny a guy his fun buzzing the crazy monks, the least you can do is back it up."

"The Aparatics have never done anyone harm," Scrape said. "Their teachings are honorable—who else would vouch for the sanctity of all life? So sue me if I admire their ethic. Just let them be. Whatever they hope to find in their excavations, it's for the benefit of all."

"Okay, if you say so. I've got a better final target in mind anyway." He lined up the nose of the Raider with the governor's compound, still 15 klicks out on the horizon.

Scrape magnified the compound with the targeting sensors, giving Tag an exquisite 3-D render of a huge octagon packed full of artificial streams flowing from a central oasis, clusters of dark green leafed bole trees, and emerald gardens blossoming with a rainbow's worth of flower colors. "You're a brave son. And a pain."

"I am indeed both. Let's make sure the good governor of Baedecker is awake." Tag poured on the speed, afterburners blazing. His only regret was not being able to see his father's outrage when he blew the leaves off every one of those stupid trees at Mach 3.

As it was, he managed to defoliate a half dozen bole trees. A pair of groundskeepers shouted skyward, tiny figures shaking microscopic fists, flanked by trimming robots that looked like small metallic samurai wielding blades.

***

Tag brought the Raider in for a swift landing at the quik-crete circle farthest from the gubernatorial mansion, and nearest the main gate. By the time he popped the canopy and climbed out, a trio of Colonial Police sprinted over. Each one wore black body armor and helmets with opaque visors that concealed their identities. They also lugged M36 rifles, standard issue for the Colonial Defense Forces and its attendant police branch.

Their formidable appearance would cow any sane civilian, but Tag, fully outfitted in the white flight suit with black trim of the Astro Enforcement Section, wasn't the least bit impressed. He doffed his helmet and grinned. "'Morning, boys. First Lieutenant Taggart Wester, AES Seventh Wing, Bronze Squadron. Don't tell me Father sent you over as an escort for his youngest."

"Sir, you are not authorized to land that craft here." The cop in front had a deep voice that buzzed through his face mask. "You need to return to your craft and depart immediately."

Tag glanced back at Scrape. His RIO watched, face impassive, dark eyed and olive skinned, with raven hair cropped close to his scalp. "Sorry, I think you're misinformed. We're AES, and as such rank a step or two above you all in the CDF chain of command. Make that three steps, right? Plus, Father doesn't like to keep guests waiting. So why don't you hose down the Raider for me —she's got a fair amount of dust caked around the pylons."

Tag sauntered off the tarmac onto the broad walkway made of quartz that bisected the compound. Shrubs lined the walk, and the boles cast comfortable shadows from the glare of the morning sun.

"I don't think they enjoyed you pulling rank," Scrape said.

"They're not supposed to. But I did."

"What do you think they're telling their supervisors?"

"Really couldn't care less." He nudged Scrape. "Check that out. Father has high priority guests."

Two more shuttles were parked at the pad opposite theirs, partially obscured by trees. It was long, and flat, with a beveled nose. One was of civilian design, painted pearly white. The five blue stripes and pale blue sphere of the Baedecker colonial flag were painted on one flank, right under silver registry numbers printed on a black bar. Six more police in body armor patrolled nearby.

The other shuttle was blocky, squat, and bulging with four railgun emplacements. Its fuselage was a digital camouflage pattern of browns, and the Colonial Defense Force emblem of a moon rising over a planet's horizon with six spheres interspersed. Four CDF soldiers stood at the points of the compass, ignoring the wandering of their police counterparts. They lugged considerably greater firepower: RG-18 Saar railguns, the Overwatch man-portable series.

"Well. Busy indeed. That white ship's an ExoTerse. Maybe a Mod Six or Seven? They aren't cheap," Scrape said.

"Someone from the Legislature."

"Really?"

Tag snorted. "Who else on Baedecker has enough money to afford one? Between that and the assault shuttle, I'd say Father's playing host to a CDF officer, too. Let's go see what's spinning."

"Ah, I don't think we can barge into your father's office."

"I think we can. And barge is such a harsh word. I prefer, surprise my Father with a charming presence and likely get the download on whatever he's up to."

Halfway up the walk they rounded the main fountain, a huge marble and metal edifice spraying water up in three columns from a statue of a Terran soldier. Tag smirked. What was it about his father's vanity that insisted on carving his likeness into the soldier's face? It was difficult to spot unless, of course, you were a Wester. The soldier's boot stood atop the ruined form of a Truppen cybernetic warrior, the bent body skillfully recreated in marble.

Let them keep their war. Tag wanted to fly, and if he had to keep up on his weaponry skills to occasionally chase pirates, so be it.

They were passing by a slew of white stone outbuildings used both as private residences and storage units, when a young woman with auburn hair came running out from a set of benches set behind the shrubs. "Tag! What a great surprise!"

"Marney!" Tag grabbed her and spun her around. She hugged him about the neck. Her laughter bubbled up, contagious to the point that Tag joined her.

"It's been months! Are you so busy with the glamorous life of a space pilot that you can no longer visit your best sister?" She smiled at him. Marney looked just like Mother when she smiled—well, except for the freckles, which she inherited from father. The blue eyes were the same brilliant shade as Tag's, but his hair was a dark brown, far less radiant than hers. She had on an elegant blue dress with floral patterns embroidered up one side and a matching vest over top of a silken, cream-colored blouse.

"Not at all! I missed you and signaled you notes every

week."

"I got them, of course, and treasured them."

"Yours were lovely. My fellow aviators think—scratch that, *know*—I'm related to the most gorgeous woman on all the Baedecker worlds."

The tips of Marney's ears went crimson, and a flush spread up into his neck. She poked Tag in the side. "You're teasing."

"Not at all." He put an arm around Scrape's shoulders. "My RIO, 2nd Lieutenant Ichiro Sakawa, can verify."

"It's nice to meet you, Lieutenant."

Scrape bowed at the waist, and kissed the knuckles of Marney's left hand. "Miss Wester. It is an honor to finally meet you in person. Tag did not exaggerate."

She giggled. "Oh, you two. Come on, now. Father's in a meeting. I'll take you to get some refreshments."

"Negative, my lady. I've got to drop in on the old man."

"I wouldn't. He's got General Wood and Speaker Zhatkowskii arguing something."

Well now. The head of CDF on Baedecker Four and the Speaker of the Colonial Legislature? "That *is* interesting."

The whine of ion engines announced the arrival of yet another craft, this one a simple, wedge-shaped civilian model. Marney's smile broadened. "Ah, the caterers! Sorry, Tag, you can have someone on the staff get you drinks, can't you? Between the caterers and the florists, it will be a miracle if I get in to my dress before the wedding ceremony."

"You'll lock them all down faster than a tractor beam set on max." Tag kissed her on the cheek. "Go have fun. We'll get dinner later, alright? You and your Navy fiancé."

He hurried off, Scrape hot on his heels. "What do you think?"

"I think, Tag, that you're only partially interested in what the general and the Secretary have to say."

"Father's likely to bore me with the details anyway. I'm skipping a step is all."

"Tag? Be careful!" Marney's voice echoed from farther down the walk. "You know how Father hates being interrupted."

Tag smothered a grin. He did indeed.

***

The mansion was a sprawling, three story structure done

in white stone, with several rooms both paneled and floored in polished planks of bole wood. The entry hall was a wide avenue lined with potted roses and red carpets that matched the shade of the petals. It led up to a towering staircase through the dead center of the mansion, stopping at a landing in front of a tall picture window that offered a breathtaking view of the Luran Plains and the distant snowpack-topped Koth Mountains.

Scrape had a dazed appearance, as if he'd had a round too many at the officer's club the night before. "Your house is, ah, big."

"This isn't my house. It's the Baedecker governor's official residence." Tag turned away from the opulence, aiming instead for a side door to the left. "My home's the barracks at Voss Flats Base."

Through the door was an anteroom, with brass coat hooks tucked in one corner and an antique end table on the other side. The door before them was shut. Muffled voices came from the other side. Tag grinned. Jackpot.

"—man's a traitor. Don't expect me to think anything less."

"General, he was on the wrong side of the Consular War. But he's as loyal now to the Terran government as my own daughter."

"Selva's a hereditary consul of the Northern Alliance! Don't matter a micrometeorite what he says he's doin' now. He's got the blood of our enemies in his veins and the blood of our fallen men on his hands!"

"Hold on, you know he never fought in the war. Blast it all, Troy, we're here to discuss security for my daughter's wedding, not Elden Selva!"

Tag sucked in a breath. Elden Selva? The man was off serving the regional Northern Alliance government underneath Terran oversight. What did that have to do with Marney's wedding? They'd pined for each other since—well, forever—but they weren't lovesick teens anymore.

"What's wrong?" Scrape whispered.

Tag shushed him. He squared his shoulders and opened the door.

Father's study was a sedate, calming place, with bore wood floors and white stone walls. Twin shelves bordered the room, one stocked full of old, worn books and the other bearing relics from the ancient conflict with Mars. A desk of glass and black metal was centered below a long window that looked out into the fruit gardens, where ripe pears hung from rows of trees.

Governor Antiny Wester sat in a cluster of three brown leather chairs, smoking a cigar. He was thickset, with a gut that bulged against the perfectly tailored lines of a charcoal gray suit. His hair was an auburn shade much lighter than Marney's, what little there was left of his, and his moustache was precisely trimmed. Bright green eyes narrowed as they locked onto the two targets entering the private meeting. "Taggart. I thought I heard you make an entrance."

"Father." Tag strolled to the mini bar beneath the row of relics. He popped the lid from a decanter and sniffed. "Crown & Scepter? You brought out the best rum for your guests."

Father frowned. "Gentlemen, my son, Taggart Wester. He's a lieutenant with AES. This is his associate, Lieutenant Sakawa. Fighter jocks."

The two men seated around Father appeared to Tag as polar opposites. Lieutenant General Troy Jarvis Wood was tall, lean, and dressed in rumpled fatigues of the same camouflaged pattern as the assault shuttle parked outside. His black boots were sheathed in dust and dirt. When he stood, Tag and Scrape instantly saluted.

"At ease, boys." Wood smiled. His skin was a dark toffee, and his hair was thick and black, save where it had turned white above his ears. "Tag Wester, right? Heard some of the boys in Recon grousing about you. Sounds like you played chicken with a training flight of hoppers out of Weyland Bay way down south last month."

"Yes, sir. We were testing the acquisition rate for our targeting sensors. I thought we could use some slow contacts for practice."

"Worked well enough. Give DeeDee my regards, if she doesn't lock you in the brig first."

"So you're familiar with General Wood." Father indicated the man on his right. "This is
Andrej Zhatkowskii, Speaker of the Colonial Legislature."

"And the only man to put up with the Governor's demands. Of which I have heard many." Zhatkowskii was short, stocky, and pale-skinned. Hazel eyes watched Tag with the intensity of an eagle on the hunt. He had curly black hair and a thick beard and moustache that obscured his mouth even when he spoke, which was in a deep, sonorous mumble. "You men are interrupting a private meeting."

"Are we? Thought it was about Marney's wedding security." Tag poured a half glass of Crown & Scepter. "Scrape?"

"No thank you." Poor Scrape stood as far away from the general as he could, seeming much more in awe by the six-pointed star and crossed railgun insignia of Wood's rank.

"Suit yourself." Tag savored the burn in his throat and the sweet, smooth flavor. "So, Father—Marney is safe, I take it?"

"Of course. General Wood himself will be here, and I'll have enough police in and around the compound that a man won't be able to sneeze without having the DNA tested."

"I'll be glad to see it."

"You are coming, aren't you?" Father raised an eyebrow. "Assuming you're not on report for whatever this is."

"This?"

"Your little flyover stunt, and unauthorized landing."

Tag shrugged. "I got my invitation, and Marney has the RSVP. As I'm sure you already know. So tell me, will I get to see Elden Selva again?"

Father's lips pinched together. When he spoke again, it was through his teeth. "Spying outside my door?"

"Soundproof your doors if it's that big a security concern." Tag downed the rest of his rum.

"Elden Selva is coming to Baedecker Four. His transport is due in later today. He's a member of the Northern Alliance Assembly and is assigned the task of retrieving identity tags from the Battle of Luran Plains."

"Don't believe a word of it," Wood grumbled. "I don't care what the Terran Graves Department says: Selva's a consul and we can't trust him."

"He's coming here as our guest, and as someone whom my family has always respected," Father said firmly. "I'll not treat him as a criminal."

"The Reittians will not be pleased when they hear of it," Zhatkowskii said. "Is no secret that they made Selva's family disappear into their gulags after the war."

"Gotta love allies like those," Tag said.

"The Reittians were critical supporters of the Terran government against the consular rebels," Father snapped. "And with respect, Mr. Speaker, is isn't a Reittian world anymore. It was ceded to our control at the end of the war."

"Tell that to the Reittians." Zhatkowskii sipped from his own glass of rum.

"They can't possibly want Baedecker back," Scrape said. "They gave it up because they said it had no strategic value. So say the political journals. Why change that?"

Father and Zhatkowskii glanced down at their laps. Wood rubbed at the back of the neck. "Geological surveys turned up some interesting finds. They reported to the Legislature last month that there may be serjaum deposits in the system."

Scrape's eyes widened.

"Serjaum? Here?" Tag wanted another drink to help him digest that bit of news, but he had to fly back to base.

"Definitely on Baedecker 2, and possibly on 3." Father tapped his cigar against the tray. Ashes rained down, and smoke swirled. "But this is classified, Taggart. You two keep it close. We don't know if the Reittians suspect, but they've definitely made inquiries about Elden. In fact, I have some diplomats on my agenda for tomorrow—in the midst of wrangling the wedding plans."

"Don't fuss about it," Wood said. "We've got the wedding security under control. Screw the Reittians. Selva's no true Terran, but I'm sure not advocating we turn him over to be tortured. Locked up, sure. But you can't trust a Reittian."

Father nodded. "My sentiments exactly. Taggart, if you wouldn't mind, I'd like to have you and Lieutenant Sakawa meet with Elden when he arrives."

"Us?" Tag frowned. "Surely you've got cops for that."

"I do, but word is the Reittians may have agents already here, preparing to take Elden when he arrives. They'd spot police a kilometer away. You and your friend have a more—relaxed approach that should throw them off."

"The Reittian presence is confirmed," Zhatkowskii said. "Intelligence knows of at least five men and women on Baedecker 4 under their employ. It is possible they have some of their own people, too, but only a close-up Bioscan would reveal them."

"There, you see?" Father smiled, a taut expression.

Tag didn't return the friendly gesture. "I'm not your errand boy, Father. Find someone else."

Father rose. He was a few centimeters shorter than Tag, but his commanding presence made Tag instinctively stiffen. "I'll see to it you comply. If you don't have anything else for me, you should leave."

Tag sneered. It was as if the man were just another commanding officer, albeit one lacking respect. "Mother would enjoy our family interludes, wouldn't she?"

"Don't you ever speak of her, not in my presence." Father stabbed his cigar. "Leave."

Tag saluted General Wood. "Sir." He nodded to Zhatkowskii. Scrape already had the door open.

Out in the main hall, Scrape cleared his throat. "I suppose

we'll have to report your father's request to Commander Dillon."

"We won't have to," Tag said. "If it's as big a deal as he makes it out, DeeDee will get a signal from him before we're even airborne."

"Then we'll be off flight duty for a while." Scrape shook his head. "Sometimes I wonder why I don't transfer out to a different unit than stay on your six."

"Because then your service record wouldn't have nearly as many commendations."

"Offset by the reprimands."

Tag smirked. "Reittians. Elden Selva. The man may be a tyrant and have a heart of ice, but Father's never dull."

***

Abbot Damal Jeopar shielded his eyes against the sun. Even with his long-brimmed hat, it near-blinded him. No doubt his ancestors from the deep sands of the Saudi peninsula on ancient Earth would be amused at his discomfort.

Jeopar wore the tan cloak over white robe of the Hirrenhausen Monastery, adorned with blood-red stripes on either shoulder that denoted him as the head abbot. He sat on a grassy hillock, overlooking the Guralve River. A pair of all-terrain transport trucks, each one with six wheels, were parked in the midst of the dirt track below. A dozen monks were spread out along both sides of the track, some holding scanners that projected holograms of whatever objects they found beneath the surface. Most were involved with the grunt work of digging.

"Do you know that the Aparatic Church believes even the souls of Truppen are welcome to the gates of Heaven?" Jeopar said to the man standing behind him. "It is a matter of faith. Those who believe and accept are forgiven. Why then cannot a Truppen's cerebral matrix do likewise? There is, of course, considerable debate as to whether or not the Truppen have a soul."

The man said nothing in reply. Jeopar listened to the sparrows tweet as they zoomed by, banking hard as the fighter-bomber he'd seen patrolling the skies. He felt the grass and dirt between his fingers, and smelled the pine sap redolent in the forests clinging to the mountain slopes. How did this man perceive those things?

"Erich, this is not a test. I merely wanted your opinion."

"It isn't for me to say, Abbot." Erich's voice was flat, with little intonation. "I believe, of course, but how do I know it's real? How do I know it isn't just programmed in?"

"There's more than just your memories and mind functions that make you human, Erich."

He sat beside Jeopar. Erich's skin was a uniform khaki hue, without blemish. Brown eyes were perfect. Not a strand of black hair was out of place. When he stared at Jeopar, he blinked once every ten seconds, precisely. "I'm not human, Abbot. Can't even tell you when I last was. I spent forty years as a Truppen warrior, and the past year in an android body. I've broken my oath. Might as well be a dead man."

"Nonsense. You have new life—both for the body and the soul. What better gift can we bring to your brothers?"

"I hope they accept it like I did."

"They will. Think of how many we have helped already. How many have been saved."

"They've only been gifted a cybernetic Purgatory. Their headpieces are active, but they're dormant—waiting for their Truppen forms." Erich pinched his ersatz flesh. "This? To them it's an abomination. I can't be revealed to them."

"You don't have to. You can lead a new life." Jeopar put his hand on Erich's shoulder. "Let me tell them of our success, when the time is right."

"If it ever is right."

A shout from below drew Jeopar's attention. A pair of young monks in brown robes wrested something from the ground. One of them handed the object, which from a distance appeared to be nothing more than a rock, to Abbot Sissok, a younger man with blond hair and a thin beard. He hurried up the hill. "Abbot Jeopar! We have found another."

Jeopar and Erich met the man halfway up the hill. Jeopar stretched out his hands.

"Beautiful," Jeopar murmured as he brushed dirt away. Silver shone beneath. "Such an elegant design, and yet for all its technical ingenuity, the real miracle is that a soul still resides inside."

He finished cleaning off the encrusted soil. The sharp-edged, armored visage of a Truppen cybernetic warrior stared back, impassive. The optical ports were a flat, smoky gray.

Erich reached behind the armor, toward the bottom of the neck. He poked his fingers between severed data connectors and power couplings. "Should be... right... there."

Something clicked. At first, nothing happened, and Jeopar wondered if, as in several dozen instances, this one had been left hidden too long.

Then a dull red glow appeared, deep inside the optical ports.

"He's alive. I'll catalog this as five hundred eighty-nine." Erich handed the headpiece back to Abbot Sissok. "Put it in the storage units."

"Of course."

With Sissok gone, Jeopar patted Erich's shoulder again. "Thank the Lord. Another for the restored host of multitudes."

Erich nodded. "Here's hoping the Northern Alliance is just as happy to see them."

CHAPTER THREE

Elden Selva sat by the large viewport in his cabin aboard the diplomatic transport Holland, watching with mild interest as Baedecker Starport blocked the stars. At four kilometers in length and almost a kilometer across its broadest diameter, the starport was a bullet-shaped station with dozens of small craft swarming about it. Lights gleamed against a pale gray hull. Holland slowed, awaiting a pair of three-engine tugs that scooted in from port side, tiny black spots on the blue and brown sphere of Baedecker Four.

"Don't look so dour, Eldi," said Andan Natour. "It isn't every day you show up to the place of our defeat as an invited guest."

"I'd hardly call my trip here invited, Nat." Elden swiveled his chair. The cabin's sitting area had four seats upholstered with blue and brown fabric arranged around a table of black metal tubing with a clear polymer top. There was a hatch ahead of them that led to a shared restroom and beyond that, four bunks. A second hatch, to the right, opened into the main passenger corridor of Holland.

Natour sat beside him, lean and brown-skinned, nose as sharp as a blade and eyes a brilliant blue. His hair was an unruly mop of black curls, cut short. Elden thought of him as his opposite —thin where Elden was broad-shouldered, dark where he was pale. With blond hair and gray eyes, there was no mistaking the two.

Both men wore navy blue trousers and brown jackets, befitting their status as representatives of the Northern Alliance government. Legitimate diplomats.

Something Elden could use to his advantage.

"Be at peace, Eldi. It's simple enough."

"Simple? We're here to collect the ID tags of our fallen troops. Terra is sullen enough about that. Can you imagine what they'd do if they found out we were taking Truppen headpieces—

still active, if the reports are correct—out with us?"

"Be glad it's Terra and not the Reittians. The devil you know and all that."

Elden shook his head. "Let's not invoke the name of everybody's favorite fascists. If the Reittians find out I'm here, they'll have me off to the gulags faster than you can order a new suit. And if I'm really lucky, they'll shoot me on sight."

Natour sighed. "Always the pessimist. Look. This mission is something we can handle."

"I've got no doubt of that."

"Then why the long face? You couldn't look worse if the captain told you we'd miscalculated a jump and were headed down the event horizon of a black hole!"

"It has nothing to do with the mission, I suppose." Elden opened his scroll and immersed himself in the encoded reports from the monks. Monks. When he'd taken on this task, he'd never guessed he'd be paired with reclusive religious types.

"Ah, you don't want to talk about it." Natour smiled. "I know what that means."

"It means, Nat, that you should shut up."

"It means, Consul, that this is about *her*."

He'd done it. Leave it to his best friend since the two were shorter than their mother's waists to pinpoint the problem with all the subtlety of a Reittian bomber raid. "I think you misunderstood 'shut up.'"

"Eldi, she's getting married. To a Terran war hero. From the war your family lost."

Elden said nothing. He swiped through the report. Hundreds of them. Supposedly reactivated. The notion accelerated his heartrate. Even at battalion strength, Truppen were a formidable force. Especially when no one else had the guts to field cyborgs these days.

Natour punched his shoulder.

"What was that for?"

"Stop locking down. Spill it. You're still in love with Marney Wester."

"So what if I am?" Elden snapped. "It shouldn't be a surprise—least of all to you. We had our lives tied together, Marney and I. She wanted to get married, and we had our parents' blessings. Then the war—it ruined everything. Cost me my Marney, my family, my father. All I have left is what he gave me: the title of consul."

"Hence the importance of our mission, I get that. But you

have to put her and the Westers out of your mind. Focus on our goal."

"I am. With the headpieces in our possession, and an army of reanimated Truppen, we'll have the seeds of a military force that the Terrans can't stop." Elden sneered. "They're soft, Nat. They've cut back shipbuilding and trimmed their recruiting for the past five years. Terra's relying too much on its alliance with the Reittians. That makes it the perfect time for us to strike."

The hatch chime warbled. Elden deactivated the scroll and pocketed it inside his suit. Even if he were searched by authorities, they'd find its memory wiped clean the instant someone other than Elden or Natour touched it. "Come in."

Franklin Goetz entered. There was no mistaking him for a diplomat, even though he wore the same jacket and pants. His shirt was black on top with a gray torso, unlike the well-tailored formal shirts of eggshell white Elden and Natour had on. He was also a hand taller than both men, and built more like a Spec Ops soldier than a civil servant. His hair was red, cropped neatly, and he had hazel eyes that flicked side to side, as if assessing the cabin for the first time.

"We really should teach Goetz the secret knock," Natour said.

"Not funny, sir." Goetz's every word was a quiet song, far from what Elden had expected the first time he'd agreed to bring along members of the Northern Alliance's euphemistically named Interventions Group.

"You have a report for us?" Natour asked.

"No signs of monitoring. No one aboard we know of who's in league with the Reittians. Everyone's backgrounds check out."

"They likely are aware of our departure," Elden said.

"Yes, sir, but there's no one aboard ship to worry over. I've got two men keeping their eyes on our luggage and cargo."

The scanners. Elden disliked carrying specialized equipment among their personal belongings, but it was necessary to get past Orbital Customs. The scanners were marked as being manufactured by a distant company that specialized in archaeological digs—when in fact they were IG's own design, mimicking the output of an archaeological scanning unit. IG promised they'd find Truppen headpieces without fail, hiding their true nature from even the most zealous Customs officers.

"You see? Goetz and IG have things well in hand." Natour gestured at the starport. "We'll catch our shuttle to Vossberg

Terminal from here and meet up with our monastic contact—Erich somebody."

"Erich Cantor." Goetz opened his jacket and slid out a scroll. Elden took note of the Ubinth Standard DK-40 9 mm pistol tucked in a shoulder holster just visible for a second. As diplomats with the trusted Northern Alliance, none of Elden's men would have weapons removed. Security precautions were the norm for all Terran government officials.

Elden had to remind himself he bore that label, and "consul" was his hidden birthright.

"The man's background is hazy. Don't know much about him before he showed up among the Aparatics a year or so ago." Goetz showed them the 3-D image of a pale man with bland expression. "But the abbots swear by him."

"I think that preferable than swearing by God," Elden said. "Make sure we're cleared through Customs, Goetz. I don't want any complications."

"Sir." Goetz saluted—right hand pressed quickly to the inside of his left elbow, first and middle finger extended with pinky, thumb and ring finger folded back. The sign of the Consuls, done only in private.

Elden scowled. Even a gesture of solidarity banned. Such were the consequences of losing a war.

***

"Yanked from the flight roster?" Tag restrained his voice as best he could. What he really wanted was to kick over the chair before him.

But since the chair faced the desk of Wing Commander Diana "DeeDee" Dillon, he figured his leg's safety would be forfeit if he did.

Dillon was in her mid-forties, and shorter than both Tag and Scrape by a quarter of a meter. That didn't matter to Tag, who regarded his superior officer—in person, at least—with as much caution as a bogey coming out of the sun. She had straw blonde hair and brown eyes that were dusty like the Luran Plains, and carried the perpetual expression of someone chewing on a lemon. Her uniform was pale gray coverall of the AES, with a slate gray long-sleeved undershirt.

Tag and Scrape stood at their best parade rest, wearing the same uniform in lieu of their standard flight suits. It didn't seem like they'd need the latter for a while.

"Your hearing failing now, Wester, along with your ability to follow orders?" Dillon grumbled. "Effective immediately, you and Sakawa are grounded from patrols, for the next 48 hours."

"With all due respect, Commander, this is the first time me and Lieutenant Wester have been singled out for extreme punishment," Scrape said.

"Yeah, and you want to hazard a guess why that is, Sakawa?" Dillon jerked a thumb. "Your flyboy pilot here has a father who loves to throw his weight around. Doesn't matter if AES answers directly to Divisional Command out of Sonderbann. The Westers have clout, leftover from the Consular Wars. So when the pressure comes down the chain of command for me to go easy on you two, I got no choice."

"So what's changed?" Tag added a hasty "Ma'am" after the question.

"The change, Wester, is that Daddy's got new duties assigned you, straight through General Wood and right to my scroll." Dillon smirked. "Which means instead of writing yet another disciplinary mark on your profile, I get to dump your ass out of the cockpit, even if only for a couple of days."

Tag just stared.

"Yeah, I thought that might douse your afterburners. Report to the MPs for your assignment. It's strictly a meet and escort—on your boots, not in the Raider, so be careful not to trip."

"Ma'am, you can't be serious. If I'm grounded I'm not combat ready."

"Combat? You expecting a pirate convoy? We've got a half dozen or more warships in system, Wester. And the last time we had a war, we stomped all over the NA resisters. Only war you're gonna get is with the regulations you keep fighting. Now get out. Dismissed."

Tag and Scrape saluted. Neither said a word until they had gone from the office and headed out the main corridor of Voss Flats Base, past the bare metal and plastic walls of offices and training rooms, and out on the tarmac. It was a half a klick walk from the AES offices and barracks to the MP station on the far corner of the diamond-shaped base. The more Raiders and assorted fighters they passed on their landing pads, the more swiftly Scrape had to walk to keep up with Tag.

"Can't believe it!" Tag finally spat. "The old man had me pulled. I should've known."

"That being the governor's son could have an effect opposite of the one you usually enjoy?" Scrape asked.

"Funny guy. No, I meant I should've know Father's request to meet with Elden Selva was anything but a request. He's never pulled strings like to that to deliberately get me onto an errand. Never."

"It seems that the governor feels it's worthwhile. Have you considered he's sending you—or I should say, us—because he's unsure of whom to trust?"

"You're a regular comedian, Scrape. Father doesn't trust anyone."

"That isn't true. Not if he's sending his son and his RIO to meet a potentially polarizing figure rather than Colonial Defense troops, or the police."

Tag hadn't thought of that angle. Maybe the old man did trust him. Of course, one would hope he'd be better trusted than a politician and a general. Neither of them were family, after all.

Yet it burned him that he could be out there, training in his Raider, tracing a path across the sky and into space, but now he was stuck babysitting a visiting official.

He supposed it really galled him that he got the punishment he was due, after all these times of pushing the envelope. But Tag wasn't about to admit that to Scrape, and he sure wasn't going to admit it to his father.

The Military Police kept a hovercraft pool for use by base personnel. Tag checked his scroll—yep, Dillon transferred over the details on Elden's pick-up straight from Father. According to that Elden had three in his immediate entourage. The remainder were diplomatic and security personnel tasked to the Terran Embassy on the south side of Vossberg.

Tag signed out a six-seater and the MP on duty gave him the starter wristband for a Ridgik Inc. Galician 40-Nine. It was a streamlined, flattened bullet of a craft, with polarized viewports and, thanks to the CDF modifications, armor plating beneath its civilian skin that would deflect most projectiles and dissipate laser strikes.

A roar of engines caught his attention. Tag watched as a pair of Raiders boosted from the base, and soared out over the Santos river, before banking east toward Vossberg.

Something brushed his arm, and next thing he knew, the hover's engines were humming. It floated a half-meter off the tarmac. Scrape sat behind the control console, smirking.

"You know, when DeeDee said she was grounded, I don't think this is what she meant." Tag slid into the front passenger seat, and confirmed that Scrape had lifted the starter wristband.

"I know. I also know I have zero traffic violations on my profile. How's yours?"

Everyone's a critic. Tag rolled his eyes. "Just drive."

***

Antiny Wester perused the list floating above the holographic generator in the center of his desk. The final wedding preparations were looking good. General Wood was true to his word—a company of the 65th Armored Division, the "Texans"—would provide backup security for the Colonial police. Wester nodded. Mechanized troops were always good publicity. The average citizen loved battle armor and heavy vehicles.

There was a note on his desk, a triangle of creased parchment. He smiled. Leave it to Marney to take the tactile approach. Like her mother, that way: she used to leave him scented notes to encourage him. When days behind the desk became too much to bear, and the political strife made him long for his youthful job managing agro-stations, he'd read them.

"Father, take heart and be cheerful! The wedding's coming along nicely. Tim has the security well arranged—he gets along with Wood infamously. What a trio you'll all make! I hope Tag's visit didn't upset you too much. He means well, but he's stubborn, too. Love, Marney."

Wester shook his head. Yes, the boy was stubborn. Like his mother—and, like his father. No point denying it. Tag had the Wester fire, from both sides.

His intercom buzzed. "Yes?"

A 3-D head and shoulders of one of his assistants appeared, floating next to the lists. "Sir, the envoys have arrived."

"Alright. Send them in, Leo."

"Yes, sir."

Wester cleared the wedding preparations. He kept the ring-trigger for his holo display on his right hand; the appropriate files were queued. For a moment, he thought about restocking the Crown & Scepter with a fresh bottle—between General Wood and Speaker Zhatkowskii, not to mention Tag, the one from yesterday had been well-drained. And Baedecker's chief export had smoothed over many difficult discussions for him in the past.

As soon as the envoys entered his office, however, Wester realized that was unnecessary. These Reittians wore the red and blue elbow bands Taldrics, of a sect that abstained from all alcohol consumption. They also took offense at its mere presence. Wester sighed inwardly. Mores the pity.

"Gentlemen, welcome to Baedecker Four. Governor Antiny Wester, at your service." He smiled and stood before his desk, hands clasped behind his back.

The Reittians were equal in height, both burly, stocky men. Both were shaven bald, also in the manner of their sect, and had well-trimmed beards—one gray, the other ash blond. They wore the white long coats and black trousers of the Reittian Diplomatic Service. The older man, who had jowls thick enough to conceal weaponry, had on a silver belt with a bronze-colored buckle studded with four red gems. His younger counterpart, by comparison, wore only a simple brown belt with a silver buckle that had a single blue stone at the center.

"First Emissary Kavinire Juren." The gray-beard inclined his head right, and bowed deeply. "This is my Fourth, Satnian Cyred."

The young man repeated the bow, though with jerky motions. In training. The boy radiated awkwardness, and the pink on his pale cheeks was obvious enough.

Wester greeted them likewise, and spread his arms wide, in the Reittian gesture of acceptance. "Please, sit with me."

Neither man requested refreshments. That was one thing about Taldrics—they certainly weren't a drain on the hospitality budget. "I am glad to see our allies here on Baedecker, though I have to say, your visit was a surprise."

"We felt it best to arrive clandestinely," Juren said. "This is a sensitive matter, and even among our government there is opposition."

"Of course. I only wish I could be better prepared."

"Our request is nothing complex, I assure you."

"By all means, I am listening." Wester enjoyed this part of the game. Terran Intelligence had tipped him off to the probable trip by Reittian envoys to Baedecker days ago. Hardly shocking, given the agents they'd sniffed out planetside and elsewhere in the system. Operatives shadowed Juren and Cyred from the moment their light corvette docked at the starport. But if they thought Wester in a position of uncertainty, even weakness, they'd be prone to boast—hopefully to Wester's advantage. Reittians were transparent that way.

"Elden Selva. He's coming here, and, if my information is correct, has recently arrived at Baedecker Starport."

"I had heard. He's here on the authority of our Graves Department, I believe."

"Ostensibly. His reasons for coming to Baedecker are irrelevant. I have been authorized by my government to demand his surrender."

Wester chuckled. "Surrender? Mr. Selva is a loyal member of the Terran government."

"He is a hereditary consul to one of the strongest ruling families of the Northern Alliance. Do not forget, Governor, the amount of Reittian blood spilled on Baedecker in the closing days of the second war. We helped your people turn the tide against your insurrectionists."

"Yes, and blasted the surface of Baedecker Four so badly it's taken us these five years to rebuilt it as a functional trade depot." Wester wished he'd gone against their preferences and had the rum. Helped him focus. Juren was being blunt, as he'd expected of the typical Reittian. It made them good soldiers, but poor negotiators. What was this obsession with Elden? "Mr. Selva played only a minor role in the conflict."

"I would hardly call a member of the NA High Council a 'minor role,'" Juren said.

"Fair point. He was a non-combatant."

"His decisions led to hundreds of deaths."

Of Reittians, yes. Wester didn't care much for them. They were hardly staunch allies, after all—Reittians looked out for their own interests, and it galled them to have Terra rebuilding Baedecker after they'd made a ruin of it. "I'm sorry. If your intent is to have me detain Mr. Selva, that's out of the question. As I said, he's an official with the Terran government, and will be a guest in my household."

"This isn't a request." Cyred's interjection surprised him. The young man still seemed ill at ease, and Wester wondered why Juren had brought such a neophyte along on a tense negotiation. "We have the wherewithal to back it up."

Wester smiled. "I seriously doubt that."

"What else would you call a battlegroup of the Twelfth Fleet?" Cyred snapped.

Wester froze his expression as his brain spun to catch up. A Reittian battlegroup was eighteen vessels. There were only twelve ships on station throughout the entire Baedecker station—

and only a handful of those were heavy cruisers. It made no sense. Threaten him with a fleet to gain one man back? No man was worth that much effort.

Ah. Unless the man were only symbolic. "You don't care about Selva, in and of himself. But his capture would provide you with just cause to retake Baedecker."

Juren's face, unlike his irritable companion, was unreadable. "This is our system, Governor."

"You abandoned it after the war. Terran sweat rebuilt it. That makes it ours." Wester had another card to play. "It, and everything of value on its worlds."

Juren pursed his lips, and Cyred looked even more nervous. So they knew, did they? About the serjaum deposits?

"Your recalcitrance is puzzling, Governor," Juren said. "The Reittians have no wish to war with Terra. It isn't good for trade. But this system is valuable, and is ours, by long tradition. The NA stole it from us. The capture and trial of Elden Selva will prove our righteousness in reclaiming what should be—and will be—our lands."

"And if I refuse to have him arrested?"

"The battlegroup will be here in two standard days," Juren said. "What it does when it arrives, is up to you."

Wester stood. Juren did likewise, but Cyred remained seated. So much for taking the hint. "I've sworn an oath to uphold Terran law and defend this star system," Wester said. "I'm not going to hand it over to you. Neither, I think, is the Terran government."

"You're making a mistake," Cyred said. "You have any idea what a battlegroup can do to this system? You've gotten so soft since the last war that we—"

"That's quite enough, Lieutenant." Juren's voice cut across Cyred's rant like a plasma blade through a bole tree's branch.

Cyred turned beet red. He stormed from the room, ignoring Wester's half-hearted bow.

"A Naval attaché? First Emissary, I'm insulted."

Juren sighed. "Hardly my choice. The Navy has its own designs. We of the Diplomatic Service must bend to them."

"So I take it that means you disapprove of their tactics."

"Tactics, yes, but we share the same goal: the return of Baedecker to its rightful owners. I would rather not see a battlegroup deployed, but my hands are tied."

Wester nodded, keeping his expression grave. It was an

old game, and he gave them credit for trying good cop and bad cop. "I will forward your request to my superiors, and await their guidance. But as far as I'm concerned, in my capacity as governor, I will not hand Elden Selva over to your people."

Juren bowed. "I regret to hear it, though I will convey your decision. Good day, Governor, and may we meet again on more cordial terms."

"Yes, of course."

As soon as Juren's shuttle lifted off, and Wester watched it soar away, he punched his intercom. "Leo? I need a secure signal to General Wood."

"Right away, sir."

He found his personal communicator and tapped Tag's frequency. The communicator was as safely encrypted as any such unit could be on Baedecker, and he sent a brief text-only message, with an eater attached that would delete it from both ends after five seconds. [*Don't be late to meet your friend. Rather he didn't catch cold.*]

Wester sagged into his chair. Now it was a matter of who at Vossberg Terminal would find Elden Selva first.

**

Tag read the message, and snorted. Be late. Right. As if he'd test Father's ire by deliberately fouling up an assignment—and no matter how he couched it, that's what it was. A job. Not a favor.

Getting back in the flight roster was payment.

He and Scrape had taken up positions about 30 meters apart inside the main hall of Vossberg Terminal. Tag thought of the half-transparent triangular tents in which he used to go camping. The hall was a monstrous version of it—a kilometer long, sloping sides of reinforced transparent polymer converging 100 meters overhead. Small transports descended from the clouds, docking at gantries that rose like denuded trees far above the hall. To the west, landing pads for shuttles of every shape and size, from sharp-edged personal yachts to bulbous passenger liners, were arranged in terraces around a pyramid of carbon fiber and metal. Numerous access tunnels branched off at ground level; above, another two dozen led away from second and third floor levels. Thousands of people mingled throughout the concourse, chattering in a slew of languages that overlapped with orchestral quality. Everything was bright and white, including the polished stone underfoot.

"Any sign of him?" Scrape's voice sounded like a whisper over his shoulder, coming as it did from the tiny communicator riding inside his ear.

"Nope. Stay sharp, though: Elden was never showy. He won't stand out." Tag loved using the subdermal vocalizer implanted in his throat; all he had to do was murmur under his breath, and Scrape could hear every word just as clear as Tag could hear him.

Elden had gone on one of those camping trips, in the Rondial Forest to the far north of Baedecker. Tag could hear him laugh over rowdy jokes.

The sound melded into boisterous chuckles from a pair of Jantari tradesmen in flowing robes of multi-hued orange. Tag shook his head. This wasn't a time for reminiscing.

The Jantari passed by, heading toward a refreshment stand. Tag spotted two men behind the stand, one seated on a black carbon fiber bench reading a scroll, the other standing just to his right, scanning the crowds. The seated one was shaved bald, and had brown eyes. The one standing wore a darkened visor and had short blond hair, plus a thin moustache.

Something triggered Tag's combat senses. Most citizens would see two men waiting idly for a passenger to arrive. Only another man with military training would see similar attributes: the way the seated man kept looking up from his scroll, every thirty seconds; the subtle bulge of a hidden weapon under the left side of the standing man's long green coat; the hand gestures passed between the two that heralded covert communication.

"Scrape. You see these boys? Ten meters to my one o'clock."

"Stand by... Yes, I see them."

"You think they're waiting for their Aunt Clara?"

"Unless they're planning to stun and incarcerate her, no."

"That's my guess, too."

"Reittians?"

"Probably. I don't see any clan tattoos, but you can hide 'em easily enough. Hang on." Tag stepped in front of a pair of tall, long-legged women—a blonde and a redhead—in black skirts. "Ladies, beg your pardon: would you mind taking a pic of me? Mom will be so glad to know I've arrived safely."

The redhead giggled. The blonde raised an eyebrow but offered a smile, too. "Oh? You having trouble figuring out your scroll?"

"Hardly." Tag grinned. "I just saw those lovely sky blue

eyes and knew they'd be far superior to mine when composing an image. Come on, do a proud son a favor."

She rolled her eyes but took the scroll. Tag turned around, with his back to the men in the distance, and gave her a thumbs-up. She saved a few images, and returned him his scroll.

"Much obliged." Tag took her hand and kissed it.

They'd barely gone on, laughing softly to each other, when Tag had uploaded the image to his father. [*Old friends of ours?*]

He'd have to wait for a reply, no doubt. Father had a direct contact with Terran Intelligence. Tag was certain they would have a man, or woman, or even drone on station at Vossberg Terminal. Someone could identify if Baldy and Visor, as he'd marked them, were Reittian operatives.

"Tag, he's here. West wall, Tunnel Five, heading my direction."

Scrape's alert spiked Tag's adrenaline. He moved through the crowd, taking a long arc, so he could still keep Baldy and Visor in his peripheral vision. The crowd was thicker here, with families reuniting, businessmen clasping hands, and lovers exchanging passionate greetings.

Elden came through Tunnel Five with two other men— one slender and dark-skinned, the other as imposing as the Koth Mountains. Tag was surprised Elden looked as different as he did. Same broad shoulders, same blond hair, although the latter was smartly fixed rather than the unruly mop Tag remembered. It was more his gait, and the solemn expression on his face. Dark circles rimmed his eyes.

"Scrape, get yourself on their three o'clock. I'm coming in on their ten."

"Roger. Watch that big fellow. I'm guessing he's hired muscle."

"Bodyguard? He looks it." Tag wove through a horde of teenaged boys and girls, their chatter drowning out all other sounds. In their midst, he hazarded a glance back at the possible Reittians...

They were gone. Where?

"Scrape. Our boys juked. Do you have eyes on them?"

"Negative."

Tag's scroll pulsed in his pocket. He pulled it out far enough to see the message glowing on one end.

[*Not old friends. Cautious neighbors.*]

Well, that confirmed it. They were Reittian operatives,

probably making their move on Elden. Speaking of...

"Got them, Tag. They're 20 meters off my three o'clock. Check the family of five, Asian."

Tag spotted them. He had to hand it to Baldy and Visor, they were skilled at blending with a crowd—at least temporarily. But they were getting too close to Elden and his entourage. "I need you to distract them."

"Copy that. Let me make a purchase."

"Scrape, I don't think we have time to—"

And time was up for Tag. Elden slowed ten meters away, his eyes widening. The men with him almost walked by, but stopped, both looking puzzled. The larger man scanned the area immediately around them, his eyes alighting on Tag—and then continuing to the Reittians.

"Tag? Tag Wester?" Elden said.

By then Tag was only a few strides away. He grinned, and spread out both arms. "In the flesh. Long time, Eldi."

"I'd say so." Elden clapped him on the shoulders. "By the stars above, it's good to see you."

"Yeah, the same here, Eldi, but we're going to have to cut this reunion short. Father's not the only one who's eager to see you."

"What do you mean?"

"Two men, moving to intercept." The big man had a curiously melodic voice. "I'll run interference, sir, but you have to move quickly, you and Mr. Natour. I'll give you time to rendezvous with Mr. Cantor."

Behind them came a crash. Tag spun, hands formed in a *dei-rinith* martial arts stance. But all he saw was Scrape, brushing nervously at the jacket of Baldy. "I'm so sorry! Can't believe I spilled all that syrup. Here, let me help!"

Tag grinned. Baedecker's Vara syrup was some of the richest in the known galaxy—and messiest. He'd fouled his clothes with tree sap that stuck less. Tag grabbed Elden's arm. "This way!"

The four of them barged through the crowd, heading for the huge arch of the main exit. The big man covered their flank, and Tag kept watch for any more operatives heading to intercept them.

"They got around me," Scrape said through the earpiece. "Watch yourself. I'm following them."

"Roger." Tag was more worried by the men who came through the entrance. They looked far less friendly than Baldy and Visor—and as he watched, two of them reached inside their coats.

"Goetz..." Elden started to say.

"On it, sir." Goetz opened his jacket, too.

But before anyone could act, a pale, nondescript man in baggy khaki clothes swept through the formation of men at the entrance. They all froze, staring straight ahead. Tag noted their quivering hands with interest.

"Elden Selva? I'm Erich Cantor. I bring greetings and welcome from the Hirrenhausen Monastery," he said.

"Thank you for your intervention."

"Those men will be free of their paralysis soon. We shouldn't dally."

"I don't intend do." Elden looked at Tag. "Though I think we need to pay the governor a visit first."

"Yeah, I think so." Tag gestured. "Your ride's this way, Mr. Selva."

CHAPTER FOUR

Admiral Daviont perused the reports from the III Corps. There was more spread across the hologram floating in his office than a lone eye could take in, but he preferred this—the wider view.

It was encouraging. The bulk of his forces had arrived in the vicinity of the Baedecker system two days ago. They'd lost a handful of ships to mechanical failure and jump disasters, but all the fuel tankers they brought along had mercifully been spared. Now they waited, three light-years out from Baedecker, in the depths of interstellar space.

His force of 70 ships would target the system itself, while nearly 100 other ships of their flying column assaulted various bases and settlements in the sector. Their mission was to keep Terran reinforcements at bay and assure Daviont of zero interference in his conquest of the Baedecker system.

The reports from the Corps quartermasters, however, was less stellar. Fuel supplies were dangerously low. If they did not secure the system, and make immediate use of the serjaum reserves, the III Corps would not return home. There was question of whether they'd even make it back across the Great Desert Rift.

Only the Ascended Masters could see to that.

A tone echoed from his office hatch. Daviont shrank the hologram to a ball of green light, its specifics indecipherable to the Naplian visual spectrum. "Enter."

A young, tall officer in the pale blue armor of the Naplian Colonial Infantry. His skin was flushed dark gray with excitement, and there was a gleam about his deep violet eye that bespoke the same. Major Rej Ad'Andra Lanviond "Sir. You wanted to see me?"

"At ease, Major. In this space, we are still officers of Their

Majesty's imperial forces, but more so we are clan kin. Please, be seated." Daviont waited until the major had sat, then took his own chair.

"Our battalions are ready for the assault, Admiral."

"I'm well aware. Your status updates have been quite detailed. The level of training to which you've held your men during this arduous voyage is commendable."

"Thank you, sir." Lanviond frowned. "But sir, if you're not interested in unit readiness, why did you summon me?"

Daviont slid his hand across a panel on his desk. Red lights outlined the desk, and the air took on a curious sensation—as if something pressed in on him, ever so gently. Lanviond grimaced, and flexed his hands.

"A necessary precaution, Rej. I want to ask you about Sov."

Lanviond's eye widened. "I... know nothing of the outlier cult. I have nothing to say about them."

"Come now, Rej, we are quite safe from the Druwei here. The emperors' internal security has a dim view of Sov followers, I realize, but I've taken precautions to secure my position."

"You?"

"Yes. I too seek the alien outsider."

"It's more than that. He has to be protected."

Daviont frowned. "I don't understand. I thought his presence would signify victory. Hence the rumors that began floating throughout the fleet at the start of the Audrian campaign."

Lanviond sighed. "I beg your pardon, sir, but this is what happens when people who are not truly called to believe jump aboard our cause. Or try to, I should say. The prophecy is clear—the alien outsider will arise among a distant nation in time of war, and his death will usher about the destruction of the Naplian Empire."

Daviont had, in fact, heard such prophecy, but dismissed it out of hand. To hear his young cousin boldly admit it was surprising. Lanviond was highly placed in the Sov cult—the Druwei had confirmed that to him. The director of internal security owed Daviont a great debt, and Daviont had called it in by demanding his cousin be left off the Druwei surveillance records that kept track of the myriad Naplian cults.

"Sir, I realize this concern blinks every time we attack a foreign system, but it is not some joke—it is a serious threat. The prophecy says devastators will absorb the alien outsider, make him one of them, and he will arise a powerful leader. It is these devastators who will vanquish Naplia."

"Who are the devastators? Surely we should target them, rather than worry about the outsider."

"No one knows. Not even our greatest mystics."

"I see." Daviont tapped the panel again. The lights faded from around his desk.

Lanviond stiffened his posture.

"Well, Major, keep me apprised. I wish to know immediately if any threats to the success of this conquest become apparent. I'm tasking you personally. I trust you understand my directive."

Lanviond nodded. "Sir, yes, sir."

"Very good. You have your orders: prepare a stealth courier and land your advance team in sight of the target. You are dismissed."

Lanviond left him. Daviont mulled over the officer's comments. He was unconvinced of any threat from this cult's prophecy, but the Druwei men secreted throughout III Corps had increased their alert. He was not about to dismiss their concerns, especially when they were about to launch an invasion of a political entity with whom Naplia had every dealt. Such were the hazards of galactic conquest.

He reactivated his holographic display and pulled up a new file, with everything the Denic agents had gathered on human history. On one hand, he was reassured that their ambitions were provincial. On the other, they had repeatedly proven themselves brave and vicious warriors, with a history of combat dating back millennia.

All factors to consider before he dropped men on the surface of an alien planet.

***

Tag was expecting Father to meet him and at least be thankful he and Scrape had pulled Elden out of Vossberg Terminal without any major complications. He hadn't figured on a half dozen Colonial police to be present at the reunion.

"One Terran Graves representative and company, delivered safely," Tag said. "No small thanks to our pal Erich, here."

Wester frowned. "I suppose I'm in your debt, Mr. ..."

"Cantor. Erich Cantor. I was sent by the monks to escort Mr. Selva on his mission."

"Is that so. Well, I'm afraid that mission will have to be put on hold." Wester faced Selva. "Hello, Elden."

"Governor."

"Let's not do that. Your father and I were good friends. His actions in the Consular wars—were regrettable. But no matter his choices, I always respected the man. I was saddened to hear of his death." Wester offered a hand.

"Thank you, sir."

"Please. Antiny."

Elden smiled. "Sir, no matter how old I get, you're always Mr. Wester."

Wester chuckled. "I suppose there's a place for that decorum, isn't there?"

Tag cleared his throat. "And, so, 'You're welcome' is in order."

"Thank you for getting Elden here, son. I understand, however, you had some help."

Ah, there it was: the start of the inevitable critique. "Well, Father, when it's myself and Scrape outmaneuvering two bogeys, and four more show up in our escape vector, some help is mighty appreciated."

"I can see that. You should have anticipated Reittian involvement, however, especially since I told you bluntly they were looking for him."

Tag shook his head. "This is typical. Is this why you have everyone gathered here? To make a public show of my humiliation? Because banning me and Scrape from the flight line for 48 hours apparently was not enough."

"This has nothing to do with you," Wester snapped. "Elden and his travelers have to remain here, in my custody."

The ripple of surprise that went through the small group was as palpable as an electric shock. The big bodyguard, Goetz, was plainly angry. Elden's buddy Natour looked perplexed, and it was Elden who broke the silence. "Sir, I don't understand. We have business with the monks."

"Yes, I realize that, but with the Reittians crawling around, I can't have you freely roaming Baedecker."

"You can't just lock him up, Father," Tag said. "He hasn't done anything."

"As a matter of fact, I can and will detain him. It's the only way to keep the Reittians from taking drastic action." Wester gestured at the Colonial police officers. Two of them flanked Selva.

"Sir, please. My work is strictly humanitarian. We're trying to locate the ID tags of Northern Alliance men killed in the war, to return them to their families. Shouldn't we be allowed to provide closure?" Selva held out his hands. "The Reittians have a blood feud against the remnants of the NA and specifically against my family."

"I'm well aware of that, Elden, which is why you'll remain here, in my custody, and as my guest. We have a cottage set aside for visitors. It's quite secure."

"For a jail?" Goetz rumbled.

"Guest accommodations," Wester said.

"Are there any further restrictions on our liberty?"

"Your liberty only extends as far as the walls of this grand estate. Colonial police are authorized to keep your persons on the premises—for your safety, Elden, and that of my entire planet."

Tag couldn't make heads or tails of the look that passed between Selva and the thin guy, Natour, but whatever it was about, Elden won. "Very well. Thank you for your hospitality, and your protection."

"More our protection than yours," Wester said. "Constable? Show these men to their quarters."

The police escorted Selva, Natour, and Goetz from Wester's office. Tag leaned against the wall, and gave the remaining man an appraising look. "Erich, was it? Much obliged for your intervention back at Vossberg Terminal."

Erich inclined his head, expression solemn and eerily peaceful. "Of course. My purpose is to serve others."

"You often get to paralyze Reittian agents? How'd you manage that, anyway?"

"A shock to their neurological systems. Nothing exotic."

"You'll have to show me the device you used."

Erich smiled. He blinked with way too much precision. That was eerier than the rest of his expression.

"Mr. Cantor, please convey my apologies to the abbot," Wester said. "I'm sure you understand this is a delicate situation where Mr. Selva's background is concerned."

"I do, Governor, and I trust this will be only a temporary delay."

Wester hesitated. "As temporary as I can make it. Good evening."

Once Erich Cantor was gone, Scrape spoke up. "Governor, I'd request that you contact Wing Commander Dillon to see if our flight status can be—ameliorated."

"I'll certainly do so, Lieutenant Sakawa. Tough business, you getting involved, but as I'm sure you're aware, that's the hazard that comes with associating with my son." Wester sat behind his desk and activated a holographic communications display. "Thank you for your assistance."

Scrape glanced at Tag. "I'll wait for you at the hovercraft."

"Check."

The Wester men stayed silent in the empty room for a full two minutes before the governor said, "You've gotten praise, and you've completed your work. What else do you need?"

"To talk about Elden." Tag pulled up a chair opposite the desk. "You're not going to turn him over to the Reittians."

"Is that a question or a statement of fact?"

"Father, they'll butcher him."

"I know that."

"So let him come and go as he pleases."

"That isn't possible."

Tag scowled. "Only if you're dealing with the Reittians."

"They are our allies."

"Only out of necessity. They'd turn on us in a microsecond."

"And what do you think will happen if we let Elden leave Baedecker?" Wester snapped. "They've got their own warships ready to pounce on this system! Elden Selva's their justification. A Northern Alliance hereditary consul, working for the Terran government: quite the PR boon if they can have him. Well, they won't. Because we won't let them have either Elden or this planet."

Tag weathered his Father's outburst. It was typical; worried so much as he was about interstellar politics, he didn't see the bigger problem beyond his office. "So now we have Elden as an extended houseguest."

"I do. Your domicile, as I recall, is Voss Flats—as you've made abundantly clear."

Leave Governor Wester to use Tag's own words against him. "You know what I mean. Given any thought to Marney?"

"What about her?"

"Come off it, Father. She and Elden were ready to be married all those years ago!"

"Nonsense." Wester paused in his composition of the holo signal, and swept it aside. "They were teenagers. Foolish. Elden's father and I never approved of—"

"It's called eloping. If it weren't for war, I'd say Marney would be planning her anniversary—or maybe her nursery."

Wester's neck reddened.

Tag pushed up from the chair. "Get DeeDee off my back, and

get me and Scrape back in the skies, Father Dear. You might also consider increasing security around our bride-to-be, unless you want to see her current suitor standing at an empty altar."

***

Abbot Jeopar knelt on the fifth story balcony of Hirrenhausen Monastery. The great central dome, hewn from sandstone, loomed behind him. Seven parapets four stories tall surrounded the dome, joined by a thick masonry wall reinforced with carbon fiber. Each parapet was adorned with intricate scrollwork hand-painted by acolytes; from his perch, Jeopar admired the patterns and colors.

Dusk turned the sky orange, as Baedecker's smaller sun set upon the horizon. The larger sun disappeared behind the Koth peaks. The first stars peeked through the darkening sky.

Jeopar knew the correct orientation for the Sol system; it was marked on his scroll, which was spread on the cool stone of the balcony. He pressed his hands together, and brought them first to his lips, then to his chest, then to his forehead, before spreading them apart. "Yours is the world and the galaxy and the universe. Grant that I might hear Your will and fulfill it to the extent my mortal frame allows."

He continued in prayer for a half hour, letting his confessions and his praises fill his heart and mind. The footfalls behind him were not a bother; he acknowledged them with a bow of his head, and a reversal of the same sign with which he'd begun.

"Sorry to interrupt," Erich said. "You received my message?"

"I did, yes."

"I did what I could. The governor's mind is made up."

Jeopar collected his scroll, and stood. "Do not despair. The governor does not realize the role he plays—the roles we all play—in fulfilling God's will."

"Wish I shared your optimism."

"It's more than optimism. It's faith."

Erich nodded. "I see. Well, Elden Selva conveys his regret that he can't be here. He's encouraged by our progress in retrieving the headpieces."

Jeopar chuckled. "If that impresses him, he'll find our latest work even more encouraging. Come with me, my friend."

They walked inside the main building, entering a broad, open floor under the curve of the dome. Its interior was emblazoned with gold foil stars and silver traceries, on a surface of polished obsidian. A huge open stairwell 20 meters in diameter yawned before them, spiraling down into the depths of the main building. Shelves full of ancient manuscripts and battered electronic reading devices bordered the walls.

Jeopar's and Erich's footsteps echoed as they descended. Silent acolytes in all brown robes and murmuring abbots in brown and white passed them in either direction as they went by the various floors. The warm smells of baking bread and cooking soup filled the entrances to the stairwell on the second floor; the aroma of wet dirt and vegetables from greenhouse permeated the first floor. But Jeopar led Erich into the basement level, a dark space full of storage alcoves. One of those alcoves was empty. Jeopar held his scroll up to the stone surface.

The wall sank back and slid aside with a soft hiss of pneumatics.

"This is odd. Secret prayer chamber? I thought the Aparatics preferred the open space from which they could see the stars?" Erich said.

"This tunnel was carved for purposes other than reflection and worship." Jeopar grabbed a battered arm-beacon from a hook just inside the hatch. It lit a long, tight corridor of twisting rock with a pale blue glow. The hidden hatch shut behind them.

The tunnel led down several dozen meters and around several sharp turns. At its end, the gleam of metal shone in the arm-beacon's rays.

Erich sucked in a breath, the sound echoing harshly off the rock walls. "What is this place?"

"A command bunker for the Northern Alliance, derelict since the end of the second war," Jeopar said. "Soldiers dug this tunnel as an emergency escape route should the base be invaded. As it were, they never used it—and the men who made it were all killed in a battle at the mouth of Iwa Valley. The previous abbot disclosed its location to me, before he left for Earth and much needed convalescence."

Jeopar reached up and to his right. A switch clicked.

Dim yellow lights snapped on, four at a time, stretching out a hundred meters from the entrance. The walls were stark metal, reinforced with armored panels, and exposed stanchions arcing overhead. One wall was lined with lockers for equipment, munitions, and sundry other supplies Jeopar had never bothered to catalog. The opposite wall was covered by huge, blank monitors.

Twelve consoles were grouped in fours along the bottom, each group centered on its own holographic projector. The far wall had another hatch. Everything was a dull, uniform blue-gray.

Standing in three rows in the center of the bunker were twelve dozen Truppen. Their bodies were tall, more than 2 meters, with armored shoulders, sharp-edged forearms ending in large, three-fingered hands, antennae and sensor posts protruding from the backs, and long, reinforced legs meant for leaping. Optical ports glowed red, dozens of eyes staring blankly.

"Remarkable." Erich stood among them, peering up into the headpieces.

"Yes. We were blessed to find so many bodies in storage, adjacent to this bunker." Jeopar brushed the arm of the nearest Truppen. "We have these in standby mode, awaiting activation commands. Another four hundred are held in the same fashion. My abbots and acolytes are reassembling another two dozen, though, and we can give form to at least another two dozen headpieces beyond that."

"But we have hundreds of headpieces."

"Unfortunately, we have not uncovered suitable parts for them. It is a shame, to come so close to having a rebuilt army and yet be unable to fulfill our promises."

"Building an army is hardly the work of God."

"On the contrary, Erich, I see it as restoring the lives of men who were stripped of their form, and cast away from life, without the chance of death. It is after death, of course, that we are fully united with God." Jeopar smiled. "How can we enter into eternal life if we never die?"

"Hadn't considered that." Erich paced the line of Truppen.

Jeopar marveled at the results silently. To think that five years ago, these had been broken, deactivated parts and lost headpieces—now, thanks to the dedication and faith of his abbots and acolytes, men were reborn in physical form. A resurrection.

"Elden Selva needs to see this," Erich said.

"I agree. It is your duty, then, to bring this reunion to fruition. Bring the consul's son—the new consul himself—to greet his worthy army."

"That'll be difficult. I've seen the security for the wedding of the governor's daughter. Only Voss Flats will be more heavily guarded."

"You are a resourceful man, Erich. I believe you can do it."

Erich sighed, a short, abbreviated exhalation that sounded

somewhat off. Somewhat artificial. "Let me see what I can come up with. There's no way he'll be able to sneak whole Truppen off-world, though. Headpieces are one thing."

"Between our status as a monastery and Mr. Selva's diplomatic position, I believe we can make it work." Jeopar stood on tiptoes, peering into the optical ports of the nearest Truppen cyborg.

"Can they—see us?" Erich stepped back from the lines.

"Not yet. Not in standby mode." Jeopar shrugged. "Or so I am told. Supposedly they are in a vegetative state. But humans in such conditions are known to monitor their surroundings."

"Then I'll take my leave. I don't need them discerning my origin."

"You're still concerned they won't accept you."

"I'm concerned they'll execute me."

"Someday, Erich, that won't be a problem for us," Jeopar said. "Someday, when the Northern Alliance restores freedom to all living sentients—not just those who are biological—you and I will stand side by side with our Truppen brethren."

"God help us then," Erich murmured.

***

The Naplian stealth interceptor designated *IFN-168* closed the distance to Baedecker with a series of precise micro-jumps. Its hull was a trimaran form of blades, each one identical to the other, and covered with a light-absorbing coating that made it appear as black as space itself. It bore no running lights, no navigational transponders, or any other identification markers.

Major Lanviond checked the charge on his Daish Kashiton-458 "Furta" energy rifle. He'd get 30 shots from the packet, fewer than 20 if he upped the blasts to their maximum damage setting. With the extra packets securely fastened to his mottled blue body armor, it would be enough to last him for several days of reconnaissance—or a few hours of blistering combat.

This wasn't a raid. It was a scouting mission, pure and simple.

"Landing zone coordinates set," the pilot said. "ETA twenty minutes."

By skillful planning and a bit of good fortune from the mystics, the target area was on its night rotation of the planet. Judging by the rough weather scans, it was also partially overcast.

Lanviond nodded. The more cover the better. "Insert us here, where those plateaus intersect. There's a ridgeline and a ledge. We can cover the vessel with adaptive sheeting."

"Yes, sir, Major."

Lanviond's men were arrayed in two columns at the back of the craft, secured in place with shock webbing. Though Lanviond commanded a full battalion, for this special operation he'd selected 40 of his best soldiers, men skilled at infiltration and espionage.

"The task is simple," he said. "Survey and surround the governor's mansion near Vossberg City. We will maintain cover during the daylight hours, and set up surveillance of the Baedecker governor and his immediate staff. His coordinates and the status of his security will be sent to Admiral Daviont. Once the invasion begins, we are to deny the humans access to and from the target. Are there any questions?"

A young soldier's hand went up. "These are Denics, sir, these Terrans?"

"Similar, yes. But not as subtle. Not as patient. Maintain your caution: Baedecker is not an undefended colony. And the Terrans are not pacifists. Though after contact with our Naplian forces, they may choose to become such."

Chuckles rumbled through the staging area.

Lights went deep red. The ride became rough. Lanviond let the nearest empty webbing station wrap him snug against a stanchion. Flames flashed outside a pair of long, narrow viewports.

The flames cleared away, and the chop subsided. Stars gave way to the deep dark of an ocean, and at its edge, the glittering jewel of a city.

"Military base," the pilot's voice said through Lanviond's headset communicator. "Running scans now."

"Compile everything for a coded burst to the flagship."

"Yes, sir."

The rest of their flight remained undetected. The stealth ship set down on a broad outcropping, at the congruence of two plateaus. No sooner had the vessel's landing pads hit dirt than the back hatch slammed open.

Naplian soldiers streamed out, separating into squads of eight. They formed a defensive perimeter around the ship, aiming their rifles into the darkness as its skin steamed. Lanviond joined Squad One at the base of the landing ramp. He pulled down his visor, covering his eye and casting everything into a pale yellow glow with Naplian body heat and animal signs glowing brilliant white.

As if caught in a wave, the outlines of his soldiers faded into the same dim yellow as the background temperatures. Their body armor deflected heat emissions and effectively camouflaged them from conventional sensors.

Lanviond flipped up the visor, double-checking his reactive camo. The mottled blue armor morphed colors into tan and brown combinations.

"Sir, the perimeter is clear. The only life signs we detect belong to small reptilians and insects," his sergeant reported.

"Good. Send up the new-eyes. I want everything within 10 kilometers of the ship charted and marked."

The sergeant relayed the order. A few seconds later, six robots the size of Lanviond's outstretched palm shot out from the open hatch. Each one was a flattened sphere, covered with clusters of transparent bumps and sprouting handfuls of antennae. Six hover-pods extended from the body, three on each side. The new-eyes slowed to a halt in front of two of the soldiers, each one of whom had a bulky, arm-mounted unit on their right wrists. After exchanging a series of soft beeps, they shot off in six different directions, rapidly disappearing into the night sky. Within five minutes, Lanviond had the information he needed.

"The governor's mansion is eight point five kilometers from our location," the sergeant said.

"Very well." Lanviond gestured ahead. "All units, move out."

The squads marched down the embankment, into the quiet night.

***

Elden Selva and Andan Natour walked the paths of the governor's compound, Goetz shadowing them by five meters to the right. There were scattered groups of people out this night. Clouds scudded across the bejeweled sky.

"Goetz is just itching to positively ID every soul within a hundred meters," Natour said. "He's convinced there's a half dozen assassins among them."

"Only a half dozen? I must not be nearly as dangerous as I thought." Elden kept a watch on those who passed by, nodding and smiling. There was one face he sought. So far, she'd remained hidden.

"It's going to get more crowded by the time of the wedding."

"Tomorrow night."

"Yes, I know. I don't suppose you warranted an invite."

"While under house arrest by the Baedecker governor? No, Nat, I'm afraid that puts me far down the list of desired attendees."

They rounded a copse of white stone, partially carved into a soaring starship, with a small fountain gurgling from one side. Lights made the pool glow aquamarine.

A woman sat beside it, trailing her fingers through the water.

Elden's heart hammered. It was as if she'd never left Baedecker, and he'd never gone off to serve the Northern alliance. She had her hair wrapped in a long braid, an auburn streak over her right shoulder. Her eyes glittered like sapphires in the light from the fountain's pool. She wore a long blue dress and a flowing white tunic with gold-lined sleeves. A sparkling ruby hung from a silver chain high around her neck.

She looked up, as if sensing him staring. "Elden?"

He smiled, astonished at how nervous he felt—infinitely more than when he'd lied straight to Governor Wester's face, and when deceiving the Terran officials who allowed him to go on this supposed mercy mission using official Graves credentials. "Hello, Marney."

"My stars!" She rushed to him, and they embraced.

She had only the barest hint of perfume. Elden held her close, not daring to let go.

Natour cleared his throat. He raised an eyebrow, a smirk tugging at his lips.

"It's so good to see you here! Father told me you'd come to collect military IDs. The monks have been gathering those in Iwa Valley, haven't they? I've seen them hard at work, no matter the weather. Such a kind thing to do for the families who lost loved ones."

"It is an important task, yes. And it's a pleasure to see you again. It's been far too long." He released her from their hug, and held onto both her hands. They were tiny compared to his. His thumb rubbed instinctively over the finger where the bronze band had been worn—in its place was a silver ring with a square jewel, the multifaceted surface of which shifted colors.

"Don't be a bore, Eldi. You haven't introduced us," Natour said.

"Of course. Marney, this is Andan Natour, my closest friend and fellow Terran Graves official. The other gentleman with us is

Goetz. He's responsible for our protection."

Goetz nodded, face as impassive as if it had been set in stone. Natour freed one of Marney's hands from Elden and pressed it to his lips. "Charmed, Miss. I wish you the best fortune this night before your nuptials."

"Well thank you, Mr. Natour. I'm afraid you've caught me hiding out here—the rehearsal dinner begins soon and I'm a bit overwhelmed by the scope of the wedding preparations. I needed some air and this spot..." She trailed off.

"I remember," Elden said. "Our favorite fountain."

Natour glanced between the two in the silence that followed. "Ah. So, Eldi, Goetz and I will mingle with the other visitors, I think. Sound like a plan, Goetz?"

He grumbled something about security precautions and followed it up with a stream of words in an old Earth language Elden didn't recognize. "Don't fret. I'm perfectly safe in the company of Miss Wester."

"Yes, I'm sure you are." Natour grinned. "Good night, then."

The two men departed, footfalls on the stone paths fading into the distance.

"Would you like to sit?" Elden asked.

"Certainly." Marney perched on the edge of the fountain, with Elden close by.

"How have you been?" Elden said. "I haven't heard much from you for—well, close to three years."

"I know. I am sorry."

"There's no need for apology. Our families and our lives went different directions a long time ago." It sounded rational, but he couldn't stop his heart from pounding, and he was terrified that if he said what he truly felt and thought, he'd stumble over his words like a lovesick teen. Which, he reflected, he'd had considerable experience being.

"I've been well. Working in the Agro Department keeps me busy. We've had great success getting crops to take hold north of the Koth range. The arid climate's a challenge but between the Hydroponics Division and the seed manipulators, I think it's a problem we can overcome." Marney brushed her fingertips across the water. "And you?"

"Well as can be expected. Work has me traveling all over this corner of the galaxy." It was true enough, even if a fair number of those trips were cover for his efforts to restore the Northern Alliance. "Unfortunately, I can't say much more about it.

The Graves work, of course, is key to mending the fences between Northern Alliance and Terra proper. I'm glad I can help."

"That's good." Marney chewed her lip.

"I have to say, Marney, this is not how I imagined our reunion."

She smiled, but there was something awkward about her expression. "I...yes. I know what you mean. My wedding is tomorrow, after all. Lieutenant Commander Timothy Ess."

"I've read of him. Lead the 61st Flotilla off Undersaw Prime, gunboat action."

"He rescued a group of hospital ships under fire. Father called it one of the bravest things he'd ever heard of."

"He sounds a like a good man."

"He is. Kind, and funny."

Elden nodded, but couldn't think of anything else more charitable to say. He knew he still loved Marney—at least, he felt the same way he did more than five years ago.

He was suddenly aware that she giggled. "What is it?"

"Oh, nothing. It's just..." She flicked a spray of water at him. The cold splashed on his cheek. "You're doing the tilt."

He chuckled. Of course she'd remember—and she was dead right. He'd tilted his head to the left, and dipped his chin. It was a habit he'd developed looking down on her across their disparate heights. "Some things never change, it seems."

"It does seem that way."

Elden couldn't stand it any longer. "Marney, you have to know I never forgot you. I've dreamed of this night for years—the night when I'd see you again, and it would be just the two of us."

"I... thought about it, too. For a long time. But..." Marney looked down at the water. Their faces were rippling reflections on the surface. "Things changed. We changed."

"Not as much as you'd think."

She placed a hand across his, but didn't meet his eyes. "You'll always be right here with me, Elden. I'll never forget you."

"Marney?"

The voice echoed from one of the paths—a commanding tone.

Marney stood quickly, her hand grazing Elden's side. He caught it, as he too got to his feet. "I love you."

She kissed him, a quick touch of their lips, and for a second, the years gone by were only in his imagination.

Then it was over, and she turned away, striding toward a

young man in dark blue tunic and black trousers. He had blond hair cropped close to his scalp, and a neatly-trimmed moustache and beard. There was no rank or insignia on his tunic, but Elden recognized military training in the man's bearing. It was like looking at a slimmer, smiling version of Goetz.

"Tim! There you are." Marney pecked him on the cheek, and looped her arm through his. Knifelike pain twisted Elden's gut. "This is an old friend of mine, Elden Selva, with the Terran government. Elden, this is my fiancé, Lieutenant Commander Timothy Ess."

"Selva. Nice to meet you." Ess held out a hand. "Marney's told me some interesting stories about you—and of course, I know somewhat of your background."

Did he? Elden doubted he'd offer to shake if he knew the full extent. He smiled back and shook Ess's hand. They played the game of warring grips for a moment before breaking off, apparently equals. "Commander. Congratulations. If you'll both excuse me…"

"Yes, we have to get to the rehearsal dinner," Ess said. "Are you joining us?"

Elden glanced at Marney, whose smile was frozen in place. "My apologies, but I have pressing matters to attend to."

He started the walk back to his quarters, hoping Natour hadn't polished off the liquor cabinet yet.

CHAPTER FIVE

T he Raider fighter-bombers broke free of Baedecker Four's gravitational pull, using the dusty red and gray moon to slingshot themselves deeper into the solar system. Tag watched their velocity spike.

He grinned. Now *this* was more like it. Far better than an errand from Father.

The Raider didn't handle like a bird out here, lacking atmosphere to make use of her aerodynamics, but rather operated more akin to a submarine. The plas-glass cockpit canopy was sealed over by an armored sheath, and Tag's immediate surroundings projected on its interior. A small hologram overlaid the squadron's position on a tiny chart amongst Baedecker's planets and moons.

"Go for ripwave in 20 seconds." DeeDee's voice was tinny over the squadron intra-comm, but no less demanding. All 12 fighters spread out from their tight formation into pairs, keeping a couple hundred kilometers between each other.

"Main drives ready." Tag popped the panel for a handle outlined in red and bearing blue stripes. "Compensator check."

"Five-by-five." Scrape sounded as excited as someone ordering dinner. "Ready for acceleration."

"Hope so, or we'll smear ourselves all over your backseat."

"Why do you always point that out every time we space?"

"Because you squirm like a cub pilot every time I do it."

"All units, mark."

Tag eased forward on the drives. The Raider's sublight engines on the wingtips were sealed up; the ripwave generator aft provided their propulsion now. A squashed sphere formed around the fighter, visible only on the ripwave generator's display screen.

Space-time ahead of the fighter-bomber contracted, and to the rear it expanded.

In pairs, the squadron leapt from the Baedecker moon's orbit at speeds in excess of a tenth of light speed.

"ETA to Baedecker Six region two hours," Scrape said. "Plenty of time for me to run system diagnoses."

"Wow, that sounds like a blast." Tag rolled his eyes. "Who've we got on our wing today?"

"Ferb and the Frog."

"Nice." Tag switched over to his wingman's signal. "Bronze Five to Bronze Six. Ferb, you copy?"

"Wester? Blast it all, Tag, why'd they stick me with you?"

"What, you're not still mad about the dry bombing run last month, are you?"

"You mean the one where you nearly bounced my ass into a gully at Mach 3? No, 'course not, why would I be?" Ferdinand Bayona said his "I" like "ah" and dropped a bunch of other consonants, befitting his heritage from somewhere on Earth called Colorado. "Man. The Old Woman must be itching to see me spaced."

"Easy, Ferb you never know if she's monitoring. Tell you what: I'll let you take point when we reach B6."

"Golly, it must be my birthday!"

"Don't be a void."

"The Frog sends you a kiss."

"That right, Katie?"

"Please. My husband would gut you like a carp, from navel to nose." Katie Delaneux had a soft lilt to her voice, and the only reason she carried her callsign was that she'd broken the nose of the last person who'd insulted the French-ancestry mining generation ship from which she hailed.

"Ten four. Stay clear of our ripwave field and let's show the rest of our pals some real maneuvers when we get there. Bronze Five out." Tag chuckled.

"Extraneous comms chatter that's against regs? Check," Scrape said.

"Worse than my Father!"

Scrape winced. "Come on, take that back..."

* * *

Baedecker Six was far smaller in diameter than Four, a cold, barren desert world scoured by high winds and covered with deep sands. It had a uniform tan color that Captain Tamara Blair found hideous. She preferred bright colors, like the purple of her crew's jumpsuits.

Not that she could proclaim beauty about a dumpy planet when she commanded the likes of the tug *Akitsushima*. Typical of her class, she was a thickset craft with a cluster at the tail end for the ripwave generator and the Serjaum jump drive. The front bulged with a huge graviton pusher and dozens of thruster ports, interspersed with tractor force emitters. Even depicted in loving 3D miniature in the hologram at the center of the bridge, Blair's ship looked like a battered metal mushroom in five shades of gray and bronze.

"You're sure the target's a derelict?" Blair adjusted her cap. Her curly black hair was cut so short the threadbare cap kept slipping forward.

"Yes, Ma'am. She's got no operational transponder, no main power, can't even get a read on auxiliaries."

"Light 'er up."

Twin banks of a dozen floodlights snapped on, casting huge ovals of white light across the hulk. It had been severed in half, at some point—an old *Cleveland*-Class star cruiser. A gaping wound midway down the hull split the fore and aft sections, with the guts of deck plates, stanchions, and pipes caught in a spray that seemed frozen. Blair realized the severing must not be complete. Something must still be holding the halves together, if they hadn't drifted apart.

"Registry number, Skipper."

She spotted it through the broad viewport of the bridge a second after Helm announced it: black letters, double outlined in white. *NAS Brooklyn*. Sounded like the name of a body of water.

"Run it through the databases. Give me everything we know on her," Blair said.

The answer came back in the form of a long, scrolling list of blue letters on the primary display screen. "Three hundred meters, three main batteries of triple missile launchers. Double that number of secondary batteries, most concentrated on the centerline dorsal and ventral. Pulsed particle cannons—six, scratch that, *eight*. She's a bruiser."

"Fighter craft?"

"None. A mix of shuttles and transports, standard for a vessel her size."

Blair nodded. "Complement?"

A pause. "Four sixty-six enlisted, fifty officers."

That was always the worse part—finding faces. Who knew how many were still floating out there, a handful of years after the Reittians killed her in the last days of the Second Consular War. Frozen expressions, desiccated bodies. Blair shivered. Hopefully most had been vaporized in whatever fires or explosions had blackened and pitted the hull.

"Bring us alongside, ready the pusher. Tractor force emitters to one quarter, reverse pull. Let's reel her in slow. Anyone get a read on the reactor?"

"Offline, Skipper," said Kando at Sensors. "Looks like the core got ejected. There's no danger of it going critical. There's nothing left, not even the reaction fuel."

"Good deal. Start the tractor procedures." Blair sat in her command chair. Lounge chair, was more like it. As with most things aboard *Akitsushima*, it was salvaged from a wreck. In this case, it was a burgundy leather off the observation decks of a fancy Class Four passenger liner that had blown all its drive systems at once off Baedecker Two. It was by far the most comfortable piece of furniture she'd ever planted her backside on, even if it still carried the faint odor of burnt plastics.

Akitsushima turned astern of *NAS Brooklyn* with all the grace of a Baedecker rhino rolling over in its sleep. For her short length of 60 meters, she hauled a great deal of mass, most of which was pent up in the bulbous pusher plate at the bow. Without it, though, she'd snap her bulkheads every time she went to nudge a wreck out of position—especially the big ones like this cruiser.

A hum built in the hull. The deck plates shuddered. A vibration rose through the chair, up into the armrests, and rattled Blair, up to and including her teeth. "Steady on the tractors. How's the feedback?"

"Manageable, Skipper. She's a big enough beast it's drawing the two of us together."

"As expected."

The burnt-out hulk loomed ever closer outside the bridge view port. Not for the first time, Blair questioned the logic in reeling in wreckage this close to her ship. It wasn't without its perils, even though she and her crew had more than four dozen salvages under their collective belts. Hence the slew of dents all over *Akitsushima*'s hull.

But when they stripped everything out of the ripwave generator and the jump drives—especially the Serjaum alloys—the profits would pay all the bills for the next three months. Plus, they would give Blair some more to stash away and pay off the loans she'd taken out to buy *Akitsushima*.

The shimmy increased. A loose plate near Blair's left boot rattled, louder than the rest. She stomped on it. "Decrease tractor force to one eighth. Standby with reaction thrusters."

"Aye, Skipper. Tractor force to one eighth. Thrusters ready."

NAS Brooklyn was so close Blair figured she could reach outside and touch the hull. "Go."

White puffs of the reaction jets sprayed out. The tiny holo of *Akitsushima* showed the thrusters firing in unison all around the forward hull. Blair braced herself as the tug closed the last few meters with the cruiser.

WHUMP.

The impact bounced everyone and everything around as if they were tossed down a set of stairs inside a sealed container. But the shaking subsided after a few seconds.

"Status!" Blair said.

"Green across all boards, Captain. Pusher plate absorbed 96 percent of the impact. Got a report of stress fractures in Section Two, but nothing the 'bots can't fix. Tractors are holding steady."

Blair exhaled. "Nice work, boys and girls. Okay. Kando, signal down to Engineering—six person boarding party to scout. We go in pairs. I'm on the lead."

Kando nodded, and relayed the message.

Blair smiled. Now came the part that always thrilled her—being the first to set foot inside a wreck. No one had touched it for more than five years.

NAS Brooklyn was hers.

***

The bewildering swirl of white light and coruscating color depicted on Tag's screens shrank, dimmed, and reformed into a field of stars, albeit a field slightly different from those Bronze Squadron had left behind at Baedecker Four. The twelve fighter-bombers slipped out of ripwave with ten seconds of each other, and twenty seconds later were formed up in a double triangle formation of three pairs each.

"Scanners up," Scrape said. "Minimal traffic—weather satellites around Six. No ships in the immediate vicinity.'"

"Mark those sats and expand the range. I don't want a

freighter traipsing into a live fire exercise."

The red-brown orb of Baedecker Six was in the distance, no bigger across than Tag's palm. Green blips appeared, demarcating the weather sats orbiting the planet.

"Extending scan out to four light-seconds…hang on." There was a pause. "Okay, looks like a salvage tug. They're pulling on something. ID comes back as *Akitsushima*, home ported at Garrick Station."

Tag nodded. Garrick was a fuel depot and trading post in the Baedecker 5 orbital slot, a debris field from a planet that had either shattered long ago or never been formed. Not too far from home. "Keep her marked and maybe we'll take a spin out to those coordinates once DeeDee cuts us loose."

The intra-comm blinked to life.

"Speak of the devil…" Tag flicked the control.

"All units, this is Bronze Leader," DeeDee said. "You know the drill: this is a live weapons training. Baedecker Six is our playground. Targeting information and coordinates are in your operational packets—I'm unlocking them now. This is imperative. You stick to the far side of the planet. Do *not*, extend your range to the eastern hemisphere. There's a handful of mining operations and independent settlements there. Western hemisphere's dead. Meet your marks and reform."

Assents trickled in over the comm. Tag added his, and watched as the combination of inertia from their ripwave exit and the draw of Baedecker Six's gravity pulled them closer to the planet.

"Unlocking packet," Scrape said. "Okay—got the targeting data. It's an abandoned smelting complex a hundred klicks north of the equator, on the cliff bordering the northern dune seas. Background says it was a Northern Alliance weapons cache before the Reittians stomped all over it."

Tag brought the information up as a hexagonal image window on the cockpit display's curve. He whistled. There wasn't much left to the complex beyond the shattered remnants of a square tower, and three crushed domes. "Well, a target's a target. Bomb load check."

"Four Keach Seekers, 230 kilograms, four Arrows, 120 kilograms. Showing a full 7,000 rounds in the 25 mm hypervelocity railgun."

"Ah, love those numbers." Tag triggered his comm. "Bronze Five to Bronze Six. You lined up, Ferb?"

"On your three, Tag."

"Like I said: you take point for this one. Strafe the target and drop your Keaches. We'll be right behind you and lay down ours. Icing on the cake."

"Happy birthday, indeed! 'Cept I don't get anything to unwrap."

"What, tungsten-diamond bullets aren't shiny enough? Five out."

The squadrons entered the atmosphere. Tag switched over to the flight controls, and spun up the engines. The ripwave generator locked into dormant mode. Halfway through their descent, he uncovered the canopy. Flames dwindled around the clear cockpit, and he could see blue-gray sky in all directions. The land beneath was cracked and barren, where it wasn't covered in heaps of sand arrayed in writhing dunes.

"Fancy a vacation, Scrape? Looks like I'd get a decent tan."

"I doubt it would do you any good, as there's probably a lack of eligible women in the mining colonies."

"Such a shame. They'll miss out."

Scrape groaned.

The fighter-bombers broke through scattered cloud cover 50 klicks southwest of the target area. Dust devil blew sand across their run, and when it cleared, Tag could see not one but four complexes spread across the cliffs. Craters littered the area, and many of the three dozen buildings were blackened.

"Somebody's beat us to the punch," Scrape said.

"I'd guess the Reittians. There's enough to shoot at, right? So let's take the pick of the litter." Tag thumbed his targeting reticule and got the familiar red double diamond pasted atop a huge set of cranes.

"Ah, Tag? That isn't one of our targets. Ours are on the ridge just beyond."

"Of course. But since everyone else is circling in an orderly fashion like infants lining up for a treat, we'll show them a little something called shock and awe." Tag kicked on the Raider's afterburners and dove for the cliffs.

"DeeDee's going to have your butt for this." Even as he complained, Scrape set up the bombing arcs, feeding the data to Tag's console.

"Sure will. Do I sound like I care?" Tag craned his neck. Ferb was supposed to lead on this one. Did he guess Tag's idea?

He did. Bronze Six roared by, taking up point a few klicks ahead and below of Tag and Scrape.

The intra-comm lit up.

"Yeah, not going to answer that." Instead Tag signaled Ferb. "Bronze Five to Bronze Six. She's all yours."

"I don't know what you're at, Five, but I'm heading for my target." Ferb sounded mildly amused. "I'll make sure to leave flowers at your funeral when DeeDee rips you apart."

"Thanks. Be sure Scrape says a nice eulogy. I'm partial to poetry." Tag snapped off the comm and, less than two klicks from the target, opened up with the railgun.

White flashes shredded the cranes. They splintered, looking for all the world like toothpicks set ablaze.

"Drop One and Two," Scrape said.

Tag punched the bomb release. A rear sensor pickup showed two fat, elongated Keaches following a precise arc into the mouths of a pair of open prefab hangars. The explosion momentarily overloaded the visual feed in a searing white and yellow flash. When it cleared, the hangars were craters filled with glittering shards.

Ahead, Ferb had already obliterated his assigned targets, and was moving off for a second run. Tag's true targets were just beyond: the tower and domes. "Three and Four programmed?"

"Locked in. all yours."

"Much obliged." Tag bracketed the tower with the railgun, chewing up one lower corner until the whole thing teetered. It collapsed, sending up a huge plume of dirt and sand and debris. Tag flew right through it and, eyes flicking to the bomb arcs, released the other two Keaches.

They slammed dead center amongst the domes, flattening the lot.

The whole area was a mess of smoke and flame and dust. Tag pulled up, g-forces clawing at him. He whooped, the yell echoing inside the cockpit.

"That was impressive," Scrape said.

"Don't sour up on me. Get the results from the scanners."

"I have them. All targets destroyed. What else did you expect? My calculations for the bomb arcs were spot on."

Tag grinned. "Nice. Always take pride in your work."

"But perhaps you should answer the comm."

"Yeah, probably." He activated it. "Bronze Leader, this is Bronze Five, go ahead."

"Don't you 'go ahead' me, Wester," DeeDee growled. "You deliberately violated the order of engagement for this run."

"Sorry, Commander, I figured by order of engagement you meant whoever engages the biggest target first and buries in a hole in the ground completes the mission."

"Your antics put others in danger!"

"By how? Eliminating a target faster than anyone else?" Tag banked the Raider, wind and sand rattling across the wings. The last of the squadron pairs finished their bombing runs. Plumes of smoke rose from the battered mining area. A whole quarter klick section of the cliff sloughed off, crashing down onto the dunes below. "Face it, Commander: if you had a whole squadron of pilots and RIOs like me and Scrape, you could mothball half your wing."

"Enough of your crap. Get back in formation for the next exercise. Bronze Leader out."

Scrape whistled. "I wonder how long of a type-up this will earn us."

"Depends on who else sees it. General Wood can always be counted on to smooth things over."

"Only if your father doesn't overrule him."

"Don't remind me."

***

NAS Brooklyn's primary airlock wasn't functioning, so the *Akitsushima* boarding party had to cut their way in.

Pink glare from the plasma torches lit up the end of the docking collar extended from *Akitsushima*. Captain Blair stood well back with three of the boarding party, while the two Engineering techs finished their cut. They stepped back, admiring their handiwork.

"Pry it open," Blair said.

The seventh member of their boarding party was a doddering Ogre Manual Labor Automaton. One of the oldest MLA's still in operation, this Ogre had been repaired so many times that it no longer had any limbs that matched the other: the left arm was pale white and the right one a dirty gray, while the right leg was a tarnished brass and the left a rusty red. The thick torso was the same collection of grays as *Akitsushima*'s hull. But its appeal wasn't in its appearance.

The Ogre jammed two sets of sharpened claws into the fresh cuts, and using arms that were as big around as Blair's head, yanked the airlock doors apart.

Their separation vibrated through Blair's spacesuit. The

tube was voided of air, and when the hatch opened, vapor crystals scattered, swirling in the beams of her helmet-mounted lights. She checked the sensor readouts on her wrist unit. "Nothing much."

"Skipper, the main cargo hold is aft about seventy meters from our position." Jake was the second mate, tall, lanky, dark-skinned, and serious as a corpse. "Suggest we investigate that compartment first."

"Sounds like a plan to me. We'll hit Engineering next and the bridge, maybe, if there's time. Move out."

They stepped into a corridor twisted and bent like the taffys Blair loved to get from Garrick Station whenever they made it back home. Magnetic boots offered them an unsteady gait. They could have moved faster if they just drifted in the microgravity, but Blair wanted to minimize the risk of someone breaching their suits on an errant projection, like a severed instrument panel.

Lights played all over the surface. The only sounds were Blair's breathing and the occasional comments her crew made in muted tones through the suit comms. Open hatches and huge gashes in the bulkheads marred an otherwise seamless corridor.

The party dropped down an open lift shaft, floating toward the deck Jake indicated. They landed in an alcove with a double-wide hatch that was still sealed. Blair took one of the plasma cutters and breached the hold.

She'd never seen anything like it.

Hundreds of shadowy forms lined both sides of a long pair of walkways, both of which were connected every ten meters by a crossway. The bodies were arranged in rows six deep, and six high. Behind them, her beacon shone on the outline of hatches that must open to space.

"Truppen." Jake made a gesture with his right hand, one Blair had seen in old vids from Earth—touching his forehead, chest, left shoulder, and then right.

"Got an auxiliary light source," one of the techs said.

Blue lights flickered on, racing in lanes down the walkway and the ceiling above. Blair's heart thudded at the sight of shining armored soldiers, hanging in racks with myriad wires and supports holding them in place. "There have to be—what, a thousand?"

"Three thousand six hundred," Jake said. "Scan confirms."

The data flowed across the screen of Blair's wrist unit. Yeah, there were. Couldn't get much more information from the scans, though. Something about the Truppen armor scrambled the instruments beyond the surface readings that told her the armor was intact. Blair started running up numbers in her head: the value of their electronics and weapons systems; the cost of the armor itself...

Jake stepped in close to one of the Truppen. He tapped on the chest.

"Is there power to the whole compartment?" Blair asked.

"Nope. Just lighting. Can't find anything else," a tech said.

"Alright. Let's finish our readings here and move out to Engineering. Serjaum's our priority. The rest of this will stay put."

Blair led the crew through the long compartment, trying to stay calm with thousands of sightless optical ports aimed at them. She kept telling herself they were statues, dead and soulless.

"Shuttle bay's just below us," Jake said. "I've got twenty landing boats so far, possibly more, on the scanners."

"Ripwave generators?"

"Looks like it."

Blair smiled. The values spun even higher. "Perfect."

In the center of the hall was a crisscrossing stairwell that led down to the hangar. Blair's beacons illuminated the wedge shapes of the landing boats. She started down.

The moment her right boot hit the first step, a white beam of light snapped on. It spanned the entire length of the hall.

It came from the panel where the tech had restored the lights.

"Skipper? We've got power fluctuations all over the place!" Jake swung around, gathering more information. "I can't tell from where but I think—"

He cut himself off as a new set of lights blinked on. Red ones.

Dozens of optical ports blinked on—dull red glows that brightened to a sharp crimson. Blair faced the nearest row, staring, her mind freezing up with fear.

The optical ports of the closest Truppen swiveled, and locked on to her. Then the head moved.

"Get out! Everyone get out!" Blair triggered her comm. "Captain to *Akitsushima*! Unhook the docking tube! We're coming back hot! Send a signal out, we've got...!"

Twenty-four Truppen leapt out from their perches. Wires flailed, and connectors sprayed bubbles of fluid throughout the microgravity. Jake shouted a warning through the comm, and yanked a bulky plasma torch from his belt and fired.

The pink beam struck the nearest Truppen, and Blair fully

expected the behemoth to get a molten hole through its gut. But the beam spattered against the armored backside, fragmenting into a dazzling prism.

The Truppen pivoted and hit Jake.

He flew backward, arms and legs pinwheeling in slow motion. His body slammed against the far bulkhead, above the hatch, and the only sound Blair heard was a sickening *crack* through the suit comm. Jake's signal went dead, and his body drifted limp back across the hall.

A warning flashed across her wrist unit. Jake's vitals, flat-lined.

Everyone was yelling in the comms. Blair shut off her magnetic boots and pushed off from a nearby Truppen. Something sharp sliced through her ankle. Her suit alerted her to loss of pressure, and clamped down. She screamed at the double whammy of the cut's pain and the seal shutting off airflow down her leg.

Another Truppen stabbed a claw deep into the suit of one of the Engineering techs. Blood bubbled out from the wound, and smeared the inside of his visor. Another tech snagged Jake's plasma cutter, which was spiraling through the hall, and fired with both of them. One beam sliced through the neck of a Truppen, and before it could get free from its tangle of wires, the headpiece lit up red-hot like a coal. It exploded, a molten spray of yellow and orange bits that left behind a sparking half shell.

Blair flailed uselessly at the Truppen who'd attacked her. He —it—grabbed her by the front of her suit and dragged her close. More alerts flashed on her comms. Her people were dying. Kondo called from *Akitsushima*, but Blair couldn't answer. She choked and gasped, unable to breathe.

A stronger signal cut across the static and overlapping signals. "Identify yourself."

The voice boomed in her ears. Blair sucked in as much breath as she could. "Captain T-Tamara Blair."

The eyes bored into her. "Not Reittian. Northern Alliance?"

"T-Terran. Salvage."

The red glowed more brightly. A second clawed hand ratcheted down around her neck. She couldn't breathe. Blackness closed in all around. But she managed to sputter. "Why?"

"I am Brigadier General Thorson Albrecht," the voice said. "And this war is not concluded."

CHAPTER SIX

The distress call rang out across the entire squadron. "Tag, do you hear this?" Scrape said. "It's the tug we marked on arrival. "Crank it up." Tag glanced at the formations. His and Ferb's fighter-bombers were linked up with two more Raiders in a mock strafing run down a wide, shallow canyon with several hairpin turns. Without even checking his distances on the laser rangefinder, Tag took the next two turns with ease, barely nudging the stick.

Static exploded in his headset, and cleared out into a panicked call: "...one, please respond! This is the salvage tug *Akitsushima*, commercial registry four eight six niner! We are under attack! Repeat! We are under attack by enemy forces! Our captain's dead! Boarding party lost! Multiple hull breaches sustained! Anyone, please respond! This is..."

The signal cut out into static. The squadron intra-comm lit up in its place.

"Bronze Squadron, this is Bronze Leader. Scrub all exercises, repeat, scrub all exercises. Rendezvous at the following coordinates, outside orbit. Ready for combat operations."

Scrape fed the coordinates over to Tag's console as Tag put the nose up. The Raider climbed at a speed that rattled the canopy. Soon enough the blue-gray sky faded to black, and stars shone overhead. Tag sealed off the canopy and switched over to the Raider's exo-atmospheric mode.

"Alright, what've we got Scrape? Tug still where we parked it?"

"Within a few hundred clicks. She's moored in close to the wreck—hang on. My stars!"

"What?"

"She's coming apart! The tug's fragmenting!"

Damn. Tag stared at the magnified view on the canopy screen. The mushroom-shaped tug was breaking up, shedding hull plates and boiling air.

"Go to low ripwave!" DeeDee ordered. "ETA to target five minutes!"

Tag dumped power into the ripwave generator and the Raider leapt forward with the rest of the squadron. Scrape put up a five-minute timer on the screen, counting down to their arrival. The use of low ripwave was understandable—activating the ripwave generator this close to orbit and hopping out into a hot zone was dangerous, Tag knew, but his excitement far outweighed any anxiety.

Finally. He was headed for a real fight.

"How's our payload?"

"Decent. Four thousand rounds in the railgun, and all the 250 pounders."

"Not that they'll do us any good in space," Tag grumbled. "So you'd better charge up the plasma projector."

"Got it." Scrape siphoned off power from the ripwave generator, building the strength behind the weapon mounted under the centerline of the Raider's fuselage.

Tag kept an eye on the power gauge as their timer and distance marker ran down. The plasma projector could run off ripwave for a half dozen shots, each one concentrated enough to disrupt energy shields and punch holes in armor plating. But it ran the risk of burning out, if used improperly.

He just hoped their targets were of the fighter-sized variety.

Their minutes fled fast. "Dropping from ripwave in thirty seconds," Scrape said.

"Roger that." Tag held his hand on the control. The other hand rested on the firing stud for the plasma projector. It held its charge steady.

Three, two, one...

Tag cut out the ripwave generator, and stars shrank back into place. The tug was ahead, centered dead in the cockpit screen. Rather, the fragments of the tug—it had broken apart into three sections, with hull plating and bulkheads swirling off among clouds of debris and sprays of air.

He hadn't anticipated the size of the hulk beyond the tug, a huge derelict warship. What was that, a Northern Alliance cruiser? Sure had the look of...

The weapons fire exploded from behind the wreck of the

tug.

"Incoming! Incoming!" Scrape shouted.

Alarms blared and more yells came across the intra-comm for the squadron. Tag swore and gave a boost with the dorsal thrusters, shoving his Raider out of the path of a missile that raced a half klick from their coordinates.

Scrape tracked it, shunted the data to Tag's console. "Locked on."

Tag gave another spray of thrusters, these on the top of the tail and the bottom of the nose, to spin the Raider over on its end, until its front faced the exhaust glare from the missile. The targeting computer bracketed the missile, and Tag punched the railgun.

A white hot stream of projectiles lashed out and peppered the missile until it exploded.

Then they were in the mix, with missiles and weapons fire everywhere. Tag slewed the raider on its central axis and boosted toward the bogeys.

"Three ships coming out—looks like armed landers, 20 meters long, four turrets, two braces of rocket pods," Scrape said. "Pulling specs now."

"Check the NA records. Got to be theirs." Tag traded fire with the nearest one, a mottled gray and black wedge that barreled straight through the tug debris. The Raider shook under the impact of railgun shots, and the curve of the Raider's shields flickered wildly like heat lightning.

"Shields holding, 92 percent," Scrape said. "Okay, the specs are in—Mark VI Lander, Balfour Industries. There's a spot under the right rear rocket brace that's habitually weakened by high acceleration stresses. Marked it off."

"Locked." Tag kept the bracket hovering over that point, even as the lander flipped over and tumbled through an evasive maneuver. What, did the pilot think he could shake him? Tag blasted forward with a one-second ripwave hop, and flipped the Raider around so fast the stars corkscrewed. He poured railgun projectiles on the hot spot.

The lander came apart in a ball of fire that was quickly extinguished, and spilled its entrails of cargo.

Armored suits? Soldiers.

Truppen.

"Bronze Five to Six, Ferb, you read me?"

"Little busy, Tag!" Alarms and thumps echoed through the

comm, and Tag heard fluent swearing in what he assumed was French. "Gotta frag this bogey before he—nailed it!"

In the distance, another lander came apart, and like with his target, Tag saw armored forms fly out.

"Tag, you seein' what I see?"

"Hence the call. Truppen, Ferb! Cut them down."

"What? But they're adrift! Can't just leave—"

The Raider bucked. More alarms. "Taking fire from those Truppen, Tag!" Scrape said. "Portable railguns and at least one suit-mounted laser!"

"Dammit, Ferb, these are Truppen cybernetic suits we're talking about! It isn't spacers adrift sending out an SOS! They can fight in space! Get back and shoot them down from farther out! Do it now!"

But Ferb was already yelling back and forth with the Frog. Tag's scanners showed a dozen Truppen converging on the Raider.

"We've got to get them off Bronze Six, Tag."

"I know it! You watch the ones trying to slice into our hull and let me worry about closing the distance!"

Shots battered the Raider from all sides. Tag boosted the fighter-bomber toward Ferb's position, then sent it into a wild spin, alternating the thrusters at random intervals. Every instant his guns lined up with a Truppen advancing on them, he shot one down. At that close range a railgun's projectile turned the cybernetic warriors into shards of molten slag.

The battle was a mess. The scanner was filled with targets —some blue, almost lost among swarms of red. DeeDee barked orders, and pairs of Raiders stuck together, sometimes back to back, defending each other from the landers and the Truppen. Tag saw debris fields—Bronze Squadron? Or the landers.

"I count twenty landers, two or three destroyed. Possibly four." Scrape muttered something sharp and long in Japanese. "Too much interference from the debris and radiation."

"Rads?"

"From the tug's reactor."

"Novafire." That reactor was probably gonna go critical.

Ferb's fighter was finally visible on his screen. Truppen limbs and melted torsos littered space around it, but Tag still counted seven swooping around the Raider—no, wait, two were anchored to the hull.

Tag sneered and opened fire.

His first salvos cut apart two of the Truppen, and two

more returned fire with portable rockets. Scrape sent out ECM in an attempt to jam communications, and must have succeeded in disrupting something because the rockets went spinning off their courses, disappearing from the battle.

"Ferb! You still with me?"

"Tag! The Frog's dead! Got a hull breach." Ferb's voice was full of liquid, as if he were drowning in tears or blood. "Can't shake 'em off!"

"Hang on, Ferb, we've got them on the—"

The Raider exploded in a silent starburst.

"No!" Tag boosted away, putting as much distance from the explosion as he could. The resulting radiation and debris still pelted his shields.

The Truppen were annihilated.

"Reactor went critical," Scrape said. "There wasn't anything you could have done."

It didn't sound true. Tag knew he could have stuck closer to his wingman. That was squadron protocol, wasn't it? But he'd burned ahead, leapt into battle, and left Ferb and the Frog on their own. That move had left them vulnerable.

The rest of Bronze Squadron was still in pairs. All ten marks still glowed on his screen, along with the eleventh that marked him and Scrape.

Only one lost.

Suddenly the large red marks turned to streaks, one after the other, and started disappearing. Tag frowned. For a moment he thought they'd self-destructed, and they'd caught a break. But then he realized—

"Ripwave generators! They've all hopped out of here," Scrape said.

The comm crackled. "Bronze Leader to Bronze Five!"

"DeeDee. Ferb and the Frog... they're dead," Tag said. "They got overrun by Truppen."

"I saw it. I know. You weren't on their wing, Wester, and they paid for it."

The words cut through Tag as badly as any shrapnel could have holed his fighter. The signal was between only he and DeeDee —she hadn't chewed him in front of the others.

"There's no time for talk. My ripwave generator's down. So's Bronze Three and Seven's. You've got to get back. Follow those marks. Report this."

"Back?"

"Those landers—they hit ripwave for Baedecker Four."

Tag's eyes widened.

"Tag, I've got our prior course pulled up."

"Right. Let's do this. Max ripwave." To DeeDee, he said, "I'm on it, Commander."

Static burst across her signal. "There's still Truppen out here. I'm going to clean them up. Bronze Eleven and Twelve are tasked to you. Don't screw this up."

"Yes, Ma'am. Five out." Tag cut the comm.

"ETA one hour fifteen minutes," Scrape said.

"Here's hoping we're faster than those landers," Tag muttered, and activated the ripwave.

Bronze Five, Eleven and Twelve flashed toward Baedecker Four.

***

Dust pounded the walls of the monastery. The storm had been forecasted for the past week, but, standing behind the stained glass windows under the dome, Abbot Jeopar was surprised by the ferocity and density of the storm. He could barely make out the courtyard below, and the monastery wall had disappeared.

His communicator chirped. "Yes? Go ahead, please."

"Abbot? We've got a situation." It was Erich, and there was an edge to his voice Jeopar had not heard since—when was it? Ah, when Erich had first awoken in his android form. Something...

Fear. Erich was afraid.

"You've got to get down the tunnel now."

The signal cut before Jeopar could respond. He hurried from the room.

Even far beneath the valley surface, the storm's intensity transmitted as a low, distant rumbling over his head. Jeopar entered the bunker, expecting the orderly rows of Truppen.

Instead, he found groups of eight.

For a moment, he was nonplused. Who had interfered with his work and rearranged the Truppen? He wanted them orderly. He reasoned it would help them maintain coherence when they awakened.

Then he realized the Truppen were *speaking*.

"They were like this when I received the signal," Erich said. "Don't know what they're discussing, because it's encoded—and I must have lost that module in my transition."

"Why eight?" Jeopar wondered if it had mystic significance.

"Squads. Truppen squads are always organized in eights. Led by octenants." Erich frowned. "Something's wrong. Something's activated them."

"How can that be? They were programmed into standby."

"Yes, Abbot, but there are other commands that override standby and bring Truppen units up to full activation."

"Such as...?"

"Combat protocols. Usually, initiated by a high-ranking officer."

Jeopar glanced at Erich. "Wait. You mentioned a signal. I sent you no such signal—you contacted me."

"That isn't what I meant. I was resting in my quarters before I contacted you. And then I felt... a command. A compulsion. An order to arms." Erich smiled. "Of course, I don't have the same internal workings as a standard Truppen, so I was under no obligation to obey. But the compulsion was strong."

"It brought you down here."

"No. That was the whispering. Dozens of voices, confirming their identification and their allegiance. I hadn't experienced anything like it since the last time I saw action during the Consular Wars."

Jeopar looked out over the gathered Truppen. They were still gathered in their groups of eight, but now, they ceased talking amongst each other. They turned and faced Jeopar and Erich, as if aware of their benefactors for the first time.

A Truppen whose gray armor bore more black markings on both shoulders stepped forward, claw feet stamping on the metal deck plates of the bunker. "Identify yourselves." His voice sounded like metal grating upon metal, with the resonance of a bell calling the acolytes to vespers.

"I Am Abbot Damal Jeopar, spiritual leader of Hirrenhausen Monastery. We have labored to restore you men to your original states as Truppen soldiers. Our goal has always and only been to make certain that your souls were protected."

The Truppen stared, red optical ports aglow. "You found this base of operations."

"We did, yes. It was shown to us by commanders of the Northern Alliance, your commanders, during the last war."

"Our orders have not changed. We are to secure the area and await the arrival of the general. Your presence is unauthorized."

The Truppen stepped closer, and raised its arm. A panel opened, and a stubby weapon barrel poked out.

"Blast it all, Jeopar, you armed them?" Erich hissed.

"I—we did not check on weaponry in any way, shape, or form." Jeopar stared down the black hole of the muzzle. He'd never faced death at gunpoint before, not even during the height of the fighting. Was this truly his end? Would God have him suffer destruction at the hands of the very men he'd worked so hard to restore?

"Wait. Don't harm the abbot." Erich stood between them, his hand upraised. Jeopar had never seen him hold himself that way—chin up, chest puffed, his whole frame bold.

The Truppen seemed momentarily confused by the interloper. "You do not command Truppen. I am Colonel Gerald Diaz, leader of the octenants of the 50th Truppen Regiment."

"And I am Major General Erich Baesler, commander of the Second Army," Erich said.

Murmurs flooded the room. Diaz took one step back, his foot indenting the surface of a deck plate. "Impossible. General Baesler died covering the withdrawal of his men."

"As did you? Why is it impossible that I live when you, too, laid down your life, only to regain it again?"

"No. You are a human. You are crude flesh, not a cybernetic form that has..." Diaz's voice trailed off. Jeopar swore the red eyes dimmed and became more like bars than round spots of light. "Wait. Scans confirm it. You are not human, either. You are a simulacrum."

"Android will do, Colonel." Erich clasped his hands behind his back and strode into their midst. "And I know what you'll say next."

"Heresy."

"By all rights, yes. According to the Truppen way, I've forsaken my oath, by turning my back on our ascended form. After all, what could be more glorious than to be transferred into a Truppen war machine? To never know hunger or exhaustion." Erich shook his head. "But we've been wrong. I was wrong. The men of the monastery brought me back from the edge of death, and restored me to that which I thought I'd lost: a human life. Well, such as it is."

Diaz's head twisted. "I do not understand. We have orders."

"Yes, you do. You have orders to reunite the Truppen here on Baedecker Four. And you don't know how to do that. And when your orders fail, what will you do then? Fight every living soul on the planet? Continue with a war that left you and your kin for dead, buried beneath the Iwa Valley?"

The murmurs washed over them again, like a wave. Colonel Diaz seemed conflicted. He also had not lowered his weapon from Jeopar's face. Still, the abbot was impressed by the conviction Erich showed. Truly, this confirmed Jeopar's righteous cause. Erich had embraced his transformation and the faith that accompanied it. If he could change—he, a general who commanded thousands of cybernetic warriors on the fields of battle—then surely that grace could extend to all Truppen.

Surely they, too, could re-embrace a human life.

"General. I make no judgment on you." Diaz put his weapon away, and faced Erich. Jeopar's heart slowed to a less frantic rate. Thank the Lord! "That is for the ranking officers to do—for the general to rule upon when he arrives."

Erich nodded. If there was fear remaining in the android, he hid it well. "I can accept that."

"Sir, I have my orders, but I do not know how to fulfill them."

"Fortunately, Colonel, I can help with that. Do you have data on the transport *Hessian*?"

Jeopar knew the rumors. A troop ship, lost among the chaos of the final days of the Second Consular War. Hounded by Reittian forces, and hiding from Terran scouts, it made for Baedecker Four. With a great sandstorm raging across half a continent, it vanished among the swirling orange clouds. Such went the stories told to children, rookie soldiers, and off-worlders pledging as acolytes.

Tales of a Truppen horror, waiting to emerge and spill blood.

"No, sir. Only that it is to be the focus of our orders to restore our units," Diaz said.

Erich nodded. "Standby."

He joined Jeopar at the entrance. Jeopar marveled at the transformation in the man. "You see, Erich? I told you they would accept your change. I told you they would not shun what you've become."

"Perhaps. But these are men used to following the commands of general staff without hesitation." Erich frowned. "My only hope is that whichever general to which they're referring—whomever has made contact with us—will be just as forgiving. In the meantime, I need your help."

"Anything, my friend. My abbots and monastery are at your disposal. We are all brothers, yes?"

"Thanks, Jeopar. I appreciate that."

"What do you need? And why did you mention the old *Hessian* tales?"

"Because they're not tales, Abbot." Erich's expression became solemn. "I need our brothers to help navigate the valley, because I know where to find the transport."

***

Admiral Daviont stood by the main tactical display on the bridge of the flagship *Narsa* as the final timer counted down. In a few minutes, they'd make the final jump into the Baedecker system. A handful of micro-jumps after, the III Corps main assault element would be in orbit of the fourth planet.

The tactical display was a huge cube, ten meters on each side, that took up half the room on the spacious bridge. It showed the position of III Corps seventy ships, with *Narsa* at the core of their eight-faced diamond formation alongside the bombard vessels. Second Division battlecruisers with long curving wings and spars made up the next layer, with the heavy and light cruisers of the Fourth Division on the outside.

Scans from Lanviond's stealth incursion confirmed the initial Denic intelligence reports: Baedecker was minimally defended. Twelve warships were posted throughout the system, with four heavy cruisers in close proximity to the capital planet. The other eight were all destroyers, tasked with patrolling the outer reaches.

They were currently in transit between postings, under thrust and moving away from their stations.

The time to strike was perfect.

"All commands, report in," Daviont said.

"Second Division is ready, Admiral, and I'll expect three rounds in *Narsa*'s officer lounge when it's completed." Admiral Hilder smirked out from the holograms surrounding the huge tactical display.

"Fourth Division stands prepared," Admiral Bouchtok said quietly. "My final meditation proved most instructive as to handling these Terrans."

"I am most glad to hear it, my friends." Daviont watched as the rosters for their divisions streamed down in twin columns, one on either side of the tactical cube. All ships gave their status as prepared.

"Time to jump, thirty seconds." *Narsa's* commander, Captain Vil Et'Tenna Kentondi sat in his command chair on the upper dais, from where he could see all operations. His crew were spread across twenty stations on two levels.

"Thank you, Captain." Daviont clasped his hands behind his back, and turned from the tactical display. "We have a single chance to salvage the great invasion. Our forces in Audrian space depend upon us to seize this system, and establish a foothold from which we can send forth Serjaum to keep our conquest proceeding. Let us not dishonor our ancestors, our clans, or our emperors. All hail Bonate and Benaltep."

"All hail the emperors," the crew chanted.

"Stand by for jump," Captain Kentondi said. "Our coordinates are set."

Daviont nodded. "Today, then, we win back our campaign of expansion, engage Serjaum drive."

"Activating!" the helm officer said.

Light and time compressed into what seemed like a tiny spot on *Narsa's* bridge. Daviont's motions were blurred, as were those of all the crew. His breaths and heartbeat were interminable minutes apart—or were they hours?

Thus was the sensation as his flagship dove through the wormhole dug by the Serjaum drive, linking points in space nearly two-light years apart.

By squadrons, the Naplian Fleet III Corps vanished from their staging sector.

CHAPTER SEVEN

uests arrived at the governor's compound from all across Baedecker. Elden had never seen so many expensive hovercraft and shuttles in one place at the same time. He did his best to appreciate the smooth, aerodynamic lines and finely polished fuselage plates rather than calculate how much money a stolen one or two of the craft could bring his secret Northern Alliance efforts.

He frowned. Those efforts would be for naught if he couldn't get away from the compound. The main gate was wide open, receiving hovercraft in a steady stream, but there were two dozen Colonial police posted in squads of four. Sneaking through was beyond the question. There were also CDF troops stationed along the walls, both at the catwalks at the top and on the base.

"One hundred forty troops and police," Goetz said.

"You're certain of the count?"

Goetz eyed him with the disdain of a teacher whose pupil just questioned his knowledge of a historical fact.

Elden smiled. "My apologies."

"Our best window's going to be late this evening, when guests leave." Natour swirled rum in a short glass. "You see that Erie Tech shuttle? I can fly those. Give me a few hours to find the owner and charm her out of her passcodes."

"Her? What are you going to do if it's a man?"

"Flying an Erie Tech? Please. It's marketed almost exclusively to rich ladies. That said, if it does happen to be owned by the rare fellow, I'll drink him under the table and steal his access." Natour tossed back the bulk of the rum.

Elden shook his head, not because the plan was ridiculous, but because it was one of the best he'd heard. Natour could get most men close to alcohol poisoning before he was mildly impaired.

The three of them sat on the balcony of a small white stone building, something that Wester called a cottage but anywhere else would be a family residence—four bedrooms, one parlor, one cooking space, and a large. The balcony gave them a tremendous view of the lush gardens, the neat rows of trees, and the mansion looming beyond.

The mansion itself was lit up with beacons, and decorated with holographic displays of shifting flowers. Fireworks boomed overhead, great starbursts of white, gold, and red exploded against the evening sky. Whoever set them off hadn't even waited for the dusk—the sky was a midnight blue, turning black, and there was still a deep red glow on the horizon where the suns had ducked below the plains.

Elden didn't feel at all like celebrating. Within a few hours, the woman he'd always loved, more than any other, was getting married. Worst of it, Ess seemed like a decent enough man. It gave Elden less cause to hate him.

"Are you going to have your sensors calibrated well enough to plan with us, Elden?" Natour finished his rum. He set the empty glass on a nearby bench.

"Yes. Sorry. I'll lock it down."

"Don't fret. I understand."

"I doubt that. But I'll..." A streak of light caught his attention. It arrowed across the night sky, trailing flickers of flame, and snuffed itself out long before it hit the ground. A meteorite? "Did you see that?"

"What?"

"I did. On the horizon, forty degrees." Goetz stood, narrowed his eyes. Suddenly his hand shot out. "There."

Two more streaks flickered, followed by four, then six. For a moment, they lanced through the darkness, then joined the one Elden had seen in oblivion.

Elden glanced around. None of the milling groups of guests dressed in fine suits and entrancing gowns seemed to notice. With the booms and flashes from the fireworks display, though, he was unsurprised.

"Meteor shower?" Natour asked.

"That's what I thought, but those lines—they were grouped too neatly."

Goetz nodded, still watching the sky. "Had to be a formation. Landers of some kind, or assault shuttles."

Elden tried to ignore the nagging sensation in his gut. Instinct told him to contact the monastery, but Wester's men had confiscated their communicators.

He put it from his mind, and focused on a plan for escape. They had to get those Truppen headpieces, or else the Northern Alliance's return to power would be aborted before they ever got off Baedecker.

***

Bronze Five lurched from its ripwave track, as near to Baedecker Four as Tag dared. As it was, the exit was so rocky and the alarms so numerous he swore they'd impacted something.

"Generator's going into shutdown," Scrape said. "I'm shunting coolant from the main engines to keep it from overheating. Should be enough."

"Should be?"

"Yes. If I'm wrong, we'll explode, and there won't be any time for you to critique my performance."

"Fair enough." Tag dove for the atmosphere. Bronze Eleven and Twelve were right on his tail. Good fliers, so far—though he knew they were rookie pilots, both. Couldn't even remember their names.

Thankfully they'd dropped ripwave in time for the sensors to pick up the remnants of fiery trails from the Mark VI Balfour landers. Twenty of them. He shook his head. "Get me a comms signal to the nearest unit."

"Hang on—got it. *TSS Confiance*, Captain Sobban Ram commanding."

"That'll have to do." Tag paused as the signal connected. "*Confiance*, this is Bronze Five, Bronze Squadron, AES Seventh Wing, First Lieutenant Taggart Wester. We are in pursuit of Truppen landing craft released from a derelict vessel. Repeat, Truppen landing craft. Enemy has destroyed at least one Terran fighter-bomber and likely killed the crew of a salvage tug. Myself and two other units are following. Request immediate scramble of any and all fighters in the vicinity. Orbital fire if available."

There was a lull in the signal. Tag didn't wait around for an answer. The Raider bounced through the outer edges of the atmosphere.

"Once we encounter severe friction we'll be off comms for 30 seconds," Scrape said.

"I know, I got it."

A static-filled answer came through. "Bronze Five, this is *Confiance*. What is your vector? Send us all data you have on this supposed incursion. We've heard nothing on the in-system chatter. Confirm."

"*Confiance*, I don't have time for your regs!" Tag snapped. "Those landers are headed to the surface of Baedecker Four, and my RIO has them impacting the Iwa Valley or the Luran Plains not far from Vossberg City. So get me some air support!"

"Bronze Five, I do not appreciate the tone you are taking with my officers." This voice was deeper, and solemn. "This is Captain Sobban Ram. You will stand by for instructions while we parse your data. Who is your commanding officer?"

"Wing Commander Diana Dillon! She might be dead for all I know! So get me those fighters!"

"You will conduct yourself in an honorable fashion, Lieutenant, and recall the chain of command. Stand by while…"

The signal fizzed out in a spray of static. Tag growled and slapped the transmitter off.

"Thirty seconds," Scrape reminded him.

"We might be solo on this one."

"We have three ships total, Tag."

"You know what I mean." Tag watched the fire lick the fuselage. "As soon as we clear this mess, get General Wood."

"I…don't think we have the authority to contact him directly."

"Screw authority!" Tag dug his communicator from his pocket and clamped it against the console. He punched the transfer control. "His direct signal's in there, courtesy of Father."

"They'll both be at your sister's wedding."

"Yeah. I know." Tag couldn't see the governor's mansion from this altitude, but he knew they'd be getting close.

He punched the afterburners.

***

The six-wheeled truck rumbled up the Iwa Valley, heading into the broadest section, where the cliffs and mountains were several kilometers apart. It was far less green than near the monastery, and Jeopar saw carbon scoring streaked across huge boulders and large swaths of the rock faces. There had been a battle here, too—he remembered the sounds of bombardment, the rumble of explosions, the rattle of weapons fire as constant as a driving rain.

Now, with everything painted deep blue under the night sky, and stars shining like grains of sand in the desert, it was serenely beautiful. Even the skeletal remains of shuttles and mechs were oddly enchanting, as if they were the ruined art of a long-dead exotic civilization, rather than the detritus of a recent battle.

Erich drove, and Jeopar sat beside him. Packed into the truck's storage compartment were twenty Truppen, pressed together close in a configuration no human would find comfortable. Their leader, Colonel Diaz, sat nearest the rear hatch.

Jeopar glanced at Erich. His features were taut, his eyes fixed on the rough trail ahead. Perhaps Diaz was no longer their leader. "I did not know you were a general."

Erich said nothing.

"A Truppen commander, yes, but not one of such import. This is truly a great blessing, my friend. Don't you see it? They accepted you. You can lead them on the new path."

"I think you're misinterpreting what happened at the bunker," Erich murmured. "It's a fluke. Diaz is willing to trust me this far. But what happens once we get inside *Hessian*? What happens when this other officer shows up? I'm still as likely to be dead."

Jeopar was puzzled. "Then why are you—?"

"Because as much as you and your abbots are my spiritual brothers, these are my *real* brothers. We were all programmed and transferred into our bodies in the same batch. We fought together, watched our comrades get blasted apart, and—died together. Our lives were supposed to be over. I'd accepted death."

"I see."

"I doubt that. If I can help them complete whatever mission they have in mind, I'll do it to the best of my abilities."

"And in doing so you can convince them of the new life that awaits when they revert to human form."

Erich didn't reply. He blinked that steady blink of his.

Jeopar lowered the passenger hatch's window, allowing cool, dry night air into the cab. The steady hum of the truck's power supply and the crunch of its tires across the dirt were the only sounds. He strained to hear beyond them, to listen for the familiar chirp of desert insects...

A noise grew from beneath all the others. It came from the sky.

Erich frowned. "Do you hear that?"

Jeopar nodded. He craned his neck, looking through the front windscreen.

Streaks of light flashed across the darkness, vanishing as quickly as they appeared. The rumble-like thunder continued down the other side of the Koth.

"Sir, those are our targets." Diaz's voiced echoed from the back of the truck. "I have received confirmation."

"So have I." Erich's voice took on a lyrical quality.

"Are you all right?"

"Yes. The signal I intercepted earlier—it's the same one, only stronger. They're landing on the other side of the mountains."

"Who is landing?"

"What's the quickest way to that side?"

Jeopar considered their surroundings. "There is the creek pass a kilometer ahead, to the north—a left-hand turn through a copse of fir trees."

"Good."

"But Erich—what were those? Spacecraft? To whom do they belong?"

"Like I said: brothers."

***

Governor Wester smiled and shook hands with the BaedCorp CEO and his wife. "Thank you for coming. Good to have you."

They slathered him with compliments about the appearance of the compound, the wisdom his policies, and all the usual flattery Wester expected from business types. As soon as they moved on to their next target—Speaker Zhatkowskii, resplendent in a black tuxedo with a red and blue sash—Wester let the smile sag.

"Looking mighty glum for the most popular man on the planet Antiny." General Wood wore his full dress uniform, khaki jacket with green pants, rank gleaming on both shoulders, medals and service ribbons so clustered on his chest Wester wondered if they could block a bullet. Wood had a glass of rum in his right hand, and clapped Wester on the shoulder with his left. "Cheer up! Marney's getting married, Ess will make a great son-in-law, you'll have grandkids before you know it—"

Wester chuckled. "I highly doubt that. Marney and Timothy have barely discussed it. Give them time to enjoy each other."

Something beeped insistently. Wood rolled his eyes.

"Blasted comm. Shouldn't be receiving any calls—my staff knows I'm at a party. Excuse me."

Wester saluted with his glass of champagne.

"Wood here. Who is this...? Slow down. I can't hear you, Lieutenant. You're where? Landers?" Wood scowled. "Dammit, Tag, if this is your idea of a prank..."

"Tag? He's called you directly?"

"Something about a tug and Truppen and landing craft." Wood shook his head. "Talk to him. I'm going to punch my code in on the secure server in your office."

"Yes, go ahead." Leave it to Tag to botch up something as pleasant as his sister's wedding. All these guests—and calling the general on his private signal! Wester put the communicator to his mouth, and it instantly synced to the speaker implanted in Wester's right ear. "You have a tremendous amount of nerve, Taggart."

"Father? Well, I suppose you'll have to do. Listen: I've got a pair of fighter-bombers with me, and we're chasing down Truppen landing craft. No idea if DeeDee and the rest of the squadron's alive —they were tangling with more Truppen at the wreck."

"What wreck? What are you babbling about?"

"Listen! Truppen are landing on the Luran Plains. I've lost them, but we're doing a flyby to see if we can spot their touchdown. Wood needs to get troops out there. They already destroyed a salvage tug and their crew."

Wester ground his teeth. The music from the string quartet tried to soothe him, in marked contrast to Taggart's yelling and the sounds of the busy fighter cockpit. Speaker Zhatkowskii motioned for Wester, appearing desperate to escape the clutches of the CEO's wife.

"I have obligations tonight, Taggart, and if this is some sort of stunt, I will see to it the wing commander never lets you touch the same tarmac as a fighter."

Taggart let loose a stream of profanity that made Wester thankful only he could hear the message. "This isn't time for a feud, Father. This is serious!"

Wood gestured for him from the doorway. The general's ebullience was gone; his glass discarded somewhere and his posture pure business.

"Hold this signal." Wester smiled and excused himself from the guests. It took him several minutes to chart a course through the crowds, and avoid a dance with the Minister for Finance.

"I got through to Voss Flats," Wood muttered. "Isn't good."

"What's wrong?"

"Defense satellites picked up unauthorized craft emerging from ripwave just outside their orbit, but couldn't get a read with sensors. By the time they'd estimated a landing point, Tag and his fighters came blasting off a ripwave course from Baedecker Six region, same as the unauthorized craft. He transmitted his data to *TSS Confiance*."

Wester nodded. "What did Captain Ram have to say?"

"Mostly derogatory stuff about your kid, Antiny—until he parsed the data. Those landers put up a storm of a fight against a full squadron of Raider fighter-bombers. Looks like one went down, and that they blew apart a salvage tug."

Wester's gut churned. "Is it true, then, what Taggart said? Truppen?"

"Yeah."

They went to Wester's office, where a pair of CDF soldiers stood guard. The office was dark, save for an orange desk lamp and the blue glow of a display screen. Wood closed the door.

Wester punched up the data feed. It was video, imagery taken from a Raider's visual sensors. A battle raged in space, with debris and the remnants of at least one ship—no, definitely two sets of wreckage—floating in the background.

Wood reached past him and paused the feed. "Right there." He swiped with his fingers until one section of the image expanded ten times.

"My God." Wester stared at the fuzzy outline. It was unmistakably a Truppen. Lord knew he'd seen plenty of them during the Consular Wars.

"Best guess: from the tug's transmissions and their trajectory out of the wreckage, it was a salvage gone wrong. Probably they were in stasis, and survived the destruction of their ship."

"What would their protocol be when reactivated?"

"Attack Terran forces," Wood said. "Northern Alliance didn't program Truppen for subtlety. Look, I've dispatched a Special Forces company to the landing area. Tag's in contact with their commander: they'll coordinate a search and destroy."

"Good."

"But we've got a bigger problem."

"I don't want to hear that."

"Elden Selva."

Wester grimaced.

"The man's still Northern Alliance—has to be, unless he's a complete traitor to his cause. If he is, then he's here for Truppen. Not just the ID badges of the honored fallen dead, or whatever BS story he's spewing."

It was difficult to chalk it all up to coincidence. Even if it was, Wester realized he, as governor of the Baedecker system, could not risk someone with the tenuous allegiances that Elden Selva held to be anywhere near the cybernetic soldiers his father and kin had used in open rebellion against Terra. Wester dug his scroll from his pocket, and thumbed the official business section open with his print.

"I'm issuing a warrant for the arrest of Elden Selva and his two companions. You're authorized to take them into immediate custody. We've already taken their communicators. Move them from their lodgings to secure holding cells—and separate them, General, especially that Goetz."

Wood nodded. He produced his scroll. Wester transferred the warrant over. "I'm on it, sir. And I'll coordinate with Tag and the Spec Forces team. Keep you apprised. You should get back to your guests."

Wester watched him leave, and considered the near-empty glass of champagne. "Yes. The festivities."

***

Tag swept high over the Luran Plains. "You see anything?"

"Hang on—heat signatures over the horizon, beyond the second ridge coming up," Scrape said.

"Right." Tag switched comm signals. "Captain, sending you the coordinates."

"Roger that." A gruff voice on the other end of the signal from Foxtrot Company, 22nd Terran Special Forces Battalion, answered. "We're 30 klicks out from your position."

"We'll provide cover," Tag said.

"Stay out of our way while you're doing it, wings. Foxtrot out."

Tag shook his head. "He's friendly."

"Probably your stellar reputation."

"Shut it, Scrape. Focus in on those readings." Tag dropped the Raider low, throttling back and coming as near as he dared to the buttes flashing by, so that Scrape got the best sensor readings possible.

"That is what I'm doing. They are definitely heat plumes —looks like the landing craft are spread out along the end of the approaching valley."

"Keep on it." Tag wasn't about to let those soldiers face Truppen without aerial support.

***

Major Lanviond crept forward among the clefts of rock. This planet was far too cold. Thankfully his armor and bodysuit had a thermal generator set to Naplian norms. "What is it, Lieutenant?"

"There, sir. Craft closing in."

Lanviond read the scanner screen, its output dimmed for night vision. Definitely fighter ships, likely Class II or III fighter-bombers. Nothing spectacular—Ffawe weaponry could easily handle an incursion. What concerned him more were the low-flying, heavily armored VTOL craft coming in close to the ground.

"Troop carriers of some kind," the lieutenant said. "The life signs are crammed together, and there's at least twenty humans in each of the four craft."

"Reduced company strength?"

"It seems so, sir. Some kind of rapid response team. They will be on our position in less than ten minutes."

Lanviond frowned. It did not seem possible they had ascertained the Naplian landing. Even if they had, why would they not pursue a stealth approach? They appeared to be rushing headlong to whatever target they'd chosen.

The lights nearby, most likely. "Anything else from those landings you recorded?"

"No, sir. Your orders were to hold this position—I did not send anyone to investigate."

Lanviond nodded. "I suspect this is an internal Terran matter. Remember: this rock was the site of a civil war. Watch the soldiers, but remain concealed."

"What of our ship?"

That was an issue Lanviond considered. Those VTOL craft could scan the stealth ship if they got too close—and given the proximity of all the action, it was entirely possible one of their squads could literally stumble across it. "Monitor their progress once they land. If it becomes necessary, we will strike."

***

The Raiders crested the ridge, flying low enough to send a herd of Trondo camels scattering.

"Coming up on the targets now," Scrape said.

"Bronze Eleven and Twelve, lock weapons and light those guys up the second we acquire!" Tag said.

The confirmations were terse, and Tag wondered how much of that had to do with the loss of Ferb and the Frog. It was entirely possible the pilots took umbrage at Tag leading them—he wasn't exactly getting commended for command level positions, and this spur of the moment battlefield appointment by DeeDee had him rattled.

"Tag? This is odd." Scrape's voice dropped an octave. "The mass readings are far too small for those landers."

"What? That can't be right. The sensors have the heat plumes right below us."

"There is no mistaking that, but the mass scanners don't lie either."

Tag scowled. "Then what's going on?"

His comm chirped. "Bronze Five, this is Foxtrot. Want to explain to me why me and my boys are gaping at an empty swatch of dirt?"

"I knew, Captain, you'd be at least fourth in line to find out," Tag snapped.

"Captain? If I may..." Scrape hesitated.

"Go for it," Tag said.

"I suspect a decoy. Something with the output to mimic the heat plume from a landing craft's power plant, at least temporarily. No one would be able to see it for what it truly was until mass scanners were brought to bear."

There was a long silence. "Yeah, that fits with what we're seeing. My spotters tell me we've got a bunch of craters scattered about. You think whatever decoy they launched made 'em?"

"Certainly a possibility. I'd read of such subterfuge being used on the Consular Wars, so if the Truppen had hardware left over from the conflict—"

The captain swore. "All right, standby. We'll investigate. I've got scouts going up on to one of the ridges."

"Hold up, Captain," Tag said. "If you go in that deep to the valley we won't be able to give you adequate cover. We can't maneuver in there."

"Yeah, your cover's been great so far. Tell you what—head on back to the governor's mansion and have your servants mop up your Raider while the real soldiers get this job done. Foxtrot out."

"Captain, wait..."

The signal cut out. Tag groaned.

"I suggest we widen our search grid," Scrape said. "There's a couple different vectors the landers could have taken."

"And with all the valleys and ravines out here it could take hours to pin down the right one, especially if they've got reactive camouflage worth a damn," Tag muttered. "Fine, then. Let's spiral outward. Give me the broadest base scan possible, and look for everything—mass, stray EM, debris, even ration packet wrappers. Give me something."

***

Lanviond watched from his perch as the VTOL craft settled at the far end of the valley. Ugly things—bulbous-like insects, with long tails that each balanced a quartet of ducted turbofan engines, and a broad set of pylons at the front that had another pair. The six-engine vessels kicked up so much dust Lanviond had to switch his scope to heat sensing.

"You were right," he said to his lieutenant. "Eighty Terrans. Spread out by squads, moving into the next valley."

"That's far too close to the stealth ship," the lieutenant said. "Shall I signal ahead and tell them to repel the intruders?"

"Negative. We have no idea how sensitive Terran listening devices are. We can't have them calling for help. Instruct the men: we move out, surround them from the ridges as they descend into the valley. Tread lightly."

"What about those fighters?"

Lanviond smiled grimly. "For them I have something else in mind."

***

Tag had barely gotten the Raiders a kilometer away when a green bolt lanced out of the dark plains.

It sheared the port wing off Bronze Eleven, and sent it into a dizzying spin before a second beam stabbed through the fuselage, just above the engine.

The entire fighter-bomber vanished in a ball of fire.

"Taking fire! Scatter!" Tag hollered into the comms. He dropped the Raider so fast he figured his lunch would come right back up. Shadowy cliffs and towering crags loomed on either side. "Scrape! Paint me a target!"

"Trying, but our scanners are jammed! Comms are wiped, too!" Scrape's hands pounded on his controls.

More green beams lit up the night sky. Suddenly Bronze Twelve exploded, showering the plains with fiery debris.

"No!" Tag eyeballed whatever the source was of the beams, angling his Raider directly into their beams, and ignored Scrape's entreaties for a withdrawal. He fired the railgun, hand shaking on the trigger, the white-blue flashes dimmed by his visor.

Something exploded at the far end of the plains, but it was too small to make much difference because the green beams kept coming.

That was when he saw the gunfire crisscrossing the plains below.

"Bronze Five to Foxtrot, come in!" Nothing but static.

More explosions—the Spec Forces craft? He couldn't tell.

A green flash rocked the Raider. Red warning lights flooded the cockpit.

"Lost lateral controls!" Tag said.

"Scanners are down," Scrape said. "We're bleeding fuel. You've got to set us down! We'll ignite for sure, even with the static discharge from a near miss!"

Tag shook his head. "We have to tell someone. Have to get word back."

He turned the fighter-bomber away from the battlefield and lit the afterburners for home.

***

Lanviond nodded. The battle could not be called by such a name. It was a slaughter.

His men, secreted in the cliffs and crags, cut down the Terran soldiers like crops ripened for harvest. The return fire was accurate enough that five of his men were killed, and another dozen wounded.

Every last Terran died.

Lanviond himself killed six men. He strode among the bodies, marveling at their short stature and bulky armor. Their weapons were all projectile based! What kind of barbaric land was this?"

"This one is the commander." His lieutenant stood over a man with strange growth from his chin—facial hair, thick and brown. His helmet and visor were gone. He spat blood, and glared with eyes as dark as the night.

Two eyes. Lanviond shuddered.

He shot the man clean between them. Smoke curled from the charred black wound.

"Secure the area," Lanviond said, "And destroy their craft. I want a full damage report from the ship—that fighter may have damaged something vital. Then ready our teams—we need to move on the governor's mansion at once."

"But sir, we haven't received orders to do so—"

"What do you think happens as soon as that fighter lands? More troops will come. We need to be on our target and prepared for the invasion." Lanviond glanced at his readout.

Soon. Very soon.

CHAPTER EIGHT

Abbot Jeopar could not believe how God's hand moved.

He and Erich got out of the truck transport in the midst of a veritable fleet of space vehicles. They were ugly sloped craft that to Jeopar seemed as if they'd sloughed off the sides of the very cliffs surrounding them. If not for the troops disembarking, he'd have wondered whether they were ships at all— their coloring matched the terrain.

But they were ships, and each one disgorged hundreds of Truppen.

Hundreds of the cybernetic soldiers formed ranks outside their craft, waiting silently in the night sky. The landers popped as their hulls cooled. There was no verbal communication between the Truppen, no speakers used. However they were relaying orders must have been by some signal.

Standing there, staring at the firepower assembled before him, Jeopar was keenly aware of twin sensations: he pitied the men whose souls were trapped inside these monstrous frames, separated from their human form; and he was terrified of what 3,600 the Truppen could do. Every one of them was armed with an assortment of large guns and weapons projections jutting from their shoulders.

Jeopar was assured somewhat by the presence of Colonel Diaz and his 20 Truppen, lined up by fours behind him and Erich.

One Truppen left the assembled horde and strode to Jeopar's contingent. His armor was a flat black, with gray markings on either shoulder. "Well. This is a surprise, Colonel."

Diaz saluted, mechanical hand clinking against his headpiece. "General Albrecht, sir. It is good to see you."

"Likewise, Colonel." Albrecht's eyes homed in on Jeopar

and Erich. "What is your explanation for the presence of these carbons?"

Carbons? Yes, of course. Jeopar wondered how odd human flesh must seem to men who'd spent years fighting a war while sealed inside artificial vessels.

"I am Abbot Damal Jeopar, sir, and as a representative of the Hirrenhausen Monastery of Baedecker Four, I must say it is an honor to meet—"

"I was not speaking to you, carbon." Albrecht pointed a clawed hand in his face. "You'll remain silent until you're spoken to."

"General..." Diaz stepped forward. "Sir, the abbot and his people were the ones who restored us."

Albrecht swiveled his gaze to the monastery Truppen. "Your last orders were to remain behind and ensure no Northern Alliance data fell into Terran hands while my forces withdrew on the *Brooklyn*. I assumed you had all fought and died gloriously. Now I find you standing here on the end of this carbon's leash. Explain."

"Every one of us here—and several more at a mothballed bunker in the vicinity—were either destroyed or left on the battlefield deactivated. We did our duty, sir, and fully prepared to pay the last price. But the abbots recovered our headpieces, and salvaged our bodies best they could." As Diaz spoke, Jeopar couldn't help but notice the rough shape of his armor—scratched, dented, paint flaking, unit numbers worn down. It was in stark contrast to Albrecht's well-kept shell. Even Diaz's movements seemed to have a stiffer quality to them. The observations tempered his pride at the abbots' fine work at restoring the Truppen. "Because of those men and Abbot Jeopar we have returned to serve."

"Serve whom? I need men ready to continue the fight."

"With all due respect, General, the fight no longer exists." Those were the first words Erich spoke since they'd intercepted these Truppen.

"You—are an anomaly," Albrecht said. "Even my basic sensors can tell me you're an android, neither human nor Truppen. Silicon instead of carbon, then? Tell me, how did you reach your analysis? I've already been shot at by Terran fighter-bombers after we were brought forth from stasis. For me, the war continues."

"What you think you've observed is irrelevant, Brigadier General. What I know—having been active longer than you—is that the Northern Alliance is a ghost of itself. We have made arrangements to meet with a man who will help us bring it back, but for now we have to act subtly."

Albrecht laughed, a harsh, grating sound through his suit's speakers. "You think you can lean on my rank and impress me? You're a failed Truppen."

"No. I am Major General Erich Baesler, and you'll yield to your superior officer, soldier."

The entire mass of Truppen stirred. Jeopar couldn't hear the conversations, muted as the speaker talk was, but it was far magnified from even the reaction Diaz's Truppen had exhibited back at the bunker. Whatever the outcome, Albrecht's mood did not alter. "Quiet!" he boomed, and the Truppen forces lapsed into silence. If they were still communicating, it was electronically.

"General Baesler? Erich." Albrecht shook his head. The red optical ports left afterglow in the night. "What have you become? A freak. A monstrosity."

"I've come closer to my lost humanity than I ever thought possible. Listen: you and your men are in danger. Pursued?"

"We are that. I have no doubt the Terrans are hunting for us, as we speak."

"Then come with me. I have the location of the *Hessian*, and the remainder of our brothers."

"The *Hessian* was destroyed."

"No. It was hidden. Buried. One of the last acts of a desperate Northern Alliance command, to prevent our Truppen resources from falling into Terran hands. I know because our soldiers—Diaz included—were among those who held out against the Terran onslaught while the transport was concealed."

"This is ridiculous. I have my—our men free. We can continue this conflict, and punish the Terrans once and for all. If we free the *Hessian*, what then? We awaken the rest of our Truppen and flee? I'm done retreating, General Baesler."

"It isn't a retreat. It's planning. It's obeying the orders of the man who can continue this fight the way it should be—slowly, with caution, cutting the Terrans with such precision that they are left wounded and weak when we're ready to strike."

"And what man is that?"

"Elden Selva, last surviving heir to Sedrick Selva and Consul of the Northern Alliance."

Albrecht went silent.

Far in the distance, a sound like cracks of thunder split the sky. Jeopar frowned; there were no storms, no foul weather due. He realized the flashes of light on the horizon were far too synchronized and of the wrong color to be natural phenomena.

"You hear that?" Erich said. "Whatever is going on out there, is something we can use to our advantage. Consul Selva is detained at the governor's mansion, the structure beyond the Iwa Valley en route to Vossberg City."

"What do you propose?" Jeopar noted the difference in Albrecht's tone—not one of submission, but touched by deference, at least grudging. He'd heard many men employ the same tone when coming to him seeking to join the monastery.

Albrecht was a soldier without a cause, and that realization was dawning.

"Place your men under my command," Erich said. "Serve myself and the Truppen again. We'll find the *Hessian*, rebuild our forces, and with the help of our consul, give the Northern Alliance the transfusion it needs to truly live again."

The sounds in the distance intensified. Whatever was happening, it was a vicious fight—Jeopar heard distinct explosions that rumbled across the plains and over the hills. His heart ached at the thought of the people who must be dying, or already killed. All he could do was implore God to examine the hearts and minds of each, and grant forgiveness as He was willing.

Albrecht appeared to have noticed the conflict, too, as had many of the Truppen behind him. Finally, he brought his right hand up to his head in a slow salute. "Very well, General."

Erich returned the gesture.

"But don't be deceived—what you've done to yourself, what you've become, is an affront to every Truppen here, and a betrayal of the principles for which all our comrades died. Once a Truppen, always a Truppen. I'll follow your orders as tribute to them. Nothing more." Albrecht leaned in, and Jeopar was struck by a sudden fear that Albrecht would kill him—and Erich—if he could. "Do not think you can betray me."

"I wouldn't dream of it," Erich said. "And you should be forewarned that I'm not going to be spat upon by our kind. There's a new future for our people, General. The abbots of Hirrenhausen have opened my eyes to that. They returned humanity to me. With the Truppen and the Northern Alliance reunited, we can spread that vision to any cybernetics who want the chance at their old lives."

Albrecht made a sound that sounded like a snort, albeit an electronic ripwave of one. Did he realize the holdovers from his human form? Jeopar saw it in how he stood, how his right claws tapped against his left forearm as he stood there with his arms crossed. Whatever the sensations one experienced when being transferred into a Truppen form, a man remained. Erich was the best proof of that.

The sounds in the distance faded. Jeopar touched Erich's shoulder. "Come, my friend. The sooner we uncover your ship, the sooner we can make your people safe."

Erich nodded. "Thanks, Abbot, for all you've done."

"I am but an instrument in the hands of a mighty God, Erich, as are we all." Jeopar smiled. "Let us count our blessings to be standing at the threshold of a new era."

***

Governor Wester paced in his office. He couldn't locate General Wood—no response to his communications. Tag hadn't contacted him again, either.

He hated waiting. Hated having to hide out here from the party. But with the wedding less than an hour away, he'd begged off from the boisterous crowds of guests. Only in his office, his sanctuary, could Wester focus on the problems at hand.

There were many.

"Sir?" One of the CDF soldiers poked his head around the door. "Your daughter to see you."

"What?" She should be getting her dress fitted, and prepared for the ceremony. "Admit her, of course."

The woman who stormed past the guard could not be his little girl. She was elegant in a flowing white dress, with white sleeves to the elbow and exposed shoulders and collarbone. Auburn hair was long and cascading in a braid down her back. Silver and diamond glittered at her neck, punctuated by a fiery red jewel. A platinum band encircled her head. Marney's freckles seemed all the redder next to the cool colors of her wedding ensemble.

It was the face that stunned him for a moment: Marney could have been her mother, in a moment of anger. Cheeks flush, eyes glaring, lips outlined in bright red and pressed into a sharp line.

"You look absolutely stellar, my dear," Wester said. "Give your old man a hug before the ceremony starts."

"Release Elden from custody, right now." There was no questioning, no wheedling, no negotiating. Wester had served in the CDF years ago—he knew a command when he heard one.

It didn't mean he was even close to acquiescing. "Marney, we've been over this. I had to keep Elden at the compound, at least for the time being. There's no need for us to antagonize the Reittians—"

"That isn't what I meant, and you know it. I went to see him and he's been arrested! Colonial police wouldn't let me anywhere near him or his friends."

"Ah. That. There's been—new developments. I don't have time to go over the details and frankly, it isn't any of your business."

"Of course it's my business. Elden is a dear friend."

Wester shook his head. "Are you certain that's all?"

Marney folded her arms. "You're questioning me, now?"

"I have that prerogative, as your father. This is your wedding night. Your fiancé is waiting for you, and the first thing on your mind is to go see Elden."

Marney blushed. "That isn't the first thing."

"I think you know what I mean. I won't even pretend to know what it was like for you two when you had to part ways. Goodness knows the war took plenty from all of us." Wester held her hands. "Marney, please: steer clear of Elden Selva. What's happening now—well, it doesn't bode well for him and his associates. After tonight, you won't see him again outside of a CD incarceration cell."

"That's ridiculous. Why have you locked him up?"

"I can't say. It's a serious situation, but General Wood's handling it. I have every confidence he can sort it out." He tried to banish the thought of the Special Forces team engaged in combat with Truppen cybernetic warriors. He'd seen what the latter could do, and wouldn't wish the confrontation on anybody. "When it's over, perhaps, I'll fill you in."

"As your daughter, I have the necessary clearance."

"I'm aware of that. You know I'd never withhold something like this from you if I didn't have good reason. Just let it be, for tonight. Enjoy your wedding. Spend time with your friends."

"Elden is one of my friends. Whatever he's doing, Father, it can't be bad enough to warrant arresting the man. Just leave him free for this night."

"So he can come to your wedding? Honestly, do you think he would?"

"I … had hoped."

Wester nodded. "I see. You still have a great deal to learn about men, Marney. However much a friend he's been to you, I think he still harbors deep feelings. Perhaps deeper than either of you are willing to admit. If that's the case, the last thing in the galaxy he'd want to see is the woman he loves married off to another man—and a Navy officer who fought on the other side of his people in the wars, no less."

Marney sighed. "I understand, I do. But it's difficult to let go of a ... friend like him. He was gone for so long and to see him now has been wonderful."

"You've a good heart, Marney. That's what I love so dearly about you."

She smiled, and smoothed out the front of her gown. "Thank you, Father. But I do want the entire arrest record for Elden tomorrow morning. If there's anything I can do to help him..."

Wester nodded. "Very well. I'll make the arrangements."

The door banged open. "Antiny, we've got a problem. The team's been..." General Wood stopped short. A hologram hovered in the air above the scroll clutched in his left hand. "Oh. Hello, Marney."

"General."

"You look lovely! Is Tim being held at bay?" Wood shifted the scroll, and dimmed the display.

Marney frowned. "What's going on? First Elden's arrested, and now you're barging into Father's office. Work on the night of my wedding."

"Nothing to worry on."

Marney put her hands on her hips. "Father, General, no more of this, please. My security clearance is Alpha One Eight Six Charlie."

Wood's smile froze in place. He cleared his throat.

"Update us both, General." Wester was perturbed, yet simultaneously proud that his daughter had not given up her training as one of the governor's children when she moved over to the Ag Department. She knew how to keep state secrets, and she was keenly interested in anything that affected Baedecker's welfare.

"Okay, then. Tag's update had the team reach the landing site, but it appears the—" He paused, glancing sideways at Marney. Wester assumed he questioned whether or not she should hear the next part, so he simply nodded to give Wood the assent to continue. "The Truppen set heat decoys down at a different site. Misdirected our forces."

"Blast it." Wester went for the rum bottle. This was going to be a long night.

"Truppen?" Marney's eyes were wide. He hadn't seen her this astonished since he used to tell her stories from the wars, when she was in primary school. "Here? How is that possible?"

"Just a second." Wood was somber. "Tag and his fighters flew cover. They were attacked. So was the team."

"What?" Wester nearly dropped his glass. "Is he hurt? Are they all right?"

"We lost contact with Tag and his RIO, but their transponder's still active—heading this way. The other two fighters were shot down, according to the sensor data. The Spec Forces team—" Wood's jaw clenched. "Dead. Every one of them."

Marney gasped. Wester set the glass down by the bottle. He didn't have the thirst anymore. "You're certain."

Wood nodded. "Vitals were all monitored by Command. Whoever took them out did it fast. No one saw the ambush coming."

"Whoever? I thought you said it was Truppen," Marney said.

"That's who we're tracking—a force of Truppen that apparently made planetfall less than an hour ago. But the sensor readings from the team, once they got down into the valley, showed no Truppen."

"Did you get anything?"

"A fragmented recording. Doesn't make sense." Wood frowned. "Alien DNA. Bipedal, tall and skinny. Single-eyed."

Wester stared at him. That didn't sound like any of the sentient species with which he was familiar—and after five years of handling trade disputes with all manner of corporations, he knew a goodly amount. "I'd say we need another unit out there but I'm hesitant to send anyone given what's apparently happened. What about *Confiance*? Did Captain Ram get us anything from orbit?"

"Negative. He's moved around in orbit for a better set of readings, but with the topography as gnarled as it is, he'd have to send someone in closer." Wood squared his shoulders. "We need to cordon off an area several klicks around. I can get my mechs and tanks into place ASAP. We'll block off every route out of that terrain."

"I don't want any more of our craft being shot down, General."

"They can circle the perimeter, at least until we get some drone scouts in there to find out what we're dealing with."

Wood scowled. "Whoever they are, they just butchered an entire company. I want them stopped."

"And we will. What other news do you have on Tag?"

"Hang on." Wood's scroll pulsed with a signal light. He reactivated it, and new words, accompanied by what appeared to be range and distance indicators, glowed on its surface. "Ah. Well, he's sustained damage, and it looks like he's coming in hot for a landing."

"At Voss Flats?"

"No. Here." Wood jogged from the room, barking orders into his communicator.

Wester reached for his own communicator. "Grounds? This is Governor Wester. We have an emergency landing imminent. Initiate safety protocols—fire suppression, force screens, EMTs. Coordinate with General Wood—he has approach vectors and the like. Send up flares outside the compound at his direction. I'm on my way."

Marney joined him. "I'll tell the guests there's been a delay—and Tim, too."

"Yes. We won't postpone your wedding for much longer." There was still half an hour before the appointed time. But Wester couldn't focus on that.

Right now, he had to make sure his only son was unhurt.

***

The Raider's cockpit was awash in red light. Mercifully, Scrape had killed every last one of those ear-shattering klaxons.

Didn't change the fact that his fighter-bomber was dangerously low on fuel. Tag knew he was going to have to ditch.

"I don't suppose I should remind you, we can't reach Voss Flats," Scrape said.

"Yeah, I think you've mentioned it. Twice before."

"Only site between here and there is the governor's compound."

"I'm not crash-landing atop my sister's wedding!"

Scrape made a choking sound. "I thought you said we could land safely! When did 'crash' become part of the acceptable description?"

"Never mind that." On the dark horizon, red pinpricks marked off an irregular circle. "Give me a reading—got something set up near the compound, just northwest of the perimeter."

"I see it. One moment." His console hummed. "Landing flares. There's a definite area—wait. There's a homing beacon. Probably from a portable unit."

The indicator showed up on Tag's console. Yes, it was sitting right outside the compound walls. Someone knew he was coming in—General Wood was right on his game. Of course, he'd like to think Father had something to do with the preparation, but wasn't holding his breath. It was even odds whether an impending fighter-bomber crash would drag his father away from a social function.

More lights flashed—this time, the starboard engine flamed out.

"Well that sucks." Tag decreased thrust from the port engine, doing his best to compensate for drift.

"Core isn't going to hold for much longer. There's time to eject."

"I've never lost a ship, Scrape, and I'm sure not starting now."

"I'd argue the insanity of that statement when measured against our current circumstances, but I know you'd just grin and not listen."

"Glad we're in agreement."

They were only a few hundred meters from the landing site when the port engine cut out, too. All that kept them aloft were the hoverjets used primarily for final approaches when landing or for a boost when taking off. They weren't meant to slow the descent of a fighter-bomber moving at high speed.

The Raider lurched and dropped.

Tag waited until the last second and triggered a full burst from all the thrusters. It took the edge off their velocity and angled the fuselage just enough for Tag to put the Raider down on the dirt plain just beyond the compound wall. The Raider slammed against the hills, banging its way down a slope and sliding into the dead center of the red flares. The screech of the fuselage against the ground echoed inside the cockpit.

Then it all stopped, and the power cut to the cockpit.

"Last stop!" Tag punched the emergency release for the canopy. Puffs of smoke and flashes of light spread in a line down the direct center of the canopy, and the whole thing disintegrated —as if someone unzipped a tent and the tent, in the process, disappeared.

Outside, the night air was full of sirens, shouts, and the cackle of flames. Harsh chemical odors burnt Tag's nose. He grabbed an emergency breather from under his seat and, having made sure Scrape had his, vaulted out of the cockpit with his RIO right behind him.

"Get foam on that right now! Force screens are up? Good! Make sure you've got a generator to back them up." General Wood led them both away, through pairs of red and silver firefighting bots and a handful of emergency workers in all orange jumpsuits lined in black. "Get these boys to a medic!"

"No need, General." Tag winced. Something jolted his lower back, and he noticed Scrape limping. Maybe a cursory inspection by a medic wouldn't be a bad idea.

Firefighting bots unleashed a flood of suppressant foam on the fighter, dousing flames coming from the aft quarter. Emergency workers circled the wreck with force screen posts, and once they had the all clear, activated them in unison. The ten posts lit up brilliant green, and Tag saw the sky shimmer in a dome that faded slowly back to transparent. Its bottom edge dug a line in the dirt.

Tag submitted to the checkup by the medic, a slender, blonde woman in white coveralls. He and Scrape sat on the lowered ramp of a medical lander's back end. The squat white transport hovered a half meter off the ground, red and blue emergency lights flashing across the plains.

"Glad to see you boys in one piece," Wood said. "Also impressed you didn't eject. It isn't like we have an unlimited supply of fighter-bombers way out here in the galactic sticks."

Tag nudged Scrape. "See? Told you."

Scrape just rolled his eyes.

More people hurried out from the compound. Tag had a moment to gawk at Marney's radiant dress before she slammed into him, making his back stab with pain. The medic frowned at them both. "Lovely to see you, my lady. I hope I haven't interrupted the biggest party of the year."

There were tears in Marney's eyes. "Tag, don't say things like that! I'm just glad you're unhurt. And you too, Lieutenant Sakawa."

"Thank you, Miss, though I'm again questioning my choice in pilots."

"As soon as you're up to it, boys, I need to debrief." Wood stood by the ramp, staring out at the smoldering Raider.

"No need to wait, General. There are Truppen out there: I have no doubt. I saw them at Baedecker Six and—" Tag's eyes widened. "DeeDee. Commander Dillon. Have you heard from her, or the rest of the squadron?"

Wood shook his head.

"Damn." Tag rubbed his hand over his face and through his hair. "I have no idea on the strength or location of the Truppen, sir, but whoever took out the Spec Forces team was not them."

"Our scans showed without a doubt that aliens were present, aliens of an unknown race," Scrape said. "Nothing in our databases matches."

"Visuals?"

"No, sir, we were attacked quickly and forced off the site."

"We're putting all our forces on alert. Captain Ram of *TSS Confiance* is moving ships into orbit to conduct a further search. I've got word to my unit to deploy. We'll cordon off the area where you found the decoys, move out from there."

"Yes, sir." Tag stood, ignoring the medic's complaint. "General, Scrape and I can do our best from the inside of a cockpit. Get us to Voss Flats and in another ship so we..."

"Hold that thought." A pair of CDF soldiers in black armor approached him. "I've got to coordinate the deployment. Don't leave."

Tag flexed his hands, wishing he were back behind his controls. But even with the flame extinguished, his Raider would be in no condition to fly for months. Assuming it was still air and space-worthy. "Marney, you should get back to the house, before Father worries."

"He's plenty worried, Taggart, but not about her or the wedding." Governor Wester walked up, flanked by a quartet of Colonial police guards.

"Father." Tag gave a curt nod. "Sorry we couldn't do better."

Wester didn't say anything. Instead, he put both his hands on Tag's shoulders, and pulled him into an embrace.

Tag was stunned. When was the last time Father had hugged him? One of his childhood birthdays? Certainly not when Mother died. Tag put his hands up, hesitantly patting Father's back.

Wester abruptly released him, and straightened out his tuxedo. He rubbed at the corner of his right eye with his thumb. "Ahem. Well. Marney, when you're through, let's get back to the mansion and our guests."

"Father, I think that—"

But Wester was already walking back inside.

Tag shook his head. "That just figures."

"Your Father's a complex man, Tag." General Wood was back, his scroll open and messages streaming across it.

"I doubt it highly. He's calculating and cold."

"I'd say you should cut him slack, but how long have I been telling you that?" Wood gestured to the scroll. "Let's deal with the facts at hand, boys, and then I'll turn you lose for the wedding in a spell."

"Yes, sir." Tag watched his Father walk back to the mansion, without glancing over his shoulder or acknowledging the police guard.

"Tag, I'll talk to him," Marney said.

Tag shook his head. He was tired—borderline exhausted. And only a tiny fraction of that had to do with getting shot at and shot down. "You know what, Marney? No one else needs to talk to him. The only person who should say a blasted word to him is me."

"Are you certain that's a good idea?" Scrape asked.

Tag shoved his helmet at Scrape. "I don't know, but I'm going to do it anyway." He pushed away from the medical lander and stalked across the plains after the governor of Baedecker Four.

***

Jeopar surveyed the plains before them, and the three mesas arrayed in descending size. Nothing out there looked as if it were home to a transport. Debris from wrecked starfighters and broken mechs littered the plains, and several craters were half filled with sand and brush. "Is this the correct location, Erich?"

"It is." Erich held a pair of binoculars to his eyes, the glass glowing green. There should be some kind of marking, some indicator."

"Unless you were completely wrong," General Albrecht said.

They were at the top of a stubby outcropping, with hundreds of Truppen spread out across the plain. A pale blue glow emanated from each one, tracing languid paths over the dirt. All their scanners fed data back to a panel Colonel Diaz held. He and General Albrecht watched it, waiting for any signs of the *Hessian*.

So far, they found only debris.

"I don't get it. I know this is the right spot. It's the exact coordinates we were ordered to protect."

"It was probably an intentional decoy, to fool the Terrans," Albrecht said. "You and your men guarded nothing, but did so with such ferocity it drew the Terrans away from their true target."

"No. Northern Alliance Command and the consul would never do something like that."

Albrecht barked a sharp, static-filled sound. Jeopar assumed it to be laughter, but it was as unholy a noise as he'd ever heard. "Do something like what? Use Truppen as railgun fodder? You always were an incurable idealist, General Baesler. The scans are clear: *Hessian* isn't here, if it ever was hidden in this spot. You've led us to a myth."

Erich scowled. He lowered the binoculars.

"Be at peace, Erich." Jeopar hated seeing a man who'd come so far in such a short time driven to doubt, especially one who held such promise for his people. "Clear your thoughts and let God be your guide. He can show you the truth of any situation; only He can lift the curtains of dark to let in the light."

"Curtains," Erich murmured. His eyes widened. "Of course. I can't believe I missed it."

He grabbed a communicator from his belt. "Units on the south side: inspect the mesa nearest you. Scan the slope."

Two dozen Truppen followed his instruction. Their scanners formed a line of blue dots along the slope of the middle mesa, waving back and forth.

"Sir! We've got something." Diaz held up the panel.

Jeopar couldn't read the results clearly, as they were in some kind of coded graphics that, he assumed, only Truppen could translate. What was obvious was the outline of something big, or at least, the sharp edges of a portion of an object.

"That has to be it," Erich said. "All units, converge on the mesa in the middle."

"What am I seeing, Erich?" Jeopar asked.

"A camouflage canopy, Abbot. Small versions are used for rapid deployments, in order to hide a unit's position—and its vehicles—from casual observation. When done right, they can even resist a cursory sensor sweep. But I've never seen it done on this scale." Erich lifted the communicator again. "You have the sensor data. Cut it down."

There was a flurry of activity along the mesa slope. With two clusters of Truppen forming on either end. Two red lights flashed on simultaneously, and laser beams flickered where dust marked their passage. They cut at the edge of the rock, spraying sparks and melting stone. Jeopar watched in amazement as molten stone oozed to one side of the beam's path, and some kind of thick covering peeled back as smoothly as the rind of the ribspar fruit.

Halfway down, the beams cut off, and the Truppen scurried back. A great tearing sound cut through the air, and the *clang* of metal banging off rock. The canopy ripped free.

The false face of the mesa was torn aside. Beyond it, was the tall, boxy shape of a ship. A huge ship.

"Jasper-Class transport *Hessian*," Erich whispered. "The last reserves of the Truppen forces at Baedecker."

He glanced at Albrecht and gave a tight smile. "So much for myth."

CHAPTER NINE

The III Corps of the Naplian fleet appeared in space less than 1,000 kilometers from the surface of Baedecker Four.

Narsa was the lead ship, with the 24 battlecruisers of the 1ˢᵗ and 2ⁿᵈ Colonial Squadrons arrayed in pairs around her.

"All craft report in," Admiral Daviont ordered.

Reports streamed in from the battlecruisers, coordinated through the tactical display. With the hologram enveloping him, Daviont felt as if he could stretch out his arms and move his fleet with sheer willpower. The blue sphere hanging in the center might as well have been a targeting reticule.

It was woefully underdefended.

"Reading three Terran cruisers, designated Type One, within 500 kilometers of the planet," the tactical officer said. "Weapons charging. Missile locks from all three. Fighter craft deploying."

Captain Kentondi twitched his head, his eye never moving from the displays. "Lot of good that will do them. Deploy our fighters, defensive screen only. Make our target the nearest cruiser."

"Yes, Captain."

"Micro-jump array Alpha on my command."

Daviont manipulated the tactical display, and opened a communications link to the battlecruiser *Dassa*. "Admiral Hilder, this is Command. Jump your squadron ahead to the starport. I want that station crippled before we begin our landing."

"Affirmative, Admiral." Hilder's voice seemed to echo out from the pulsing green circle that denoted his flagship among the 1ˢᵗ Colonial Squadron. "Fear not, Tir, we'll show the two-eyes how to conduct a proper naval exercise—with themselves as the unfortunate targets, of course."

"I trust in your abilities. *Narsa* out."

The twelve ships of 1ˢᵗ Squadron blinked from existence. Seconds later, their indicators reappeared only 200 kilometers away from the huge space station orbiting the planet. Streaks of light denoted missile tracks as the squadron opened fire. Almost immediately, red lines returned the favor from the station. Daviont frowned. There were far more batteries firing than the Denic agents had indicated. No matter. If the exchange became too lopsided against the Naplian force, he could withdraw and reorganize. The bombards and transports were waiting a jump back with the 3ʳᵈ Colonial Squadron: more firepower could be brought to bear later.

The enemy ships, no matter how few, were the greater threat. They were mobile. As the Ffawe hunting aphorism went, there was no sense hunting a treed *nuiraska* beast when the smaller, craftier, and poisonous *jolar* hound was stalking you from the crags.

Alert klaxons blared. "Incoming missile salvos from the Terran ships."

"Launch countermeasures."

"Yes, Captain, deploying drones. Picket lasers charged and targeted."

"Concentrate our fire on the lead of the three, Captain," Daviont said. "Whichever craft is receiving and sending the most communications—whichever's maneuvers are mimicked by its companions."

"Understood, Admiral." Kentondi snapped his fingers at the tactical officers. "You heard the man—less blinking, more action!"

Dozens of missiles swept in from the Terran ships, but they were hardly a match for the Naplian's armament, by Daviont's accounting. Half the battlecruisers threw out a swarm of drones, each one 10 meters long, that sprayed defensive clouds of shrapnel and fired lasers that overheated and exploded the incoming missiles. Those that did make it past this screen met a veritable fence of laser beams that swept space, cutting apart any missile which they intersected.

To Daviont's surprise, the squadron's defenses only accounted for half the missiles fired by the enemy. As his ships launched more than 70 missiles in response, 24 Terran missiles breached the invisible wall.

"Where in the great suns did those come from?" Kentondi snapped.

"Captain, they evaded our pickets! We're reading across the board navigation and targeting failure on at least three handfuls of them. Some kind of disruption from the enemy projectiles—we can't bring the affected pickets back on line."

"It seems the Terrans are more resourceful than we gave them credit for, Captain." Daviont tapped on three squadron vessels in the tactical display. "Move these ships to correct for the imbalance. Ignore the disabled drones. Have these three sweep across the following coordinates and concentrate all their fire on the incoming missiles."

Tactical officers relayed the orders to the appropriate ships, while Kentondi reoriented *Narsa* so she was less vulnerable to the strike.

The three ships at the tip of Daviont's improvised spear took the brunt of the incoming missile's fury, drawing the attention of the rudimentary artificial intelligence guiding the projectiles. A flurry of laser beams and particle blasts filled space around each ship on the tactical display as red arrows mobbed them. Several got through. After a few minutes, none remained.

On the tactical display, all the Naplian ships exhibited twitches and shivers that, to any other species, would have seemed the result of a sensor malfunction. But they were the outward signs of precision micro-jumps, so perfectly timed that it gave the illusion of a Naplian vessel being at one set of coordinates when in fact it had shifted off that position by dozens of kilometers. Daviont was pleased to see it played havoc with the Terran sensors, too, as the bulk of their missiles were on erroneous vectors when they detonated.

"Damage report," Daviont said.

"*Soton*, *Diam*, and *Eilan* have all taken hits. *Soton* has a severed drive sail. Crews are hauling out a replacement. *Diam* has hull breaches in several sections but patches are holding. *Eilan* lost its forward particle turrets and one missile tube. Remaining missiles are being shunted to the secondary and tertiary tubes. Minimal casualties."

Daviont nodded. Acceptable, though not ideal. He was not about to lose a single Ffawe to these Terrans—though, he'd already begun reforming his invasion plans in the face of their surprising ingenuity. Terran technology was not as backward as Denic agents had led them to believe, and now he was faced with an even greater conundrum.

"Sir, the three Terran cruisers sustained damage in our

opening salvo but all are still combat operational," the lead tactical officer said. "I...Admiral, they can't possibly have destroyed all of our missiles in that first wave!"

"Maintain your composure, Lieutenant," Daviont said. "We are used to facing a determined adversary in the Audrians and the Briddarri, are we not? Then it should come as no shock the Terrans are just as stubborn, if not more so. The worst mistake an officer of the imperial fleet can make is to underestimate an enemy, no matter how seemingly primitive. Wars have been lost because of such errors."

"Yes, Admiral."

Daviont did not need to tell the lieutenant the reminder was spoken for himself, just as well.

He ordered a second salvo, then a third, with nine of the squadron's ships firing upon the Terrans. *Narsa* added her missiles to the attack, under Kentondi's direction—targeting the enemy's lead ship. Though the Terrans resisted well, and scored a handful of hits upon Naplian ships. *Soton* and *Diam* suffered considerably more damage in part because their commanders were slothful in responding to Daviont's command to withdraw. As a result, the squadron found itself with two battlecruisers crippled.

"Brainless," Kentondi snapped. "I'd space them myself if they were on my bridge."

"I suspect their near-disaster will be reminder enough." Daviont frowned. "In case it is not, however, I will reinforce their shame by demoting them one grade in pay. Make a note of this."

"Yes, Admiral."

An alert came across the tactical display—Admiral Bouchtok's Fourth Naval Division had jumped further in-system, and split off into its constituent squadrons. Bouchtok's flagship, the heavy cruiser *Catinal*, led the 15th Dragge Squadron of six ships and the bombard vessel *Solon* to Baedecker Six.

"There are a handful of settlements here," Bouchtok reported via hologram. "Easily subdued. I have the 17th and 27th Squadrons chasing down the Terran destroyers patrolling the system. You were correct, Admiral—your initial assault at Baedecker Four spurred them into responding, and we were able to pinpoint their exact coordinates and approach vectors."

"Very good. I trust there's no complications."

"None, Tir. There is, however, a great deal of debris not far from orbit—appears to be wreckage of a warship and another commercial vessel. Nothing of concern. I will report back in when

Baedecker Six is ours. Fourth Division signing off."

The tactical display broadened to include the individual movements of Bouchtok's four squadrons, shrinking down the groups to smaller pricks of light. Daviont reached for Admiral Hilder's force assaulting the space station. Sections of its shield system had collapsed, and text marked each destroyed missile battery as it fell under the onslaught of the Naplian ships.

"Admiral Hilder informs us Baedecker Spaceport will be defenseless shortly," the tactical lieutenant said. "And the three Terran ship are pulling back behind the curve of the planet."

"As well they should. The damage they've sustained is grievous." Yet, they continued to fight. From the communications station, a steady stream of intercepted chatter flowed. There was no sign of panic from the Terran captains—and whenever it cropped up among their officers, it was tamped down immediately.

Daviont smiled. There was nothing so satisfying as the defeat of a worthy enemy. The Terrans of Baedecker were shaping up to be just that.

***

TSS Confiance was in geosynchronous orbit above Baedecker Four's night side, searching for the Truppen landing below, when the attack began. She was, like her three siblings drawn into the initial brawl, a Monsoon class heavy cruiser, 300 meters long, armed with an array of short and medium range torpedoes, plus nine batteries of long range missiles. Twin engines stacked atop each other aft of a gracefully sloped hull reminded Captain Sobban Ram of the fish he'd caught out on the family lake with his uncle.

He was a tall, slender man, dressed in the dark blue jumpsuit of the Terran Navy. His shoulders bore the four silver bars and four-point star of a captain, with a pair of collar slashes that denoted starship command. With thinning black hair and deep brown skin, Ram would not have stood out discernably from his ancient Egyptian ancestors. Yet it was his devotion to the old gods, whose resurgence quietly spread across the stars when his people left Earth centuries ago, that he knew kept him calm while his officers shouted commands at subordinates.

Ram did not race out to join the brawl, which he knew from the start would be lost. One cruiser would not make the difference when the Terran ships were outnumbered by a factor of eight. He stood at the front of *Confiance*'s bridge, a long chamber built like an amphitheater, atop the dorsal hull. From there he could see the battle unfolding in the holographic display tank, a tall cylinder of ever-changing vectors and swarms of lights that indicated not only combatants, but civilian ships fleeing the Baedecker Starport.

The starport was the linchpin. If it could ward off this initial attack by 12 alien ships—and by all rights, it should have had the armament to do so—then he could sweep in and lead a counterattack. All he had to do was stay hidden while the eight destroyers farther out in the system raced to join the fight.

Except, the enemy's intelligence was far better than he'd anticipated. Whomever these aliens were, they'd dispatched more squadrons to cut off any such rendezvous.

Ram watched the sensor data trickling in from Baedecker Starport, bouncing off a satellite at one of the Lagrange Points. It was troubling, in terms of the sheer number of the attackers, and also puzzling in their behavior. More than once the station had targeted an enemy ship using its particle cannon, only to find the ship was not actually where the coordinates provided by the sensors said it should be. Some kind of scan interference? Ram had no way to tell. There was no way the station would survive another salvo, even having disabled two of its attackers. His options were limited.

"HV cannons charged, Captain. Pulsed particle turrets online." His first officer, Commander Allison Vollan, was a stocky, pale woman nearly his height. She had straw blonde hair and eyes pale blue, like chips of ice. "Missiles racked all batteries and ready for launch."

"Very good, Commander." He used his scroll, which was linked to the main tactical display, to etch out his plan. When it was complete, he swept it across the link and overlaid it onto the display. "Pass the word to the battery chiefs: this is our targeting spread. Have the helm set our course accordingly."

Vollan's eyes widened as she took in his vectors, and a smile spread across her face. "Aye, Captain."

Ram listened closely to the ebb and flow of orders and input around his bridge. They were a good crew. But they'd never faced anything like this—an alien invasion by a force of overwhelming strength. Ram knew war. He knew it well enough from the Consular conflicts, both of them. Maintaining cool was key to winning the battle.

The tactical display alerted him to the failure of Baedecker

Spaceport's primary shields. Its defenses were collapsing. The enemy ships sensed this too; their formation closed in, and reduced their fire.

"They mean to take the spaceport intact," Ram murmured. "A wise move. Even damaged a station of that mass makes for an excellent forward base, until they can construct something to their native specs."

"It sounds as if you don't think this is a hit and run, Captain," Vollan said.

Ram shook his head. "No. I fear this is an occupation."

He turned to the tactical officer. "You may fire when ready."

***

The spread of torpedoes that shot around Baedecker Four and plunged into the pack of Naplian ships surprised Daviont but only mildly. He knew they were short one heavy cruiser.

"She's hiding on the dark side of the planet." Daviont activated the indicators for the 1st Colonial Squadron. Two ships, *Bellon* and *Fare*, were bending their courses away from the space station. Both had suffered critical damage to their shields. "Send to Admiral Hilder: the incoming fire is from a Terran heavy cruiser. Peel off *Ardente* and *Mobello* to intercept."

The order was acknowledged and relayed. *Narsa's* deck swayed underneath as the flagship took fire from the lead Terran heavy cruiser.

"Have to admire their squint to come up this close and live long enough to punch it out with us," Kentondi muttered. "Forward guns: let them have it."

Narsa soaked up a peppering of shots by some kind of hypervelocity projectile cannon, the kind Ffawe forces used on Naplia long before they developed reliable shipboard energy weapons. But the *Narsa* was also getting hit by pulsed particle weaponry. Apparently the Terrans had a mixed bag of new and old technology. Did that make them a scavenger species?

Bravery aside, for a 300-meter heavy cruiser to engage *Narsa* at that range was tantamount to suicide. Daviont watched *Narsa's* shields decline, but they were nowhere near as badly affected as the Terran was by the shots scored by *Narsa's* gunners. Their particle cannons were far more devastating, and before long, gouts of flame erupted from the spots at which the Naplian weapons penetrated Terran shield.

However, the exchange of fire this close did interfere with his scanners, leaving Daviont temporarily blind to the fight. If that was intentional, the Terrans showed considerable cunning.

Captain Kentondi bounced both fists off a console as the opponent exploded in a silent nova of white light and yellow fire, that blinked out faster than a cinder doused in water. The two remaining Terran ships turned their backs, and fled along a vector that would take them near to Baedecker and its moon.

Daviont nodded. As he suspected, the lead ship's destruction had taken the fight out of the Terrans. He pushed aside that portion of the display and focused on Hilder's contingent at the station. Interference from the particle weapons fight of a few moments ago lingered, scrambling his view of the battlefield. He could discern enough, however, to see that the spread of torpedoes was easily countered by the squadron's defenses. Only a handful struck home.

"None of Admiral Hilder's ships report significant damage from the torpedo strike," the tactical officer said. "Another wave of missiles and torpedoes is incoming."

"Tell him to be cautious: our micro-jump capabilities are obviously not enough to prevent the Terrans from causing injury." As was apparent by the crippling of four of their ships already. Something about that new spread of Terran torpedoes tickled Daviont's senses, though. As much as he spread his eye, he couldn't see what the enemy had planned. Two spreads: the remaining heavy cruiser should have followed them immediately, seeing as how the Terrans demonstrated a penchant for close-range slugging with their hypervelocity railgun cannons.

Even as the interference with the scanner dissipated, Daviont realized what was amiss. He reached past the tactical officer's shoulder and opened a direct comm signal to Hilder's *Dassa*. "Go! The Terran is coming around the opposite side of the planet! Redirect your vessels!"

It was too late for *Ardente* and *Mobello* to alter course—they were well on their way over the wrong side of the planet. That left eight of the 1st Squadron with their attention squarely on the station.

A new red circle popped into existence as *Narsa's* scanners detected. The Terran dove at the squadron, unleashing a devastating salvo of short range torpedoes and larger long-range missiles of greater yield. The weapons swept in, with the heavy cruiser hot on their heels. Whoever the captain was did not wait for his shots to fail or succeed; he simply blasted away with every projectile and particle cannon he had.

The battlecruiser *Suverein* was at the back of Hilder's pack. She scrambled out of the incoming barrage as best she could, and launched a mob of countermeasures, but still took the impact of eight torpedoes. A few gasps escaped the bridge crew as *Suverein's* jump sails shredded, and she split along her spine.

The Terran was merciless, beating on *Suverein* until the vessel's reactor core failed and it exploded.

Kentondi swore in *ffawe-kresh*.

"All ships, move in," Daviont said.

"Sir, what of the escaping Terrans?" the tactical officer asked.

"You want the wounded *comper* herbivore when the *jolar* has us by the heel?" Daviont snapped. "Leave them! Do as I command!"

Spinning up the short-range jump took agonizing minutes, during which the Terran interloper managed to cut a swath through the Naplian ranks. She took a pounding, but considering her position it was risky indeed for the Naplians to fire on her without inflicting friendly fire. As such she managed to score several hits on *Arcole* before lunging away from the starport.

Daviont narrowed his eye. A bright mind, that one, and not willing to sacrifice Terran naval power to defend the station—which he must already know was lost.

Before any of Hilder's force could do more than hammer her shields, the Terran ship had jumped away from Baedecker.

"Short range FTL ripwave," Kentondi said. "Well, we know their propulsion's on par with ours. Thank the War God and his Brutes they don't have micro-jumps."

"Reserve your thanks for later, Captain. Tactical, send word: the transports may close. Prepare the bombards."

With the station silenced and surrounded, their invasion could begin in earnest.

***

Captain Ram coughed to free his lungs of the smoke pooling on the bridge. Ventilators whirred as they struggled to pull the acrid remnants from the air. Several consoles had shorted out. Emergency lightning colored every surface and every crew member a lurid red.

"Engineering reports one of the shield generators is down for repairs," Commander Vollan said. "Compartment Sixty-Six is open to vacuum. Torpedo tubes Three and Four are down."

"Casualties?"

"Two dozen with major injuries, ten dead."

Ram closed his eyes. It was a painful loss, but the results could have been far worse. Coldly balanced against the outcome—one of the alien ships was destroyed—he would not trade.

As it were, he could sense the shift in attitude. His bridge crew were tense, and tired, but the fear was gone. He opened his eyes and could see the change in their expressions. They now knew the enemy could be defeated.

He would need every bit of that improved morale to survive what was coming.

"Send word to *TSS Akron* and *Shinsoku*, and any destroyers that have survived," he said, circling the two remaining heavy cruisers on the main display. "Withdraw from current stations and rendezvous at Station Golf Echo Five, in the cometary debris belt. The farther away from Baedecker Four, the better."

Vollan pursed her lips. "Sir. We're abandoning our planet?"

"There's nothing more we can do. If we remain here and continue the fight we will be destroyed—and we will not be so fortunate as to repeat our first attack, now that the enemy has seen our improvised tactic. Our best course of action is to retreat and repair. Station GE 5 is remote, and though it is only a sensor and refit depot, it will provide an adequate base of operations." Ram gestured to the communications officer. "Send word to General Wood and Governor Wester of our actions. We'll standby when they're ready to initiate."

"Initiate what, Captain?"

Ram stared at the tactical display, watching the red circles of the enemy fleet spread out, a plague encompassing the space around Baedecker Four. "The insurgency, Commander. Our objective now is to harass and destabilize the enemy. They will have our planet—but we'll make them bleed slowly, every day, and they'll find the cost too great to continue."

TSS Confiance ripwaved away from the battlefield, for the black depths of the outer star system.

***

Admiral Hilder was in a fury when Daviont contacted him

from the privacy of his office.

"Blinking two-eyed scum destroyed one of my battlecruisers!" Hilder snapped. "Their treachery is intolerable, Tir! Too many loyal Ffawe have lost their souls between the stars today."

"While I agree with the sentiment, Gol, it's hardly treachery. The Terrans are skillful warriors; whatever intelligence the Denics sent our way, that is the key thing to remember. I take full responsibility for the loss of *Suverein*. Had I not underestimated our enemy, in spite of the violent history which I know they've led, I could have seen the misdirection sooner."

"All the more reason to unleash my squadron and let me hunt down those aliens!" Hilder said.

Daviont shook his head. He paced his office, with two life-sized holograms of Hilder and Admiral Bouchtok watching him. Between them floated their summaries of the respective battles. Both were encouraging, though not without complication: Hilder's 1st Colonial Squadron was the hardest, with *Suverein* lost, *Bellon* and *Fare* in dire need of repairs. The 2nd Colonial had *Soton* and *Elian* crippled, plus *Diam* heavily damaged.

Bouchtok's forces were less impaired: of his four squadrons amassing 24 ships only the 19th Dragge had lost a vessel: the light cruiser *Quinet*, caught at the convergence of two salvos from Terran destroyers who showed considerable coordination. A handful of other ships had sustained heavy damage, enough so that Daviont recalled them to Baedecker for repairs. But his results were reassuring: half the eight Terran destroyers had been eliminated.

"We are still left with seven of the twelve Terran ships in the system." Bouchtok stood with his hands behind his back, posture relaxed, eye fixed on Daviont.

"That's far too big a pack to leaving roaming about." Hilder had his arms crossed, and a healing patch affixed to a bruised portion of skin above his eye.

"I heard you the first time, Gol. Our telemetry indicates that the Terran survivors have fled toward the fringes of the system. It's riddled with cometary debris. Tracking ships out there will be difficult at the least." Daviont held up a finger to forestall further comment by Hilder. "We have damaged ships, and injured crew. For our primary forces those are the priorities: repair and healing."

"Third Colonial hasn't even a single scratch," Hilder said. "I'll transfer my flag to *Noul*, and take those battlecruisers—"

"That's enough, Vice Admiral." Daviont used the rank

instead of the familiar name in his final effort to warn Hilder off his vendetta. The subordinate admiral shut his mouth, though the lines furrowed around his eye told Daviont the matter was not settled. "I need the Third here, to guard our backs as we secure the planet itself. With the bombards stationary and the transports disgorging their troops, we'll be stationary targets."

"Speaking of which, Tir, might I suggest we use this time to investigate the Serjaum deposits?" Bouchtok said.

"Of course, Kiv." Daviont consulted the fleet rosters. "Take *Catinal* and the 15th Dragge to Baedecker Two and secure the region. There was nothing on our initial scans but scattered merchant and mining traffic—I sincerely doubt any are still there, given the battle, but send a fast scout ahead to be certain."

"Your will for our victory, Admiral." Bouchtok said. "Admiral Hilder, I trust upon my return we can conduct a joint memorial for our lost crews, to see their souls found by the Ascended Masters."

Hilder returned the bow, but stayed silent. Daviont found Bouchtok's tacit reminder that he, too, had lost a ship more effective a stay against Hilder's bloodlust; it certainly seemed to shame him from making further comment about the losses he'd sustained.

Bouchtok's image shivered and disappeared. Daviont mimicked Hilder's defiant posture. "Well, Gol? Anything more, or can we move on with the occupation?"

"Nothing more, Admiral."

"Don't be fooled by my orders into thinking the Terrans will not pay for their impertinence," Daviont said. "As soon as the planet is ours, I'll dispatch one of your squadrons and one of Bouchtok's together on a hunt for the remaining enemy ships. We will not seek revenge, however, but justice. If any of the ships and crew can be captured, I want them. They will provide far more valuable intelligence than even our Denic spies could manage. Is that clear?"

Hilder relaxed his arms, and gave the bow of subservience. "Abundantly, Tir. Thank you. Hilder out."

With his hologram dissipated, only the list remained. Daviont frowned at the red marks. Two ships lost. Several more damaged. With the Briddarri, the outcome of such a lightning invasion would be far harsher. But he knew he'd face intense inquiry from Bonate and Benaltep when he returned to the Naplian front.

Of course, by extension, the Baedecker system was the new front.

Daviont returned to *Narsa*'s bridge. The tactical display was focused on the 3rd Colonial Squadron, the only one not to see action in the initial strike. Twelve battlecruisers formed a spherical perimeter beyond Baedecker Four's moon, and Daviont summoned the four bombards and four transports into a low orbit around the planet.

"We're all set for the show, Admiral." Kentondi preened worse than a *siru* bird in mating season, chest puffed, uniform straightened, rank shining.

"Very well, Captain." Daviont stepped into the midst of the display. He swept his hand about the ships, touching each bombard and each transport. Their indicators flashed with white rings and pulsed. They were prepared.

"All bombard vessels: This is Admiral Daviont. Take up position over the primary military bases and population centers. Your orders are to eliminate all military infrastructure, all ground to space transport, all ground-based defensive weaponry, and major communications networks. Leave civilian population centers intact. We will need labor for Serjaum extraction, after all. Limit your fire on the cities to demoralizing strikes."

He paused. "Transports, you are clear to make your deployments. All assault pods and landers, commence. For the glory of Naplia and her emperors."

"For Bonate and Benaltep!" Kentondi bellowed, and the bridge crew joined in his cheers.

Daviont watched as the huge bombard vessels, each one a bulk rectangle twice the size of *Narsa*, took up orbits that allowed them to fire on their targets. Sheets of green energy discharges and streaks of missile exhausts rained down on Baedecker Four. Beyond them, the smaller transports emptied wave after wave of cone-shaped assault pods. They gave the appearance of a highly regimented meteor shower as they blazed into the atmosphere.

"Signal Admiral Hilder," Daviont said. "Assign fighters from *Frislant, Arcole, and Imperial* to patrol the skies and engage any enemy fighter craft. I want nothing in the clouds to hinder us."

"Yes, Admiral."

As the tiny, claw-shaped fighters raced out from their ships, Daviont smiled. Soon, he'd have this world between all six of his fingers. And enough Serjaum to win a war.

CHAPTER TEN

With fifteen minutes left before his sister was to get married, Tag caught his father at the entrance to the Grand Hall of the governor's mansion.

Beyond the open double doors of solid bole wood, he saw hundreds of guests crammed into chairs and onto benches. Mansion staff in formal attire lined the walls. There were even a pair of Colonial police stationed just inside the doors. At the very front, a Colonial justice of the peace and a CDF chaplain stood, both clad in crisp versions of their respective uniforms. Beyond them, a huge window that curved overhead gave everyone a stunning view of the fireworks display that reached a fever pitch.

Wester was startled when Tag seized his arm. "I thought you'd still be with the medics. I didn't want to disturb you any further."

"Disturb me? I about died out there!" Tag snapped. "Maybe you and the general didn't get my full report—there are Truppen out in the plains."

Wester pulled Tag away from the door, toward an alcove. A painting of Baedecker Starport loomed above. "Keep your voice down! I know exactly what your report says. I read every word, and I also read how those Special Forces soldiers died. How your fellow pilots died. General Wood's unit is on its way as we speak. But my role, as governor of this colony, is to keep my citizens safe. That includes putting on a pleasant public face so as not to incite them to panic."

Tag scowled. "Sounds to me like another excuse for walking away from the real problem."

"What do you suggest I do? Pick up an M36 and follow you out into the desert, where we can singlehandedly fight all the

Truppen?"

It was a sharp comment, meant to cut Tag's pride, and no matter how he steeled himself against it—even when he saw it coming a kilometer away—it still sliced through his defenses.

"You can't fly in and take out every target on your own, Taggart," Wester said. "There are times when the greatest way in which you can serve is to be just a small part of the larger picture. When you have to acquiesce to someone else's plan, someone else's orders, to ensure the achievement of the greater goals. Until you can do that, you'll never understand me."

Tag felt cold, and weary. Some of it must be the exhaustion of the past day, but he knew some of it was trying to talk to Father. "Following orders can get you killed, if they're the wrong orders. Look at Commander Ess—Tim." Tag pointed into the hall, where Ess had entered from a side door. He stood stiff and proud in his Terran Navy dress whites, cap tucked under his arm. "He saved hundreds of lives on those hospital ships, by taking the initiative when no one else did. If he'd stayed put, following orders, they'd be free-floating particles."

"Yes, but with every such action, no matter the good that results, comes more risk and more pain. Ask Timothy about the twenty men and women who died aboard his ship when he gave the order to rescue the hospital ships. Ask him if he's still haunted by their loss, even though he did save forty times as many lives through their sacrifice. That's the difference between command and cavalier."

Tag lapsed into silence. Every time he tried this, it devolved into the same old arguments about Tag's career. He turned away.

Wester's hand rested on his shoulder. "You and Marney are the only family I have left for a hundred light-years, Taggart. No matter what it takes out of me to run this planet, I would never want anything to separate us. I never had. Your mother was always so much better at being a parent. Management was my strength, but management doesn't show a child he's loved and doesn't encourage him to be his best."

"I was surprised you even came out to the crash site," Tag said.

"If it had been in the middle of the desert, I would have walked." Wester stood in front of Tag, and smiled. "Come. Be here at least for Marney's ceremony. Sit by me. Your seat's empty. As I am sure your RIO knows, every man can use a good co-pilot."

Despite his frustration, Tag smiled at that. "Okay. For

Marney, and Mother. And... well, for you too, Father. When it's done let's—"

Explosions rumbled beyond the windows. At first Tag mistook them for more fireworks, and glanced instinctively at what he supposed would be the grand finale. What he saw, however, were streaks of light. He instantly recalled the Truppen landers.

Only, there were far more than twenty.

Murmurs arose among the guests. Tag started for the door, away from the Grand Hall, when a series of tremendous impacts rattled the entire mansion. Chandeliers swayed. Lights flickered. Somewhere deeper in the mansion, glass shattered. Shouts of alarm echoed from the hall.

"What in the stars is this?" Wester got on his communicator. "General Wood, respond."

Nothing but static.

He switched frequencies. "CDF patrol Alpha, report."

Still nothing.

Wester stared, wide-eyed at his communicator. Tag didn't know what was going on inside that mechanized brain of his, but Tag had already figured out the problem.

Someone was jamming communications.

"Sir!" A pink-faced Colonial policeman in full body armor ran up to them, huffing. Tag caught a whiff of bole wood and fragrant greenery—the man must have been on guard duty outside. "Assault pods! We can't identify their origin but they're hitting the plains all around the mansion."

Wester glanced at Tag. "More Truppen."

"Damn."

Guests were streaming out of the Great Hall. Timothy Ess pushed his way through. "Sir, what's going on? It sounds like a combat landing."

"We don't know anything yet," Wester said. "I have to find Marney. Tag—you and Timothy find General Wood."

"And Scrape. Right, we're on it. C'mon, Tim." Tag took off at a run, weaving through clusters of confused servants. Ess stayed close on his heels.

They jogged down the stairs of the mansion, and collected a half dozen armored CDF troops on the way who had been headed inside. "Everyone's okay in there," Tag said. "Our priority is finding General Wood."

"Saw him last at the landing site, still supervising the

cleanup," one female corporal said.

"Right then. Two of you, with us. The rest, maintain your positions on the wall," Ess said.

"Yes, sir!"

They split off into two groups. Tag led them to one of the stairs that mounted the compound wall, climbing them two at a time. He wanted a better vantage point, so he could see what was going on and hopefully locate the general and Scrape faster.

He crested the rampart and stared.

A half dozen craters were spread across the Luran Plains to the northwest, each one emitting smoke and steam. Shapes like squashed eggs—eggs surrounded by thick, ribbed shells of black and forest green—split open, casting a sickly green glow from their sides. Within seconds, hundreds of soldiers poured out of the dozen pods.

Alien soldiers.

"My God," Ess murmured.

"You ever seen those before?" Tag wished desperately he'd stopped at the armory first. Both Colonial police had M36s, and the idea of having a flechette-firing rifle loaded with 150 rounds in the magazine appealed to him.

"No. Never."

The troops wore a mottled blue-gray armor that reminded Tag of urban camouflage, but before he could classify it further the armor changed color, matching the hardscrabble terrain. They were tall and lanky, with three fingers on each hand. Their weapons fired green energy discharges tinged with white and yellow.

Great. Handheld particle weapons.

And then the mechs trundled out, eight-legged monstrosities as big as a Ghamsara bison, flat gray and blue armor plating, a single orange eye glowing at the front. A cannon mounted on the back shot bursts of the same color energy discharge. The impacts made the compound wall ring like a gong.

"Let's go!" Tag had to get weapons for them—M36s, SAAR railguns, portable grenade launchers, anything.

The strange screeches of the aliens' energy blasts crescendoed. They were joined by the whine of railgun shots and the rapid chatter of flechette bursts. The armory wasn't far away. Tag's boots pounded the pavement. His lungs burned. They rounded a cluster of bole trees—

And he collided with Scrape.

"Man! Am I glad to see you." Tag slapped him on the back.

Scrape smiled tightly, and handed over an M36. There was a second one slung across his back. "More so because I brought a present, I'd wager."

"Also yes." Tag hefted the weapon. The power pack was at full charge, according to the green light. Good. He could get 5,000 rounds fired before it died, and the strap attached to the M36 had 10 more magazines secure in pouches. Fifteen-hundred rounds of ammunition.

"General Wood's here." Scrape gestured behind him.

Wood was indeed there, firing off orders at the soldiers coming and going. The armory door was wide open, and the men and women charged with defending the governor's compound were bringing out every weapon Tag had hoped.

"What's the situation?" Ess accepted an M36 from a CDF soldier.

"We don't have a clear count, but there's at least 300 enemy soldiers, plus a dozen mechs," Scrape said. "There's a defensive line just beyond the wall. It won't hold."

The resignation in Scrape's voice startled Tag. But with the sounds of battle increasing he couldn't blame his RIO for letting pessimism win out. Still, Tag would rather have his fighter-bomber in one piece. That would make short work of these invaders.

An explosion near the gate caught everyone's attention. The exterior doors had been blown away, twisted metal with blackened edges the only evidence that half meter-thick armor had once guarded the primary entrance into the governor's compound. Now all that was left was the force field barrier on the inside of the wall.

Two of the alien mechs trundled forward, hideous mechanical spiders. They pounded at the field with their energy cannon.

"Get up on that blasted wall! Destroy them!" General Wood hefted an M-199G grenade launcher and scrambled up the steps to the compound's rampart.

"Come on!" Tag was not about to be left out of the fight, but he turned to Ess first. "Get back to the mansion and find my sister."

"I'll get her and your father out, I promise." Ess sprinted back for the house.

Scrape found them a spot where the rampart was highest, and a blast from someone's weapon had torn a huge chunk away —perfect for a firing slit. Tag took up a position on one end, with Scrape on the other. He flipped the selector on his M36 to six round bursts and found the nearest alien.

Tag shot him down on the run. Pale yellow liquid sprayed as the creature flailed in is death throes.

Yellow blood. Definitely no species he knew of.

He and Scrape took turns, one firing, the other covering while the shooter reloaded, and so forth. They took out a half dozen soldiers that way, but their success made them targets. The fusillade of fire directed their way became so great Tag had to hunker down behind the rampart and quit shooting.

"They outnumber us," Scrape shouted, "And those energy weapons pack a considerably greater punch than our rifles!"

To their right came a *whump* and a flash of light, followed by an explosion that shook the wall under their feet. One of the alien mechs was destroyed, nothing left but a jagged crater in the gate pavement and flaming bits around it.

But there were far too many dead Terran soldiers and police strewn about for Tag to be comforted by that small victory.

The wall swayed again as a second blast, this one of a decidedly alien pitch, lit up the entrance. The energy field flickered and died.

"The shield's down! Fall back! All troops fall back!" General Wood shouted.

"That's our cue!" Tag slapped Scrape's shoulder and scurried for the steps.

They were halfway down it when a blast ripped the bottom of the stairwell off. Tag tumbled through the air, landing flat on his back amidst the scorched bushes. Scrape landed heavily an arm's length away.

Dizzy and nauseated, he shook away double vision and grabbed his rifle. Strange, almost musical sounds drifted underneath the sounds of battle. In his semi-delirium, Tag wondered why Father had permitted the band slated for Marney's reception to move outside. Didn't they know it was dangerous out here?"

When he looked up, there were a trio of the alien soldiers less than five meters away.

One of them pointed at him, yelled something in the strange, warbled tones that Tag realized was their language. The alien—a guy, he assumed—had slate gray skin and a single, pale blue eye, three times the size of any human's.

Tag stared down the double muzzles of the soldier's energy rifle.

A burst of flechette fire tore through the soldier from

behind, severing his right arm at the shoulder. Yellow blood sprayed everywhere, and its scream made Tag grind his teeth.

The other two soldiers turned and fired, giving Tag the chance he needed. He brought the M36 up and took them down with three bursts.

General Wood limped over. There was blood smeared on his side. "Graze, nothing bad," he said. "Get up."

"Wait!" Tag shuffled over to Scrape. His RIO was unconscious and... not breathing? "Scrape? C'mon, get up!"

He shook his shoulder. Wood didn't say anything, only slung his rifle over his back and picked up one of the alien weapons.

"Scrape? Scrape!" He checked for a pulse. Nothing. The man's eyes were wide open, staring through him, straight up at the sky.

Wood knelt beside him, and examined his neck, of all things. "Broken. Snapped when you two fell. I'm sorry."

Tag stared. It couldn't be real. They'd survived way worse—crashes, malfunctions, and a shootout with spaceborne Truppen. Now Scrape, the only worthy co-pilot and RIO—the best friend—he'd ever had, was dead? From a fall?

His chest constricted. He gasped for breath. Focus, Tag. He gripped the rifle.

"Listen up, Lieutenant." Wood grabbed his collar and jerked him close. The rum on the general's breath was worse than engine exhaust. "A lot more of us are going to die tonight if you don't snap free. Take your gun, follow me, and shoot every one of these blasted invaders we come across!"

Tag nodded.

They got up and ran.

***

The cell was as drastic a change from their so-called "guest cottage" as Elden Selva could envision. Bare quik-crete walls, polished stone floor, metal bars reinforced with a low grade energy field—strong enough to give a powerful shock and nasty burn to anyone curious enough to test it. He'd seen the results on prisoners of the Northern Alliance; the same manufacturer made incarceration units for both sides during the war.

But right now he wasn't worried about the pain that could be inflicted by the field. It was the sounds and tremors outside the jail that had him anxious.

There was a battle.

"Of course they'd have to make these blasted things without windows," Andan Natour snarled. "So we can die in complete ignorance."

"Steady, Nat." Natour's cell was directly opposite Elden's. Goetz was to his right; the other five cells were empty. The door at the far right of the narrow corridor between the cells was sealed tight, a pale gray hatch, also windowless. He shared Natour's worry, but unlike his urbane friend, being locked up with an unseen fight raging outside did not strip away all civilization's polish from Elden. He'd seen war, up close.

Fortunately, so had Goetz.

"Don't recognize the sounds." Goetz voice was muffled. Elden could picture him with an ear pressed an exterior wall of his cell. "Pitch is strange. Guards have M36s..." He paused amidst a salvo of particular shrill shots. "SAAR railguns. The whole works. But the other weapons, they're energy based. You can hear the impacts sizzle when they hit dirt, or flesh."

"Oh, perfect," Natour said. "Advanced weaponry. That means assassins—or aliens."

"Aliens. Someone out there's either using a very high-end scrambler for voices, or it's a xeno language. I've never heard it. Give a listen."

Elden pressed his ear to the wall. The sounds were deadened, but unmistakable: weapons fire, both the strange screech Goetz mentioned and the familiar rattle of flechette rifles. Occasionally the *whump* of a grenade launcher and the *boom* of the resulting explosion interrupted fire. Screams and shouts mingled among the harsh mechanical sounds of the weaponry.

Marney. Was she still in the mansion? Likely in her gown, standing at the head of the aisle, wed to a Terran officer.

But he imagined her dead, body rent by terrible wounds, blood soaking a white dress.

He pounded his fist on the bars. Damn Antiny Wester and damn the Reittians for this mess!

Thumps sounded dangerously close to the jail. Human shouts and rifle fire answered, but were cut off mid-stream by the screeching blasts. When the sound faded, a musical warbling overtook it, faint yet still audible.

"Someone's outside the hatch," Natour hissed through his teeth.

More blasts. These were much louder, and the last few made

the hatch ring as a bell. The entire jail shook. Lights flickered, faded, and failed. The dim glow of orange emergency beacons set in the floor took its place.

The power was gone. Elden edged closer to the cell door. Did it mean...?

He eased his fingers toward the bars. No warning spark, no crinkle of static on his skin. He shoved his hand out.

Nothing. The field was down.

Something banged against the bars in Goetz's cell. His shoulder, Elden guessed. "Lock's still in place. It was backed up by the field; should be easy enough to break."

A spray of sparks emanated from the side of the hatch, just above the controls.

"Hurry on that," Natour said, and he too shoved hard against the locking mechanism.

Goetz grunted with each hit. The mechanism twisted, but held in place.

The sparks exploded into a blinding spray, and suddenly stopped. The hatch banged open.

Soldiers. Alien warriors in camouflaged armor, the coloring of which seemed oddly familiar. Elden realized it was the same pattern as the leaves of the bole trees. Even as he stared, that pattern faded away, replaced by the pitted gray of the quik-crete jail walls.

The aliens had helmets, and visors that covered their eye—a single, huge, glaring eyeball. They were like giraffes, gangly, all skinny limbs and thick joints.

Natour shrank back against the wall of his cell, emitting a choking sound.

The aliens zeroed in on him. One had darker gray skin than his companion, mottled with discolorations similar to human birthmarks. He sang a note and pointed. The other one bobbed its head, and used its weapon to bash open the lock on Natour's cell.

"No! Stay back!" Natour scrambled into the farthest corner, as if he could claw his way through the quik-crete.

One more *bang* from Goetz's cell, and the barred door swung open. Goetz collided with the mottled skinned alien, arms grappling for the gun. The alien shrieked, the sound stabbing at Elden's ears, and the weapon discharged. A green pulse left a smoking crater in the far jail wall and a glowing blob afterimage in Elden's sight.

The gun clattered on the stone floor.

The alien in Natour's cell turned, ignoring his prey. He was ready to fire, and shouted something unintelligible at Goetz.

The bodyguard had both arms around the alien's slender neck, bracing his head in a lock. "Drop it or your buddy's neck gets snapped," Goetz said. "Your call."

Whether or not the alien understood the language, the intention was unmistakable. He did not, however, relinquish his weapon. He shouted back.

Elden's fingertips grazed the gun. His second attempt snagged the stock.

The alien reached back into Natour's cell and dragged him out. Natour's shoes squeaked on the stone. The alien pressed the double muzzle against Natour's head and snarled words that were far less musical than his interaction with his superior.

Goetz's eyes narrowed.

"For star's sake, don't let him shoot me, Goetz!"

Elden got his hand through the rounded handle underneath the gun. There had to be a trigger in there somewhere. He fumbled, squeezed, and pressed. Nothing...

The gun fired. The green discharged gouged a trough in the floor and burned across the legs of the alien holding Natour hostage.

It screamed and collapsed, and dropped Natour, but not its gun.

Elden heard a sickening crunch of bone. Goetz threw aside the first alien, its neck bent at an impossible angle, and that single eye listless. He slammed into the second. They both hit the open bars of the cell.

Goetz clamped one hand over the alien's tiny nostril slits and small mouth. His right arm shoved hard against where the diaphragm would be on a human's torso. He held fast with the hand and pushed with the arm, body bent, shoes scraping the floor for traction. The alien tried to hit Goetz with the gun; the bodyguard pressed against that wrist until the alien let go.

Eventually—to what Elden seemed like hours—the alien's body went limp. Choking sounds from under Goetz's hand cut off.

He let go. The soldier slumped against the wall. Goetz's chest was heaving, his arms tensed at his side.

"My stars," Natour muttered.

Goetz grabbed the alien rifle, and gave it a once over. He regarded the trigger mechanism with what Elden thought was a childlike curiosity. Apparently satisfied, Goetz shot both alien bodies in the chest, point blank.

He was right. Flesh did sizzle when the energy discharges hit a person. Or alien.

Goetz mashed the lock off Elden's cell. Elden grabbed the rifle he'd used as a distraction. It was two-thirds the weight of an M36, even though it appeared bulkier.

"There may still be shuttles on the landing pads," Natour said. "Goodness knows I heard enough of them flying in for tonight. We should there."

Elden glanced at Goetz.

"He's your friend, sir."

Natour scowled. The disdain was evident in Goetz's tone. "May I remind you that we are the officials, and you're the hired gun, even if you're Intervention Group."

"Understood, sir." Goetz said the *sir* as if he were regarding a slug he'd squashed underfoot. "That's why I get the gun, and you stay out of my way."

Natour bit back whatever retort he had coming, for which Elden was glad. "The middle of an invasion isn't time for a quarrel, gentlemen. We have to get to the mansion."

Both Goetz and Natour stared at him. "Last I checked, that was in the opposite direction of the shuttles," Goetz said.

"What he said." Natour prodded the nearest dead alien with his shoe. There was a sidearm strapped to the alien's belt; Natour reached down and, after fumbling with a strap, removed it. "I know what's on your mind, Eldi, and let me preface any argument with you by saying this: Don't do it, you madman."

"I'm not leaving Marney Wester here to die," Elden snapped. "So either stick by my side like you always have, or fight your own way to a shuttle."

He stepped through the hatch. The night air was filled with the stench of charred meat, and the sweet stink of blasted bole trees. The sharp odor of ozone drifted on the breezes. Gunfire lit up the sky, flashed between trees and hedges. Shadows ran back and forth. He had no idea where the enemy positions were, or where his side was.

Colonial police. CDF troops. And he, the consul for the Northern Alliance, technically their prisoner. Not sure *who* was on his side.

Goetz drifted up on his left, silent as a wraith. The alien weapon hummed in his hands. "Recommend I stick close, sir. The mansion's bound to be a target."

Elden nodded.

"Blast and damn." Natour was now on his right. He glanced this way and that, flinching at every explosion and exchange of fire. "Let's not stand here and converse! Find the girl!"

***

Great Hall was empty, save for a few police guarding the corners.

Two were incinerated by the blast that shattered the curving window that had been the planned centerpiece for a grand wedding. The fireball consumed their bodies, the altar, and the first row of seats.

Naplian energy blasts struck down the other two police before they even turned around.

Major Lanviond led sixteen of his best men in through the gap. He consulted the scanner readouts on his arms. Human life signs everywhere. Like vermin—*shirish*. Exterminating them all would take time.

Fortunately, he needed to concern himself with just one.

He brought up the data file provided by Admiral Daviont, acquired by the Denic spies. The image of an older Terran's face flashed on the wrist units of every soldier.

"Find Governor Antiny Wester and bring him to me," Lanviond said. "Alive, for now."

CHAPTER ELEVEN

There was little Abbot Jeopar could do while Erich and the Truppen started reactivating their brethren lodged inside Hessian. There were more than 10,000 cybernetic soldiers in standby among those crowded, darkened decks; it would take considerable time to get each one not only reactivated, but updated. Five years of being in their equivalent of a coma produced side effects that crippled their combat abilities until they could be fully reconditioned. And Jeopar was not a technically inclined man—there were far more skilled individuals among the acolytes who would have been of assistance.

What he could offer was spiritual guidance to Colonel Diaz, who seemed the most curious among the revived Truppen. Was it coincidence that the soldiers who had been reassembled and kept safe by the abbots and acolytes were the ones most inquiring about the faith? Jeopar did not believe in coincidences.

"There is grumbling among the men about General Baesler," Diaz said. "If not for the courage and cunning he showed during the war, I think they would let General Albrecht execute him immediately—and would encourage him to do so if he wavered."

Jeopar watched Erich issue orders among the ranks of Truppen. Hundreds were lined up outside *Hessian*, which stood like a giant cliff of metals and plastics. Dirt occasionally trickled down from some deposit long shielded from Baedecker Four's winds by the camouflaged curtain that had hidden the ship. A long line of Truppen cordoned off the area.

"I understand, from what Erich as told me, that you see his transformation as the worst betrayal of his oaths as a Truppen soldier."

"We're not supposed to long for the life we left behind."

"Why? Surely remembering your physical humanity can do

no harm to you as a soldier."

"It dulls our edge. We cannot fight as effectively if we lapse into our pre-transferred thinking. When you start pining for the human life, you picture yourself as frail. Truppen are more powerful than any sentient biological soldier. We should never give up that advantage by entertaining thoughts of weakness."

Jeopar shook his head. "The body and soul are not to be despised in combination, Colonel. All of us were given both at the same time. You were born, body and soul, and when the body is gone, is it not right to long for it with the soul?"

Diaz stared off at the cordon of Truppen warriors. "You imply that we are something far less than human."

"No! Far from it. You have a soul, Colonel. That much is undeniable. Are we not taught that first we join God in the form of our spirit, only to be reunited in body and soul when the final resurrection is at hand?"

"Who's to say I haven't been resurrected already?"

"Neither you in this shell nor Erich in his android form have been reborn in the glorious state God has planned for all of us." Jeopar smiled. "But I can help you—all the Truppen—set aside the crudity of war and embrace the body of peace."

The ground shook with a tremor that brought more dust and dirt down the side of *Hessian*. Jeopar heard the distant rumbles —sounds of ships, and weapons, he now realized.

"General!" Diaz trotted over to Erich.

Was the CDF looking for them again? That would complicate things unnecessarily. Jeopar activated his communicator, and signaled the monastery. "Open up the adjacent bunkers. Yes, all the ones which are mothballed. We may need the space in which to secret out friends."

Lights spread across the horizon, toward Vossberg City and the governor's mansion. Green lightning streaked down. Flashes lit up the sky. Strange craft that Jeopar had never before seen filled the skies, descending like hail among the lightning.

Erich and Diaz joined him. "It's an orbital strike, there's no doubt, sir," Diaz said.

Erich held up his binoculars. "All I can get is a hazy view, but I've never seen those fighters before. Not Reittian. Not Northern Alliance, either."

"Alien design."

"Definitely." Erich frowned. "Get me General Albrecht."

The Truppen general joined them. Together the four

crested a small ridge, the top of which gave them a broader view of the Luran Plains and Iwa Valley. Jeopar's heart sank. The green lightning—weapons fire, according to Erich—definitely targeted Vossberg City. More of it came down in smaller batches to the north and south.

"What's at those points?" Albrecht said. "They're targeting more than the city."

"I believe they are refueling depots and landing facilities," Jeopar said. "We've used them ourselves, for the monastery's vehicles."

"Those are landing pods of some kind." Diaz pointed at rows of neat streaks that arrowed down from the sky. They hit the ground in the middle of the desert, intersecting with the splotch of light Jeopar knew belonged to the governor's mansion.

"No." He faced Erich. "Elden Selva. He's being held at the compound."

"Selva? Sedrick's son?" General Albrecht's voice rose an octave. It sounded even more static-filled. "You have the consul himself on Baedecker Four!"

"He was to meet with us and retrieve Truppen headpieces for covert transport back to the Northern Alliance," Erich said. "Plans changed."

"He is still there, Erich. We must save him."

Erich chewed his lip. The gesture reignited Jeopar's pride in the designers of his android body. "All right. General, supervise the reactivation of the rest of our men."

"While there's a battle afoot? If you think—"

"That's an order, Brigadier General."

Albrecht's speakers buzzed. Indignation? "As you command, Major General."

"Do whatever you can to get *Hessian* operational, too. If she can fly, I want her up. If she can't, find out how to fix her."

"Yes, sir." Albrecht loped back down the hill.

"Colonel Diaz, round up your men. Only the 20 we brought from the monastery."

Diaz nodded. "Yes, General. Armed?"

"With light weapons, so we can move quickly."

"There are hover-sleds in *Hessian*'s bay. I will power up a few for us."

"Good."

Once Diaz was gone, Erich glanced at Jeopar. "Abbot, I have no right to ask this…"

"Do not despair, Erich. If I were not willing to sacrifice this earthly form in the service of the Lord, I would not have chosen the monastic life." Jeopar smiled. His insides shook, and his heart pounded. Fear, of course. But he would not be stopped from helping these people achieve their destiny.

"Glad to hear it. Because you and I will rescue Elden Selva, while our Truppen escorts do whatever they can to disrupt these invaders."

***

Tag ducked behind a fruit tree. The top exploded. Burnt wood splinters sprayed everywhere. Sap adhered to his flight suit, and leaves caught afire. The aroma of the destroyed fruit reminded him of fresh jam being made in the mansion's kitchen. He could still taste the warm raspberry that he'd filched from under the cooks' noses.

General Wood was behind a low stone wall that surrounded the orchard. He shot off a couple bursts. An alien soldier went down. "They've got the way to the mansion blocked off!"

A mix of a dozen CDF soldiers and Colonial police were there, too, shooting over the top. SAAR railguns cut bright white streaks through the darkness of the garden. The muzzles of their M36s flashed. Green bursts from the aliens' energy rifles responded and took chunks out of the stone wall.

"At least none of those mechs are up here." Tag tracked sudden movement—an alien, sprinting with that ungainly, long stride from one point of cover to the shattered remains of a cottage where the rest of his comrades were. Tag waited for the moment when he was clear of the tree branches.

His flechette burst ripped into the alien's side, a weak point in the armor.

By now the courtyard separating the two forces was slick with blood, yellow and red, mixing into a sickly brown. Sap from the trees oozed between the paving stones. Dead men, women, and aliens were sprawled up and down the paths leading to and from the courtyard.

"Try the governor again," Wood said. "And someone get the mortar up here!"

Tag fumbled with his communicator. "Father? Do you read me? Father, respond!"

Nothing but static. Whatever the aliens were using to jam

communications was still in place. Tag switched to Timothy Ess's communications signal, but got the same result.

A volley of energy blasts forced him to duck even lower for cover. The top centimeters of the stone wall near his position sheared off. A handful of shards sliced across his face. Blood dribbled down his lips.

"You okay, Tag?"

"Yeah. Good." He couldn't give a damn about scratches. All he saw was Scrape, staring up, never again to see the sky or space or the inside of a cockpit. Tag leaned around the corner of the wall and switched over to full automatic. He drained the entire magazine of 150 flechetts in a matter of seconds. The trigger seized up the instant the ammunition ran out.

"Reloading!" Tag pulled another from the belt. He was down to three of the original ten—eleven, if he counted the magazine that had already been loaded when Scrape handed him the gun.

Pounding footsteps caught his attention.

"At your backs! Don't shoot!" Three men burst through the shrubbery, slipping and skidding on the sap and leaves. One of them wound up on his side, right next to Tag.

"Elden?" Tag stared.

Elden Selva's diplomatic garb was torn and stained. His jacket had been lost or abandoned. Shirt sleeves were rolled up. He had an alien rifle in his hands, and even through the grime smeared on his face, looked more determined than some of the police and soldiers.

"Hello, Tag. Nice to see you again."

The other two men—the bodyguard and Elden's associate Andan Natour—crouched with them. Both had alien weapons, and Goetz had a lot of blood soaked into his shirt. Yellow blood.

"Boy. I'm glad you're here." For the first time in what felt like an eternity, Tag grinned.

"We're trying to get to the mansion," Elden said.

Tag nodded. "Marney and Father were in there, last I knew. Her fiancé Tim went after them, but the aliens have the comms locked out. We're stuck here."

Elden looked crestfallen. "Our opponents?"

"Half again our number." General Wood joined them. If he noticed Elden Selva was one of them, he didn't let on. Instead he gestured with his rifle. "You boys figure out how to work those bug zappers?"

Goetz nodded. "Got enough similarities to our guns."

Wood smiled grimly. "Okay then. Here's the plan..."

Tag pressed himself as close to the wall as he could, and as far to the edge as he could manage without exposing himself to enemy fire. A couple police officers squished in next to him. Wood and the rest of the CDF soldiers and police took up the opposite end of the wall. A handful continued firing, but they did so in lackadaisical fashion.

Elden and his two companions slunk back to the hedges, keeping low and hidden in the darkness. There they waited for Tag's signal.

"Lookout! They've flanked us!" he shouted.

Wood and his troops turned around and repeated the alarm. They fired, but aimed high, sending all their shots over their ersatz attackers. Tag only hoped Elden and his fellows were good enough aims they wouldn't hurt anyone on their side.

Elden, Natour, and Goetz fired back using the alien weapons they'd acquired. The energy bursts ripped smoldering troughs in the ground, some of them hitting the wall between the two groups of defenders.

Tag yelled. He made it as strangled a cry as he could imagine. The police with him followed his lead, and Wood did likewise. Their surprised shouts and sporadic weapons fired dwindled to nothing.

After a few seconds, it was silent in their corner of the garden. Tag crouched, as still as the stone wall. No one breathed.

Soon after, footsteps padded on the courtyard. Strange, singsong language drifted through the air. Tag had no idea what the aliens were saying, but they advanced quietly. He could hear at least a dozen sets of footprints.

He couldn't see Elden, Natour, and Goetz, still concealed in the hedges. But General Wood gestured: Be ready.

Tag nodded.

The footsteps were so close he could hear individual pebbles scrape between the soles of their boots and the pavement. A sour smell overtook him. It reminded Tag of ripe fruit on the edge of going rotten.

Wood counted down with his fingers: three, two, one.

Tag leapt up and fired.

All along the wall, the CDF soldiers and police did the same. Flechette fire ripped through the aliens, and in a frozen moment, Tag saw them clearly up close: the gray body armor on spindly bodies, the one eye wide open like a human's but huge by comparison, the viscous, yellow blood spattering in the air.

Flashes of green screeched between the two groups of defenders, cutting down the aliens with devastating effect. When Wood called a halt to the shooting, sixteen aliens lay dead on the courtyard. Most were slashed open where the flechette rounds had hit their armor and limbs; others had deep craters in their torsos, the edges burnt and smoking.

Wood made everyone hold position for a moment longer. No other aliens emerged from the broken cottage they'd used for their cover. "All right, boys and girls, secure the area."

Elden and his men came forward. "Your general is a madman, Tag."

"I'm told he learned a bag of tricks during the Consular Wars. Glad we've got him on our side for this mess."

Elden seemed grim. "So long as he doesn't get us all killed."

"Tag! Get yourself one of these. You men, too." Wood passed alien rifles to a handful of others, and one to Tag.

The weapon was lighter than he expected, and warm. It pulsed with an electronic heartbeat. Was there even a power indicator? He found an orange light that filled up about two-thirds of a shiny strip. Getting a hand around the trigger was difficult, but doable: the aliens had such long, three-fingered hands that they could reach both the trigger and the ring-shaped grip behind it. The power pack—Tag assumed that's what the box labeled with odd curling script was, on the other side of the grip—bled heat. He picked up a couple more from the ground.

The mansion loomed behind the ruined cottage. There didn't seem to be much weapons fire from there, though smoke wisps rose from a few windows and several more were broken in. Tag had heard an explosion from somewhere behind the mansion —at least, he thought he had. Keeping track of which forces were fighting whom where became an impossibility with the failure of all the lights in the compound.

"Listen up: the governor and his daughter are still inside, as far as we know. ID trackers and communicators are on the fritz." Wood shouldered the alien rifle. "It's room to room searching. We find them, we get to whatever air or ground transport's remaining, and barring either one, we walk. Understood?"

Lots of "yes sirs" greeted his orders. Tag nodded, daunted by the prospect of looking in every room of the massive mansion. It was hard enough to find someone when every system was online. With them all down…

Wait. "General? When the dust storm of last spring swept in, and pounded everything out here for a week, Father had people gather in the billiards room. It's between some of the thickest masonry of the mansion—only one window from the outside, and a single set of doors from the inside."

"You think that's where the Governor went?"

"He called it the safest room above ground," Tag said. "And if the power's down, he wouldn't have access to the emergency bunker under the basement, or the rooftop sanctuary."

"You heard the man. Move it!"

***

Wester and Marney had two dozen guests secured in the billiards room, in the west wing of the mansion. A few carried hand beacons that lit up the entire room with a hazy yellow glow. Paintings of desert scenes and holo-images of Ghamsara bison decorated the walls, which were painted a soft red. The floor was polished bole wood planks.

"Give me a hand with this." Wester and a CDF soldier heaved on a giant, stained oak cabinet. Pool cues rattled inside like a load of lumber. Its legs squealed against the floor, dragging gouges. Wester wondered how much it would cost to have them finished. He also wondered whether the cabinet, which was taller than he or the soldier, would hold up against blasts from the alien weapons.

"Father, there's a woman bleeding." Marney ripped a long strip from her dress, and quickly bound the charred and bloody skin of a plump, elderly lady's arm. She lay on one of the pool tables. Her pallor was alarming. The green felt beneath her was soaked dark brown. "We need to get to some medics."

"Do what you can. We'll find help soon." Wester wiped sweat from his brow. The soldier had perspiration beading the lower edge of his helmet rim. "Private, go check the window. We might escape that way."

"Yes, sir." The young man pushed his way through the civilians, ignoring their pleas for help and the scattered complaints. The window was 30 meters away, at the opposite end of the room. He sidled up to the frame and peered around the corner.

Wester tried his communicator. Still nothing. Whatever General Wood was up too, he had no idea if it was successful. There was gunfire all over the place, the sounds filtering in through the broken window, but Wester needed a status update.

And Tag? No word from him, either.

He could not lose his son. Not to these one-eyes.

Brilliant green flashes blew apart the window frame. They stabbed through the soldier, jerking his body, and stray bolts cut down a man in a three-piece black tuxedo standing near him. Smoke and plaster dust billowed into the room.

"Marney! Get over here, away from the window!" Wester had a gun—a DK-40 9 mm pistol—and he pointed it now at the window.

Six aliens burst in, tall, slender, and sheathed in armor so dark it was almost black. They fanned out into the room, and swept their aim around to every person.

Wester's gun hand shook. He could take one, right now, but even if he successfully killed one of the invaders, Marney's life would be forfeit. So would those of the guests.

A seventh alien stepped through. Wester recognized him as the commander—he had to be, with the bearing and surety of movement. His helmet had a different shape, and there were more markings on his armor. He spoke something to the two soldiers in front, nearest Wester. They moved aside.

The alien stopped a couple meters from Wester. It pressed a set of three long fingers to its throat, and a white light pulsed at the chin of his face mask. "Governor Antiny Wester. I detain you by right as conqueror of Baedecker Four." This voice was mechanical, with a buzz behind the words. A translator unit. "You and your daughter, Marney Elizabeth Shannon Wester, are prisoners of the Naplian Empire and the Ffawe people. Your compliance will ensure a swift consolidation of our rule over your planet."

Wester scowled. "I don't care who the Naplians or the Ffawe are. I'm not going to surrender a novafired thing to you."

The alien spoke again to his subordinates.

One of them hauled Marney to her feet, and aimed the muzzle of his gun at her chest.

"No!" Wester moved, his gun up—

The lead Naplian hit him in the gut with the stock of his rifle. Wester gasped for breath, the wind knocked from him. A steel grip broke his gun free of his grasp.

"Do not resist, or everyone in this room will die."

Behind him, someone pounded on the billiards room door. Gunfire hit it, again and again. Energy pulses, from alien weapons.

Wester's heart sank. Surrounded. He had to give in, for the safety of the people around him. For the life of his daughter.

Marney glared at the soldier. Tears streaked the dust on her cheeks. "I love you, Father. Don't surrender to these aliens."

"I have no choice, Marney. I'm sorry." Wester collapsed to his knees. The pain in his gut was unbearable.

The lead alien spoke again to his men. Two soldiers went to move the cabinet out of the way of the door, and warbled to the shooters on the other side as they began to push. Of course—they wouldn't want to be shot by their own people.

The shooting stopped. But there was no reply.

The Naplian leader hooted something that sounded like an alarm. He pulled Wester off his knees, and pressed Wester's back to his armor. The alien's forearm choked Wester.

Suddenly the cabinets blew apart in a flash of green light and spray of wooden shards. One of the aliens was thrown back. Guests yelled and scrambled out of his way. The second alien was struck down by blasts from—his own kind? Wester blinked, confused.

But it made sense when General Wood and Tag burst through the doors, shouting for people to get down. Six more people followed them, taking up positions behind the broken cabinet and nearby pool tables.

By the stars. How had Elden Selva gotten free?

The alien leader backed to the window. He and his men, the other four aliens, returned fire, while the civilians between them lay flat as they could and more than one screamed in terror. Murmured prayers in Hebrew, Arabic, and what Wester assumed was Mandarin mingled with the cries.

The defenders took hits. Andan Natour, Elden Selva's associate, was hit in the side by a Naplian blast. A CDF soldier was beheaded by a shot. But one of the aliens was also cut down.

"Cease firing your weapons!" The Naplian's translated voice boomed in Wester's ear. "We have your governor hostage! End the attack and his life will be spared."

The weapons fire stopped, on both sides. The only sounds, in the seconds thereafter, were the cries of the guests and Wood's florid swearing.

The Naplians backed toward the window. The leader pulled Wester along, and another soldier dragged Marney—literally kicking, but not screaming. The other three Naplians covered their withdrawal.

A DK-40's report broke the silence. Wester couldn't see who fired his gun—then he realized it was Timothy Ess, firing not

Wester's gun but his own, from just outside the window. He had the pistol braced in a two-handed grip, and fired a handful of rounds at the back of the alien who held on to Marney.

They dented his armor but otherwise did no damage. Marney broke free and ran back to the civilians huddled on the floor. The leader twisted his arm and shot Ess through the leg.

Weapons fire exploded once more, and this time, no one paid any attention to any entreaties or demands. Tag shouted something Wester couldn't hear, and in an instant he was covering Marney. He and Wester saw each other through the chaos, but it was too late, and Wester was out in the darkness of the compound's gardens. The alien leader dragged him away; one of the others had Ess slung over his shoulder. The Navy officer's teeth were gritted in pain; blood trickled from the corner of his mouth.

More aliens joined them. There was a great rush of wind overhead. The next thing Wester knew, a light shone down on their group, and he was forced through the opening of—something. More lights nearly blinded him.

He was shoved to the deck of an alien ship, and Ess was thrown down next to him.

The alien leader removed his facemask. The lone eye glared at him, and the tiny slit of a mouth moved with what Wester assumed was contempt. "The actions of your men endanger your life, Governor. You should have called them off. Now they will all suffer."

He leapt away, out into the black rectangle of night, and the shadow of the mansion beyond.

***

Tag didn't let Marney out of his sight as their group, which took almost two dozen guests from the billiards room and another two dozen from elsewhere in the mansion, streamed along the edge of the compound wall toward the landing pads.

"There's four shuttles, maybe five that aren't destroyed. Speaker Zhatkowskii's is that one." Wood pointed through a gap in the trees.

Tag saw it—the flat nose of the ExoTerse high-performance shuttlecraft was unmistakable. Scrape had been right, it was a Mod Six.

He tried not to think about his RIO at all, and focused on Marney. "Are you sure you're okay?"

"I'm not hurt. But Father—those aliens took him, Tag!"

"I know. We're going to get him back."

There were ten CDF soldiers around. Their armor and uniforms were in various states of upkeep—some broken, some bloodied. They stayed close to the trees, white and black garb blending well in the shadows of the garden.

"Haven't seen much action for a while, sir," one of the women said to General Wood. "Suspect they're all up at the mansion."

"I know. They took the Governor."

"Oh. Speaker Zhatkowskii's here. In the shuttle. He won't come out—don't think his wife will let him, sir. They tried to take off but—" The woman patted her M36. "I persuaded them to wait."

"Nice work. Load these people up." Wood turned to Tag. "You pilot that bird. Get these people out to Station Golf Echo Five."

Tag frowned. "The repair depot?"

"Emergency rendezvous. Captain Ram of *Confiance* was supposed to round everyone up to that point."

"What about you?"

"I've got the Armored Cav out there, somewhere, looking for blasted Truppen. If we pound dirt for a ways, we can get free of the jamming and link up with them."

"On foot? In the desert?" Tag shook his head. "That's crazy."

"Relax, Tag. I have backup. And our pal Selva."

"He's right, Tag." Elden and Goetz helped Natour walk, the latter of whom grimaced and held on to his injured side. "We stand a good chance of it."

"Good chance of what?"

"Following that alien ship. It flew off toward Vossberg City. There's a whole pack of them swarming out there." Wood scowled. "We'll get the governor back."

"And Timothy." Marney slid the magazine out of a DK-40, checked it, and reinserted it. She chambered a round. "Father's gun. I'm taking it, and going with you."

Elden took her hand. "Marney, don't. Go with Tag. You'll be safe with the other refugees."

"I'm not one of them," she said firmly. "I'm the governor's daughter. I have to try to bring him back."

Behind them, soldiers shepherded civilians aboard the shuttles, including the Zhatkowskii's ExoTerse. Tag heard a woman's protests, and a man's deep voice try to soothe her. Hopefully the Speaker would win out.

"Marney, I can't leave you. Not now," Tag said.

"She'll be all right," Elden said. "I'll keep her safe."

"You're not going to argue her out of this?"

Elden glanced at Marney. "There isn't a moment that passes that I don't wish for the chance to save my father from the Reittians. But that's gone. We have that chance for your father."

Tag gripped the alien rifle. DeeDee, Scrape, his father—if Marney were lost he didn't know what he'd do. But there were people's lives at stake. A whole world in the balance. "Okay. You take care of her."

Elden clapped him on the shoulder. "I will."

"Let's get going," Wood said. "Dark will provide us the best cover."

Marney hugged Tag. He pulled his arm around her tight. "You come back to me," he murmured.

"I promise." She kissed him on the cheek. Warm tears wet his collar.

And just like that, they slipped away into the night.

CHAPTER TWELVE

Captain Sobban Ram read the reports from the Terran ships that had joined him so far. The summary was devastating.

They'd lost four of the twelve ships defending the Baedecker System. The aliens had seized control of the spaceport, and were bombarding the planet. Baedecker Six was occupied as well, and ships were making forays toward the suns.

Baedecker Two. The Serjaum deposits.

Ram frowned. Though the list of people who knew of the serjaum's existence was limited, he had friends in the Colonial Legislature.

"Problem, Captain?" Commander Vollan stood by his chair, hands clasped in front of her. The sleeves were rolled up, and there were stains all over her arms.

"Potentially. You have seen the Lagrange-sat indications of invaders moving into the Baedecker Two region?"

"Yes, sir. I didn't know what to make of them. Could be they're angling for heavy metal deposits."

"Indeed. Run off a couple of strike scenarios for me. Fighter-bombers, escorts, but no ships. Harassment has to be our strategy for the time being."

Vollan crinkled her nose. It gave the appearance she'd smelled something unpleasant, but Ram recognized it as an indication she was concerned over a problem. "Yes, sir. If I had more to go on in terms of what the aliens wanted—"

"Irrelevant at this moment to planning a strike. Sow chaos, do not seek answers. Not yet."

"Aye, Captain." She held up a scroll. "Our damage assessment."

"And?"

"Going as well as can be expected. Station Golf Echo Fiver has limited repair facilities. The cruisers are receiving the bulk of the attention, which is good. The last of the hull breaches should be sealed within a few hours; replacing armor and shoring up bulkheads could take days."

"As I suspected. I don't think any of our ships are ready for operational duty beyond patrols."

"Correct, sir. We can put a pair of destroyers in a wide orbit, but that's it."

"What's our small craft complement look like?"

"Good, considering the hammering the units at Baedecker Four took. There's three dozen Raiders, all in decent shape, minor repairs needed. We also have two squadrons of SF-107s, the single-seat fighters."

Ram nodded. The nimble Warhawks would be perfect for fast strikes against static positions and slow ships, even if their limited armor made them far more vulnerable. "I'm assuming we have pilots with them."

"Yes, but with more armament and damaged ships trickling in, we're going to need more trained personnel. We lost a lot of pilots at the starport."

"Very well. Keep me apprised."

"There's another issue, Captain. Refugees."

"Oh? I thought you had the group brought in by those civilian ships bunked away aboard the station."

"I do, but as I said—there are more and more ships coming in. That isn't limited to military units. I have a collection of freighters, yachts, and passenger transports clamoring for our attention. Most just want to jump out of here to the nearest safe station, but they won't budge without an escort."

"I cannot spare a single Warhawk or Raider, let alone a capital ship."

"That is what I told them, Captain. But we're running out of options."

"So." Ram turned and faced the communications station. "Any response to our distress signals?"

"None yet, Captain. If it got through to Van Sutton, they haven't replied or acknowledged. Whatever the aliens are doing to FTL transmissions, it's mucking up the signals pretty bad."

If they couldn't get backup from Van Sutton Naval Base, 30 light-years away, Ram knew his planned insurgency wouldn't make it off the ground.

An alert blinked on the communications board. The officer pressed his hand to his earpiece. "Sir, I've got an incoming message. Pilot says he's AES."

Before Ram could inquire who was using an open comm in a restricted area, Vollan intercepted another alarm, this one from the tactical display. "Eight small craft on approach, Captain. They're ripwaving in at top velocity."

"Run out the mains," Ram said. "Prep short range torpedoes. Helm, get us clear of our moorings ASAP. If we can't move, we'll shoot them down from here."

"Sir, they're signaling friendly!"

"And we are in the midst of an alien invasion. Do we have transponder confirmation from any of these approaching craft?"

"Negative, sir."

"Then they are targets until we determine otherwise."

A few minutes passed. The deck hummed ever subtly under Ram's boots as *Confiance* moved from the station dock, secondary engines pushing her slowly away.

The communications officer winced, then dug out his earpiece. Someone rather irate was hollering on the other end. "Ah, Captain, that pilot wants to know what the—frig—we're doing targeting civilians."

"Where is my transponder confirmation?"

"Got it," Vollan said. "It's—sir, says it's Speaker Zhatkowskii's official shuttle, an ExoTerse Mod Six."

"Andrej? What is he doing out here? Comms, put the signal on speakers."

The officer did, and a voice came on in mid-shout. "...the novafired space is going on with you people? I've got the Speaker onboard and a bunch of ticked off...!"

"This is Captain Sobban Ram." He grimaced, because he recognized the irate voice without needing further reflection. "Lieutenant Wester. Have you finally been demoted to flying passenger craft rather than Raiders?"

"Oh. Hey, Captain. No, sir, I've got orders and data from General Wood. Plus eight shuttles full of civilians and officials who'd rather not get vaporized by a heavy cruiser's particle cannon. So maybe you could stand down and escort us in?"

"I think that is prudent." Ram gestured to Vollan, who passed the word to the bridge stations to step back from combat status. "You've been planetside since the invasion hit?"

There was a pause, and Lieutenant Wester's reply was

tinged with something Ram couldn't pin down. "Yes, sir. The aliens call themselves the Naplian Empire. I heard them when—they have the governor, and a bunch of other hostages. Took them right from the compound, in the middle of my sister's wedding. I don't know how many troops and police were killed, but it's a lot."

Ram clenched his jaw. They had the governor. No doubt the Legislature would be another target. "What about groundside military strength?"

"Sorry, Captain. I'd better show you in person." Wester cleared his throat. "It's bad."

***

The initial bombardment by Naplian warships destroyed their targets before any response was possible.

Communications stations across Vossberg City and at the nearby Voss Flats Base were reduced to glassed-in craters. Electromagnetic discharge from the energy blasts ruined local and personal communications networks in the immediate vicinity, and played havoc with computer systems.

The bombardments took out missile batteries and ground-to-space particle cannon, next. While CDF gunners were able to get off a few return shots—at the locations where the personnel sacrificed their lives even though they knew their destruction was imminent—it was not enough to stop the deluge of strikes made from orbit. A pair of cannon north of Vossberg managed to score hits on the bombard *Napliae*. It lost shielding in the bow and internal fires forced the bombard to cease its attack while it moved out of orbit.

But the other three bombards shifted their orbits enough to cover for their injured comrade.

AEF fighters took to the air as quickly as they could, but two squadrons were wiped clean from the tarmac in the process. Swarms of Naplian starfighters, their wings shaped like claws with particle weapons protruding from underneath, descended into the atmosphere to counter them.

It was the most uneven of matches.

Without Wing Commander DeeDee Dillon to lead them, the Baedecker planes did their best to shoot down as many invading starfighters as they could. Raiders and Warhawks dove into clouds full of the alien ships. The sky flashed and rumbled with the white of railgun projectile bursts and the green of Naplian particle weapons. The battle raged for an hour and a half over two continents.

In the end, a squadron's worth of mixed starfighters and fighter-bombers limped into orbit on the far side of Baedecker Four and ripwaved away.

Three squadrons were gone. The Naplians lost one and a half.

Vossberg Terminal was gutted. The magnificent hall was reduced to a skeletal frame of blackened ribs, the windows shattered and melted. Any aircraft on the ground were destroyed in place. No one would use the terminal and its many tarmacs for the foreseeable future.

Troops on the ground didn't fare any better. Naplian landing pods dug into the plains around Vossberg City. Aerial units skydived into the center of the city, securing city blocks. Colonial Police were overmatched; after being cut down by scores in lopsided battles with the invaders, their goal became one of withdrawal and rescue. The police evacuated as many civilians as they could, but links out of the city were rapidly closed off by the Naplian mechs. Most civilians were rounded up and herded into makeshift detainment camps—in parks, in the sporting stadiums, in large warehouses.

Colonial police who weren't killed or captured went into hiding.

The few remaining CDF platoons in the area banded together at Welder's Bridge, the largest of five crossings over the Santos River. It led up to rocky plateaus just above the city, giving the CDF troops a high grand advantage they couldn't afford to abandon.

It seemed as if they would be pushed off this last battleground, too, until the mechs leading the march across the bridge blew up in spectacular fashion. Sappers with the 101st Engineering Battalion had lined the path with cordo-thermite charges invisible to nearly all known sensors. CDF troops cheered the fact that this included the alien invaders.

With a dozen mechs heaped in flaming piles, the Naplians withdrew to the city side of the bridge. The CDF got a working shield generator in place, and were able to absorb punishing enemy fire with ease. General Urs Ri'Nan Falloram considered a concentrated orbital strike by the bombards to reduce their position to rubble, but Admiral Daviont overruled him. Firstly, the plateau was home to the largest power source for the city—a double core fusion generator.

CDF knew this and made it their base, with the shield generator tucked inside the power station.

Daviont didn't want to wreck a power source that could be easily coopted. He also didn't want to destroy the city as a threat to the Terran holdouts. They knew so little about this small empire; it was possible they could still be coopted as allies or, at the least, conscripts for the Naplian campaign of expansion. Unnecessary civilian slaughter was unacceptable.

So instead General Falloram ordered the bridge held against the Terrans. Meanwhile he personally led a strike team to Voss Flats, which was a collection of broken buildings and cratered tarmac. CDF and AEF had abandoned it; the few units remaining on guard were easily dispersed.

The morning suns broke over the horizon and bathed the sky in blood. Both were brilliant red when viewed through the plumes of smoke and dust clouding the base ruins. It was the perfect picture of a successful conquest.

But when Falloram dismounted the mech he rode into the base, his temper rose. Most of the weaponry and equipment were accounted for. Whatever the Terrans didn't scurry off with was either destroyed or captured—with one glaring exception.

"Where are the portable anti-starship batteries that were reported to be here?" Falloram snapped at his subordinates. "Where is this Armored Division?"

***

Fifteen kilometers to the northwest, hidden among the dunes and ravines of the Luran Plains, the 65th Terran Armored Division—the Texans—could have been just another bit of the dusty landscape.

Major Frand Sikora Bond walked a narrow trail beaten by the boots of hundreds of soldiers. The sand was worn away, revealing red-brown stone underneath. Bond was a short, wiry man with black hair buzzed close to his scalp, skin tanned by years of outdoor service on Baedecker, and a single hazel eye. This right was gone, lost to Northern Alliance rebels in the last war, with the flat black and gray panel of an optic interpreter implanted in its place.

This war was different.

He'd rather be pummeling the one-eyed spindly buggers

with his mechs and tanks and battle-armored troopers, but all that tech was hidden under camouflage tarps that hid the Texans from visual inspection as well as scans. When the attack had come, Bond was already in the field, en route to investigate some emergency involving no-longer-dormant Truppen Landers. So General Wood insisted. The invasion changed priorities—Bond knew he couldn't get back to Vossberg in time to do any good, so we went to ground. Their hover-sleds and transports were grounded nearby, concealed in the same fashion as the weapons and men.

Fortunately, he'd gotten word to the rest of the division to evacuate their remaining strength. The Texans had been preparing to ship off planet in the next week or two, so the anti-starship batteries were stripped down and loaded for transport. That made it easy to tuck them into the desert, out of the reach of the attackers.

Downside? They were stripped down. It would take days to get them operational.

Bond finally found his comms officer, a tall, broad-shouldered soldier named Vinh who was part Vietnamese and part Scandinavian.

"Major? Got some good news for you."

"Lay it out, Lieutenant. I could use some of that."

"Our company that stuck behind linked up with CDF remnants and have the heights over the Santos bridge. They've got possession of the fusion plant and have a shield generator up."

Bond grinned. "Can't wait to tell the general. The sooner we can get the A-S batteries live and bring them back to town, the better. Speaking of..."

"I haven't been able to raise General Wood, sir." Vinh scowled at the rows of portable comms equipment stacked like so many shipping crates on a folding table. "Someone's got a massive jammer set up at the governor's compound."

"The general will find a way to circumvent, I'm sure. Send up a couple Whispers. Add a secondary communications package to its payload."

Vinh's eyes widened. "Ah! Bounce the signal off!"

"Precisely. We can avoid the jamming field at ground level that way, but we can also stay low enough to keep off the enemy scanners. I don't want to risk them finding this location. Send our signal to the general in short bursts. Let the Whispers wander autonomously." Bond knew the stealth drones were notoriously temperamental unless on a leash, but even a tight-beam link for control purposes could be traced back.

"I'll see to it, Major." Vinh hollered at a few of the enlisted men nearby and gave instructions in technical speak Bond barely translated.

Instead he surveyed their makeshift camp. The A-S batteries hunkered underneath long tarps. Sand blew over them, dusting the long, rectangular barrels. Each battery had two guns the size of a Vossberg City hover-bus, a good 40 meters long, rigged up on eight huge wheels with an independent suspension built for traversing rough terrain. Four of the A-S batteries were in Bond's possession. One was enough to punch a hole through a lightly-shielded ship.

Now he just needed the chance to use them. First, though, he had to find his commander.

***

Elden's legs were rubber. It had been far too long since he'd had to do anything this strenuous, and he was thoroughly embarrassed by his lack of endurance. The group that had escaped the governor's compound with General Wood trudged through the Luran plains; the civilians huddled together as best they could against the chill desert night air. CDF soldiers and police formed a cordon around them as they followed a sloppy zig-zag among the dunes and cliffs.

General Wood didn't look or sound any worse for wear. He stayed at the lead of the column, which had swelled to include 80 people. His dress uniform was sheathed in dust, and black dress shoes were caked with dirt. Both red and yellow blood were dark blotches on his jacket.

Elden knew he appeared equally a mess, but it irked him that the 60-year-old general marched along as if he were on parade, rather than delving a dozen kilometers or more into Baedecker's desolate regions.

"Thought we had a signal a moment ago," Wood murmured. "Virgilio! Take two men and branch off south-southeast, 10 degrees. See if you can pick that up."

"Yes, sir."

"Is your division nearby, General?" Marney's voice was dry. She held onto Elden's arm. Somehow she'd fashioned a belt from a torn strip of her dress; the DK-40 pistol was tucked into the impromptu waistband. In the dim light of dawn, Elden made out the barest of smiles as she looked at him. He smiled back, trying to appear as reassuring. It was a tough act.

"They should be. They were on their way to investigate the Truppen landing but they didn't check during transit. My guess is Major Bond saw the attacks, dug in somewhere. Problem is, he can't just fire up a communicator and holler for me." Wood shook his head. "Those one-eyes would crater the entire division, and then we'd find them real quick—by the plume of smoke left in the air."

Elden turned. There was a different plume visible: the governor's compound, aflame. He could still smell the sweet aroma of bole sap as it burned, crystallized. The bonfire that had once been several square kilometers of the most opulent residence on Baedecker Four had lit their backs the entire march. Now, it was a towering column of black smoke on the distant horizon behind them.

Goetz was at their backs, watching everything and everyone. He especially kept close to Natour, who was walking with greater speed than when they'd started out. His wound was bandaged, though his face was still pale. Natour nodded at Elden and winked, though it was followed immediately by a wince. He stumbled; Goetz's hand shot out, prevented him from falling.

"Nat's going to need better treatment for his wound," Elden said.

"I'm sure we can take him to a doctor in Vossberg City," Marney said.

"What makes you think there will be any left?"

She was silent for a while after that. Elden cleared his throat. "Sorry. I've seen this kind of fighting before. It doesn't leave much room for hope."

Marney nodded. "I understand. But we shouldn't give up. Hope is one of the few things we have left. It keeps us human."

Elden recalled the alien invaders who'd overrun the compound. Humanity was going to have to be their strength, if nothing else.

***

Major Lanviond slithered over the rock outcropping. He ignored the sharp edges digging into his legs, and propped his arms up on a round stone as big as his head. His Furta energy rifle hummed, the entire weapon warm from near constant use.

General Falloram was in command of the invasion, and

Lanviond was glad to have turned his hostages over. Taking prisoners was not his standard operation—this was.

He and the 33 remaining men of his company had tracked their quarry by splitting into four platoons. They kept in contact using light signals and the high-pitched whistles that only Ffawe could hear. It had taken all night, but it was worth it.

Eighty humans trudged through the desert, down a narrow ravine that followed a dry creek bed. Boulders protruded from the sides of the ravine and were obstacles in the middle that the group had to wind around. It slowed their progress.

Lanviond watched the heat signatures displayed on his visor and smiled grimly.

"Sir, Units Two and Three have taken their positions at the head of the ravine, 100 meters south," one of the corporals said.

"Good. Take up your aim and wait for my mark." Lanviond whistled—a series of bursts and trills. He'd read that the Denics knew of a human code named for a man called Mores. It was eerily similar to the Ffawe *syllasonna*.

He waited. The desert sounds around him were muted— lizards scratching the sand nearby, insects buzzing about as the early morning air heated up. His breath fogged his visor.

Whistles echoed back, three of them. The platoons were all in place.

Lanviond thumbed up the power level selector on his rifle. His sights bracketed the lone human walking a few paces ahead of the group. The man held a Furta rifle, something no human—no alien—should be allowed to touch. The thought of *shirish* fingers soiling the very weapon Lanviond held repulsed him.

With a well-placed blast he'd remove General T.J. Wood from the human's chain of command and cease his interference with the Naplian conquest.

***

Abbot Jeopar could not believe a new day was dawning. It felt as if he could go on forever without sleep, even though his body must be exhausted. When the adrenaline wore off, he supposed he would crash worse than an acolyte who'd prayed without ceasing for days.

Erich passed him a water tube. Jeopar drank greedily, thankful for the provision for his health. They sat alongside a butte with long, corrugated sides. Jeopar could see the Truppen waiting in the shadows, ghostly statues without a single light active. That bothered him more than the intense red optical ports, because he knew what the lack of illumination heralded.

"Are you certain they're aliens?" Erich whispered into a communicator.

"Affirmative. No idea what species. But they're ugly." Diaz's voice came back clear. Jeopar marveled at the advantage they had over conventional troops—being able to speak directly from their minds and have that thought transformed into an electronic signal. It let them stay deathly silent.

"All right. Stand by." Erich rubbed his chin.

"What is the matter?"

"The aliens—they're the force that destroyed the governor's compound."

"Is that not why we followed them here? To capture one and question them as to their motives?" Jeopar did not understand military tactics well, but he knew the governor and Baedecker's military commanders would be grateful for whatever intelligence could stop the invading creatures.

But now he wondered if Erich shared the same goal. This was an army that had attacked his enemy—the Terrans, who defeated and absorbed the Northern Alliance at the conclusion of the Second Consular War. By all rights he should sit back and let the aliens escape, or actively help them.

Jeopar saw twin difficulties: they had no idea of the aliens' motives, making it suspect as to whether they'd accept help from someone who looked human; and in the face of such conquest, the divisions between the Terran government and former Northern Alliance supporters seemed trivial.

"The problem, Abbot, is that there's a group of Terrans down there." Erich passed Jeopar the binoculars.

Yes, there were people walking through the desert. Refugees fleeing the compound? And among them... "Elden Selva!"

"Yes. Selva, and General T.J. Wood, the man in charge of Baedecker's defenses. He was at the governor's office when I got Selva there from Vossberg Terminal. They seem to be escorting people through the desert. What you don't see are the alien troops lining the ravine, from those cliffs overlooking the route." Erich scowled.

Dawn's pink light bloomed on the horizon. Jeopar was suddenly worried. "The aliens have not seen us, have they?"

"No. We can strike now, and save that group." Erich paused. "That's the rub."

"There is not any conflict, Erich. You have the chance to save lives. You must take it."

"Terran soldier lives? The same ones who killed so many Truppen last time around?"

"I cannot fathom the grief that causes you, my friend, but that is the past. If you are to lead the Truppen to accept transformation as you have done, you must give them an example to follow. Spare the Terrans. Stop the invaders."

Erich twisted the communicator in his hands. He stared out at the horizon, where Baedecker's twin suns were peeking over the rugged terrain. His jaw worked. Finally, he swept the communicator to his mouth. "Take them out."

Jeopar heard Diaz's reply, and the barest whisper of metal feet shifting sand.

He did not want to watch, God help him.

***

The shrill sounds of railgun weaponry and the humans' cursed flechette rifles made Lanviond jerk his arm. His Furta rifle's blast went awry, carving a chunk out of the ravine.

The humans below shouted and scrambled for cover.

By all the skin-burning fires of a giant star!

"Sir, we're under attack! They're coming in from...!" The call for help was cut off by weapons fire.

Panicked cries and shouts of orders overlapped in his communicators. Ffawe whistles went unanswered, and ended abruptly in gurgles. Choking on their blood.

Lanviond rolled into a crouch, and moved forward among the rocks. He could see towering, shadowy bipeds leaping about, shooting at his men and fighting hand-to-hand. They were massive, and armored.

Red eyes gleamed. Two red eyes.

Fear scythed through Lanviond. He fired at the new targets as best he could, but they moved too fast, killed his soldiers too quickly. How had they missed the attackers? He'd had the entire area scanned, made sure they weren't followed.

They were ravenous spirits.

***

The single shot that hit the cliff wall sent rocks and dirt spraying. People around Elden screamed. He grabbed Marney and ducked behind a boulder, even as a rough hand shoved him forward. Goetz, no doubt—yes, the bodyguard joined them, with Natour wedged between himself and the cliff face.

"Check that ridge!" General Wood crouched behind another rock, his confiscated enemy rifle up. He didn't seem worried about the fact that an alien sniper could be stalking them from above; Elden had seen men who'd received botched haircuts more annoyed.

CDF soldiers sprinted up and down the ravine, seeking a better vantage point. There was no further incoming fire. Elden aimed for the top of the ridge, where the shot had originated.

He nearly pressed the firing stud when more gunfire erupted, but Goetz grabbed his shoulder. "Hang on. Those are ours."

It took Elden a moment to realize he was right. The new sounds were from railguns, as best he could tell.

General Wood joined them. "Everyone okay?"

"No injuries here," Elden said. "I suppose we have your Special Forces men to thank for watching our backs."

Distant cries echoed and flashes of green flickered. The men up there must be giving the Naplian invaders quite the fight.

Wood was quiet. This bothered Elden more than the attempted attack. "General?"

"The only Spec Forces team I have operational was killed earlier today, fighting Truppen," Wood murmured. "Whoever's killing the Naplians isn't us."

Truppen.

For the first time since they landed at Vossberg Terminal, Elden felt a stirring.

What was it Marney said? *Hope is one of the few things we have left. It keeps us human.*

His hope was in something far greater, far more powerful, than mere humans.

Pain lanced through his right shoulder, and his left leg. Lanviond stumbled, and fell face forward onto a pile of rocks. His visor spiderwebbed with the impact. He could taste blood.

Something heavy impacted his gut. Lanviond rolled onto his side, desperate for a weapon, but his rifle was gone. There—it was cut in two, lying a couple meters away. He pulled his pistol from its holster. Six shots were all he managed.

They sparked harmlessly off his attacker.

A blade whispered through the air, and Lanviond stared at the stump where his right hand had been. Yellow blood fountained. He jammed it hard against his chest and groaned, trying to staunch the flow.

When he opened his eyes, one of the spirits towered over him. He'd never seen anything like it—taller than any Naplian, armored as fully as one of their combat mechs, and bearing a visage of sharp lines and angled plates. Those red eyes bored through the darkness.

That was when Lanviond realized: the prophecies were true. He'd believed them, of course, and dedicated himself to finding the home of the alien outsider.

Baedecker Four was that place. And these... these were the devastators.

Naplia must never fall!

It was his last thought before the blast killed him.

***

Jeopar had no desire to see the outcome of the carnage, but Erich brought him down to the site of the battle as soon as Colonel Diaz said they had finished.

Battle. It was a slaughter.

He knew it was ordained that they should be there, to save the people fleeing the compound, but it had resulted in nearly 40 of the invaders being killed. Jeopar was physically ill. Why must the preservation of life often entail the ending of another? Surely even these aliens with their advanced technology and desire to conquer his home must hope for something beyond this life. They must have families. They must have a god.

It was something over which he must diligently pray.

For his part, Erich stood silent, watching as the Truppen dragged the invaders' bodies to a single location. Colonel Diaz approached with a pair of the enemy weapons. "Pulse rifles of some kind. The design's far more advanced than standard-issue flechette rifles."

"Arm yourselves with them," Erich said. "They could prove useful."

Diaz moved off and relayed the order. Jeopar made the sign of the cross. "For what do the Truppen need those weapons?"

"For whatever war it is we are now fighting," Erich said.

The thought of another war did not encourage Jeopar—yet, he reflected, Erich was right. They were already involved in one. "But Elden Selva—now that he is safe, we should make contact with him. He must know that his plans have come to fruition."

"No, not yet. Not with a Terran general and CDF troops crawling around him." Erich gestured at the dead aliens. "We scavenge what we can, then we return to *Hessian*. To prepare."

***

The refugees waited for nearly 20 minutes in hiding before Wood's soldiers signaled all was clear. Wood wrangled Elden as a "volunteer" along with himself and five CDF troops to investigate the ridge.

Elden wouldn't leave Marney's side until Goetz promised to guard her with his life. He'd done the same for his consul; Elden knew he'd keep that promise.

The seven of them crept up the ridge, as slowly as they could, until they crested a low-lying butte. There had been a battle, all right—one which the Naplians had spectacularly lost. The dead were lined up in neat rows. Yellow blood soaked the dirt. It was the only blood Elden could see. The red of dawn turned it a stomach-churning orange.

Elden examined the ground nearby. There were overlapping footprints, some the strange two-toed, narrow feet of the invaders. Most of those were trod underfoot by sharp-edged claws that were twice the size.

General Wood shouldered rifle, and spat in the dirt. "Truppen."

Elden didn't reply, but masked his feelings with as stern a countenance as he could manage. It *was* true, then. The monks had been far more successful than he'd dared dream.

This could change everything.

"General!" One of the young soldiers held up his communicator. "I've got a signal coming through. Set of coordinates, nothing else—well, actually, there is some gibberish caught in there."

"Give me that." Wood held the communicator close to his ear. He suddenly barked a laugh. "That's not gibberish. That's a specific code—same one Major Bond and I cooked up on Imsara Three back in 'Seventy-Two, when the NA broke our comms.

Where'd the signal originate?"

"Looks like a Whisper drone, but they bounced it to prevent tracing."

"Then let's get a move on. These coordinates aren't far off." Wood grinned at Selva. "Our luck's changing for the better."

Elden smiled back, but for an entirely different reason. The claw prints in the sand had done more than rekindle his hope in their survival.

They had sparked his belief that the Northern Alliance would rise again.

CHAPTER THIRTEEN

Three Days after the Naplian Invasion

C aptain Tag Wester pulled back on the ripwave generator controls. Stars shrank back to their normal size, and ahead of him, a small, pasty gray moon filled his displays.

Those displays were a lot more compact than he was used to, set on a console that fit him like a tight glove rather than the roomy old boot of his Raider.

But the Raider was gone—sitting in a heap of dirt outside the Baedecker Four governor's compound. Tag snorted. Probably blown to bits by the one-eyes.

Sensors altered him to the presence of eleven other fighters. Tag switched off the alter sounds. "Give me a range—" He stopped, the words caught in his throat.

He didn't have a RIO anymore, either.

Instead he was wrapped up tight in the cockpit of an SF-107 Warhawk, a starfighter only 10 meters long and carrying far fewer bombs than his Raider. What he did have were two railguns, mounted along the centerline ventral fuselage, and a small defensive laser turret mounted aft of the cockpit. The Warhawk, shaped like an arrowhead with four small engines at the rear, carried six RS-18 anti-matter warhead missiles massing far less than the bombload of his raider.

"All fighters report in." The voice over the intra-squadron comm was of Major Chok, squadron leader for the re-constituted Bronze Squadron."

The announcements trickled in, more voices Tag hadn't even heard until a few days ago. But one battlefield promotion by Captain Sobban Ram—check that, Commodore Ram, thanks to Speaker Zhatkowskii and the few Congressmen in exile—and Tag found himself the wingman for their new squadron's new leader.

Everything was new. Except his flight suit, and the old Bronze Squadron insignia. The patch adorned with an inverted Raider amidst 12 explosions was discolored. Naplian blood.

Anyone wanted it off Tag's uniform, they were going to have to try and cut it out themselves.

"Bronze Two, report." Chok's tone was calm, cool, far from the harsh snap of DeeDee's snipes.

"Bronze Two, reporting in," Tag said. "All systems good."

"All right, ladies and gentlemen. Proceed to Checkpoint 1. Range, ten thousand kilometers. Coast in—no acceleration. Let's get the lay of the land and proceed from there."

Lay of the land, indeed. As the sensor data trickled in, and the gray lump expanded on Tag's display, he saw for the first time why there was such a fuss about this raid.

Two squadrons of Naplian warships ringed Baedecker Two, barely visible around the curve of the moon. It was a dark, pitted planet, barren of all life. Way too close to the system's stars, which blazed among the star field brighter than Tag had ever seen. His training and patrols never took him this deep in-system

The Naplian vessels were huge, three different types of cruisers ranging from 200 up to 600 meters in length. All of them had the now familiar design—wide jump sails shaped like the fins of some seagoing leviathan, curved, sharp-edge hulls. Mixed among them were boxy transports of some kind. Those hadn't been present during the invasion.

"There's our mining complexes," Chok said. "Busy pulling our serjaum out of the planet, no doubt."

Tag nodded to himself. Yeah, there was a steady stream of small craft flitting to and fro—shuttles, at least based on the preliminary scans. He couldn't tell from the complex data sets whether they were armed transports or simple bulk carriers.

"You'd have it pinned down, Scrape," Tag muttered.

He could still hear the wry counterpoint from his RIO, before the image faded from his mind. It was replaced by the picture of Scrape dead, wrapped in darkness.

There hadn't been time to bury him.

Bronze Squadron crested the moon, pulled along by its gravitational field. Tag shook his head. "Twelve ships—six in each squadron. That's not counting the mining complexes."

"You're not getting cold feet, are you, Tag?"

Chok Full. That's what the squadron members who disliked

their new commander called him behind his back. His official call sign was Mongoose. Tag didn't care one way or the other—the man was lukewarm as hours old coffee. "Negative, Major. Just making sure we know what we're up against. And verifying what I have to blow up."

"It's twelve of us Warhawks versus two Naplian squadrons. Our objective is to harass them and inflict as much chaos on the mining operations as we can, while gathering intelligence. A sensor sweep close in should tell us to what capacity the mining complexes are loaded."

"And if we can sink one on the way out, more's the better." That would be Chasm—1st Lieutenant Camille Castelano, Bronze Three. Tag actually had met her once before, during some of his first weeks of flight training. She'd maneuvered through the Farhold Ravines southeast of Vossberg City with such ease—and twice as fast as all the other pilot trainees—that the call sign stuck. "Permission to put a missile up their exhaust ports, Mongoose."

"Stick to our objectives. All fighters, attack vectors."

Tag stuck close to Chok's wing. Chasm was behind and "above" him, trailing with Bronze Four. The rest of the squadron paired off by wingmen, then grouped into two more fours.

A ship-to-ship comm light came on. Tag punched it. "Chasm, if you're bored, I'm sure there's something on your console you can occupy yourself with."

"Light off, Tag. Chok Full has us coming in too slow."

"Yeah, I imagine that's so we don't show up like Winter Sol house decorations in the middle of the night," Tag said. "Brighter than all get out."

"What kind of raid is this? We gonna do damage or what?"

Tag didn't have time to argue this nonsense with a subordinate, and he, too, was impatient for the fight. To have Chasm needle him about it made the urge difficult to restrain. "Cut the chatter, Bronze Three. You have your orders."

Chasm snarled a "Yes, sir," and the signal went dead.

Tag switched over to Chok's frequency. "Bronze Two to Leader. Natives are getting restless, Major."

"Chasm, I take it?"

"Yep."

"I'm not worried about her. Princess will tractor her in."

Tag wished he could share Chok's confidence that Bronze Four could exercise that pull on her wingman, but he found Princess too soft-spoken. "Yes, sir."

"Don't fret, Tag. We'll get our shot. Closing slowly to those mining complexes and scanning them does not mean we have to avoid the chance at crippling one if the opportunity presents itself. Besides, I've seen your aim: I'd be a fool to waste you on this run."

Tag smirked. Maybe Chok wasn't the vacuum-brain the others thought.

They'd barely made it a few thousand kilometers nearer when the sensors went crazy with alarms. Bright flashes rippled across the sky, packed together in one place. Tag gaped. Starships, jumping in? From where?

At once the intra-squadron signals overlapped. Chasm's voice cut through the mutters and questions. "Major! Since when is the commodore sending heavies to the party?"

"Since not as far as I'm aware." Chok sounded stern, as if he were an instructor who'd caught the perpetrator of a simulator prank. "Capital ships are not part of our plan."

Tag watched the ships emerge from the jump, and the light show faded. They were Terran, all right. Even from this far out, he could make out the hull shapes of heavy cruisers and... wait a second. He remembered a trick Scrape had shown him for lensing the sensors, feeding of the bandwidth from other planes in the squadron. It would foul theirs for a bit but boost the range and resolution of his own. The results were instantaneous.

"Major? Those aren't ours, but the good news is they aren't the one-eyes' either."

"What?"

Tag packaged and distributed the data to the squadron. *Nicely done, Scrape.* "Reittians. ID comes back for Battlegroup Five, Twelfth Fleet."

Chok sighed. "Well, that's interesting."

Not good. When Chok said "interesting," that meant "bad." But Tag didn't agree. There were 18 warships heading in—eight of those were cruisers, the Reittian equivalent of Terran heavy cruisers. Talk about a bruiser: 360 meters, 12 long range missile launchers, more particle cannon than the Terran equivalent. They were fast, too. Tag read they were pulling acceleration 10 percent greater than *Confiance* could manage. Along with them were two much larger ships that he guessed to be carriers, judging by their bulk and inferior acceleration, plus eight destroyers as escorts, four per carrier.

This, he realized, must be the force Father had warned the Reittians would send after Baedecker if Elden Selva were not restrained. The Reittians must have grown tired of waiting for him to be turned over.

"That's what I call ironic," he muttered to himself.

The Naplians weren't dumb. Six of their heavy cruisers—the big 600-meter types—swept out of orbit. Missiles streaked out like schools of razor-sharks.

"So much for pleasantries." The quiet voice in the comm was Princess, Bronze Four—2nd Lieutenant Naomi Wyss.

The Reittian ships didn't take long to react to the fleet they'd stumbled upon. The eight cruisers altered their vectors to fire upon the Naplian ships. Before long space around the planet was filled with the pinpricks of missile exhausts, the flashes of particle weapon bursts, and the bright blooms of explosions.

Tag shook his head. Typical Reittians. Lumbering in with their heavily-laden warships. He noted that two larger vessels—carriers, his sensors told him—accelerated away from the fight. They were screened by eight destroyers.

"Well, the die, as they say, has been cast. All fighters, accelerate to attack velocities," Chok said. "Same plan as before: get in, cause as much havoc as possible and gain our scans, get out. Only now, do be mindful of the crossfire."

Tag grinned. Finally.

Chok led the squadron on a vector that bypassed the melee between the Naplians and the Reittians, but he wasn't kidding about crossfire. Stray particle blasts from both sides zipped across their approach. Tag dodged a bracket of Reittian blasts that went 500 kilometers from his position—a huge gap by planetary standards, but considering his speed was four times that, it was a hair's breadth.

The remaining six Naplian ships finally noticed their presence, but it was at such a close range they resorted to particle blasts. Tag set the nav computer for evasive maneuvers, keeping a light hand on the control surfaces. The targeting reticule drifted over the nearest mining complex. Stars, what an ugly beast that was—nothing more than a rectangle of browns and grays, lined with green lights and pale yellow running stripes. Data poured in over his sensor panel.

"Sweet novas! They're full up to the brim with that one!" Chasm said.

"Forty percent is hardly 'to the brim,'" Princess said. "Tag, are you receiving the same results?"

"You bet I am. Between the two of us I think we're good to

go. What say we light this firecracker off, Chasm?"

She chuckled. "Men first."

"What a lady you are." Tag spun up two of his missiles. The targeting scanners had no problem finding a weak point on the mining ship's haunches.

"Steady on, my children—we have incoming." Chok's voice cut across the intra-squadron. "Sixteen fighters, from the planet's surface."

"Novafire," Tag spat. "You ladies hear that?"

"Just like you to cancel a hot date, Tag." Chasm sounded as forlorn as if she really had been denied a candlelit dinner. Though Tag had trouble picturing her at any kind of genteel establishment. More likely it was a fighter hangar.

"What did I say about chatter?" Chok sighed. "Split off into pairs. Draw them up into the firing lanes between the two forces."

Chok's fighter burned ahead of him, forcing Tag to keep up. Whatever complaints his squadron mates had about the major, he was no slug when it came to flying. His Warhawk dipped and scooted out of the incoming missiles from the Naplian fights, picking off strays with his counter-fire laser and jamming others with electronic counter-measures.

Tag bracketed the nearest fighter and loosed a missile. He didn't stick around to see if it hit, but spun the Warhawk with its axial thrusters and pulled in out of the way of an onrushing alien missile. It streaked by in a blink; the rear-facing laser turret tracked it on a separate, circular holo display by Tag's right knee. Seconds later the missile exploded.

So did Tag's, and his was no more successful: detonation without impact or destruction of a Naplian fighter. "Perfect," he muttered.

The range closed swiftly. His sensors enlarged the Naplian fighters, and he whistled as he examined them. Long, curving wings, stubby cockpit in the middle, three engines—one to either side of the cockpit, with the third slung underneath. They were maneuverable, and heavily shielded. In fact, Tag's sensors indicated a decrease to one of the fighter's shields. So his missile had hit the target. And hadn't destroyed it.

He grinned. Nothing like a challenge.

Bronze squadron swept into a barrage of energy blasts from the Naplian fighters, and cut into the enemy ranks in kind with their railguns.

"Watch it, Four, you've got one on your tail," Chasm

snapped.

"I see him. He's quite skilled at evading my laser." Princess could have been announcing the solar wind forecast rather than describing a Naplian fighter attacking her from behind. "If you're not too busy, Chasm—"

"Shut up and bank, your port!"

Tag's display kept the blue arrowheads delineated. Chasm's Warhawk swept in from the perpendicular to Princess and her pursuer. The Naplian must have realized there was another Terran on an intercept vector because he spun to meet Chasm while still racing after Princess. It was too late.

Chasm's railguns peppered the enemy's shields enough to put him off-course, and the missile that followed blew the fighter into a cloud of smoldering particles.

In those brief seconds, Tag had brought his fighter around in an arc that put him after the damaged Naplian. He opened fire with his railgun, pounding away at the depleted shields. Blast, but they had to have a monster of a generator for those things! The counter for the number of rounds in his gun was spinning down fast.

The Naplian juked to starboard but Tag shoved his fighter the same direction, with his port thruster bank. Flashes from a rear-facing particle gun arrowed in at him. The nav computer jerked the Warhawk back and forth along his pursuit vector, allowing it to narrowly evade the incoming shots.

The Naplian's shields went down, and Tag's last burst caught it square on an engine nacelle. It exploded, the fire dying out swiftly in the vacuum of space.

"Good shooting!"

"Thanks, Chasm."

"Bronze Leader to Bronze Two. I could use some cover."

Chok was "above" him, the belly of his fighter visible outside Tag's canopy. He was headed straight for the nearest mining complex, dragging along a pair of Naplians.

"Dammit, Mongoose." Tag flipped his fighter and boosted off after his squadron leader. Those two Naplians were right on his tail. He'd been so focused on chasing down his own target…

Chok abruptly cut his acceleration and spun his fighter in a gut-wrenching pivot. Railguns flashed as he hurtled along, backwards, firing on his pursuers. A missile shot out from Chok's Warhawk.

The Naplians eased apart, hardly seeming bothered by the

act. Simple enough for two planes to evade one weapon.

That is, until the missile exploded in a hailstorm of glittering fragments.

Tag shook his head. The shrapnel from a BX-44 warhead had to be traveling in excess of 10,000 kilometers per second. It didn't matter that they were just dumb shards of composite; at that velocity, they hammered the Naplians' shields until both sets of defenses collapsed. One of the fighters managed to maneuver free, angling "down" from Chok, while its partner was obliterated by the BX-44's shards, the plane shredding like a dried up leaf.

Tag caught the one headed his way with a burst of railgun projectiles.

Someone cried out across the comm: Bronze Six. Who was that? Tag couldn't remember a name, a rank, blast, even a gender. But his—or her—arrowhead disappeared from his display, caught in a sweep by three Naplian. Bronze Five, the wingman exploded alongside him.

A signal chimed pleasantly from his board: the sensors were done with their evaluation of the mining complex. A detailed readout of the ship's capacity, its armament, and its defenses scrolled down the screen. "Bronze Leader, this is Tag. I've got my fill. Chasm was right—final numbers come back as 43 percent full up on serjaum for that first complex."

"Good work, Tag. And much obliged, by the way, for not letting me die out here." There was dry humor behind Chok's words. "Not yet, at any rate."

"No problem, Major. What's the word?"

A Naplian ship's jump sails shattered like a small nova, momentarily blinding Tag. New alerts clamored for attention—the Naplians and Reittians engaged in battle had drifted nearer the planet, and consequently Bronze Squadron.

"It appears the action's coming to us. Steady on, keep to your objectives."

A Reittian destroyer came under heavy fire, caught between two Naplian light cruisers. It beat off the barrage, but an explosion just aft of the main hull—right between the pylons joining the two long engine nacelles—sent it shuddering off course. Lights flickered across the dorsal hull, but stayed on. The top nacelle went dead.

Tag glanced at his HUD. Chok was headed back toward the mining complexes, with four other fighters trailing him. Naplian fighters looped around to pursue. In the melee Tag nailed another enemy fighter, catching him under the starboard wing with a missile that shorted out his shields and destroying him with railgun fire.

Suddenly there was a corridor in space hemmed in by ships from both sides and hedged by weapons fire. Those Naplian light cruisers altered course toward the limping Reittian destroyer.

"Chasm, you still flying?" Tag flipped the Warhawk onto a new vector. Three missiles left, and half his railgun loadout.

"What kind of question is that? Of course I am!"

"Thanks in part to me," Princess said.

"Yeah, she did swat one off my rear," Chasm grumbled.

"And you're welcome."

"We've got a target of opportunity, ladies. Check that light cruiser at 046 mark 27. Portside shielding's running yellow."

"That Reittian's still not gonna make it."

"He might if we give him a chance. Form up and follow me."

"Tag, what about Mongoose?" Princess asked.

"He's fine. Got the whole rest of the squadron at his back, right? Let's make this run count."

The trio of Warhawks accelerated into the midst of the capital ships, dodging the weapons fire the two sides intended for each other. It didn't seem the Naplians would pay them heed, as intent on the Reittian battlegroup as they were.

But Tag's proximity alert squawked—four Naplian fighters followed them.

"Tag, let me loose. I'll cut 'em down while you two go for the cruiser," Chasm said.

"Negative! Maintain form and target the weak shielding on that light cruiser!" Tag highlighted his sensor readouts and transferred them via tight-beam. More kudos to Scrape for teaching him multi-tasking.

The Warhawk shook around him. Space outside his canopy blazed with the reflected energy from a Naplian blast impacting his shields. Ninety-percent—just a graze.

His squadron intra-comm was keyed to Chasm's and Princess's signals: another signal clamored for his attention, but Tag blocked it out. He glanced at the HUD: Chok was okay. He had plenty of fighters at his back, even with Naplians swarming about.

Even as he thought it, his sensors registered two explosions on the aft hull of one of the mining complex. "Nicely done, Mongoose."

The Naplian cruiser loomed ahead, busy pummeling the

Reittian destroyer with energy blasts. Tag had to hand it to the aliens: they made ships of eerie beauty. Giant fish, he thought, but very mechanical in their appearance. If they were going for size and grandeur with which they could impress enemies, they'd succeeded.

More shots from behind. A pair of missiles streaked in. Tag bucked himself off course. Focused ECM did its best to scramble the brains operating the Naplian missiles, while his aft laser lashed out. The first missile veered completely off course, disappearing in the midst of the crossfire between the capital ships. The laser vaporized the second one.

"Tag, if we're gonna do this, you'd better not wait until they put out a welcome signal!" Chasm hollered. "I'm holding off these one-eyes but they're persistent!"

"Just hold on! Targeting now." Tag put his sights square on the cruiser's damaged shielding. He keyed up his remaining three missiles. A red light flashed: the weapons systems warned against launching the last of his loadout. It was standard battle ops to leave one missile.

"Nothing about this counts as standard," Tag muttered, and launched all three.

Less than five seconds later, three missiles each from Chasm and Princess joined his. The projectiles streaked in, spaced widely, broadcasting jamming signals.

"Go! Break for the Reittian forces!" Tag led them out of the Naplian phalanx, through open space between the aliens and the Reittian battlegroup.

The missiles tracked clean—and at 30,000 kilometers from their target drew the full brunt of the light cruiser's defenses. Tag watched as the ship rolled and pitched, trying desperately to accelerate out of the path of the missiles. But they didn't need inertial compensators like biological payloads—missiles could accelerate at 30 times or more a standard cruiser. Tag gambled on the Naplians sharing the same need to protect from g-forces as humans; sensor data sure indicated that was the case.

Only two of the missiles were blotted out. Of the other seven, two applied one-shot braking thrusters at the last moment. The first five missiles hit the shields full on. Invisible most other times, the shell around the ship flared, bright as a sunrise, and then dimmed. The last two missiles struck home right after that, but they encountered no shields—they hit hull. Gouts of flame, air, and debris billowed out.

"Yes!" Tag thumped his console.

Chasm whooped over the comms; even Princess added a pleasant, "Oh, good shooting!"

The light cruiser's acceleration died. It had been mid-way through an arc that would bring it toward Baedecker Two, but without the constant push of its engines it drifted straight into the Reittian formation. The damaged Reittian destroyer and a cruiser savaged it with every weapon they had available. The Naplian couldn't withstand the salvoes, not with their weakest point so helpfully highlighted by a tail of white vapor. A series of explosions ruptured the light cruiser at the centerline; starboard jump sails broke apart, and the hull split. The halves tumbled away from each other, and in the next instant the aft was obliterated by a white hot nova. Main core failure.

A new signal requested contact with Tag—Imperial Reittian Destroyer *Wombat*. "Terran fighters, this is *IRD Wombat*. That was nice throat-cutting—worthy of a Reittian stalker squad. We could have handled them on our own, of course, but we appreciate the assist all the same."

Tag snorted. Assist? He would make sure the squadron tally chalked the light cruiser up as a kill for all three of the Bronze pilots. "Captain Taggart Wester here, Bronze Squadron, Terran AEF. Don't mention it, *Wombat,* though next time we won't leave you anything to shoot at."

The rest of Bronze Squadron was homing in on Tag, Chasm, and Princess, bringing them all back into formation among the relative safety of the Reittian battlegroup. Tag suddenly realized the Reittians were down several ships: three destroyers were gone. He saw only debris fields, and background radiation from their destruction. And a cruiser was broken in half. A second cruiser appeared to be retrieving escape pods while two more provided cover, but overall the Reittians weren't faring well—especially since the Naplians had only lost two ships.

Chok's signal continued to pester him. "By the stars, get over it." Tag punched the receiver. "This is Two, go ahead, Leader."

"I see how you earned your reputation, Wester." Chok never called him that, in the past few days. He always referred to him by call sign, as he did with all his pilots. The familiarity was gone, replaced by a cool, stern tone that made Tag suddenly, irrationally want to salute. "Yours may be the shortest-lived battlefield promotion in the history of the AEF."

"Major, I get that you wanted me to engage the mining

ships, but I'd already completed my scans and the Naplian—"

"Enough." One slice of that word, and Tag clamped his jaw shut. "You deliberately disobeyed my orders. You abandoned your wingman."

The HUD screamed for attention. Six more lights appeared on the display—and Tag swore as Naplian battlecruisers jumped into the fray. They were too far off to see, but the sensors told him they were powering weapons and prepping batteries for launch.

"Standby. We'll continue this at base." Chok switched frequencies, and opened a link to the Reittians. "We're going to make a series of jumps to our command post. I strongly recommend you follow."

Tag's ripwave generator was spooled up. He locked in the coordinates for the first of a half dozen jumps they'd make to throw the Naplians off their trail, and dissuade discovery of Station Golf Echo Fiver. He gave the squadron roster a final glance.

Three planes lost.

He didn't know those men and women.

As he engaged the ripwave generator, Tag wondered whether that would have made a difference when it came to his actions.

***

Tag stood at attention before Major Chok. The man was shorter than him by head and shoulders, with brown hair turning silver above his ears. But the eyes—they nailed Tag to the bulkhead of the squadron's makeshift ready room inside a Station GE5 maintenance cabin. One was pale green; the other was dark brown.

It was the green one, Tag thought. Like a targeting laser.

"What makes you special?" Chok asked. "What makes you exempt from our discipline? I lost three people out there, and even though we fulfilled our mission parameters, it was no thanks to you."

Tag remained silent. He'd said his piece, given his rationale —it was all there in the after-action report he filed.

"I'll not blame Chasm and Princess—they were following your lead, and your rank. Which is what I wanted the squadron to do when I asked Commodore Ram to assign you to me. I wanted the other pilots to follow you, Tag. You have a gift to make bold decisions, but you're too rash. You rush off on your own. It's as if you don't even understand the concept of a squadron."

Tag stared at a set of rusted bolts above the hatch a few centimeters over Chok's head. He tried to clear his mind but he kept remembering Baedecker Six—the mock bombing run, DeeDee's admonitions, the discovery of the Truppen and the chase thereafter.

They'd never found any remnants of the old Bronze Squadron. Those eight planes were considered MIA.

"Wing Commander Dillon was a friend of mine." Chok never raised his voice throughout his tirade. That made it worse. "She hated your cavalier attitude but marveled at your skill— marveled, you understand? She, a veteran of *both* Consular wars. I want to give you a chance, Tag, but you won't let me. You can be a good commander, and a great pilot. You don't have to choose between the two."

Tag finally cleared his throat. "Am I grounded from combat duty, sir?"

Chok stared at him. The green eye blinked once. "No. You're staying on as my exec. You, Chasm, and Princess will get the kill for that light cruiser—you deserve it, of course. Commodore Ram is none too thrilled that the Reittians are here, but ... well, they're finicky allies. Stubborn, rash. Should sound familiar. However, given the fact that we've heard nothing back from Terra, we've resigned ourselves to enlisting their aid. Once they've repaired, of course."

"Yes, sir. Thank you, sir."

"Don't thank me, Tag. Improve. Trust your leaders." Chok folded his hands behind his back. "Now come. We have a memorial service to officiate."

Tag followed him out. His heart sank. If this is what being a leader entailed, it was a far more difficult job than he'd imagined.

CHAPTER FOURTEEN

Elden had never seen anything quite so ugly as the double core fusion reactor looming over them from the heights outside Vossberg City. But as tired as he was, it could have been a transient's rusted shipping container converted into a bunk for all he cared.

Twin towers eight stories high leaned over the column streaming into the power station's boundaries. Each one was a rhombus, slanted to the northeast. They were a deep slate gray so dark as to be almost black. A blue glow pulsed through transparent walls on all sides, adding much-needed illumination to the late night arrivals.

Elden's skin itched for a moment as the group of refugees, in tandem with General Wood's armored division, trundled between a pair of HM-2116 hover-tanks. He had a vague recollection of slippers—his father's, sitting by the electric hearth in their house. The tanks had the same long, rounded shape, albeit topped with twin anti-personnel lasers and a long, 160 mm railgun barrel. He knew it wasn't sand fleas this time that made him scratch, but rather the sensation of walking through an opening provided in the huge, invisible shield that protected both the power station and the soldiers using it as a base from orbital and aerial bombardment.

A cheer went up from the CDF soldiers inside the power station. They were a raggedy bunch—most had stains and dents on their armor, and many were lacking pieces of the equipment. Weapons were stacked about in seemingly random collections, propped up against or inside storage containers. Tents of torn plastic, broken quik-crete slabs, and lids from the aforementioned containers were strewn about, in some places arranged in groups of eight and in others, simply pushed up alongside the dozen buildings of the reactor complex.

General Wood strode in ahead of the Armored Division's vehicles, leading the four anti-ship cannons. He held up his hands, which must have signaled to the awaiting soldiers to stop cheering, for they lapsed into silence. Elden dropped the pack he was wearing and took a long, drowning drink of water from his jug. It left him gasping but burn it all, he was thirsty.

"You guys and gals have done a tremendous job of holding this position," Wood's voice boomed across the reactor complex. Elden figured there had to be a couple hundred CDF troops—and scattered groups of both police and civilians—streaming over to the entrance to see the new arrivals. "I couldn't be more proud of your fighting spirit."

A roar like thunder rolled through the crowd, but Wood cut it short with another gesture of raised hands. "But this is the sloppiest excuse for a forward operating base I have ever seen in my forty-four years of soldiering! I want all officers to report to Major Bond here on the double! Non-coms! Get those weapons properly stowed. Those tanks need to be moved back from the perimeter. All debris not being used as a bunk needs to be cleaned up, on the double! Get your asses in gear!"

Troops were moving before Wood's tirade ended. The civilians and police seemed nonplussed, but at least a couple handfuls of officers made their way to the Texans' column, ready for work. So did groups of civilians, ranging from burly techs in grease-stained coveralls to people Elden assumed were clerks, or administrators, dressed in the rumpled remains of their office attire.

"The general has a way with words," Marney said.

Elden turned. She hopped down from an armored truck, and gave Goetz a hand bringing down the stretcher to which Andan Natour was strapped. An Armored Cav medic was right there with them, a short, dark-skinned woman with curly black hair. She spoke with Natour while checking readouts on the hovering med-scanner by her left shoulder.

"He certainly does. How was your ride?"

Marney smiled, and shrugged. Her hair, a duller shade of auburn now, was frizzy from days of ill care and tied up in a ponytail. She'd washed off the wedding makeup; it was replaced with dirt. Even her gorgeous wedding dress was gone, packed into a spare bag she'd been afforded. In its place she wore fatigues of a desert camouflage pattern, the same digitized design as the other

Texan soldiers. "Bumpy. But your friend Andan kept me grinning the entire way."

"I do... still maintain my ways with the fairer sex." Natour coughed, and gave them a weak version of his smile. He was far too pale, and his face had thinned considerably.

"Ma'am? Could you please take the patient along to the med-tent over there?" The medic pointed at a tall, slope-sided pyramid of grey-green plastic. The red outline of a cross with a silver caduceus—twin snakes wrapped around a pole, topped by sharp wings—was the rare splash of color in the otherwise drab encampment. "That'd be a great help."

Goetz checked the hover unit on the underside of the stretcher. It hummed, lifting the stretcher a meter off the ground. "I'll escort you, Miss Wester."

"Thank you, Goetz, but I'll be quite safe here." She patted the holstered pistol strapped to her fatigues. She readied to push the stretcher but stopped. Then Marney kissed Elden on the cheek. "And thank you for helping us get this far."

"I'm not through yet. We'll find your father." Elden touched her hand. He abruptly remembered it wasn't just Governor Wester whom they sought to rescue. "And Timothy."

"Yes. I know." Marney smiled again. She pushed Natour's stretcher away. Elden could hear him take up a joke—one to which he'd heard the punchline a dozen times. Marney's laughter carried through the milling crowds.

"How bad is he?" Bless Goetz. The man was as blunt as a seismic-hammer.

"You gentlemen want me to fudge it, civilian-style?" the medic asked.

Elden shook his head. "No. Even if you haven't told Nat, we must know."

"Oh, I told him. He's far too canny—I couldn't have hidden the truth if I tried. Those one-eye weapons are nasty. Never mind the necrotic tissue and organ damage; the radiation from the blast did an awful number on his central nervous system. His body isn't responding to the first aid regen I can provide. He needs full-on surgical care, probably nanite treatment."

Elden turned away. He stared out at Vossberg City, far below the escarpment. The spires and skyscrapers were beaten and battered—broken windows everywhere he looked, smoke rising in both thick black plumes and thin gray wisps. There were fewer tall buildings, he noted. Vossberg Terminal was the most disheartening. Hadn't he just escaped Reittian entrapment in its crystalline hall, a few days ago? Now it was a burnt corpse.

"What are those odds?" he asked. "Of finding a functional medical center with its nanite treatment suite still intact."

"Major medical facilities could have been at the top of their target list," Goetz said. "I wouldn't put it past them."

"Either way, gentlemen, it may be too late to investigate." The medic's face was impassive. "I gave Mr. Natour something for the pain—which is considerable—but don't put money on him lasting the night. He's lucky he made it this far."

Lucky. To die of grievous wounds, away from his home planet, not having accomplished any portion of their mission? They couldn't even contact the monastery. General Wood had forbidden all communications from their column while they were in the desert.

Elden fumed. He wouldn't let Nat die in vain. They had to get through to Abbot Jeopar, and his lackey, Erich. Find out the extent of their Truppen successes. Based on what he'd encountered in the desert, Elden knew they'd restored at least some of the cybernetic soldiers.

"Anyway, if you need something more from me, holler. I'm going to go check on the patient."

"Thank you, Sergeant." Elden nodded.

Once she was gone, Goetz moved closer. "Don't like this, sir. If Mr. Natour dies, and we're stuck among the CDF, it's going to make our objectives harder to achieve."

"I understand. That's why we need our outside help as soon as possible."

Goetz slipped something small and black from his pocket. "Here."

Elden palmed it, watching the people around them. No one seemed to notice. "Do I want to know which Texan is missing their personal transmitter?"

"None. It's a spare, borrowed from the maintenance truck."

"Borrowed?"

Goetz's mouth quirked into a tight smile. "Temporarily loaned. It needs some fiddling—and if you use it here at their base..."

"Too risky. I have no doubt General Wood's monitoring all communications traffic, or at least one of his officers is." Elden put the communicator in his pocket. "There's another option. We can send a signal without interference from the city."

Goetz stared at him. He pointed at the city. The smoke was lit by the red glow of a fire burning somewhere—several somewhere, Elden realized, and the intermittent flashes of green energy blasts from Naplian weapons. "Down there? We can't stroll over the bridge, sir. There's just a handful of Naplian companies, complete with those blasted mechs, blocking the route."

"I promised Marney we would rescue Governor Wester—"

"Plus her fiancé."

Elden ignored the jibe. "And I mean to keep my promise. There has to be a way into the city, across the Santos River, that a handful of people can find and use, quietly. Once there, we can contact the monastery."

Behind them there was considerable activity. One anti-ship cannon stood nearby, at the edge of the shield protecting the power station. The other three were deployed elsewhere—one to the far end of the station, off to Elden's left, was visible as a toy-sized version, its muzzles aimed skyward. The other two were likely on the other corners, but all he could tell was they were in transit, huge wheels rumbling.

Anchors slammed down from the mobile platform of the nearest cannon. They cracked quik-crete and churned up dirt. The gun mount motors whined as it angled up.

General Wood approached, grinning. Elden tucked the communicator into his trousers pocket, smiling back. "You seem in good spirits, General."

"Oh, yes. These babies are the reason we took as long as we did to get back here, traipsing past every itching sand dune and scrub cactus this side of Vossberg." Wood put his hands on his hips and craned his neck. The stars were peeking out, high above the reactor towers. "Time to show those one-eyes what it means to tangle with Terrans."

***

Admiral Daviont sat behind his desk and let Vice Admiral Bouchtok finish his report on the status of operations at Baedecker Two, and kept his irritation concealed behind a serene mask.

"We lost several hundred thousand tons of the serjaum, along with the mining complex in which it was stored," Bouchtok said. "Fortunately the second mining complex only suffered drive damage—none of its contents were lost. The same cannot be said of our ships. The light cruiser *Veloce* and cruiser *Lutin* were both destroyed. Several others sustained damage to vital systems."

"More damage." Vice Admiral Hilder's head bobbed. "These two-eyes have caused more havoc than can be counted on six fingers, Kiv. Especially with that surprise attack fleet of theirs. It's a good thing I brought in the 3rd Colonial Squadron when I did."

The three of them were seated in Daviont's office, off *Narsa's* bridge. The huge holographic display floating between them showed lists of ships, their crew complements, armament, and individual reports from the captains. A separate column of green, set off to the right, was General Falloram's surface update.

"Yes, it is indeed." Bouchtok stayed impassive, fingers steeped, and did not make eye contact with his comrade. "As I already said three times, you have my thanks."

"Just so we know who owes whom." Hilder smiled.

"But I do not think the fleet is a backup force of the Terrans. Communications intercepts revealed the term 'Reittians.' Do we have further intelligence on this group?"

"Human allies of the Terrans," Daviont said. "According to our Denic spies. And they are not always the best of friends. Apparently the Baedecker system belonged to the Reittians prior to the last war the Terrans fought among themselves. Only after the radiation settled did the system become apportioned to its current occupants."

"Assuming that's true, and I don't like assuming anything where two-eyes are concerned, what's the likelihood they want it back?" Hilder asked. "If they have any idea how much serjaum is hidden away on those inner planets, I'd imagine they'd be quick to act."

"That is what I surmise. Take their arrival." Daviont gestured to the holographic display. At his motion, it replayed the start of the Baedecker Two battle. Daviont froze the imagery seconds after the Reittian ships arrived. "Consider their vectors. You see the data? They jumped in close to Baedecker Two, and given its orbital alignment to Baedecker Four, the ships would have been difficult to spot as a war fleet."

Hilder's eye narrowed. "What are you saying? We weren't the target?"

"I think Baedecker Four was the target. Consider the size of their fleet—eighteen vessels. A pittance compared to our fleet, but an adequate show of force against the Terran's twelve."

"They couldn't have conquered the system with eighteen ships, even if two of them looked like carriers," Hilder said. "There wasn't a transport among them, so far as our sensors could determine!"

"Perhaps they did not seek conquest, but intimidation." Bouchtok stood, and stepped closer to the holo. His hands cupped around one of the Reittian ships, and he spread his fingers, which magnified the image. "Yes. It was a diplomatic move, of sorts. Meant to put pressure on the local government."

"That is my feeling. *Savionta urs Tash'Nal.* 'Gunboat diplomacy,' as the humans would say." Daviont expanded a smaller hologram on his desk, this one a quick rendering of the Baedecker system. "Whatever their motive, we must assume these Reittians have variable loyalties. As such they must be swayed to our cause."

"If we can find them." Hilder sighed. "Sorry, Tir, but wherever the Terrans are hiding, it's got to be on the far fringes of the system. Ice chunks all over the place, millions of them, and every one could support a small depot or dry-dock. I have my ships combing the region, but every time we think we're on the right vector, those *shirish* gnat fighters pop up and pound us."

"They make quite the mockery of your missiles, Gol." Bouchtok's tone was neutral, but Daviont smiled at the intended barb.

"And yours. And the admirals. I'll give them three fingers up—the Terrans have impressive countermeasures. Firepower? Lacking, and crude. But they can scramble a missile's brains with the best of them."

"We'll concentrate our efforts around Baedecker Two and Four," Daviont said. "Word from the rest of the fleet in the region is that the Terrans put up quite a fight, but this sector of space is well on its way to being subdued. No major fleets have been dispatched to eject us from Baedecker. The Naplian Empire enjoys a strong foothold on this sector, including several major systems. We need only keep the Terrans away for the next few months while we reap every bit of serjaum we can from that rock. Kiv? Send your damaged vessels here to Four in order that we may conduct repairs."

"Of course, Admiral."

"Gol?" Daviont tapped his desk. Many possibilities with these new humans. How better to eliminate the burgeoning resistance than by driving a wedge between tenuous allies? "Send a few stealth ships out. Broadcast to the Reittians, quietly. If we can win them over with promises to control this system, perhaps they —"

An alert blared throughout the office. Emergency lights flashed. "Admiral to the bridge!" Captain Kentondi's voice snapped under strain.

"Excuse me, my friends." Daviont left the office, not at a run, but not at his leisure, either. There was nothing to be gained by showing his worry to the crew—it was harmful to their morale. Bouchtok and Hilder did not wait idly, either. They followed at his heels.

Daviont strode onto the bridge, hands clasped behind his back, as if he were arriving in time for an inspection. "Report, Captain."

"Energy surges from the human's capital city," Kentondi said. "Sensors are having difficulty pinpointing what's causing them. They're emanating from the fusion power station on the contested heights above the city, but the technicians assure me the readouts do not match those created by a fusion core."

"Sacred ancestors," Bouchtok whispered. "Do they seek their own destruction by sending the reactor into a critical spike?"

Hilder scowled. "The humans fight like crazed *viash'tul* scavengers quarrelling over the last morsel every time we engage them in combat. I don't see them as the suicidal type, and definitely not in the business of endangering their civilians."

Something clicked into place in the recesses of Daviont's mind. "Send to all commands, priority signal: pull all vessels out of low orbit. Get them 100,000 kilometers away from the planet immediately."

Kentondi made a face. "Admiral. A retreat?"

"Do as I say!" Daviont snapped. "Now!"

The outburst was enough to shock Kentondi and the bridge crew into action. Voices overlapped as the commands were relayed. Ships displayed in the tactical hologram moved from their positions, albeit slowly.

Far too slowly. "Micro-jump if you have to," Daviont said. "We must get out of range!"

Before anyone could further question his orders, a proximity alert sounded, and red lights flashed throughout the bridge. Blue-white energy blasts lanced out from Baedecker Four, cutting through the dark skies. Three of the shots speared the bombard *Tancrede*. They gutted the forward hull, tearing through armor plating and spewing debris, before shields were raised.

More blasts knifed into the fleet. Two battlecruisers took hits, and though their shields held, Daviont saw red indicators light up their readouts on his tactical displays. But the rest of the ships reacted accordingly, spurred on by the sudden weapons fire from the planet's surface. Daviont's view of Baedecker Four shrank as *Narsa* leapt away, followed by dozens of other warships.

"Bombard *Tancrede* is listing in orbit, sir," Kentondi said. "Escape pods launching. She's coming apart at the seams."

Hilder swore. "Cursed two-eyes! Falloram should have caught their artillery. It's unacceptable that he allowed them to escape."

"General Falloram had men searching every valley and cliff shadow for a hundred square kilometers," Daviont said. "But have you seen this planet's topography? There are myriad places the Terrans could have burrowed in. Which they obviously did."

"Sir, the fleet's moved off," Kentondi said. His face was flush with anger. Deep grays built up on his neck and cheeks.

"*Tancrede* is a loss."

"Yes, Admiral. Fifty dead, at least. We're still getting reports —and the battlecruisers *Bellon* and *Tepare* also sustained damage."

Hilder groaned. "Not *Bellon.* She's still undergoing refits."

"It appears she's no longer spaceworthy." Bouchtok pulled forth a diagram from the cloud of the holographic displays. "Look at this failure of structural supports—if she attempts micro-jumps, she'll be torn to pieces."

Daviont nodded. "Strike *Bellon* from the list. Send word: we need a tug in-system as soon as the rest of the fleets in the outlying star systems can spare one."

"Word is there's a repair base set up 20 light-years from here."

"That will suffice." The weapons fire from the planet ceased. Daviont faced his companions. "Keep your ships outside the 100,000 kilometer mark, unless you're sufficiently far enough around the arc of the planet to avoid the range of those guns."

"Negates the use of our bombards, doesn't it?"

"It does indeed. Unless General Falloram can take the heights and eliminate those guns, our campaign on the ground will not finish as soon as we'd hoped." Of course, this meant more casualties. A protective shield such as the one surrounding the Baedecker fusion plant was hard to crack—it deflected most ground-based energy and kinetic weapons. Daviont knew more soldiers would die. It had to be left to artillery, mechs, and troops to take the station.

He brought up a display of the region around Vossberg City,

with the power station highlighted. Many Terran lives—soldiers and civilians—would be lost, too. At some point, the losses would prove unbearable to the Terrans, and they'd be forced to sue for peace.

One thing was certain. Daviont felt a glimmer of fear, not for himself, or the outcome of the campaign, but for the battles ahead in the Naplian war of conquest. Because whoever converted the Terran worlds into allies would make them a tenacious enemy of all Ffawe and the great emperors.

He thought of the scrambled, frantic last transmission from Major Rej Lanviond. Whatever had killed his unit was something unrevealed by the Terrans in combat. They had slaughtered the special forces team—much like Lanviond had done to the Terran force, in a separate skirmish—and disappeared into the desert.

Rej's warnings about the devastators unleashed by the alien outsider did not sit well with him. If some portion of this prophecy were true—if it were even possible that such a threat to Naplia existed, Daviont would raze the planet.

He'd rather face nightmares for the last centuries of his life, haunted by the deaths of two million people, than let his empire perish.

***

The Naplian ground forces retaliated promptly.

Less than fifteen minutes after the ground-to-space cannons ceased fire, alien artillery opened up from the lower end of the Santos bridge, pummeling the shield around the power plant with green energy blasts. Simultaneously mechs and soldiers swarmed the bridge, making a rapid advance that they hoped would both overwhelm the Terrans with its surprise and intensity.

General Wood had been waiting for them to make such a move.

He had snipers armed with SAAR portable railguns stationed on the rock faces leading from the upper end of the bridge to the base of the power plant, as well as laser squads and two-man rocket launcher teams. They lit up the advancing ranks of Naplians—white-hot flashes of railgun projectiles, orange blossoms of fire from exploding rockets, and glowing red mech body parts where they were overheated and sliced by the laser teams.

The Naplians pressed forward, using their mechs as fodder and armored shields for the troops. Artillery in the rear ranks scored several hits against the entrenched snipers. Their blasts tore great gouges in the cliffs.

Two squadrons of Naplian fighters roared overhead. They hammered the shield, causing the huge dome to flicker wildly above the defenders. CDF troops returned fire with the handful of anti-aircraft railgun emplacements they had, but they weren't much good against the heavily shielded, fast fighters.

"Major Bond!" Wood snapped into his communicator. "You're up."

Four squads of six HM-2116 hover-tanks each swept down from the west, ripping up the desert sands and burning the dirt underneath with their engines. They fired down onto the bridge, sweeping the advancing mech hordes clear, while taking care not to damage the bridge structure itself. It was the Terrans' only route into the city, too.

At the same time they brought the Naplian advance to a standstill, Wood allowed a small section of the shield opened at ground level, facing north. Six assault shuttles shot through, each one stripped of its troop-carrying capacity and replaced with rocket pods. They banked over the desert, sending up a huge cloud of sand and dust, and their engines fanned it higher than the crest of the shield dome.

The Naplian fighters changed course to avoid the blinding dust, and ran straight into a wall of rockets. Three exploded on the first pass, and two more lost wings. Their pilots ejected as the wrecked fighter spiraled into the darkness below before slamming into the desert plains.

***

It was in the midst of the battle that Elden Selva said goodbye to his best friend.

"You look terrible, Nat." He tried to smile, but it wouldn't stay.

Natour shook his head. "No...not my best...day." He gasped, and coughed. Blood oozed from the sides of his mouth.

They were in the medical tent, among two dozen other injured or dying personnel. The medic who'd helped earlier was nearby, running a dermal stitcher over the gaping thigh wound of a soldier. The young man—boy, really—had taken a hit from a

Naplian rifle, and the stench of burnt flesh turned Elden's stomach. The medic glanced over at Elden. There had to be something more she could do for him.

She frowned, and focused on the soldier in front of her.

"Eldi...sorry about all this." Natour grasped his hand. Such a weak grip. A far cry from his hearty handshakes.

"Don't say that. You helped us escape. You fought off invaders."

"Invaders of...what? Not...my home." Natour closed his eyes and exhaled, a long, rattling breath.

For a moment Elden thought he'd passed. But Natour gasped again, choking. He pulled on Elden's hand, urging him closer. Elden leaned in. Natour's breath was faint.

"Be...cautious. If there...are Truppen...dangerous..."

He sagged against the cot. His last breath faded.

Goetz stood by the foot of the bed. Marney held on to his arm.

Elden's throat tightened. Tears burned the corners of his eyes. After all they'd been through, and after all the plans they'd made for the rebirth of the Northern Alliance...now Elden was on his own. He closed Natour's eyes, and placed his palm on his friend's forehead, his fingers forming the sign of the consuls. "Go safely to the stars."

The medic sedated the soldier next to them. He was unconscious in an instant. She came over to them, stripping sanitary gloves as she walked. "Sorry about your friend. If we weren't in the middle of a war he'd have had more of a chance."

"If we were not in the middle of your war he would never have been shot," Elden said.

He didn't acknowledge her questions or Goetz's as he strode from the tent. Outside the sound dampening field of the medical tent, the sounds of battle pressed in from all around—the ground shook with explosions, the air vibrated as the shield absorbed blasts, and weapons shrieked, making it nearly impossible to hear voices.

Impossible, that is, until Marney whispered in his ear. "Elden, I'm so sorry."

He squeezed her hands. "Thank you."

Goetz was behind her, unflinching as Naplian blasts flashed across the shield. "Sir. If we want to move—"

"Yes. Now's the time." Elden pulled Marney closer. "Are you ready to rescue your father?"

"Of course." Her eyes widened. "Now? In the middle of the battle? I don't have any idea where in the city he's being held."

"That's not our first problem. We have to get out of the camp, and we have to find a way into Vossberg without using the bridge."

"If you can accomplish the first, I know a way in."

Goetz frowned. "Can we go unnoticed? That whole area's lit up with Naplian weapons fire."

"I've done it before—it's been a couple years, but I remember the path."

Elden trusted Goetz's judgment, but Marney was the one who knew the terrain far better than any of them. And he'd known her much longer—and in greater detail—than Goetz. He'd trusted only Andan Natour more highly.

And Nat was dead.

"Goetz. Get us our weapons. Meet us by the section of the shield where those assault shuttles left."

"Yes, sir." Goetz disappeared among the groups of soldiers hurrying across the station grounds.

Elden and Marney ran for the north end, back toward where they'd first entered the shield, dodging medics and the wounded and soldiers moving to the front lines. A second wave of assault shuttles roared forward, whipping up the grounds in a windstorm. The soldiers manning the shield gap checkpoint held up their arms to protect their eyes.

Goetz was back in an instant, with both Naplian rifles slung on his back, along with a pack bulging at the seams.

"Go!" Elden said.

He and Marney and Goetz sprinted through the exit, the exhaust of the assault shuttles buffeting them from all sides.

And they were out, boots churning the sand. Elden heard the telltale buzz of the shield sealing behind them. Darkness closed in as the lights from the station faded. Elden slowed his pace. He had to give his eyes time to adjust.

But he didn't have to wait long to be able to see, because the flare of explosions and weapons fire lit everything back up as clear as day.

"This way!" Marney pulled ahead. She ran toward the edge of the escarpment and scrambled down the lip.

"Better stick close to her!" Elden said.

"That was my plan," Goetz muttered.

They worked their way down the escarpment, letting loose

an avalanche of rock and dirt. The battle raged above them, atop the bridge and on its west side. Marney hurried like a champion grav-ball runner, barely pausing on the way down, and twice almost stumbling over the sharp outcroppings that lead in straight drops to the river below.

Elden had no idea how they were going to cross. The surface of the Santos River shone like a mirror in sunlight where the battle's fury reflected. Everywhere he looked, as he slipped and slid down the escarpment, was deep churning water.

Except for a long, broad patch far from the Santos bridge. Marney headed straight for it.

Elden and Goetz caught up with her. They crouched behind flat rocks the size of dining tables, half submerged in the river.

A tremendous explosion rocked the bridge. Naplian forces backed off. And a trio of Terran hover-tanks pushed their way into the center, pounding at their adversaries.

"Right here!" Marney put her head close to Elden's to be heard. "There's a sandbar that's built up over the years. The water's no deeper than a meter at this time of the year."

"What about drop-offs?" Goetz seemed concerned. His face looked paler than usual.

"None. It's safe. Tag and I raced across it a couple of times, when the river had dried up even more."

If she was wrong, they could drown. But Elden wasn't about to turn his back on Marney now. "Lead on."

They slogged across, moving as quickly as they could. It was shallow, and biting cold. Elden was soaked up to his thighs. Water and mud pooled in his boots, making them heavy as a depowered mech exo-skeleton. He trudged along.

The sounds of battle diminished. Hoots and warbles cut through the noise.

"They're retreating," Goetz said. "The Naplians are reforming behind their barricades."

And the Terrans backed up to their fortified position at the upper end of the bridge. If either side had planned to seize the bridge that night, both failed, but Elden suspected Wood just wanted to whittle down the Naplians.

How long could they last, though, tucked under their shield?

They reached the edge, freezing and sopping wet, but unhurt. Marney gave Elden a hand, and together they pulled Goetz up. The three hunkered by a quik-crete retaining wall, hidden in shadow and gasping for breath.

"Well done, Miss Wester." Elden smiled at her.

She grinned back. "Thank you. What's our next move?"

Elden glanced upriver at the flame-lit towers of Vossberg City. "We find others who can help us. And then we find your father."

He touched his pocket. The communicator was still there, and dry.

Natour's warning about the Truppen arose in his memories. His smile disappeared. The only ones who had to fear the Truppen, he thought, would be the enemies of the Northern Alliance—both of this world and those who invaded it.

PART TWO

CHAPTER FIFTEEN

Seventeen Days after the Naplian Invasion

The reports from Baedecker Four were discouraging. But Admiral Ergen of the Briddarri Ninth Stellar Fleet was used to being discouraged. After all, the war against the Naplians had winnowed the best and boldest officers from his ships over several grueling years.

And now here he was, on the bridge of *Winter Scourge*, breathing in the stink of Briddarri body odor and musk that worn-down ventilators could not filter, while he stared at a star system full of one-eye starships.

It had taken them two years to get here. Two years of skulking through the galactic backwater of the Great Desert Rift, dodging Naplian scouts and avoiding black holes.

"Three weeks late," Ergen growled. "Three weeks, and we might have held the line."

The main tactical display of *Winter Scourge* was a depression in the deck, dead center to the bridge and the surrounding stations. Baedecker's twin stars glowed in the core; planets drifted lazily on pulsing white tracks. His frustration lay with the clusters of red dots grouped at the second, fourth, and sixth planets.

"It's pretty bad." This from Commander Ziran Zol Happar, lead pilot for the Ninth's fighter squadrons. Happar was more appropriately Briddarri height—short, stocky, skin flushed a deeper green due to years spent pulling high-gee maneuvers. He had Brown hair buzz cut to his scalp and streaked with twin lines of fluorescent orange above each ear.

Ergen frowned. Entirely against protocol, that was, but it encouraged esprit de corps among Happar's pilots, so Ergen let it slide. "Thank you for that observation."

"Sure thing, Admiral. There have to be sixty warships in that system. We brought along twenty. Does that strike you as a fair fight?"

"Only if our fighter pilots miss their marks."

Happar snorted. "I am cut, truly, I am."

"There's no indication our arrival was noticed. Hence my order for us to jump to the very fringes of the solar envelope."

"A wise precaution. If you need more detailed scans, I have a squadron prepped for insertion. We can dive in, see who's where, and be gone before they have time to check their scanners."

"Somehow I doubt that. Doesn't matter. We didn't bring along enough firepower to dislodge the Naplians."

"Anyone we know?"

Ergen handed him the scroll. His gazed remained fixed on the display. Something about the outer shell of comets and other frozen debris encasing the Baedecker system bothered him. A cluster wasn't orbiting as it should.

"Oh. Daviont and the III Corps."

"Exactly. Too much to hope he'd change his mind, the rascal, yet here he is. And they've got ships down at the second planet—probably scraping it clean of serjaum."

"We can blast them," Happar said. "Let us loose, Admiral."

"Enough of that. I'm not about to throw away men after we've near killed ourselves to get this far." Ergen stroked his moustache. "Tactical?"

"Yes, sir?"

"Focus on that region at quadrant 15-6. You see it? The debris is clustering in a strange fashion."

"Sir...? Oh, I see it. Bringing hi-res sensors on line."

Happar peered past him. "What's your target?"

"We haven't picked up any Terran ships in the vicinity," Ergen said, "Save for a handful that appear to be converging on Baedecker from surrounding systems. And all the other systems in this sector were hounded by the Naplians, so we know the Terrans who were here didn't flee to one of them."

"So Daviont destroyed them all," Happar said. "Flaming engines."

"No, not even he's that good. Remember the reports from Everett Lind? He said the humans are dug in outside the main city, raising havoc against their occupiers. There were also rumors of damaged Naplian starships and incursions against their mining."

"Ah." Happar grinned. "The humans went into hiding."

"I'll bet a month's *rietsu* cigars they're skulking around with whatever they've got cobbled together, sniping at Daviont's heels every moment they get. Lind's been clear: the humans might be on the technological downslope and somewhat savage, but they can fight. Boy, can they fight."

"Admiral! I've got something."

He joined the tactical officer at his console. The young Briddarri magnified the selected region of the Baedecker outskirts. "Concentration of metals and energy signals. Confined to that area, mostly, but now that I know what to look for, there's traces throughout the system. Could be ripwave activity, and fusion engines."

"Good work. How many?"

The officer shrugged. "Best estimate? Couple dozen warships, give or take, if you include the scattered signals with the rest."

Ergen smiled. Got them. "Comms? Send out a low-burst transmission, signaling friendly intentions, to the location provided by Tactical. I have a frequency for you to use."

"Lind provide you with that?"

"He's eavesdropped enough on their communications to crack the basics. At least they'll know it isn't the Naplians." Ergen handed the Comms officer his scrolled. "Make that link on the lower left, Lieutenant."

"Yes, Admiral." There was a pause. "I'm rolling it over. Should be ready to record any moment."

"Good!" Ergen clapped his hands together. He sucked in his gut, and ran a hand over the hair clinging to the sides of his scalp. "Tuck in, Commander. We'd best look presentable."

Happar straightened to a parade rest position.

The communications officer nodded, and gestured with his index finger. Go.

"This is Admiral San Sett Ergen of the Ninth Stellar Fleet. We hail from a distant realm, and call ourselves the Briddarri. All you really need to know is that we're their enemies—and we're here to help you beat the scum back…"

***

The Naplian fighters swarmed them like mosquitos along the banks of the Santos River in high summer. "Get 'em off my back!"

Chasm screamed. "I can't shake…!"

Her signal vanished.

Princess was gone too. So were Bronze Seven and Eight. Tag was in the midst of the swarm, firing on every target. His railgun ran down to its last hundred rounds. They'd be spent in a few seconds.

"Form up," Chok said. "And hold fast. We have to complete our mission…"

He was gone, too.

Only Tag remained against the horde. There was nothing to do but dive for atmosphere. Flames licked the cockpit of his Warhawk, and the passage battered him worse than being in a bar fight.

He emerged from cloud cover over Vossberg City—but there was nothing left. The towers were black as a stand of trees after a forest fire. More Naplian fighters flew over the plains. Wrecked Terran hover-tanks and the smudges of dead bodies littered the land.

One of those smudges was Marney. The other, Father.

The Naplians overtook him and as his shields collapsed, Tag emptied his railgun. Screams rattled the cockpit. Flame overtook him…

Tag sat bolt upright in his bunk. Sweat drenched his T-shirt. He gasped.

He was bunked in another of Station Golf Echo Fiver's former maintenance closets, one that had been retrofitted with a single bunk. All the weapons and repair tech crammed under, around, and atop the bunk gave him a few square meters of personal space. His flight suit was draped over a crate of frag grenades.

A chime rang out from his communicator. He'd left it on standby. Didn't want to miss an alert, even if he was due some sleep after two back-to-back patrols.

Tag glanced at the time index on the communicator as he picked it up. Six hours. Could have been an eternity.

Marney. Father.

It'd been weeks without hearing any news from or about them. Weeks since General Wood said Marney and Elden Selva had fled the CDF's base for the city. The Naplians had not made any demands of the Baedecker government, nor had they paraded their captives, so Wood had nothing to say about Father.

The chime rang again.

He frowned. It was not an attack alert, nor was it a summons for patrol. But the small screen displayed Major Chok's signal. "This is Wester."

"Tag, I know you're on rest, but I need you upstairs in the

Atrium."

That burned off the rest of his sleep fog. The Atrium was for Command—well, the cobbled together Command Group headed by Commodore Sobban Ram and Speaker Andrej Zhatkowskii. Pilots and other low-ranking officers didn't get called up unless they were in trouble.

Tag sighed. Entirely likely, for him. "I'll be right up, sir."

***

Station Golf Echo Fiver had a radial design, with eight spokes coming off one huge core that was saucer shaped and a kilometer across. Each spoke was 700 meters long and 200 meters in diameter, and currently crammed full of civilian refugees, military personnel from units all over Baedecker, and of course, the station's original crew of 200.

The Atrium was at the very pinnacle of the dorsal saucer. It was a dome 100 meters across, armored and shielded against space debris like the rest of the station, but the techs had upgraded its standard display systems with something Tag found far more awe-inspiring. The interior of the dome used data, both visual and scanned, to recreate space around the station in such detail it appeared to people inside the dome that there was no dome—only the stars above and nearly 100 ships docked at the station. Several hundred more were scattered around the surrounding region. All those ship captains, staying put rather than risking Naplian interception if they tried to jump out of the system. Tag couldn't believe they were so paralyzed by fear.

Only the tall, arcing braces painted pale blue and white reminded Tag that he was not in fact about to drift off into space. Many groundside personnel would find it disturbing—Scrape would have hated it, Tag realized.

But he could have moved his bunk in right that second.

Whatever Major Chok had in store for him there was not an inquiry, but some kind of planning session. Chok stood at the far edge of a huge, ring-shaped table with a polished black surface. Officers clustered around him—CDF colonels, AEF captains and majors, Navy brass. Tag would have felt more comfortable with Naplian fighters screaming around him.

That sparked the memory of his dream. Tag quashed it hard, and sidled up to Chok. "What's the word, Mongoose?"

Chok put a finger to his lips, and lifted his chin, indicating the seated participants.

There was Commodore Ram, with his second, Commander Vollan. Speaker Zhatkowskii sat to Ram's left, and a handful of civilian men and women Tag didn't recognize. Their clothing was flashy, and that meant expensive—must be Congressional remnants.

Their Reittian allies sat farther around the table, separated by a few seats. The six men wore black uniforms with silver piping, and wore gray caps. Each one was tall, packed with muscles that bulged under their jackets, and sitting ramrod straight. There was a uniformity to their gray and blue eyes that hinted at a very shared genetic background. Tag recognized Commodore Loronere Yost, the leader of the Reittian battlegroup, by his square jaw and long, narrow nose. Twin scars traced jagged paths down his face from each eye. Along each scar, maroon tattoos added to his fierce visage —one of a dagger, and one of five slash marks that looked like claws.

The ones who surprised Tag were the green-skinned fellas.

Granted, their skin was more a pale green—as if someone had turned the contrast on a vid of humans too far in one direction. Two men sat separated from everyone else, one a towering, massive man missing most of his hair and bearing a moustache thick enough to clog a Warhawk's atmospheric intakes. He and the shorter, stockier guy with orange stripes in his hair both wore gray uniforms with gold braid differentiating their rank. The big guy was in charge: Tag could feel it the way he sat at the table. The one next to him? He seemed more relaxed, but something about his gaze prodded Tag's intuition—and when he saw the pair of stylized silver triangles branching from an arrowhead on the man's chest, he knew.

"Orange strip over there's a pilot," he muttered to Chok.

"I know. Commander Ziran Zol Happar. Their equivalent of a Wing Commander. And the big one is Admiral Ergen."

"Yeah but... what are they?"

"Briddarri." Chok shrugged. "More aliens. But they've got 20 warships, and eight of those are battleship tonnage."

"So...what're they doing here?"

Chok again pressed his finger to his lips.

Tag tuned out the murmurs from the officers around him and focused in on the debate at the round table. Zhatkowskii was in rare form. "...Doesn't matter to me whether you say you're here for our good, Admiral Ergen. Baedecker doesn't need another alien force vying for its resources." He glanced at the Reittians. "Or a human force, either."

"Our claim to this system is not in dispute," Commodore Yost said. "Baedecker is ours. It has always been ours. That is the only reason we have agreed to remain here in service of this alliance and clean out the alien *shirish*."

Ergen, the Briddarri admiral, chuckled. "Use of talk like that makes a sailor think he's unwelcome." His mouth moved in patterns out of sync with his words; Tag figured he must have a translator adapted to his comm, or maybe an implanted speaker.

"Your arrival certainly is coincidental," Zhatkowskii said. "After we've already been conquered by a hostile alien force, a second one shows up."

"If you think for one second we're here to aid the one-eyes, you're as oxygen-deprived as I first suspected," Ergen said. "Our nation took the lead resisting the Naplian's unchecked advance across the galaxy, and without us the Grand Alliance would be overrun in days. My ships traveled for two of your years just to follow them here, and by the great host of our spirit warriors prevent them from seizing the serjaum deposits you humans were too daft to exploit."

"Now, see here—"

"Gentleman," Commodore Ram interjected. "Of all species. Please." He held up his hands, and smiled. "I think we can agree than nothing has worked out as foreseen for any party involved. The fact is simple: The Naplians control this system. I am reduced to seven warships. Our Reittian colleagues have 15, having lost several to our mutual enemy. Admiral Ergen, if you were to add your force to ours, that would bring us to 42—not an even match but certainly gaining."

"The Naplians are getting reinforcements," Ergen said. "You have to realize they hold this entire sector, not just your system. Our scans upon arrival show another squadron of battlecruisers en route. They could have more than 80 ships. Can't very well fight them. Unless you're prepared for months of guerrilla action."

"Why should we?" Yost said. "They will strip us of our serjaum and leave Baedecker a useless husk. We must act now to preserve our resources."

"Those would be *Terran* resources." Zhatkowskii pointed a finger at the Reittians. "Don't forget it."

"Resources you can share with allies, unless you decide you do not require our assistance," Yost said coolly.

"That's blackmail, Commodore."

"So we need a plan of action that does not entail all of us dying, and our fleets being destroyed," Ram said. "As you can see, we have a few more Terran assets at our disposal."

He gestured at the far end of the dome. Tag could see several boxy Terran transports docked on one arm of the station, along with a handful of cruisers and destroyers. "These units have trickled into Baedecker over the past weeks, able to slip through the patrolling Naplians in small numbers where a fleet would surely be intercepted. As a result, we have two battalions of orbital jump soldiers and mechs at our disposal."

"But not enough to retake an entire planet," Yost said. "Not nearly enough to dislodge the Naplian armies from Baedecker Four and Six. Not even if we add our Marines from our battlegroup."

"We don't need them," Zhatkowskii said. "There's enough orbital jumpers to surprise the Naplians and give us the advantage."

"Forgive me, Mr. Speaker, but you don't have a scissor-rat's idea what you're talking about," Ergen said. "These are military matters. Let the men who have served figure it out—the ones who have the guidance of the departed dead warriors living in Bridd Barra. Now, I have plenty of soldiers in the Ninth Fleet who can reinforce both your little battalions."

"Not that we will allow more aliens to have arms on the surface of Baedecker Four," Yost said.

"And you think you'll get to plant whatever Reittian troops you want there?" Zhatkowskii scowled. "You're as mad as the green-skinned arrivals."

Tag rolled his eyes. Some joint force. At this rate they'd do better to just turn their ships over to the Naplians.

"Gentlemen, you're misinterpreting my point—by trying to state it before it has even left my mouth." Ram leaned forward, elbows resting on the table, fingers steeped before the tip of his nose. "I do not mean to retake Baedecker's worlds. I mean to evacuate them."

If Tag thought the group around the table was unreasonable before, Ram's pronouncement confirmed it. Recriminations and insults flew. The Reittians got to their feet, with Yost pointing at the Terran contingent and chastising them for apparent cowardice. Zhatkowskii's face was beet red, and he shouted loud enough to rattle the glass of water in front of him. The Briddarri interjected, trying to sway Ram toward an all-out-invasion, and when he simply shook his head no, Ergen resorted to his native tongue. Tag guessed by the sharp-edged sounds of the words that they were profanity.

He couldn't stand it. Worse than fighting aliens—fighting among people who were supposed to work together against the invaders. He turned away, and glared out the dome at space around Station GE5.

And the horde of civilian cargo haulers drifting there for safety.

"I'll be spaced." Tag grinned.

"What is it?" Chok asked.

"We can do it. Commodore Ram's right. Those ships out there..."

"Are not nearly enough to get two million people off of an inhabited planet."

"It's only 1.8 million now, remember?" Tag snapped. "The Naplians made sure of that."

"Captain Wester." Ram's voice cut through the arguments like a laser through a pursuing missile. The cacophony died down, and Tag was keenly aware that all eyes at the table had targeted him. Novafire. "Do you have something to contribute to our exchange of ideas?"

Tag sealed his mouth tighter than an airlock. No way he was going to get himself skewered by the Navy brass from three different nations.

Major Chok elbowed him. "Captain Wester has thoughts regarding a potential evacuation of Baedecker Six."

Ram raised an eyebrow. "By all means, address us."

Blast you, Mongoose.

Tag stepped up to the table, behind one of the vacant chairs. He cleared his throat. "Ah, Commodore... I was discussing with Major Chok how we already have a ton of empty cargo vessels gathered around Golf Echo Fiver that could be used to lift civilians off my world."

"I'm sure your major pointed out that you're only going to get two-third evacuated that way," Yost said. "There is nothing to be done for the Terran settlers there."

"Yeah there is," Tag countered. "We can use the combined fleets for a distraction—something to occupy the Naplians while freighters pull people off the planet."

Ram nodded. "My thoughts precisely. The bulk of our forces can engage the Naplians with what appears to them to be an all-out attack, while an escort group oversees the rescue."

"As much as I hate to agree with a Reittian," Zhatkowskii

said, "Our colleague and ally does have a point. Even if you could fit a thousand people onto one ship each—"

"More like 2,000," Tag said.

"Yes, fine. Two thousand. That still only accounts for around a half a million people. There are nearly four times that many left on Baedecker." Zhatkowskii threw up his hands.

"Just a moment." Ergen stroked his moustache. "The young human's using his mind. Let's muse on this. I have eight battleships. Their towing capacity's far better than anything your fleets can handle right now."

Yost frowned. "I fail to see your point."

"If I keep back two battleships from the distraction Commodore Ram plans, they can be used to haul two huge objects with large capacity." He raised an eyebrow.

Tag slapped the table. "The station!"

Ergen smiled. His face got darker green around his forehead, ears and neck. Briddarri satisfaction?

"We can't tow the entire station!" Zhatkowskii said.

"Won't have to." Tag's mind was churning with crazed plans. "We could detach a couple of the arms, tow them in..."

"Except, unlike the freighters, they cannot affect a planetary landing," Ram said. "And I doubt we have enough shuttles."

Tag scowled. Yeah, he was right. It would slow down their effort way too much. What they needed was something just as big as one of the station arms, but independently mobile and shielded enough to survive atmospheric passage.

Bingo.

"Sir... can you bring up a holo of the Naplian movements in and out of the system over the past few days?"

Ram reached for a control. The empty center of the ring-shaped table lit up with red lines. The sheer number made Tag's head spin.

"They've been busy in the past week, bringing in new ships and sending out the damaged ones for repairs in more secure parts of the sector," Ram said.

"Right. Narrow the lines down to just the serjaum shipments. Sir."

Chok grunted softly.

All the red lines vanished, and the few that remained overlapped each other on courses that took them out of the Baedecker system by heading straight "up" from the ecliptic plane.

Tag pointed. "See? They've been sending those complexes out full of serjaum, and bringing them back in empty. In pairs. Three times now, and the vectors stay the same."

Ergen slowly nodded. "Right. They're sticking to a schedule. Admiral Daviont's probably trying to get as much shipped back to the main Naplian fleet in Audrian space as soon as possible. It'll take years to get them back there."

"But they can't be unguarded." Chok stood at Tag's side. "Commodore, what kind of escort can we expect?"

Ram pulled up a stream of data. "A battlecruiser and a light cruiser. It seems they meet the incoming complexes at between 3 and 5 AUs distance from Baedecker Two, above the ecliptic."

Tag glanced at Chok. "What do you think, Mongoose?"

Chok smiled. "I think we've sunk a cruiser before."

Tag grinned.

"An empty mining complex," Ergen said, his voice tinged with awe. "You ever seen the inside of one of those? They've got cargo holds 1,000 meters long, and 500 to 600 meters wide, plus the same height again."

"Give everyone a couple square meters," Tag said, "Especially if the thing has multiple decks."

"Three levels, I think, inside each one."

"And they are atmosphere capable?" Ram asked.

"Yep. Been a long time since I've seen one set down, but usually they do it on planets with thicker atmospheres. Less risky for shuttle traffic. Your Baedecker Two is a different case, I take it."

"It's an airless world. We've only observed them using shuttles." Commander Vollan spoke up for the first time since the meeting began. "All of our after-action reports indicate the mining complexes have minimal crew and armament. They're dependent on their escorts. Send in two squadrons—Raiders and Warhawks—and that would handle those ships. Of course, we'd need our own strike force to tackle the blasted battlecruiser."

"We can handle them." The other Briddarri with Ergen, Commander Happar, grinned in a cocksure way Tag found way too familiar. "What do you say, Admiral? One of our battleships and two squadrons of our best fighters?"

"I say more than that, I'll bring *Winter Scourge* herself." Ergen chuckled. "Just so the one-eyes know we're serious."

There were a few good natured chuckles at that, even from the Reittians. It seemed to Tag the gloom had lifted—well, partially cleared—from the table.

"We have precious little intelligence from Baedecker, other than what bits General Wood can slip our way," Zhatkowskii said. "I can't even tell you where the bulk of the refugees are. They could be scattered over every square kilometer of the city."

"I can help with that," Ergen said. "We've got a man down there."

"We? As in, Briddarri alien?"

"As in, loyal Briddarri operative," Ergen grumbled. "Man's a snake, as in cunning, but he's loyal to a fault. According to him, most of the refugees are cooped up in some sports arena."

Tag nodded. "Got to be the Castillo Fields Coliseum. That place can fit a couple hundred thousand, easy."

"That's where we should aim for the main landing site," Chok said. "On the city outskirts, as near Castillo as possible."

Commodore Ram was listening to whatever it was Vollan whispered at him. His expression brightened. "It seems we'll be able to put this to the test sooner rather than later. Based on their current schedule, the Naplians should have a new pair of mining complexes arriving in two days. I am giving us 24 hours to prep for this mission. Admiral Ergen, your *Winter Scourge* may carry the honor of leading the operation, with the *TSS Independence* as the secondary vessel. Commodore Yost…"

"*IRD Badger* and *IRD Wolverine* will accompany the task force," Yost said. "*Wolverine* carries three squadrons of starfighters."

Ram shook his head. "I don't want that many fighters thrown in on a small mission such as this. We must ration them. One battleship, one heavy cruiser, one destroyer, and another of your heavy cruisers—*IRD Hammerhead*. Plus Bronze squadron, I think. Major Chok, your pilots are on the tip of the spear for this one."

Chok saluted. Tag stiffened and copied his gesture. "We stand ready, sir."

"Good."

"Can we count on any outside help from the rest of the Terran systems?" Ergen asked.

Ram frowned. "We have limited contact with the nearest base. But if we send a brief, coded transmission, I suspected we may gain more transports. Commander Vollan?"

"I'll get it done, sir," she said. "We can rustle up some more fighters in the process."

Ram leaned forward. "Our task is daunting. Some no doubt

think it borderline impossible, and foolhardy in any case. But I take solace in a story from long ago, during one of Earth's wars. It is the tale of Done Kirk. A huge conquering army—a horde of invaders—surrounded a smaller army at the last stronghold on their allies' continent. It appeared they would be overrun and slaughtered. But the leader of that small nation called on any owner of a seagoing vessel, even the lowliest fishing boat, to traverse the channel between the two lands and evacuate the soldiers in peril. The legends say more than 300,000 men were pulled off the beaches and out of the harbors in eight days."

Ram stood, as did the rest of the attendees. "I pray that by our efforts we will live up to that grand history of courage. Dismissed."

The meeting broke up into knots of Congressmen and women talking with both the Reittians and Briddarri. Commander Vollan gathered Terran officers around her and issued orders.

Ram shook hands with Tag. "Thank you for having my back, Captain. Sometimes it takes the perspective of a lone pilot to cut through the fog."

"Yes, sir. Thank you, sir."

No sooner had Ram left than Chok elbowed Tag again. "I do not think I've heard that many 'sirs' from you in one sentence before, Tag."

"Must be all the brass chafing me." Tag relaxed. "Seriously, Mongoose. It seems like a good idea, but I don't know if we can pull it off."

"You had a flash of inspiration, Tag, and we're going to run with it. But you may not enjoy the consequences."

"What do you mean?"

"The Naplians cannot know we have those mining complexes. If they learn we captured empty ships—"

"They may suspect we're trying to evacuate the planet." Tag ran a hand through his hair. Man. He didn't even want to think about how exhausted he was. The adrenaline of the planning session was wearing off, and he could feel his body aching.

"Correct. Extrapolate."

Tag stared out at the stars. "We can't leave any survivors."

CHAPTER SIXTEEN

Nineteen Days after the Naplian Invasion

E lden Selva rubbed at the burgeoning beard encrusting the lower half of his face. He never grew beards. Preferred to be clean shaven. But this was an extenuating circumstance. One of the first things he'd had to adjust to upon becoming a refugee was giving up certain amenities. Shaving—and bathing once a day —were the first things to go.

He was under no illusion that he was anything but a refugee. He sat cross-legged on the crumbled quik-crete of a subterranean mag-rail station's platform, the communicator cradled in his hands. It was dusty, and dented on one side from one of the several drops it had suffered. But it still worked.

Now if he could only make contact.

Footsteps indicated Goetz had returned. The smell of blood and meat confirmed it.

Goetz plopped down on the rock. He wore camouflaged trousers and combat boots, with a sweat-stained short sleeved brown T-shirt. He'd tied a strip of gray and black fabric from his old bodyguard shirt around his forehead. It stood out in stark contrast to his red hair, grown much longer than his usual tidy cut.

"Hungry, sir?" He slapped down an—animal on the quik-crete.

Elden made a face. "Saarno fox, again? I thought they were wild creatures. What are they doing in the city?"

Goetz shrugged. "Last thing I'd read before we got off the transport was that Saarno foxes are scavengers, and have a keen sense of smell that can detect rotting flesh at 10 klicks. I'd bet Vossberg smells like an open barbecue to them."

Leave it to Goetz to sum up catastrophic ruin as succinctly

as possible. "Yes, I suppose." As foul as the Saarno fox smelled, Elden's stomach rumbled. Of course he was hungry. They were always hungry. "I'll prep it this time."

Goetz raised an eyebrow. A frown creased his beard, which was thicker than Elden's and just as bright red as his hair. Elden felt a tiny surge of jealousy that Goetz had managed faster facial hair growth. Funny thing, considering how dire life was now.

Elden set the communicator aside and unsheathed the knife from his belt. It was one he'd looted from a destroyed market, rationalizing that the previous owners—whose corpses were nothing more than blackened ash in a crater—wouldn't need it anymore. He cut through the hide and the skin with practice born of fourteen other field dressings.

His cutting was so much muscle memory that Elden glanced up when he heard Marney laugh. She stood at the other end of the platform, her smile illuminated in the pale yellow glow of emergency beacons. Ten were placed at intervals all around the platform and at both mouths of the mag-rail tunnel. It made it easier to see the hundred refugees sharing the space, which had been divided up by tents that ranged from brand new camping models complete with price coders to shredded bits of tarp. The people wore a mix of ripped up and stained police uniforms, casual civilian clothing, and formal office attire. The youngest was an infant of one year, who mercifully did not cry much, and the oldest, a 106-year-old woman who played the guitar with such skill that she both overpowered the crying and soothed it with her music.

All of them were hungry, and tired, and run into the ground by the distant sounds of Naplian energy weapons and explosions.

Only Marney seemed capable of spreading cheer with every laugh, every light touch, every liter of water she lugged down through the shambled steps from the surface. Elden knew he and Goetz, plus a handful of men and two teen girls, provided the food on scavenging runs, but it was Marney who held their group's morale together, even when supplies were light.

Elden wiped the blade clean on a rag. To think, it hadn't even been a month since they entered the city.

He checked the communicator. Like every time before, the signal had been sent. Like every time after that, he received no response.

"Could be it's jamming." Goetz cracked open a pyro-stick. It flashed bright enough to leave a spot in Elden's vision, then dimmed as the flare top burned down. He set it in the midst of a pile of rags, and broken wood furniture, hemmed in by quik-crete. Within seconds he had stoked a decent fire.

"No. It wouldn't send if it were jamming. But something could be interfering with receipt on the other end. Or the monastery could be overrun." The image of dead monks and burning domes filled his mind. He banished it by focusing on the division of meat into portions for each group of refugees. They wouldn't get much from the fox. But it would supplement the mealy rations they had stockpiled behind Elden's post.

Goetz unlimbered the Naplian rifle and propped it against the rubble. "Spotted a patrol. Just the one—three Naplians."

"They're thinning out."

"Seems like it. Haven't seen more than one or two patrols each day, since mid-week." Goetz stared into the fire. The reflecting flames made his eyes appear ablaze. "I don't think there's been any major action on either side, though. Last look I had at Santos bridge yesterday confirmed it: they're at a standstill."

"And meanwhile who knows how many people are starving." Elden sliced the last of the meat with such vigor his blade hit rubble.

"Easy, sir."

"Don't give me that. Not when I know there are Truppen out there, courtesy of our allies at the monastery. They could have swept the city clean of Naplians by now, and—"

"And what? You'd fight the Naplians and the Terrans?" Goetz shook his head. "No. If they haven't answered, there has to be a reason, either by malfunction or design."

Elden didn't agree, but wasn't about to start up that old debate. They'd had it too many times to count in the past week. He stood. "I'm going up for a look."

"Take your knife. And your rifle. But favor the knife." Goetz picked up a charred metal rod from the ground, and speared some of the fox meat. Blood oozed down the blackened stick. "Those Naplian guns pack a punch, and run cool, but the noise is a terrible trade-off."

"Yes, sir." Elden gave him a sloppy mock salute and clambered off the pile.

His rifle was propped against the tent pole of a domed, three-person model of an ugly tan and green. Supplies were stacked in the middle, delineating sleeping areas for him and Goetz. Mattresses liberated from destroyed homes made for lumpy bedding. Elden strapped on a backpack containing a jug of water, a medical kit, and a couple extra Naplian power packs. He fitted a DK-40 to his hip.

"Elden? We're down to 200 liters of water." Marney walked around the side of the debris pile in front of the tent. She patted Goetz on the shoulder as she passed. "If you're headed up, can you keep an eye out for more?"

He smiled. "I will do that, Miss Wester. Though I can hardly bring back another 200 on my own."

She shook her head, but was smirking as she did. "Of course not. If you find any, send a runner back and we'll start up the Spindler."

Elden saw the eight-legged, vaguely arachnid robot hunkered by the stairs leading up from the station. It was half the height of a man, with articulated appendages that let it cross all manner of obstacles and clear rough terrain at speeds in excess of 30 kilometers an hour. It was also sufficiently low-tech so that Naplian scanners ignored it, or misidentified it as a malfunction. "I will do so. But I won't head out alone."

As he passed her, she held his arm. "Don't forget—if you hear any news of Father or Timothy, even a whisper..." Marney's voice trailed off.

Elden brushed a strand of hair from in front of her nose, and tucked it behind her ear. Even in the accumulated grime, her beauty shone. "I always do. You know that."

"I know. Sorry." Her cheeks reddened.

"No need for sorry. If I were you..." He stopped. What would he do if he were in her place? For Elden there was no choice to make. He longed for her to make the better one. "I'll take Rett with me. He's good for a scouting run, for a data pusher."

Marney nodded. She opened her mouth, as if to say something else, but one of the women in the large family nearby called for her. She waved back. "I have to go. Be careful."

"I will."

Elden walked to the Spindler. A young man was crouched there, pulling at wires dangling from an exposed compartment. He was of tanned skin, with dark brown hair and brown eyes, unremarkable otherwise. Elden would never have remembered him if they'd met before three weeks ago—and who knew, perhaps he had, at Vossberg Terminal or Baedecker Station or anywhere else in the galaxy. Rett was short, but trim, like an athlete.

"Hello, Elden." Rett's voice was monotone, with a hint of the Baedecker accent to which Elden had become accustomed—clipped consonants, soft vowels. "I fancy you're not here to help me tuck these innards back."

"Not at all. I'm off for a scout."

"Need company?"

"Goetz will have my head on his spit over that fire if I don't take any."

Rett laughed. "He's a cheery fella, that Goetz. Sure, let me get my gear." He slapped the compartment shut. "One fixed Spindler."

Elden shook his head. "I thought you were a data pusher for an economic analysis firm."

"What can I say? I tinker in just about everything. The single life can be a boring one." He smiled. "That's why Everett Lind is an adaptable man."

***

The abandoned mag-rail station was on the east side of the city, perhaps two kilometers from where Elden, Marney, and Goetz had crossed the Santos River. This quarter was desolate, except for a few enclaves of refugees. Most of the buildings, from the tall spires to the three-story apartment blocks, had suffered damage in the initial Naplian bombardment and the subsequent fighting. Raids by Terran forces into the city—and their repulsion by the Naplians—added daily to the wreckage.

After several blocks they were both sweating. Baedecker's suns blazed through the early morning haze of smoke, a pall that never left Vossberg City these days except when the desert winds kicked up. Elden's neck burned after an hour, and he took a swig of water much sooner into their expedition than he'd planned.

"That must have been a fight to see." Rett pointed out a market for agro-station produce that had lost all its windows, its door, and half its walls. The smell of burnt vegetables and fruits cut sharply across the pervading stench of sewage and dust.

Elden held his rifle ready. "See if anything's worth taking. I'll stand watch."

Rett settled on a bag full of assorted fruits, and an armload of carrots—a decent haul. They divvied the food up amongst each other, loading down their packs.

Crumbling rubble snapped Elden to attention. He swung his rifle around.

A man and woman in Colonial police uniforms stood there, aiming M-36s, with a group of eight civilians behind them.

"There's more in there," Elden said. "We have all we can carry."

The female officer nodded. She was in her 40s, twice the age of the male officer, and bore a resemblance to several of the people grouped in their protection. Family, then. "Okay then. We don't want any trouble."

"You'll have none. We're moving on."

The group did not make a motion toward the ruined store until Elden and Rett were a block away. "Skittish," Rett said.

"Understandably so."

"It's not as if we're Naplians in disguise. That'd be difficult to pull off."

"It doesn't matter, I suspect. We're competition—human or otherwise. Until some kind of aid can arrive on Baedecker, every person here has to survive."

"Don't hold your breath. I ran into a few soldiers the other day. Word is there's some ships, all right, far out in the comet fields, but there's no way they can beat off the Naplians." Rett made a face. "Worst of it is, a Reittian battlegroup is supposedly in the mix now."

Elden's mouth went dry. Reittians? He thought back to his meeting with Governor Wester, at the mansion—not that long before it was set aflame. They had come to retake Baedecker, no doubt, and whatever resources they could find. Arresting Elden would have made the best pretext; perhaps they'd decided to act and then haul him in.

No matter. He allowed a grim smile. They had bigger problems than one Northern Alliance consul.

He and Rett followed 41st Street several blocks south, before heading west on Rojas Avenue. There'd been a water transfer station in the vicinity; Elden had seen it on their lone map back in the camp. It, too, had been bombed, but it was surrounded by several storage facilities. Those facilities were bound to have supplies untouched by the attack and fighting.

So he hoped.

They were eight blocks out when the familiar soft warble of Naplian conversation drifted through the air. Elden ducked behind an overturned hover-truck. Rett crouched beside him.

Footsteps. Boots crunching on debris. The warbles grew in volume, overlapping.

Rett nudged him. He held up four fingers, and raised an eyebrow.

Elden lay on his side. He scooted to the edge of the hover-truck's frame, ignoring the stench of an empty fuel cell dangling over his head.

Yes, there were four. Their armor shifted from light to dark gray, rippling like the surface of the Santos River, as it adapted to the changing facades of the buildings lining Rojas. All four carried rifles, and a sidearm. Power packs for both were strapped to their waists.

Elden scooted back. He patted his rifle, and repeated Rett's sign of four.

Rett scowled. He jerked his thumb over his shoulder.

There was an open alleyway, 20 meters from them. The hover-truck was large enough, it should shield them from the Naplians' view if they made a run for it.

But they also needed water, badly. Two hundred liters was a lot, when one saw it all stored together. For a hundred people, though? They could stretch it over a few days. After that, dehydration would set in.

Lack of water was far more dangerous a threat than starvation.

Elden shook his head. He got to his knees.

Rett rolled his eyes, but nodded. He must know Elden well enough by now to hazard a guess at his plan.

It wasn't complex, really, and it depended almost entirely on Rett being a good shot with the Naplian rifle.

The Naplians walked the street slowly, sweeping their guns toward every opening they passed. There was a pattern to their motions. Elden watched it. Memorized it.

When they turned right, he bolted for the open door of a law office.

The inside was pitch black save where the light through the dust-covered front window admitted it. Plenty of places to hide. He found a good spot behind a desk, and its low partition.

Hoots of alarm sounded outside. A sharp whistle cut it off. A single set of warbles issued new orders. Footsteps increased their pace.

Two sets? Elden couldn't tell. He slipped the rifle's strap over his back, and unsheathed his knife. Forced himself to breathe slowly, calm his heartbeat—which was no mean feat given it pounded as fast as if he were sprinting a footrace.

He could hear Goetz's instruction, along with the visual memory of their practices: *Grab them from behind. The necks are weak. Bring the knife across, dig deep on the left—that's where the main artery is. Be fast, but sure. You get one cut. Do it right, they're bled out in seconds.*

Elden shivered. A far different reality than political infighting during the Consular Wars, but the same concept.

The footsteps changed in pitch. They walked on the tile floor of the law office. Elden could hear their breathing—quick sniffs through those tiny nostril slits.

All right, Rett. Any time now...

Energy blasts shrieked. The Naplians outside cried out, but those cries were cut short. The two inside pivoted, their boots squeaking.

Elden launched himself off the floor. He got his left arm hooked around the nearest one's neck, and yanked him back deeper into the shadows. One quick slash was all it took to kill him. He dropped the body.

The second Naplian was in mid-turn toward Elden when he slammed his shoulder into its side. Together they banged off the hallway wall. Elden stabbed him, but the blade gouged along the armor, its tip scraping the surface.

The Naplian brought his rifle muzzle up under Elden's chin.

He jerked aside.

The blast blinded him, and his ears howled with the sound of the discharge. But Elden dragged the knife up the armor, searching...

There.

It slid between segments, plunging deep into the Naplian's body. The alien screamed at him, and let go of its gun. It clutched the wound with both hands.

Elden drew his DK-40 and shot him above the eye.

The Naplian slumped against the floor, fingers still curled at its abdomen.

Elden wiped the blade off, and sheathed it. He stripped as many power packs from the body as he could affix to his rifle strap, and repeated the process with the first alien he'd killed.

He assumed at some point he'd feel terrible about ending these lives, but right now he could focus only on the people waiting for him to bring supplies back to their refuge. They were the innocents who'd done nothing to deserve an attack by an alien empire. They were the ones who didn't deserve to starve, or worse —watch their children suffer.

Elden grabbed one more thing each from the bodies: their communication devices, and the implanted tracking sensors in their armor. He set them down on the floor and bashed them to pieces with the stock of the rifle. Quite the sturdy weapon, that.

"Elden!" Rett was inside the doorframe. "We'd better continue on. No telling if they've got mechs on backup. Remember Dorset Road?"

Elden winced. "I'm not looking forward to a repeat of that ambush. You're right, let's go."

They hurried along Rojas. Elden agreed with Rett that they should stick close to the buildings, using alley entrances and traversing the open floors of abandoned offices. It was best to stay off the street, now that they'd left a Naplian patrol dead in their wake.

**

The water transfer station's triple domes were shattered like eggshells. Two of the storage facilities were marked of with bright pink spray paint—empty. Elden led them to one of the other three they'd yet been able to investigate. Fortunately, the area was empty of patrols other than the one they'd seen.

It was the motherlode.

Rett shouldered his rifle. "Unbelievable. How many liters, do you reckon?"

Water jugs were strewn about, some still in neat lines, others buried and scattered under collapsed segments of the warehouse roof. Elden counted the rows, then the columns. "There have to be four hundred, at least." He bent, and brushed dust off the closets jug. "Four-liter containers."

"Sixteen hundred liters, or more." Rett grinned. "Looks like we need to holler for Spindler."

Elden glanced up. There was a metal staircase that zig-zagged to the roof, up through the gaping hole that let in morning sun. "You do that. I'm going to take a look up top."

"Suit yourself."

Elden climbed the steps two at a time, pausing only on sections where the staircase swayed dangerously and bolts creaked. Pigeons cooed back and forth at each other, from nooks in the scaffolding he couldn't see. A warm breeze blew over his face. It was welcome relief from the stagnant, swampy air at street level.

He emerged from the steps onto the roof, seven stories up. Sunlight blasted around him, but the wind made the intense heat bearable. Elden shielded his eyes.

Vossberg City retained some of its beauty, even after a month of war. Though hundreds of buildings were damaged or destroyed, thousands were still largely intact—missing windows, sporting impact craters, but otherwise upright. The city resembled a field of crops, white and tan and pale gray stalks with blackened, truncated stems interspersed. From here he could see Vossberg Terminal, once a stunning crystalline palace but now something ugly, resembling a cage. Naplian fighters and shuttles lifted from and landed at the area of the terminal every fifteen to twenty minutes.

Out past Vossberg Terminal was the great broad loop of Castillo Fields Coliseum. It sat like a monstrous bowl, shining silver in the morning light. Naplian troop activity was heavy there; no wonder, considering Rett had scoped it out two weeks ago and had seen thousands of refugees trapped inside. They were receiving rations, yes, and basic medical care, but to Elden they were no better off than prisoners.

Santos Bridge loomed beyond the center of the city, dusky red frame still tall and proud, though scarred all over by weapons fire. Elden caught a glimmer from the power station's shield, high atop the escarpment. The CDF barricades were white walls at the upper end; the Naplian fortifications, pale green and brown at the lower, peeking from between the buildings at the city's edge. No movement today, it seemed.

He couldn't watch the Terran base for long. It reminded him of Andan Natour. By rights he should have contacted Natour's parents as soon as their son died. Being stuck in a war zone complicated such things. It also explained why Elden felt no sympathy for every Naplian he killed. The aliens had shot his only friend, a key advisor to the underground Northern Alliance movement. Revenge was on his mind. Fine. He would have it.

Activity at the center, however, drew his attention back that direction. The Naplians appeared to have set up their headquarters in the former Baedecker Colonial Courthouse. It was a sandstone and steel building 12 stories tall, an octagonal tower with windows that reflected the sky for kilometers around. Troops and mechs patrolled the blocks around it. Even from here, he could see checkpoints set in those blocks and especially at the entrance to the large courtyard in front of the building that was the same size as its footprint.

The Naplians would be terribly difficult to dislodge. Even for Truppen soldiers.

That thought dampened his spirits further. He supposed he should try another time. Perhaps up this high the signal had better chance of getting out. Elden activated the communicator, and triggered the signal.

He waited.

The roar of Naplian fighters overhead made him crouch by the stairwell. They were several blocks away, flying along the west side of the city, but the presence of the claw-shaped starfighters made him anxious, nonetheless. He watched them, feeling the coolness of the communicator's shell against his palm.

Nothing. No receipt, no response.

Elden shook his head. He had to keep trying. He knew the Truppen were out there, and unless he had proof the entire monastery had been blasted from the face of Baedecker Four, he'd not give up.

Suddenly the communicator hissed static. Elden's heart jumped. Incoming signal? Could it really be them?

No. The frequency displayed on the readout was wrong. He frowned. It was the open civilian bandwidth, accessible by anyone from schoolchildren to military personnel.

"People of Baedecker Four." The voice was synthesized, with a musical tone to it. Elden knew it instantly—Naplian, translated. "This is General Falloram speaking on behalf of the Baedecker Occupational Command. Your continued resistance to our annexation is not in the interests of either party. Since you are unwilling to lay down arms and submit yourselves for processing at our internment centers, we offer you this opportunity to witness the fruits of continued resistance."

Elden was on his way back down the stairs before General Falloram paused. The impact of his boots rang out in the silence of the warehouse roof.

"Elden!" Rett's voice echoed from below. "You'd better get down here!"

"I know, I'm coming!"

The communicator hissed again. "At 1200 hours tomorrow, local time, we shall execute by firing squad 150 prisoners captured at the governor's compound on the night we captured your planet —beginning with Governor Antiny Wester himself."

Elden's foot slipped and he almost fell down the rest of the steps, two stories from the warehouse floor. Stars above. Wester? He was still alive? Elden realized then he'd long since given up hope at rescuing either the governor or Marney's fiancé, the Terran

Navy officer. He'd become content, in an odd way, living by her side among the refugees.

"Among these 150 prisoners are Colonial government officials who have failed to take our generous offer to rule in tandem with the Naplian occupation," Falloram said. "If any wish to join our forces, and help oversee Baedecker Four in an orderly fashion, come to the Colonial courthouse and sign the pledge of fealty to our beloved emperors, Bonate and Benaltep—all hail. This offer of amnesty is extended only to the time of the execution."

Falloram rambled on about futile resistance to Naplian occupation, inevitable defeat of the Terran forces outside the city, and a litany of propaganda intended to whittle down morale. Elden ignored it, listening instead for more information about the execution. By the time he reached Rett, he saw the other man fiddling with a scroll.

"It's receiving data," Rett said. "Thing hasn't picked up so much as a stray entertainment post in weeks. Now I'm getting a full on dump."

Elden oriented himself so he could see the pale blue glow of the holographic surface. "What is it?"

"A list." Rett turned it.

It was a long list of names. Elden didn't recognize any of them, though he saw some must be CDF because they carried ranks. Wester's name was at the top of the list.

"Most of them are civilians," Rett said. "They're going to kill all those people."

"It could be a bluff—an attempt to get the resistance fighters or the CDF on the hill to surrender."

"You really think so?"

Elden shook his head. "The Naplians could easily do both. No. I think it's…"

He stared at the list.

"What? Elden, what's wrong?"

"Marney's fiancé, Timothy Ess. He's among those to be executed."

Rett groaned.

"I'm going to have to tell her, if someone hasn't already shown her the list."

A heavy stamping sound came down the street. Elden reached for his rifle, but relaxed when he realized it was just the Spindler. The robot paused inside the open bay door of the factory, waiting to be loaded with water cargo.

"More than that." Rett tucked the scroll away, and reached for the nearest jugs. "The CDF's gonna have to figure out how to rescue the governor."

Elden thought about the impasse at Santos Bridge. "Yes, someone there will."

They had only 26 hours.

***

Fifteen thousand Truppen.

That was their grand total. Jeopar walked the yard of the monastery, past the Saint's Well, past the open stalls of the smithy and the rug-weaver and the baker—all trades taught to the young acolytes that had been lost for centuries. He took great pride in sending these men out into the world with skills that could earn them a living—for who among the city dwellers of Vossberg and more modern locales beyond—would not pay a premium for handmade goods, rare as they were?

Yet among them stood 80 Truppen, arrayed in ten octants. They followed Colonel Diaz through a series of exercises that Jeopar gathered were meant to insure proper calibration of sensors and servos. Jeopar found them similar to the martial arts and calisthenics combinations found on Seyruz Three.

These were the elite Diaz trained, the ones who had been on multiple forays into the desert outside Iwa Valley and the monastery's walls.

The massive number he contemplated was the tabulation completed by Erich's scroll. He accompanied Jeopar on his walk, but hardly noticed anything but the data streaming across the digital surface. "General Albrecht says we're ready to deploy the entire unit, soon," Erich said.

"Do you agree?"

"I do. They've been through countless scenarios and have rotated out with Diaz's team against the Naplians enough to give them a taste of true combat. Can't do better than that, in this environment."

"I suppose so." Jeopar didn't feel he had anything more to add.

Erich finally noticed the silence, because he stopped in his tracks and folded up the scroll. "Something's on your mind."

Jeopar folded his hands. "I knew when I began the quest of gathering Truppen headpieces what the outcome would be. We were recreating an army. Do not mistake my actions for naïveté."

"Your goal was restoring life, Abbot."

"So it was. But I wasn't blind."

"Are you having qualms about it now? It's late in the day for that." Erich gestured. "These men have already engaged the enemy on dozens of raids. Each one, we send out more and more Truppen, slowly increasing the numbers, switching out veterans for trainees, gaining combat experience. How much longer before the Naplians figure out we have a legion of Truppen out here and come calling?"

"You have done admirably by keeping our involvement hidden, between the bunkers under the valley and *Hessian* camp. That is not my concern." Jeopar shielded his eyes from the son. "What I hope is that the Truppen are not intended as a weapon for oppressors. They can be protectors of the innocent. That is where their greatest strength lies."

Erich nodded. "I can understand that. Look, Abbot, I want the Northern Alliance restored. That's all. Who then are my enemies? Terran soldiers? Probably? The people of Baedecker? They've done nothing wrong. The Naplians have thrown a wrench into the works, of course—they need to be excised before they can do more harm."

There again: the need for violence to save lives. Jeopar was nauseated, but found himself better able to reconcile with the necessity than a month ago. Surely prayer alone would not rescue people from the invaders.

Still, the prospect of so many being slain filled him with dread.

"General Baesler." Diaz joined them. Something about the colonel's electronically modulated voice seemed more vigorous. "Sir, I have good news: we've intercepted a signal from Vossberg that was intended for the monastery."

Jeopar's eyes widened. "Is it the same frequency as the ones before? The ones which died before we could pinpoint them?"

"Yes, Abbot. And General, there is no mistake or supposition this time: we have confirmed Elden Selva's signature."

Erich smiled. Jeopar would never forget the expression of hope—it was unlike any the android had ever exhibited. "That's it! The Consul *is* alive."

"Thank the Lord," Jeopar said. "Can we bring him to us?"

"You'd better believe it." Erich slapped the armor plating on Diaz's arm. "Colonel, break up your exercises. I want a triangulation done on Selva's coordinates. Then I need to see the scout reports from Vossberg and the surrounding area for the past several days. We leave nothing to chance."

"Yes, sir." Diaz loped off to his men.

"I can be of help, Erich," Jeopar said. "I know the city well— or did prior to the invasion. The acolytes and I would venture there twice monthly to trade and sell goods, as well as bring donations of food for the poor."

"I'd hate to bring you into further danger, Abbot, but you've shown courage thus far."

Jeopar held Erich's shoulders. "This is the path the Lord has set before me. Far be it for me to shrink from the way now."

Erich nodded, and followed Diaz off to a conference with his officer. Jeopar watched them huddle. No, he would not stray from the path.

Not even with death surrounding him on all sides.

CHAPTER SEVENTEEN

Nineteen Days After The Naplian Invasion

T ag had to hand it to Commander Vollan—the first officer of TSS Confiance was shaping up to be an intelligence analyst as ace as any pilot.

She had to be, to get the timing of their raid down so precisely that when *TSS Independence* and its task force dropped from ripwave, they were three light-seconds away from the arriving Naplian mining complexes.

Tag's Warhawk was nestled in the starboard launch tunnel of *Independence*, with five other Bronze squadron fighters racked behind him. Major Chok and the rest of the squadron were queued up portside. All Tag could see outside the cockpit were the curved stanchions, pale white like an animal's ribs picked clean, and the dark gray surfaces of the bulkhead and deck. Stars filled the open hatch ahead. He thought he saw a pair of flashes in the distance.

"Targets are up," Chok said. "Two mining complexes. They are decreasing thrust and certainly moving as if they're hauling empty. Contact with both a Naplian battlecruiser and light cruiser."

"That'd be the escorts, right on schedule." Tag pulled the data over from *Independence*'s sensor feed. His display lit up with red triangles for the enemy warships, and red squares outlined in pulsing white for the mining complexes. *Independence* was a blue triangle; the Reittian destroyer *IRD Wolverine* and heavy cruiser *IRC Hammerhead* were yellow ones. Someone with a sense of humor up on the bridge had marked the Briddarri flagship, *Winter Scourge*, as a green triangle.

"Standby for launch." The voice was from Captain Mariana Rocha. "Godspeed and good hunting, Bronze Squadron."

"Bronze Leader acknowledges. All right, boys and girls, stay sharp—remember, take the communications arrays first. We have to keep this operation as quiet as possible."

"Roger that, Mongoose." Tag checked the release triggers for his RS-18 missiles. The point defense laser was drawing power from the core nicely, without excess heat buildup. The railgun was zeroed. "Ready."

The timer just over his display marked down from five seconds. At one second prior to his launch, Tag felt the ship vibrate around him. His sensors showed Chok launching first.

Zero.

The acceleration rail slammed him out the tunnel, bulkheads blurring. Only the Warhawk's compensators kept the g-forces from mashing him into paste against his seat. In an instant he was clear of the tunnel, out amongst the stars. Chok's fighter was already far ahead.

Within 20 seconds the entire squadron had launched, and formed up into its constituent flights. Tag had Chok's wing, and together they were paired with Chasm and Princess. His sensors balked at the approach of another squadron that he took for Raiders, until he realized they were Reittian knockoffs—Cossacks, 5 meters longer on the centerline and able to carry two 230-kilogram bombs more than the Raider loadout. Judging by their lackluster acceleration, however, a Raider would spin loops around them.

The Briddarri fighters joined them, a two dozen craft that Tag found funny looking. They had very short, very tall fuselages, with four engines—two at the top, two at the bottom. Each engine sported a stubby wing and tiny clusters of maneuvering jets. The cockpit was nestled between the top two engines. Wherever the weapons were mounted must be internal, because Tag didn't spot any external hardpoints. They slewed nimbly into formation, and though Tag was impressed, he figured they wouldn't fare as well in an atmosphere—they were born for spaceflight.

"Squadron Kazh and Squadron Mun, forming up." Commander Happar sounded as pleased as a man would be relaxing at the bar after the mission. "We have the escorts in our sights.'

"Very good, Commander." This voice was solemn, and just above a murmur, from the Reittian frequency. "This is Squadron

Captain Orn. I stand ready to cripple the mining vessels."

"Cripple only their communications and defenses, Captain Orn," Chok said. "Stay away from their propulsion systems."

"Of course." Orn spoke as if Chok were a dim student who'd chastised his teacher. "My squadron is one of the most highly decorated in the empire."

With that, the Reittian Cossacks surged ahead.

"Bet his mama's proud," Chasm grumbled.

"Cut the chatter," Tag said. "Our task force is lighting them up."

Indeed, they were. *TSS Independence* fired a salvo of eight missiles, and *Winter Scourge* loosed 12. Tag couldn't help stare at the Briddarri battleship—even as far away as Bronze Squadron flew, the battleship dwarfed *Independence*. It had a long hull with smoothed edges, clean lines all around, that Tag was sure must have Terran techs salivating. Sure wouldn't mind if they showed the Terran Navy how to build a few.

The Reittians fired missiles, too, and brought the total to 26. The Naplian ships didn't sit around for them to arrive—they boosted onto an evasive course and fired their own swarm of 14. Tag's display filled with marks. He increased the magnification, banishing the ship-to-ship fire from his field of view.

There was only one set of targets he needed.

The mining complexes appeared ahead—as did a cluster of new marks.

"Incoming fighters," Chok said.

"I count 36 targets," Princess said softly.

"Then move over and let's burn 'em down!" Chasm snapped.

Tag found his nearest target and locked a missile. C'mon, Mongoose, don't wait forever. It was that familiar itch to dive into combat, to fly loops around the enemy and score his kill—except this time he couldn't help seeing Scrape when he glanced at his instruments.

The Naplian fighters launched missiles.

"All units break, Starburst Five!" Chok said.

Tag executed the maneuver without thinking. All 12 starfighters in Bronze Squadron cut their forward acceleration, and spun their engines to face each other. The star-shaped formation hurtled on, until they all boosted away from each other, and spiraled off into a series of pre-programmed evasive maneuvers that made good use of the main engines and auxiliary thrusters.

Tag's put him farther out of the reach of the onrushing

Naplians, but he maintained his missile lock. He fired as his Warhawk slid sideways along its vector.

The Naplians appeared surprised by the Starburst Five, because they continued on their original course for 15 seconds longer than Tag would have advised. Finally, they broke off into flights of five, seeking out their opponents.

Tag's target used a defensive laser to shoot down his missile, though the explosion was at a hair-raising 100 kilometers from him. Just a second longer...

His sensors screeched. Missile lock. Here they came: two, bearing oh six seven, mark one one nine. Tag checked on Major Chok. He was shooting by a Naplian fighter, which exploded a second after his passage. "What's the tally, Mongoose?"

"Terran one, Naplian zero. My preferred score. You've picked up some tails."

"Two of 'em. Yeah, I see." Tag's heart was thumping. Sweat slicked the inside of his gloves. The missiles were gaining. The point defense laser fired, rocking the Warhawk. Power levels dipped.

Tag grinned. That's it. Close in.

The first missile exploded. Second one. And here came the fighters who launched them, two Naplians, racing up on him. Green flashes lit up the cockpit display as the targeting and visual sensors combined forces to let him know that he was, in fact, being shot at.

Tag knew the onboard ECM could only scramble their targeting sensors for so long, and the closer they got, the more negligible the effect. But he wouldn't need it for much longer.

When the Naplians got within a thousand kilometers, Tag cut acceleration and spun the Warhawk around.

The Naplians were moving so fast—2,500 kilometers per second as opposed to Tag's 2,000—that they raced up on him without time to register that Tag's railgun was firing into their faces.

The lead fighter exploded at 10 kilometers away. His partner zipped by so fast that Tag's sensors couldn't translate it visually except to paint a claw-shaped blur on the inside of the canopy's display.

Tag wrenched the Warhawk around to its original vector, with barely a second's pause, and then fired again.

The Naplian was already 2,600 kilometers away, decelerating, but Tag winged him—literally. The red indicator flashed, and the sensor readouts told him his railgun projectiles had torn off the right wing. A subsequent explosion meant that one of those blasted energy guns had gone critical.

"Yes!" Tag chalked those up as two kills.

Except the fighter pulled the same trick he did, only after he turned to face Tag, he decelerated, which meant that Tag was now the one racing up on him. Green energy blasts rattled the Warhawk's shields. Warning alarms blared.

And suddenly the enemy fighter exploded.

Tag exhaled. "Nice shooting, Mongoose."

Chok's fighter flashed through the space the Naplian had occupied. "You seemed to be doing well without assistance, but I can't let you hog all the kills."

"Fair point."

Chasm and Princess knocked down three between them —though Princess had the greater number of kills, which irked Chasm. A quick scan of the battlefield revealed the Naplian fighters were cut down by a third, while none of the Terran fighters had been lost and three Briddarri had been destroyed. A Reittian fighter-bomber was gone, but the Cossacks were swarming one of the mining complexes. Even as he watched, they blew out the last of the weapons emplacements on its aft hull.

The escorts? The light cruiser was listing, and even as it valiantly swatted at *Independence*'s missiles with its lasers and energy weapons, the heavy cruiser delivered the death blow with pulsed particle cannon and a few hull-rending shots from railguns. Somewhere deep in its hull, the light cruiser's reactor failed. It ignited like a small sun, lighting up space for a moment before it dimmed. Nothing but molten fragments remained.

The Naplian battlecruiser was beset by *Winter Scourge*, though it was holding its own. Tag's sensors plainly showed *Winter Scourge* was taking more damage at a faster rate. No wonder. The Naplian's sensor signature was doing the crazed dance they were fond of. The only thing saving *Winter Scourge* from failure was *Independence* and *Hammerhead* concentrating their fire on the same ship. Tag shook his head. Multiply the scene by a dozen, or a hundred, and that's what the war between the Naplians and Briddarri looked like. He was thankful Terran space was far from their empire's clash.

Though, it didn't seem that would last.

"All right, boys and girls, let's see if we can give our Reittian comrades a hand," Chok said. "Bronze Leader to Commander

Happar. We've culled her a bit—feel like tangling with the rest?"

Tag watched a nearby Briddarri fighter juke its way out of a Naplian's pursuit with far greater finesse than he could manage. The fighter obliterated its attacker with a few well-placed shots, then got itself lined up for an attack on another. "Can do, Major. Have to say—I'm impressed. If this is the way all Terrans fly, I may have to reassess your status as a savage backwater."

"I'll assume that was a compliment. Bronze Leader out."

Chok and Tag led their squadron toward the second mining complex, which was doing its best to accelerate from the battle. New data streamed in, this time from *Winter Scourge*: the spin-up time for the Naplian jump drives. Tag grinned. Good. He liked deadlines.

"Some of our dance partners decided to follow," Chasm said. "Six of them, coming in at mark two oh two, bearing two eight five."

She was right—a half dozen Naplian fighters had split off from the group tangling with their Briddarri counterparts.

"Well, then, let's not keep them waiting. Bronze Three and Four, take—"

Chok's signal cut off in a haze of static. Tag frowned. They hadn't been shot at yet, and there wasn't any jamming he could detect. "Lead, this is Two, copy?"

Nothing.

"Lead, this is Bronze Two, over. Mongoose, you copy?"

Again, nothing.

Voices overlapped on the comms, but Chasm's cut through them all. "What's doin', Wester? The major out of it?"

"Negative." He swept in as close as he dared to Chok's fighter. Sensors showed life support, power, those were all good. Fire control seemed operational. Comms—

Tag scowled. "He's got a burnout on a batch of circuits. Whatever happened, it killed his communications and junked the ripwave generator."

Chasm groaned.

"Is the major himself unhurt?" Princess asked.

Tag magnified his view of Chok's cockpit. The major appeared all right; looked like he was wresting with a bunch of wires. "Yeah, he's good."

"As warm and fuzzy as that makes me feel, we still got fighters closing on us and a big old mining ship trying to bail."

"I know, hang on."

"Captain Wester, I think Chasm is trying to say, what are

you orders?"

Tag's mouth opened and closed. His orders? He didn't have orders. He had to knock out that complex. Its comms were already toast, thanks to the first strike by the Reittians that hit both mining ships. But if it could activate its ripwave drive, or jump completely out of the system...

Orders. Yeah, he had to give them. Chok was incommunicado.

Regs made Tag the acting squadron leader.

He blew out a breath. "Chasm, you and Princess take Bronze Five and Six. Run interference for us. The rest of you, with me. Knock down the weapons on that mining complex!"

The acknowledgments echoed through the intra-comm. Chasm and Princess's fighters swept back around toward the Naplian planes, followed by two more Warhawks. That left Tag with himself and six others, not counting Chok.

Scratch that: Chok's fighter took up his wing. Though he couldn't talk to the major, the posture was unmistakable—attack run.

The mining complex opened fire with short-range torpedoes, wiry little weapons that corkscrewed at them. Bad enough the ECM had a terrible time trying to scramble their brains, but they exploded shrapnel warheads in their path. Tag let the laser sizzle as many shards as it could, but when it became obvious he was still going to hit a hailstorm, he bounced the Warhawk "over" the spreading cloud.

"Bronze Elven picked up damage! Lost port engine!"

"Steady, kids, watch that shrapnel." Tag let the sensors bracket the energy weapon emplacements on the dorsal hull of the mining complex. Stars above, the ship was *huge* this close up. It was like strafing rock formations on the Luran Plains again, only this time the Luran Plains were trying to get away.

He could hear Scrape behind him: *Range to target... Weapons locked...*

Tag thumbed the trigger.

Two missiles swept out, weaving their way through the green flashes. More missiles streaked past him, and he grinned. Bronze Squadron dumped a dozen missiles on the mining complex —even Chok shot a pair, incapacitated to command as he was.

Several got blasted down, but eight impacted. Results immediately scrolled past on Tag's screen, and he whooped. Energy guns off-line, port and starboard, dorsal and ventral. Atmosphere leaking—someone's missile, no telling whose at this point, had penetrated the shields near a destroyed gun mount and poked a hole in the hull.

The mining complex cut its acceleration, but let them have another round of frag torpedoes.

"Chok! Incoming swarm—" Tag cursed. No way Chok could hear him.

But Tag could warn him.

He edged his fighter as close as he could. Proximity sensors howled, right up until Tag shut them down. He only needed to get within a few hundred meters. It was a kilometer now, and the numbers spun down—

The Warhawk shook violently, as if seized in a giant hand and thrown. The shields sparked and flashed around him. Warning lights indicated the shield projector was critically damaged. The feedback from the collision of Tag's shields with Chok's was enough to impair both.

But he got Chok out of the way of the frag spread, even as a spray pummeled the underside of his shields and sliced holes in the wings.

"Shut up already!" Tag growled, and killed the rest of the alarms. Blessed silence.

"Bronze Three to Two," Chasm said. "Tag, you're off your course! That's some crazy flying they teach you boys at Voss Flats!"

Tag sagged back into his seat. The Warhawk limped along, but the rest of Bronze Squadron took out its torpedo launchers, rendering it impotent. Chasm and Princess were on their way back, and the Naplians pursuing them were nowhere in sight—thanks in part, Tag assumed, to the half dozen Briddarri escorting the four Terran fighters.

"Nice work," Tag said. "Now, if you don't mind, somebody point me back to *Independence*. I could use a stiff drink and a shower, in that order."

***

With the two mining complexes disabled, it was up to the 75th Orbital Jump Battalion under Lieutenant Colonel Laura Macken to secure the vessels.

Tag circled the ships, providing cover and observation for *Independence* and the operations command stationed there. Two companies of 80 soldiers each deployed from wedge-shaped assault shuttles that were coated in flat back stealth panels. The jumpers spread out like flies over a corpse, tiny gray forms scooting from one end of the mining complexes to the other. Orange light flared where they cut their way into airlocks and cargo hatches.

Within five minutes, it was all over.

"Negative casualties," Macken said. "Only 30 crew on each ship, rest was run by robots. We've detained the crew and are transferring them to our custody."

"If it were me I'd space every one of them." Admiral Ergen's voice grumbled over the communications link. "But you humans have peculiar ways. Right, fine, bring them in and we'll keep them locked up until this whole thing is over."

"Understood. Jumpers returning to *Independence*. Thanks for the cover, Bronze Squadron—not that we needed it."

"Glad to be of help, Colonel." *And glad to land*, Tag thought. The holes in his wings weren't critical damage, but he didn't feel good about banging around space for one minute more.

First thing he did after his Warhawk was safely landed and stowed in a repair bay was find Major Chok. The squadron leader had his helmet tucked under his arm and was conferring with a tech about the ventral access compartment for shipboard systems.

"Sir." Tag saluted. "They get your comms mess squared away?"

Chok returned the salute. "Not yet, but I told them I'd rather have all the guts pulled out and reinserted rather than get a new bird. For one, we don't have many spares. Second, I'm attached to this Warhawk—it's been mine for three years."

Tag thought of his Raider, and what was likely its burnt out shell on Baedecker Four's plains—assuming the Naplians had let it be. "I understand that."

"I spoke with Chasm and Princess. You did well out there. You kept to the mission objective, and kept your pilots safe."

"Thanks, sir." Tag grinned. "Felt good."

"Command isn't easy, but it is rewarding. If this thing drags on any longer, we're going to need more pilots who aren't only just skilled at knocking down Naplian fighters, but who can lead others into battle at the same time."

They took a set of crisscrossing stairs up a deck to the main hangar. Tag spotted the assault shuttles behind the transparent bulkheads that separated the hangar from the corridors on either side. Macken's jump troopers brought their Naplian prisoners down the ramps. These weren't soldiers in body armor like Tag had fought at the governor's compound. They wore simple, pale green and tan jumpsuits, and seemed even more slender than their armed counterparts.

Each one of them stared at the inside of *Independence*'s hangar and the Terran jumpers with what Tag figured was outright fear, judging by how they clustered together and how wide their eyes got. Not surprising. If Tag had been under escort by the Terran jumpers—armored like statues with glowing blue optical ports—he would have been near panic, too.

"I hope this whole thing works," Tag said. "And I'm glad none of these guys had to die."

"Oh? Plenty were killed when we destroyed that light cruiser and battlecruiser."

"Yeah, I know. Those were soldiers and pilots, like us. They picked this fight. But those transport crew? They're more like civilians. None of them even drew a weapon on the jumpers." Tag shook his head. "And plus… I don't think Scrape would have liked it. Those weren't the guys we were trained to take out."

Chok nodded. "There's wisdom in that. If we are to end this war, we'll have to make tough choices—and leaving our enemies alive may be the toughest of all."

Tag watched the Naplian prisoners until the last one was led out of the hangar. No, he didn't want to kill them.

But he'd make damn sure they wouldn't hurt any of his people again.

***

Admiral Daviont walked *Narsa*'s hangar bay, following the path set between two rows of 12 Jarra Fol Starfighters. Sparks flew from arc torches as technicians repaired damaged weapon mounts. A few crew noticed Daviont's passage and saluted him; the rest did not, and for that he was thankful. He'd rather have people who focused on their work than have them tripped up by every bit of protocol.

"The sooner we can get these planes back into Baedecker's skies the better." General Urs Ri'Nan Falloram was a few centimeters taller than Daviont, broader at the shoulders as most ground troops were, with dark skin the shade of slate. His face and hands were marred with white loops, a patterning rare among Ffawe. Combined with the piercing yellow of his eye and the thick padding of his mottled blue armor, it gave Falloram a more fearsome appearance than most everyone else on Daviont's ship.

A fearsome visage would not save him from critique, however. "Would you throw them at the Terrans' shield on the heights above Vossberg City? That strategy hasn't borne fruit."

"With all honor, Admiral, I will not have to continue fruitless attacks if you'd bombard the *shirish* from orbit."

"I cannot do that without exposing my ships to the Terrans' guns," Daviont said. "And I will not risk losing another like with *Napliae*."

"Bombarding the city would certainly entice the Terrans into surrendering their fortified position."

"Would you gamble with the lives of those civilians? I will not. From everything the Denic spies have passed to me—and by that, I cannot stress again the volumes of historical data now lodged in my memory—the humans will only fight with unchecked ferocity if we threaten the people they have sworn to protect. Your occupation of the city has only worsened matters."

"Navy floaters are all the same," Falloram grumbled. "You drift up here outside gravity's pull and think you understand two *ryzak* about what it takes to subdue a world. Martial law is necessary to root out all pockets of resistance and keep the populace under control. Now you may argue with my methods, Admiral, but you can't dispute my results."

"These are your results." Daviont waved his hands at the busy hangar bay. "Seventeen damaged fighters, all undergoing repairs for things as small as vandalism and as great as anti-aircraft fire. Your martial law has succeeded in riling the very populace you hoped to subdue. Instead of a city full of people who may cooperate with our rule you have refugees starving—"

"That's propaganda foisted by the *shirish* resistance!"

"And you have a resistance that, when it isn't destroying our patrols one by one, is painting slurs on our craft!" Daviont stopped by a Jarra with a single, grotesque eyeball spray-painted in red, with a black double slash through it. "The situation is intolerable, General."

"I have a solution that will quash the will of the people," Falloram said. "Don't worry about these malcontents. They'll soon be sorted out. From the sounds of it you have your own problems up here."

"I do. Wherever the Terrans are hiding, their base has eluded us for nearly one of their months. And now this latest raid..." Daviont held up his scroll. "A light cruiser and battlecruiser lost, along with two mining complexes."

Falloram's brow contracted, and he pursed his lips. "That's more than they've managed in weeks, even with the second outsider group of Terrans arriving. What changed?"

Daviont let a holographic image, distorted by lag, play from the sensor data report. The outline of a long, smooth-hulled warship floated.

"Briddarri," Falloram said.

"Yes. It seems they followed III Corps several months after we departed. Unsurprising—our intelligence from conquered Audrian space indicated as much."

"But this data makes no sense. Why take empty mining complexes? If I were trying to smash serjaum extraction, I'd destroy the loaded ones. Like they did in their first raid."

"You assume they wanted to destroy all four ships." Daviont shook his head. "The debris field and radiation dissipation from the site of the battle is inconsistent with the destruction of four ship's cores, though the battlecruiser's loss masked it fairly well. I've seen this trick pulled before; the Briddarri are fond of it. No, I am certain they took both empty mining complexes intact."

Falloram frowned. "What for?"

"I do not know. It could be a means of shipping more materiel and weapons into the system, a covert action meant to bypass our forces in this sector. Or perhaps they think the complexes will prove useful in a raid. I'm conferring with Vice Admirals Bouchtok and Hilder on the matter."

"I see." Falloram walked beside him to the end of the row of fighters.

"As to your situation…"

Falloram stopped. "I suppose you have new orders, Admiral."

"No. Only advice. Do not further antagonize the Terrans."

"After the damage they've caused? Do you know how many patrols I've lost outside the city limits? The *shirish* must have battle armored units or mechs out there—no survivors are left, and there are great tracks like claws all around. The men mutter superstitions to me, nonsense about 'devastators,' but I know it's Terran trickery."

Daviont did not say anything. After Lanviond's death, and reading Falloram's reports, he wasn't so sure. Something was wrong. Something other than the Terrans stalked Naplian soldiers in Baedecker Four's desert plains.

"You know I have the governor slated for execution."

"Yes. Continue with your plans. If you are correct, and the Terrans are crestfallen by his death, I will let you operate as you see fit." Daviont held up a finger. "But if they rise up with even greater fury, General, you will be removed from command of the ground forces."

Falloram saluted. "Understood Admiral. And the *shirish* holdout at the power station? What of them?"

"Destroy it within the week," Daviont said. "The same consequences apply."

CHAPTER EIGHTEEN

The ninth iteration of their plan to rescue Governor Wester, Timothy Ess, and the rest of the prisoners from Naplian custody prior to tomorrow's execution did not turn out any better than the first eight. Elden wondered if anyone truly realized the complexity of such an operation.

"What about the CDF hover-tanks?" This came from a man twice Elden's girth, who'd made his living as a housekeeper robot salesman. "I've seen them up on the rise—they can put up a good fight."

Goetz frowned. "What about them?"

"We need to get word to General Wood or Major Bond or whoever's in charge up there. They send a column down the streets, and while the Naplians are busy fighting the tanks, we sneak in and free the prisoners." The man beamed, and made eye contact with the refugees around him, searching for approval the way a prospector pans for gold.

"You're an idiot," Goetz said.

As depressed as Elden was by their lack of a feasible plan, his bodyguard's candor made him smirk. It was by the far the lowest opinion he'd ventured on any plan submitted so far.

"Oh yeah?" The man folded his arms. "It's a better plan than anything you've come up with."

The others around him backed up a step. They knew Goetz. This man was a newcomer, and he did not.

Goetz stepped right up to the man's face, and glowered down at him. "Hover-tanks are terrible at urban warfare. You send them in, the Naplians will have the streets mined with explosives in less than an hour. Every tank driver and gunner the CDF has left will be destroyed. And do you honestly think the one-eyes will be stupid enough to leave hundreds of valuable prisoners—especially the captured governor—unguarded while they rush off to fight? Then there's the matter of penetrating automated defenses: sentry 'bots, force shields, sensor-operated gun emplacements. If you're keen on getting yourself and whatever volunteers you can muster chewed up into ground meat, by all means, carry out your plan."

The man's bravado had all but disappeared by the time Goetz snarled the words "ground meat," and after that he was downright pale. Sweat beaded his brow.

"Besides," Goetz said. "You don't have a gun, and I'm not lending you mine."

He must have considered the debate closed, because he stood quietly, hands on his hips, watching the other man like an eagle targeting its prey.

"Well...it was just an idea." The man wandered off, muttering under his breath. A knot of a few men and women joined him, arguing among themselves about the merits of his dismissed plan.

"Don't be too hard on them, Goetz," Elden said. "We've struck out so many times you can't blame them for wanting to score."

"No. But I can smack them down when they want to try something that's going to get everyone killed, sir." Goetz scratched his beard. "Hover-tanks? Listen to that guy. He doesn't know the first thing about military tactics. If we are going to come up with a successful plan, it has to rely on stealth."

"Except we've already discarded three of our best options, all of which relied on stealth."

Goetz frowned. "The courthouse is a fortress. Was that way before the Naplians took it. You've seen the scout reports."

Elden nodded. He'd seen it firsthand, and up close. There were sensor-operated energy guns on the courtyard walls, and mounted higher up the courthouse building. Sentry mechs plodded around the entire block surrounding. He'd counted six patrols of four Naplian soldiers apiece.

"See if those police we contacted the other day have any ideas," Elden said. "I won't discount civilian input just because of their lack of experience. Sometimes their creativity can surprise the stiffest military minds—even yours, Goetz."

"Hmph. All right, sir."

They split up, Goetz heading for a group of two women and two men conversing near the steps of the mag-rail station. The small group Elden and Rett encountered at the wrecked market had appeared on the streets again, with 30 refugees and police in tow. Rett brought them in, and Marney had decided they should stay under their protection, though Goetz had argued against the inclusion. More stress on the supplies, he said.

Elden agreed, but was not about to turn anyone away from Sanctuary.

Marney sat atop the rubble pile near Elden's tent. She was swiping and tapping a scroll, the glow lighting up her face and hands. Elden recognized it as Rett's scroll: the list of prisoners to be executed by the Naplians today.

It was 0700 hours. Less than five hours from now, Governor Antiny Wester and Timothy Ess would be dead.

Elden sat beside Marney. Her faced was pinched. "What's the verdict?"

"Nothing. Absolutely nothing." Her forehead creased. "I've been over the scans you and Rett brought back, and there isn't any way past their security."

"There have to be entrances less guarded than others."

"No. They rotate their patrols perfectly." Marney touched a map diagram. She must have built it—Elden didn't recognize it as one of Rett's. "See? There isn't a gap. They always overlap their routes. And if there is a gap, the mechs close it up."

"I know. I've seen it." Elden had been over the data he and Rett had brought back dozens of times in the past day. It didn't change anything.

Marney switched off the scroll and set it on the rubble. "You're going to tell me we can't get them back."

"No. I'm going to tell you it's a possibility."

She shook her head. "I won't accept that. There has to be some way to save Father, and Timothy. You've gone through all this information. Isn't there anything we can do?"

Elden didn't reply. He wanted badly to help Marney, to reunite her with her father. But there was a quiet whisper at the back of his mind, from the same recesses that prodded him to attempt contact with the monastery and the Truppen that had to be there. *If the governor and Ess die, then she's with you alone. There'd be no one else to interfere.*

The thought excited and sickened him simultaneously. He didn't know Ess, other than that they'd been on opposite sides of the Second Consular War. By all accounts he was a stalwart man. And Antiny Wester had been like an uncle to him. Even when Elden had shown up on Baedecker, Wester had taken steps to protect him from the Reittians seeking his capture.

Even if Marney were not in the picture, he owed Wester that much.

Marney stood. "Fine. If there's no way to break them out, I'll go talk to them."

"Talk to them?" Elden frowned. "This isn't the colonial Congress, Marney. The Naplians have locked down Vossberg City. Martial law is in effect. That means the military run the streets."

"I know what martial law means, Elden," she snapped. "But I am the governor's daughter. That ought to gain me at least a chance at speaking with whoever is in charge."

She started down the rubble.

There was no way he was going to let her waltz right into the arms of the invaders. Elden scrambled down the pile. "Marney, wait. Be reasonable about this."

"I've been reasonable. I've listened to you and everyone else come up with plans that won't work, and talk through what we can and cannot do." She pointed up at the steps. "There's less than five hours until they kill Father and Timothy. I won't let them."

Marney turned away, but Elden grabbed her arm. She stared at him.

"I won't let you go alone," he said. "It's too dangerous."

"It's the only way!"

Someone cleared his throat. Elden glanced over his shoulder. Rett approached them, hands stuffed in the pockets of his jacket. "Sorry. I'd say I was eavesdropping, but frankly your voices were starting to carry."

"It's private, Rett."

"See, it isn't, Elden. I think I have a solution. And I know you'll hate to hear me say it, but Marney's right."

Elden let go of her arm, and poked Rett in the chest with his finger. "One person isn't going to free hundreds of prisoners slated for execution."

"Oh, one person can," Rett said. "In a manner of speaking."

***

They followed Rett outside, up into the crumbled ruins of the rail station. It reminded Elden of a smaller version of Vossberg Terminal, with narrower windows and lacking the ostentatious décor. Most of the walls were intact. Birds flew about the roof, opened to the sky by a Naplian blast.

Goetz was with them. As soon as he saw Elden and Marney head up the exit with Rett, he'd been on their tail, rifle in hand.

Rett sat on a black metal bench that was oddly set precisely parallel to the main walls, even though it was the only bench not blistered by weapons fire or broken into fragments. He rested his elbows on his knees, and stared at the wall opposite, which was painted with a mural of jovial passengers on their way to some destination across the southern Luran Plains.

"Not safe doing this out in the open." Goetz watched the numerous entrances and gaps in the walls, as if he expected a Naplian patrol to pop up from behind one at any second.

"Take it easy," Elden said. "We wouldn't be up here unless Rett had something to say he didn't want everyone else to hear. Isn't that right?"

Rett grinned. "Hard to pull a fast one on you, Elden. Yes, it is sensitive information."

No one said anything else. Marney in particular seemed anxious for him to continue.

"So, the Naplians have a custom," he said. "A particularly peculiar one from among a bunch that are weird by any being's standards. This one is called *saia ki maranvion*. It's Ffawe Naplian, the language of their ruling minority, and it translates as 'bad blood shed for those who would be dead.' Happens to rhyme in your language. It's a custom we can use to free the governor and the rest of the captives."

Elden's mind seized on a few key points. "Your language? You mean 'our.'"

"No, I mean 'your.'"

Goetz stuck his rifle in Rett's face.

"What are you doing?" Marney put her hand on the barrel.

"Step aside, ma'am. This man's a Naplian spy."

Elden didn't want to believe it was true, but it certainly explained the growing sickness in his gut—a feeling he was not one to ignore.

"Hey, now! I'm no lover of the one-eyes!" Rett scowled, but he didn't make any sudden moves. Smart plan for a man with a Naplian energy pulse crackling centimeters from his nose.

"Then how do you know about their customs? Their language?" Elden said. "That isn't something they bandy about over the airwaves."

"Because I've spent a lifetime studying their ways, so I can work against their forces. They're my enemy, too, Elden, and that's why I'm helping you guys out." Rett waved his hand. "This *saia ki maranvion* is a substitutionary punishment—one person takes the penalty for a crime in order that another may go free.

"The man asked you a question," Goetz said. "If you're not a Naplian spy, who are you with?"

Rett sighed. "A race called the Briddarri. That's who I am. We've been enemies of the Naplians for a long time, and as we sit here, you're wasting time holding me at gunpoint, the Briddarri are on the front lines of a Grand Alliance stopping the Naplians from overrunning this entire region of the galaxy."

Elden glanced at Goetz. "What do you think?"

"Frankly, sir?" Goetz thumbed the power level up. "I think he's full of crap."

"Elden, hear me out—if I were working for the Naplians, would I have helped save your hide? Wouldn't I have turned over our entire enclave?"

"It depends on whether any of that worked to your advantage."

"Staying in the guise of a human served my advantage, because it let me gather intelligence on you and the Naplians, and pass both along to my superior."

"Who is...?"

"The commander of the Briddarri forces that have entered the Baedecker System and allied with the leftovers of your fleet." Rett made a face. "But that's irrelevant. This substitution is our only hope for getting your governor back."

"Not just him—I won't choose between Father and Timothy," Marney said. "We have to save them both."

Elden held up his hand. "No one's suggesting that. Rett, is there any way around that? We do need to free two people—and preferably all of them."

"Well, the *maranat*, the one who substitutes, can free all of the people accused by the Naplian officials if that substitute is an enemy of the very people he or she wants to rescue. That's one of the more obscure aspects of the tradition, but one that the Naplians honor."

The sinking feeling in Elden's gut intensified. He could end this, and rescue all those people. Rescue Wester—and Marney's fiancé.

And what would it matter, really, if he died? With Andan Natour dead, and Elden having no way off this planet, the mission was a failure. Coupled with the lack of communication from the monastery, he'd seen the last of his hopes dwindle.

There would be no return of the Northern Alliance, no matter how badly he and people like Goetz wanted it.

But the question remained: Could Rett be trusted? "That all sounds well and good, but we have no way of knowing if you're telling us the truth."

"I agree," Marney said. "I'm not pinning my father's and my fiancé's survival on your say so, Rett. You've deceived us all along—you could be lying about this, too, as a means of drawing us out of hiding."

Rett stiffened. "You have my word as a servant of the Briddarri state that I am an ally of humanity."

Goetz shook his head. "Nice speech. Try again."

"Fine. Elden, give me your knife."

Elden drew it from its sheath, and held it out, hilt first. "Goetz, refrain from shooting him."

"Don't worry, sir. No chance he could stab you before I vaporize his brains."

Rett took the knife, and chuckled. "When this is all said and done, I'll miss you the most, Goetz."

He cut his palm.

Marney gasped. Elden understood why, because the blood welling in a thick line across Rett's hand was an emerald green as dark as the pine branches of the Koth Mountains.

"I'll be spaced," Goetz muttered.

"You can scan me too, if you like, and it will show you my internal organs are, well, out of place compared to yours." Rett held up his palm, letting green blood dribble between his fingers. "The scrambler implanted in my hand is now disabled—otherwise your scans would have shown you a healthy human male."

"I think we can wait on that." Elden reached for Goetz's weapon and lifted the barrel. Goetz let him, without protest or resistance. "Would you two give us a moment?"

Marney frowned. "I can hear whatever it is he has to say to you, Elden."

He smiled, but inside he knew he wouldn't reveal his involvement with the underground Northern Alliance until it couldn't be avoided. The last thing he wanted was Marncy despising him for such plotting, especially after he'd gone to such great lengths to build a respectable career in the Terran Graves department. "I'll explain later, Marney. Trust me."

She kept her frown, but nodded. Goetz joined her as the two walked away, back to the entrance of the rail station. He flashed Elden a warning look, as if he knew what Elden was about to do.

Truthfully, he hadn't decided. "Rett...I don't suppose that's your real name, is it?"

"No. Everett Lind is the cover, and the name my handlers use, for safety's sake. Not the name gifted by my clan and my parents." Rett smiled. "But it sounds close enough. And I'm not a different person."

"Sometimes we have to be different people," Elden said. "If you deceived us in order to spy on the Naplians, I could understand that. Just as you can certainly understand when I tell you that my entire background is not with the Terran government."

Rett's smile faded. "Oh?"

"I am the hereditary consul to the Northern Alliance."

"That had something to do with your last war, didn't it? The NA was the losing side."

"Yes. Sedrick Selva was my father."

Rett's eyes widened. "Ah. I see."

"Surely you studied our history when you were sent here for the Briddarri."

"I did. I've been here about a year. But it was forward-looking research, mostly. So when you say Northern Alliance—"

"I mean I am an enemy to the Terran people. The Reittians have already tried to capture me."

"What are you doing on Baedecker?"

Elden saw Natour in his memories, dead, and the promise of a Truppen resurgence wiped away like footprints in a sandstorm. "It doesn't matter anymore. The fact is, I should be the one to substitute myself for the prisoners."

Rett nodded slowly. "I see. You'd reveal yourself?"

"I would."

"Those people—"

"Are not my enemy. They're human; that's what matters. With a threat like the Naplians hanging over our heads, bringing the Northern Alliance back to power matters even less than it once did." Elden glanced at Marney. She stood by the front of the station, arms folded, watching the sky. Goetz still had his rifle at the ready; he watched Elden and Rett. "The governor was—is an old friend, and a good man. If I can convince the Naplians to spare his life and free him, along with the other prisoners, perhaps there's hope to bring this occupation to a peaceful conclusion."

"Okay. If that's what you want." Rett gave a half-smile. "I didn't think any of you would be willing. It was a last-ditch attempt, on my part, but given that my handlers are working on something to break the blockade, well..."

"What is their plan?"

Rett shrugged. "Don't know. They haven't shared. It's better I don't know much, you see, in case I'm captured."

Elden nodded. His heart pounded. He was ready for this.

Rett jerked a thumb over his shoulder. "You going to tell her?"

"I am."

"Good luck with that." Rett rose, and held out his hand. "We'd better get prepared."

Elden shook it. "Yes. We'd better."

***

They left the refuge silently, slipping out as the man with the hover-tank plan launched another vociferous lobby. Two dozen people including Marney and Goetz were occupied either with the argument or trying to prevent it from coming to blows.

The ruins of the mag-rail station were a dozen blocks from the Colonial Courthouse. Elden didn't bother with sticking to the alleys and the abandoned storefronts; he was going to turn himself in, so stealth was pointless.

He should have told Marney his plan, but he didn't want her to worry any more than she already had. It would be enough if Wester and Ess returned to her, with Rett escorting them.

Elden glanced sidelong at his walking companion. Everett Lind, aka Rett, aka ... well, he hadn't bothered to ask the Briddarri spy's true name. It was possible he'd lived under an assumed name for so long he didn't have any use for it. Elden had a hard time imagining what it would be like to hide behind a false identity for months; it was bad enough the handful of times he'd had to do so for a few days when he'd traveled incognito.

Then there was the matter of physically disguising an alien as a human.

"What do you look like?" He blurted.

Rett raised an eyebrow. "Come again?"

"Your physical appearance, as a Briddarri."

"Oh. Pretty close to human. Skin's got green behind it instead of red. When we get angry or blush, it's a deeper tinge.

Other than that..." He shrugged. "And, ah, this might be a good time to tell you we were followed."

Elden looked over his shoulder. Marney and Goetz were a block back. It was even odds as to which one looked angrier, but Elden had enough experience with both to know they were equally so.

"I can't believe you!" Marney said once they'd caught up. "What were you thinking, leaving us without saying anything?"!

"I have to take the place of the prisoners, like Rett explained. It's the only way to get the people back," Elden said. "Goetz understands."

Goetz snorted. "Tactically, yes. But it's still a stupid idea. Sir."

"Thank you."

Marney folded her arms. "Talk to me, Elden. Why are you doing this? I already said I won't be put in a place to choose between my father and my fiancé. Don't add yourself to the equation, too. I couldn't bear to see any of you dead."

Rett cleared his throat. "Maybe Goetz and I should walk on a bit."

"No. I need to come clean with both of you," Elden said.

Goetz grumbled something under his breath, and trudged ahead. Elden was grateful. This was going to be difficult enough.

"Marney, you know why I came to Baedecker Four."

"To find the identity tags of the fallen soldiers," she said. "Yes, Father told me, and I read the report from the Terran Graves department."

"That's only part true. I came here because the Hirrenhausen Monastery has uncovered Truppen headpieces, and I was tasked with retrieving them."

Marney's eyes went wide. What did she see, just then? Possibly the statue at the governor's compound, the one of a soldier stomping on a toppled Truppen? "You—that's not possible."

"It is. I've been working for some time now to rebuild the Northern Alliance, albeit as an underground organization." He sighed. "None of that matters anymore. Andan Natour —Nat— and I were the ones who knew the most about the project. All my attempts to contact the monastery have failed. If there were Truppen here, they've been long destroyed."

Rett frowned. "Truppen?"

"Cybernetic soldiers. The Northern Alliance used them when they rebelled. Huge, armored, robots with the minds of men and the force of an entire squad of CDF soldiers." Marney opened her mouth, as if to say something more, but apparently thought better of it. Instead an icy calm settled over her expression. "I can't believe you lied to us all this time. Father protected you from the Reittians. Do you know they threatened to bring a battlegroup on our heads if he didn't hand you over?"

Elden took her hands and pressed them between his. "That's why I have to do this. I have to make amends, especially with your father—and you. There's nothing I want more at this moment than for you to be happy. And if that means freeing Timothy Ess from death, then I have to do it."

Marney shook her head, tears welling. "Elden. You're as stubborn and impulsive as you ever were." She pressed against him. "It doesn't matter to me what you've done, the lies you've told—they're things I would have done to protect Baedecker and my family. You were just on the wrong side. But all those years, I thought you were safe, even when you were nowhere near. Now...I don't want you to die."

He hugged her. "Neither do I."

Rett cleared his throat. "I hate to interrupt, but those cyborgs—we could use them here. Now."

"I've been unable to contact them," Elden said. "That's part of why I'd stayed silent."

"Yeah, but...Marney, you said minds of men. People can be turned into cyborgs?"

"It's a dangerous process, but yes."

Rett's eyes took on an odd stare.

A shout from the other end of the block drew their attention. A Naplian mech stomped around the corner, one of the massive eight-legged beasts Elden had seen the night they attacked the governor's compound. The orange eye front and center blazed like an emergency vehicle's beacons. Goetz and Rett stood before it, weapons set on the ground, hands behind their heads.

A squad of four Naplian soldiers came around the corner. The one with the palest skin was also the tallest, and chirped orders at his men.

Elden walked directly to them, heart racing, palms sweaty. Marney stayed by his side.

"State your business." The Naplian's voice was full of static, and the words didn't match the motions of his lips. Translator device, Elden guessed.

"My name is Elden Selva, and I am surrendering to your

forces," he said. "I wish to speak with your commanders about the prisoners scheduled to be executed."

"There is no speaking with the general," the Naplian said. "Submit peaceably or join the rest of the *shirish* for extermination."

Elden bristled at the use of the word *shirish*.

Marney stiffened beside him. "We are not vermin, and you will release the governor and our people," she said.

The Naplian's single eye, a pale brown, focused on her. "Bold words for a new prisoner. You have no authority."

"That is why I invoke your tradition of *saia ki maranvion*," Elden said.

His voice must have carried enough for the other three soldiers to hear, because their heads bobbed around on skinny necks to face him. They hooted and murmured.

Their leader snapped off a sharp warble that silenced them. He lowered his weapon. "You would be *maranat*?"

"I would."

They stood there for what seemed like forever. Sweat trickled down the back of Elden's neck. He realized the Naplians could just shoot all four of them and leave their bodies for the Saarno foxes, and in a bit of dark humor appreciated the irony.

The Naplian leader warbled something else. His soldiers forced Rett and Goetz to their feet, and started them walking again. One of the three came back and jerked the end of his rifle at Marney.

"You will all accompany us." The leader slipped a pair of binders around Elden's hands—soft, pliable green and gray material, like cotton or cloth, that stiffened into a heavy, almost metallic substance as soon as the two halves joined together between his wrists. "The general and the magistrates will decide your fate."

As they marched deeper into the city, Elden reflected that he had suspected his journey would end in someone's custody, but never had he dreamt it would be at the hands of alien invaders on the world where the Northern Alliance died.

***

The courtyard was surrounded by walls 5 meters tall, and topped by dark green Undershear plants, hearty desert scrub that bloomed with bright orange flowers. Naplian soldiers patrolled the sandstone wall at its corners and above the gatehouse, a metal and quik-crete structure large enough to admit two hover-tanks side by side. Elden craned his neck for a view of the Colonial Courthouse. The mid-morning sky turned its windows a brilliant sapphire.

The rumble of conversation from a large crowd drew his attention back down. The four soldiers and attendant mech led Elden, Marney, Goetz, and Rett through the gate and into a broad, flat area paved with white tiles. It was full of hundreds of people—men, women, children, former officials and police, civilian workers. They gathered under the arches set in the wall, seeking shade where they could. A few clustered under the pale green leaves of date trees arranged in two rows.

The prisoners were lined up between those rows. At the head of the 150 were Governor Antiny Wester and Lieutenant Commander Timothy Ess.

Marney stifled a cry, but she didn't run to them. She stood her ground, beside Elden, with Goetz to his left and Rett on Marney's right. The mech took up station with a counterpart inside the gate; the soldiers formed a loose cordon behind Elden.

The prisoners looked haggard, but Elden couldn't see any bruises on their faces or other signs of overt mistreatment. West had lost weight. Ess guarded him, standing stiffly at attention, leaning on a cane. He'd grown blond scruff on his chin.

A portico overlooked the courtyard from the second floor of the courthouse. Four Naplians stepped up to the railing made of copper mesh that had long ago turned green. One was a soldier, wearing the signature mottled blue armor. He must have had the adaptive camouflage option switched off, for it didn't shift color to match the sandstone walls and pillars. This Naplian was bigger than any Elden had seen before, and had bizarre white markings on dark gray skin. His eye was bright yellow and targeted the people below with the same intensity as the optical port of a mech.

The other three Naplians were all pale, with eyes varying shades of purple, but they wore robes instead of armor. Each robe was emerald green, with silver and gold patterns woven throughout. Though they shared the same colors each one was unique in its design.

"General Falloram." The Naplian officer who'd brought them in kept up a translation. "We have with us the Terran who invoked *saia ki maranvion*."

His voice hushed the human crowd, but touched off a round of warbles among the Naplians. The yellow-eyed Naplian put both hands on the railing. "We received your communication. This is a bold statement coming from the *shirish*. Which one?"

The Naplian officer shoved Elden forward. He raised his chin, and drew back his shoulders. If this was to be his death, he'd face it like a Selva, with the pride his father showed. "I am Elden Selva, and I will be *maranat* for these people."

"I don't think you understand the gravity of the situation, human," General Falloram said. "You die, and one of yours goes free. What of the other 149?"

"I am here to submit my life for all the accused." I'm sorry, Marney—and you too, Goetz.

Falloram's brow furrowed atop that glaring eye. "Is that so. Magistrates? What say you?"

He turned away, and conferred with the three robed Naplians. The silence in the courtyard was as unbearable as the blazing heat, and was interrupted only by the buzzing of cicadas. Elden glanced back at Marney. She smiled, though tears dripped down her cheeks. Elden tilted his head left, and dipped his chin —then smiled, too. Rett fidgeted; Elden wondered what would happen should the Naplians discover his true identity. And Goetz— Goetz just nodded at him, as if that gesture summed up all they'd been through with a single implied, "Right here, sir."

"Approach the prisoners," General Falloram said.

Elden stepped to the front of the group, his hands still bound. Wester shifted his position, grimacing and gripping his cane. "Elden! By the stars, thank you for keeping Marney safe."

"You're more than welcome. I'm glad to see you're both unhurt."

"Relatively."

Timothy Ess tapped his cane. He scanned Elden up and down. "Selva."

"Commander."

"You have my gratitude for rescuing Marney."

"That was part your doing, Commander. If you hadn't shot through that wall, we might not have gotten her out of there."

"Nevertheless..." Ess held a hand. "You kept the woman I love alive."

Elden shook it.

"Elden Selva." Falloram's voice boomed. "You are the supplicant in this process. Do you fully comprehend what that means?"

"I do."

"Are you friend or enemy?"

Elden squared his shoulders. There was no backing down.

"I am Elden Selva, heir to Sedrick Selva and consul of the Northern Alliance," he said, making sure his voice carried throughout the courtyard. "I fought in opposition to the Terran government, to which these people swore allegiance, and continued that work beyond the peace accords to which many of my Northern Alliance compatriots fraudulently agreed. I have betrayed that allegiance by my intents and actions; I am an enemy of all here condemned."

Gasps and murmurs spread throughout the crowd. Some of the politicians among the prisoners scowled. Wester himself went pale. He shook his head slowly, but made no comment. Ess wore an expression that seemed torn between disgust, and amazement.

Elden understood; he couldn't decide where he stood on his own actions. He just knew it had to be done. "Forgive me," he muttered to Wester and Ess, "But it is the only way I can atone for my wrongs."

The Naplian magistrates talked among themselves, then conferred again with Falloram. Elden didn't know much about Naplian facial gestures, but he guessed by the wide open yellow eye that Falloram was surprised by their answer. "The magistrates have ruled. Divider? Step forward."

Naplian guards stationed behind the prisoners split their ranks. A lone alien clad in all black armor marched out between them. He had one of their sidearms in a holster on his belt.

The prisoners made way for him. He ignored their presence as one might ignore crickets underfoot. His boots clomped on the tile.

Ten paces out he stopped.

"The petition is accepted," Falloram said. "The prisoners scheduled for execution are now free to leave the courtyard."

Cheers erupted from the people gathered around the courtyard.

"Kill the supplicant!" Falloram shouted.

The Divider drew his sidearm and aimed.

Elden took a deep breath. All he got was a lungful of Vossberg's hot air.

I'm sorry, Marney.

Light flashed green, and the energy weapon shrieked.

Elden felt an intense burn in his chest that rippled through his body. Everything went black.

The last thing he heard was Marney screaming his name.

***

The shot echoed to the rooftop of a commercial structure two blocks away. Erich lowered his binoculars. "They've killed him."

Abbot Jeopar fell to his knees. Not Elden Selva. All hopes for the Northern Alliance were surely dashed, like pottery dropped on the banks of the Santos River. He made the sign of the cross. "Commend his soul into the hands of Our God and Savior."

"You take care of the soul, Abbot. We'll tend to the body." Erich slipped the M-36 from his shoulder, and signaled to Colonel Diaz, who stood behind him with a squad of Truppen. "Let's go."

CHAPTER NINETEEN

Antiny Wester hugged his daughter so tightly, he thought he'd never again be able to breathe. "My dear Marney." His voice was gruff, and choked with tears.

She was crying, too, her body wracked by sobs. Warm tears soaked his shirt. "Father! Oh, Father, I missed you so much."

"It's all right now. We're together again. It's all right."

"Why did he do that? Why did he have to die?" she whispered.

Wester couldn't bear to look at Elden Selva's lifeless body. The Naplian soldiers who'd brought Marney and the others into the courtyard had draped a sheet over him. Wester hadn't counted on a gesture of respect from the one-eyes.

"Marney!" Timothy Ess laid a hand on her shoulder. "My God, Marney, are you hurt?"

Wester let her go, so the two of them could embrace. It did his old heart good to see them reunited, and a part of him ached at the thought that what should have been their wedding night was forever tainted by the invasion and assault on his mansion.

Prisoners streamed out of the courtyard, accompanied by the crowds of refugees who'd come to watch the execution. All around him, reunions were in progress—grandparents weeping over their grandchildren, wives kissing their husbands, fathers clinging to their sons.

Elden made it possible.

It couldn't be avoided. Wester knelt by the shrouded form laying on the hot courtyard tiles. He rested a hand on the nearest arm. It was still warm, as if Elden would push back the sheet and hoist himself up, startled at the commotion around him. Wester waited a full three seconds in which nothing of the sort happened.

"I'm so sorry, Elden," he said. "I never wanted any harm to come to you. Say hello to your old man for me, should you see him again,"

Shadows loomed over him. The Divider, the executioner himself, stood at Elden's head. His pistol was holstered. The four Naplian soldiers stood behind him. More footsteps approached.

"I cannot make sense of you humans," said General Falloram. "You fight and rebel and cling to your individual safety as tenaciously as scavenging reptiles, yet one of you displays the urut—the sacrificial courage—to set down his life for enemies who would surely see him vaporized."

"Our contradictions are our greatest strength," Wester said.

"They are troublesome."

Wester stood. "As is all of humanity. That's why you'll never fully conquer us. We'll fight you to the day we breathe our last."

Falloram squinted. "That may be. But the Ffawe are not without tenacity. I would have you ask the people of the star systems against which we've waged long, brutal campaigns about that tenacity, but there are none left alive to question."

Wester glared at him.

"Divider, take the body of the supplicant to the stasis pods."

"There are none in this complex, General, but there are transports parked around the backside that have a few." It was the first the Divider had spoken. His voice sounded like bole tree leaves skittering across the stones of the governor's compound. "Those are intended for our honored dead."

"This human is worthy of that title. Put him in stasis. We'll bear his remains to the temple of Omiat where the martyrs sleep."

The Divider saluted. He warbled in Naplian, and the four soldiers behind him gently picked up Elden's body. The latter's hands dipped beneath the edge of the sheet.

"No!" Marney ran up to them. It took all Wester's strength to hold her back. "Where are you taking him?"

"They're interring his body," Wester said. "It's…a custom of theirs, I suppose."

"They shouldn't touch him," Marney snapped. "One-eye scum!"

Falloram moved close enough to Wester and Marney that Wester could smell a strange, sour odor coming off him. His breath reeked of bitter herbs. "I am bound by Ffawe Naplian law and custom to release the prisoners intended for execution, and to let them go freely from this place. The magistrates demand it.

But don't mistake my honorable actions as weakness. If you make yourself my target, you'll be destroyed."

"We shall see who is destroyed," Marney said coolly, "And I would not count on it being the people of Baedecker."

Falloram stood as stiff as a statue. "Leave, *shirish*."

The Naplians withdrew, carrying Elden's body with them. Wester kept a firm grip on Marney, lest she break free and charge after them—something he could vividly imagine her doing, in her current state. "Marney, please. There are others we have to look after."

She closed her eyes, and took a deep breath. When she opened them again, the fire had cooled, but only just. "You're right. We have a few hundred in our shelter who need our guidance."

The three men waited for them just outside the gates. Ess spoke quietly with—what was his name? Gertz? No, Goetz—the bodyguard. Another man, stocky with dark hair that reminded Wester of Tag's, watched the activity in the compound with a gaze that bespoke attentiveness.

Tag. Not for the first nor last time did Wester wonder what had become of his son. "Have you heard anything from your brother?"

Marney shook her head. "There's been rumors of our ships making raids on the Naplians—at Baedecker Two, and elsewhere in the system. Nothing quik-crete. But he can't be dead. Not Tag."

"No. Of course not."

Marney touched Goetz's arm. "I'm so sorry."

The bodyguard stared off at the Naplians, ignoring everyone around him save for Marney. "Didn't think he'd go through with it. Mr. Selva had—a lot of things on his mind. A lot of questions of what he should and shouldn't do. Guess I know which won out in the end."

He looked down at her. "I have to go."

Before he got far, the stocky man blocked his way. "Look, don't do it. It isn't worth it."

Goetz scowled. "It is to me, Rett. Move over, or I'll move you."

Rett sighed. "Fine. But let me come with you. Backup. I owe Elden that much."

"Okay by me." Goetz walked off into the crowds streaming through the streets outside the courtyard.

"Rett, be careful. Get back to the station as soon as you can," Marney said.

Rett smiled. "I will. Look, I said before I can't tell you much about what the Briddarri have planned, but whatever it is, they want us to stick as close to as many refugees as possible. That means Castillo Fields. So if you can..."

"We can't move there. It's a prison camp."

"I don't think it will be for long. Just trust me: get near the camp, and watch it. You'll know when to act."

Marney hugged him. "Thank you. Take care of Goetz."

"Hopefully he doesn't do anything stupid." Rett looked sheepish, and Marney noticed that he hadn't blushed at all—red or green. He hurried off after Goetz.

"What's this station? Do you have a place of safety we can go to?" Ess asked.

"Yes. The mag-rail station at Forty-First and Kiva," Marney said. "The Naplians overlooked it."

"That should suffice, but we have to consider the refugees at the coliseum, too. They'll need your Father."

Wester blinked. "Me? What for?"

"You're the governor, Antiny. You have to show them you're still alive."

"I'm no governor, Tim. That post has been forcibly terminated."

"It doesn't matter if there's nothing left of the mansion but a hole in the sand. Your presence will reassure people that Baedecker lives on, even while the invaders step on their freedoms." Ess stood at parade rest. "There are plenty who will follow you to the end, sir."

Wester smiled. There was that possibility, wasn't there? "Well, Rett there said we should be near the station—though I'm not fond of submitting to capture again."

"Then don't. Call to them from the nearest building." Ess returned the smile. "Rekindle their fight."

"Marney, is there any way we can contact General Wood?"

She frowned. "If we sneak back across the river, at the sandbars—that's how I led Elden over here in the first place."

Wester nodded. "Good. Well, my dear, what's your orders?"

"My orders? Father, you're—"

"The governor, yes, even formerly." Wester held her chin. "Much has changed, daughter. I've been a prisoner for a month. You? You've shown leadership, and the fire needed to survive. I'll not take your place with the people you've rescued. Elden wouldn't want that."

Marney leaned into his hand. "I won't let you down. Any of you."

"That's my girl." Wester smiled at Ess. "Commander? Let's follow her lead."

***

Jeopar spotted the activity around the two Naplian transports the same moment Erich whispered his commands to Colonel Diaz and the eight Truppen with them.

The transports were ugly things—bulbous, pale green edged with dark brown, as appealing to the eye as Luran dung beetles. They hovered in place, held aloft by a technology that operated with the barest whisper, unlike the roar of Terran hover-vehicles.

There were five Naplians below, four of whom wore the typical color-shifting armor. The fifth one was clad in black, and directed the other four with something wrapped in a sheet.

A body. Elden Selva's body.

"Stay put, Abbot," Erich murmured. "Let Diaz handle this part."

Jeopar nodded, though he found the statement silly. He would do nothing but stay put, as Erich suggested, for he was not about to take up arms against another sentient being.

There was a cry of surprise from below. A burly man struggled with one of the four Naplians, and as Jeopar watched, slashed the soldier's neck in a spray of yellow blood. He bellowed a cry, diving for the next one.

The black clad Naplian shot him down, without hesitation.

A second human was nearby, and opened fire with a dropped Naplian rifle. A second soldier collapsed, and the human retreated behind one of the transports.

"Blasted nuisance," Erich said. "Diaz, make it quick!"

The Truppen converged on the parked hover-vehicles without any sound other than the tread of their metal claw feet on the pavement. They tore the weapons from the hands of the remaining two Naplian soldiers and punched deep holes in their armor using clawed hands. In seconds all four were dead, yellow blood staining the pavement around them.

The Naplian in black armor drew a hilt from his belt and depressed a switch. A blade leapt out to half a meter in length, the same obsidian as his armor, at least until it began to vibrate with such ferocity it became a blur. The Naplian dodged a blow by one of Diaz's Truppen, and severed its arm. He made no sound of triumph, nor did the Truppen cry out in alarm or pain—he could feel nothing.

Though he put up a far more spirited defense, Diaz stabbed his claws deep into the Naplian's chest armor. The blade jabbed through Diaz's torso, coming clear out the backside, with servo fluids and wires dripping from its edge. The Naplian's eye went unfocused, mouth slack. He slumped against Diaz.

"Let's go." Erich slapped Jeopar's shoulder.

Together they scrambled down the escape ladder of the nearest building and joined the Truppen in the alley. Diaz's body was already stitching itself back together; Jeopar wasn't familiar with the repair process, but understood from Erich that nanites embedded in the Truppen's armored frame acted as the cells of a human body do, healing what damage they could. Diaz would likely require more permanent restoration back at the Iwa Valley bunkers.

Jeopar hurried to the body. The sheet had fallen half off. It was Selva. His face was pale, placid. He could have been asleep.

"That's him." Erich shook his head. "There isn't much time, is there?"

"No. If we are to transfer him into a Truppen body, his brain must be rebuilt. He has already been dead for a long time, and without the benefit of a Truppen headpiece to preserve the tissue."

"Get him in the back of that thing," Erich said to the nearest Truppen.

"Yes, General." That one lifted Selva into the open hatch of the transport. There was a long, white container inside. Its sides were ribbed with green lights and the interior hollowed out, like an empty eggshell. No sooner had he laid the body in the container than it sealed up, without a discernable seam. The lights went red.

"Stasis module, by the looks of it," Erich said. "Well, here's hoping we can figure out how to open it again."

"It looks like standard Naplian technology," Diaz said. "Our mechanics should be able to make it work—with help from the Hirrenhausen acolytes, of course."

"Sir? We caught this one." Two Truppen advanced, with a stocky, dark-haired man suspended between them. His eyes were wide with terror, as if he expected the Truppen to rip his arms from his sockets at any moment. They could, Jeopar reflected, do just that if ordered.

"Who are you?" Erich shoved the M36 under the man's chin. "And the other one, the one who nearly fouled our plans?"

"R-Rett. Everett Lind. That one's Goetz, he's Elden's bodyguard." His Adam's apple bobbed. "You can't—he didn't want them to take Elden's body. I told him it was a bad idea but he wouldn't listen. The man's loyal to the bone!"

"Do you know who we are?"

Rett shook his head. "I've never seen anything like you— them. Whichever? This new Terran tech? Special forces?"

"General," Diaz said. "I've scanned him. I don't know what he is, but he isn't human—nor is he Naplian."

Erich stared. "Neither? You'd better come clean."

Jeopar touched his arm. "Bring him to the valley with us. Surely you can question him there, not out in the open. Someone is bound to have heard the shots."

"Right. Let's not fool around anymore. Diaz, get the pod removed and let's clear out of the city. Take the prisoner along."

"Sir, yes, sir. What of the wounded human?"

Jeopar saw that the man named Goetz was barely breathing. "Take him, too. See if he can be stabilized. Come on, Abbot."

They left the Truppen to handle the stasis pod and two humans. Jeopar backtracked the route they'd taken through several alleys, ending under the broad awning of an abandoned hover-car sales lot. A hundred vehicles in silver, white, and gray—with scattered sleek red and blue models—were crammed together. Half of them had been knocked about, as if a giant child had grown bored with his toys. Deep craters from weapons blasts pocketed the slick black parking surface.

Jeopar got their transport, a gray civilian model hover-car with tan markings, started. The hover engines hummed to life. Once Erich was seated next to him, he drove it out of the lot and down a narrow side street.

"Diaz will have Selva's body back to our transport in no time," Erich said. "We can ditch the car at the landing site."

Jeopar nodded. They were five minutes from the Truppen craft.

"Are you certain this is the right thing to do?"

"I am. Elden Selva is the last consul of the Northern Alliance. If he dies, it will never recover. The only way to revive him at this point is to make him Truppen."

"He may object to that."

Jeopar didn't say anything. That was the quandary. Every

one of the Truppen—from Erich and General Albrecht through Colonel Diaz down the ranks to the lowliest enlisted man—were volunteers. They had traded their human bodies for war machines, willingly. But to force someone into the transition, someone who had just died...

That didn't even begin to solve the difficult issue of Selva's soul. Would it be drawn back to his body? Jeopar believed the soul was present with God in the moment after death—and shut away from His presence if it belonged to the unbeliever.

He glanced at Erich. The former Truppen turned android kept watch out the hover-car's windscreen, unblinking. Had he not seen evidence that Erich's soul was reunited with his body, even though it was a fabricated body? Or was that just the eerie efficiency of the Truppen transition process mimicking a true man?

If Erich died, where would he go?

"The consul must live so he can lead," Jeopar said. "He can then free us from the Naplians and usher in a new era for the Northern Alliance."

"Hope you're right," Erich said. "Because as soon as Albrecht can get the *Hessian* operational I'll be hard pressed to get him to stick around. He wants us ready to attack the nearest Terran base—you know that."

"Madness. Can he not see there is a new enemy?"

"Doesn't matter. Unless Selva can convince him otherwise." Jeopar prayed it was so.

***

Albrecht was not pleased when they arrived at the primary bunker, buried deep below Iwa Valley.

"You can't be serious. Fight the Naplians? They aren't the ones we spent years trying to overthrow. Our target should be the Terran tyrants!"

"How long do you think the Terrans will last if the Naplians stay?" Erich snapped. "Those aliens are the top dogs now, General. If we lend a hand, there might be a chance to stop them."

Albrecht made a harsh, buzzing sound through his speakers. "With all due respect, *sir*, we should put it to the men. They can decide where we should go. *Hessian* needs only a few engine tests, and she can be ready to lift tomorrow. After that we're home free, and in position to strike at any Terran outpost we please."

Erich threw up his hands—a very human gesture.

Jeopar and Rett waited by the window into the bunker's medical center, watching as a robotic surgeon with 30 appendages deftly removed Selva's brain and spinal column from his body. Though the sight of Selva split open sickened him, Jeopar forced himself to watch the entire procedure. The robot surgeon placed the brain inside a waiting Truppen headpiece, and neatly severed the spinal column with a laser scalpel glowing from one appendage. Next it began the long process of implanting thousands of electrodes into the brain, while deploying nanites from two other appendages around the implant sites.

"What are they doing?" Rett asked.

"Transitioning Selva into Truppen form."

"These Truppen—they're cybernetic soldiers?"

"Yes."

"We—the Briddarri, that is—don't use them. Neither do the Naplians. How many do you have?"

"The generals have 15,000 at their command."

"Thousands," Rett murmured. "Interesting."

In the adjacent medical bay, Goetz lay on an operating table. He was conscious, but barely. His vitals refused to stabilize, no matter how the pair of acolytes tended to him.

They should prepare his soul at this point.

"The men will follow our orders," Albrecht said. "You'd better see to it we're on the same side when it comes down to that."

Erich's face was a mask. "Are you saying you won't obey me, Brigadier General?"

"I'm saying, Major General, that they will see the orders coming from a true Truppen as superior to one who's lost the will to face the Terran scourge." Albrecht loomed over Erich. "Wait until Consul Selva rises in his new body—in the same form as I. Our Truppen won't drag their tails behind a castrated general."

"This isn't the time for dissention, Albrecht. You heard this Rett—there are other aliens allying with the Terrans, still holding out against the Naplians. If we can join them we can still fight the good fight, and free the people of Baedecker!"

"Our brothers on *Hessian* and the oppressed remnants of the Northern Alliance are the only people I care to free."

"Abbot?" Abbot Sissok came out of the medical room, his robes stained with blood and his hands sheathed in surgical gloves also turned red. "Mr. Goetz wishes to speak with you—all of you."

Albrecht stomped for the bunker exit. "I'm going to brief the men. Let me know your decision. Sir."

Erich scowled. "That Truppen will get everyone killed."

Jeopar, Erich, and Rett followed Sissok back to Goetz's bedside. He was deathly pale, and the Sissok ran a scanner over the bandaged wound on his chest.

"We've stopped the bleeding but the energy blast was too destructive," Sissok said. "He's suffering from organ failure."

"Should've guessed." Goetz voice was reedy. "Elden... is he...?"

"I am sorry," Jeopar said. "But your friend has died."

Goetz sighed. He twisted his head far enough so he could see into the adjacent suite where Elden's transition continued. "They're working on him."

"Yes. We thought it best if the consul were given one last chance—as a Truppen commander. He could continue his work, that way."

"His work." Goetz chuckled, and the sound morphed into a hacking cough. Blood bubbled from his lips. "The NA? Forget it. You've seen what's out there. He'll be a soldier, yes, but he'll pick his own fight to lead."

"Listen Goetz, these guys can help you." Rett grasped his shoulder. "Right? They can put you into a Truppen body, too. Then you could continue on."

"Wait a sec." Erich pulled his hand back. "We never discussed that."

"No, but... hey, let go." Rett tugged at Erich's grasp but Jeopar knew he might as well be trying to free himself from a mech's pincers.

"Becoming a Truppen isn't something you randomly decide to do because your bored or depressed," Erich snapped. "It's a deliberate severing of all physical ties to your humanity—or your Briddarri nature, whichever. You do this, and you'll never go back to being a biological sentient being. I know what I'm talking about."

Jeopar frowned. "Erich, Mr. Goetz has no options left. If he chooses to do nothing, I will of course commend his soul to the Lord. But if he elects transition, then it is our duty to help him live. A Truppen life is still a life, is it not?"

Goetz grimaced. His vital signs dipped on Sissok's scanners. "Look...whatever you have to do, do it. I'm not going to abandon Elden if he's alive."

"Very well. Erich?"

Erich stared. "Fine. Another soldier is another soldier. Prep him."

As they exited the room, a second surgical robot lowered from the ceiling and extended its arms to Goetz. Rett watched, mouth parted. "You said another soldier is another soldier. Sign me up too."

"You're insane. Don't you have a commander to whom you have to return? A family?"

"My family's all dead," Rett snapped. "Naplian casualties. I've got no one. Why do you think I made such a good spy? And I know what the Briddarri rank and file think of me: a snake, a conniver. They use spies as well as the next empire, but Briddarri despise anything that isn't open and blunt confrontation. They hate me because they have to use me and I'm good at it. Well, if I'm a cybernetic soldier, I'm nobody's snake—and the Briddarri Command will see the benefit of using Truppen of its own."

Something about the tenor of the man's voice bothered Jeopar. Yet his earnestness was evident.

"There is no reversing this. Not back to what you are now. And I'll warn you flat out—we've never done a transition on your species before," Erich said.

"Doesn't matter. If I go back without being a Truppen, I won't be fit for anything else other than being an operative. And I'm done with that."

Erich nodded. Though his android features were difficult to read, Jeopar couldn't help wonder if he was exhausted. "All right."

Jeopar led Rett back into the medical suites. "May the Lord God bless and preserve you, Everett Lind."

Rett watched the robotic surgeon sedate Goetz, and approach his body with a pair of laser scalpels. "Never was much for that stuff, Abbot, but I hope you're right."

***

Elden was perplexed.

Darkness? Or was it light?

Nothing made sense, not even his senses. Hot and cold, pain and peace—all were interchangeable. He was overwhelmed by voices, and stunned by absolute silence.

Rett? Goetz? Nat?

Marney?

No one answered his calls—and no matter how he shouted,

he couldn't make a sound. The conflicts frustrated him, and he lashed out, but couldn't touch anything.

It was as if he didn't exist, yet he knew that he did.

Suddenly something dragged him away from whatever trap he'd been locked in, pulling him down through dizzying depths. Colors swirled up, and light grew from a pinpoint to the blazing corona of a sun. Heat suffused his body. He gasped...

And he heard his gasp rife with static.

"Consul? Consul Selva?"

That voice. Familiar. He opened his eyes.

Or—not. No eyelids responded. Instead, he saw a line of gibberish. Numbers and letters. Code?

Even as he puzzled, its meaning translated. Not eyes. Optical sensors.

He activated them.

Bright blurs resolved quickly into a room. A medical operating center. Pale colors, brilliant lights, young men clad in white. Except their whites resembled religious robes, not doctors' tunics. Beyond them, a window into a darker room with a spare, military appearance. Vaguely familiar.

Elden sat up—or rather, he leapt up, a full meter, and banged his head off the ceiling. His feet slammed down onto the floor so hard he cracked the tile under foot.

Not foot, or feet. Claws. Metal claws.

His head didn't ache. The was a dent in the ceiling panel— which was so close Elden marveled at how cramped the room was.

And the men before him—small. Short.

Horror struck him. The men weren't short. He'd grown far taller.

"Consul Selva." It was the bland-faced man who'd helped him escape the Reittians at Vossberg Terminal a month ago—Erich. He was the contact with the monastery.

Was he there? Had he finally made it? "Where am I?"

His voice, again, sounded filtered through a machine. His throat felt constricted. Elden rubbed his hand against his neck—

Metal and plastic scraped together.

Elden staggered against the wall, and caught his reflection in the windows. A Truppen. Him? His form? He raised his hand again.

The Truppen in the window did the same with its right claw.

Impossible. He'd been transformed. Power surged through

his body. Even as he reveled in the feeling of strength, streams of data overlapped in his field of vision. Too many—he separated and parsed, whittling them down to the basic modes he wanted.

"I ... am Elden Selva," he said.

Another man, bearded and dark-skinned, placed both hands on Elden's arm. "A marvel. You survived, Consul—you survived your transition and have returned to your people."

"My people?" Out the window, more Truppen filed into the room.

It was true. The monks had succeeded.

The Northern Alliance had a chance.

Yet, even as he thought so, he remembered the Naplians, and his head filled with more data. Each stream had an identifier code that originated with one of the other Truppen—and one with Erich. He saw the reports they'd gathered about the Naplian activities, and how much damage they'd inflicted. So many lives lost.

The NA would have to wait.

Two more Truppen were laid out on the tables in the medical suites. Elden knew, without asking, to whom the bodies belonged, for their identifiers—though still dark and blank of data —appeared in his mind. "Goetz? And Rett?"

"One was near death. The other chose to join the cause," Erich said.

"The cause is no more," Elden said. "We can't put our hope in the rebirth of the Northern Alliance, not when the Naplian Empire threatens to conquer everything we vowed to protect."

Erich stood stiffly at attention. A Truppen behind him, identified as a Colonel Gerald Diaz, did likewise. "We stand ready to serve, Consul. What are your orders?"

"He'll give no orders!" The voice boomed throughout the room. The others made way for a Truppen bearing general's markings. "That's no more your leader than the apostate formerly calling itself Erich Baesler! I'm putting an end to this mockery once and for all."

The Truppen slashed at Erich with a bladed claw—and Elden blocked it, surprised at how quickly he'd produced his own blade from his forearm and brought it into the path of the blow. The Truppen—General Albrecht, the data informed him— counterattacked, managing to slit part of Elden's armor, but Elden pivoted and severed his arm. He pinned Albrecht to the wall with a swift stab.

"Release me!" Albrecht demanded. "You've no right to pretend to be consul and lead us from our true mission. We serve the Northern Alliance and—"

Elden stabbed his blade deep into Albrecht's right optical port. Sparks and smoke burst out. Thick fluids oozed down onto his shoulders. With a second motion, Erich swiped his headpiece free of his shoulders, and crushed it beneath his foot.

Silence prevailed. Elden turned around. Everyone else, Truppen included, stood staring.

"I am Consul Elden Selva, Truppen commander," he said. "From this moment forth, you serve only me."

CHAPTER TWENTY

Twenty-One Days after the Naplian Invasion

Tag sat in his cockpit, ripwave generator primed. He grimaced, fidgeted in his seat, and ran what had to be the hundredth check on his sensor resolution. Weapons systems were ready. Everything was ready. Especially him.

Nothing worse than drifting in the black empty of space when you were ready.

"All units, this is Wing Commander Chok." The voice over the wing intra-comm was calm and measured as usual. Tag's jitters subsided. "Standby for ripwave in two minutes. Squadrons, report in."

Chok himself was the fighter lead for this plan—Operation Dunkirk Reverse, the brass was calling it—and commanded Nova Squadron. Four others listed their readiness down the line, until it was time for the final squadron to weigh in.

"Bronze Leader, standing by," Tag said.

He grinned, pleased at not having stuttered or said anything moronic when it came to his turn. It would take time to get used to the title. In the past two days he'd managed to answer to "Bronze Two" enough times that his pilots gave him a ribbing—good-natured, of course, because he was now their commander.

His wingman was the new Bronze Two, Naomi Wyss, now a freshly-minted first lieutenant. Tag shook his head; when this mess was all over, they'd have a raft of battlefield promotions to sort through.

With Chok promoted and heading the entire wing of six squadrons, Tag had needed a new wingman and a level-headed second. Princess was the best choice.

And she'd needed a new wing, as well. Chasm was gone,

her body and her fighter blasted to free-floating atoms somewhere in the Baedecker Six region. Tag's grin subsided. Squadron morale was still down after that loss, though the joke circulating among the barracks was that if you listened hard enough in the silence of space, you could still hear Chasm's caterwauling.

"This is Commodore Ram to Strike Force One. Ready for ripwave."

Tag watched as the bulk of the combined Terran-Reittian-Briddarri fleet maneuvered into position. Their courses were plotted for Baedecker two. Tag pulled up the latest scans by Briddarri scouts distributed among the fleet by Commander Vollan. There were plenty of Naplians to play with out there—three squadrons of a mixed variety of six ships each, plus one of battlecruisers.

But Tag and the fighter wing had another target.

"Mark," Ram said.

Flashes of light rippled like the surface of the Santos River across space. Stars ripwaved and streaked as the 32 warships of the fleet ripwaved out of the area. Within seconds Tag was staring at a starry void.

His counter started over. Ten minutes until their move. "Bronze Squadron, this is Lead. Take up escort positions around Miner One, over."

"Roger that, Captain." Princess was a half klick away, her Warhawk a slate gray arrowhead barely visible on his cockpit's optical readouts. "All pilots reporting ready."

Bronze Squadron's Warhawks dispersed around the hulking mining complex. Tag's sensors confirmed to him that it was no longer sparsely inhabited by a Naplian crew; instead, hundreds of Terran orbital jumpers from the 76th Battalion were stashed aboard. His job was to shepherd the mining complex in, and keep Naplian fighters away from both it and the jumpers when they deployed. Gold Squadron had Miner Two.

The remainder of the ships comprised Strike Force Two, but Tag found that a misnomer. He'd have termed it Escort Force; it included hundreds of freighters of every imaginable size, shape, and hauling configuration, plus the two captured Naplian mining complexes that dwarfed all comers. The only warships were the heavy cruisers TSS Confiance and TSS Independence, plus the destroyers TSS Soldati and TSS Kashin, accompanying six Briddarri vessels led by Admiral Ergen's battleship Winter Scourge.

"All fighters, this is Wing Commander Chok. Keep your eyes

open and your sensors trained for Naplian fighters. Commodore Ram will take care of whatever warships are still hanging around Baedecker Four. Anything comes up out of the atmosphere, we're to knock it down. Understood?"

"You got it, Mongoose," Tag said. "Make sure you share with us—no sense in being a glory hog when there's plenty of targets."

"I'll set aside a spare warship for you, if that'll do, Tag."

***

The raid had to be precisely timed.

Strike Force One cut its ripwave generators 4 light-seconds from Baedecker Two. Intelligence provided by the Briddarri scouts was spot on—three Naplian squadrons of six vessels each, plus one of 12 battlecruisers, for 48 enemy ships. Most of them were spread throughout the immediate gravitational sphere of the planet, with the cruisers paired up as escorts for mining complexes.

Commodore Yost of the Reittian Battlegroup Five, Twelfth Fleet, struck the moment the vessels stood down from ripwave.

Dozens of salvos of missiles swarmed Naplian targets, and at that close range of 1.2 million kilometers evasion was difficult at best. Two light cruisers were destroyed in that first salvo, and two heavy cruisers crippled.

"Send to Strike Force Two—we have engaged the enemy." Yost turned his chair at the center of the bridge aboard *IRD Wolverine*, his flagship and one of the Reittian carries. All three squadrons of fighters dove into space, heading toward the mining complexes with orders to cause as much chaos as possible. "Tactical, watch for a response from Baedecker Four. I do not want us caught with our eyes turned the wrong way when they show up."

"Yes, sir."

"Signal the Terrans in our group: have them vector off to guard possible approach routes from Baedecker Four."

The Naplians, though caught unawares, were no slouches. The battlecruisers grouped into formations of three within the first moments of the attack. Yost admired their precision—even if it made them easier targets.

The next wave of missiles did less damage. Whatever it was about those Naplian ships that made them shudder and shiver out of existence, thus confounding Reittian scanners, proved maddening to both the targeting computers and the tactical officers operating them.

Yost checked the timers. Their FTL communications reached Strike Force Two instantly. As soon as the rest of the Naplians showed up to play, Commodore Ram could implement the other half of their plan.

"Incoming fire, sir!"

Yost nodded. Now the battle had begun.

***

Admiral Bouchtok surveyed the holographic display of the battle from *Catinal*'s bridge. This was certainly different than the Terran's usual approach. He had to admit, he'd become used to their slashing raids conducted with a handful of ships and a few fighters. But 32 warships?

And the cursed Briddarri were with them.

"Send to Admiral Daviont: we've engaged the main body of Terran forces and their allies," Bouchtok said. "Situation is— manageable, but we request further support. The sooner we crush them here, the better."

Manageable. Less than a couple minutes had transpired, and he was down five ships. Those losses brought the odds perilously close to even. That was not the Naplian way. From Day One at the academy, he'd been drilled in the twin naval principles of technological and numerical advantage. That is what ensured Naplian victory, and was the basis for their entire drive into this corner of the galaxy.

Well. They'd soon regain that advantage.

***

A light flashed across Tag's board. One minute. The ripwave generator produced a low hum that vibrated his Warhawk.

"All craft, we've received word from Commodore Yost that the Naplians have called for reinforcements from Baedecker Four. Ready to ripwave on my mark."

Tag grinned. Wait until they get a load of this."

The timer spun down, and at Commodore Ram's sharp "Mark!" Tag engaged the drive.

His fighter, and the rest of Strike Force Two, leapt for home.

Admiral Daviont paced the command center of *Narsa*, watching the first scans trickle in from Baedecker Two. The Terrans had managed an effective surprise. Bouchtok was out of his element. The man was a steady commander, but when things became chaotic, he often couldn't see through anything other than one eye. The Terrans and their allies—Daviont spared a moment to curse the Briddarri to the deepest depths of the darkest black hole—kept shifting their vectors, and switching targets. Those Briddarri fighters were everywhere, like blood-sucker *iyiris* bugs, with human heavy fighters that did considerable damage close up to the Naplian warships.

The advantage of micro-jumping to confound enemy sensors would not be enough, especially against the wicked ECM of the Terran missiles.

Daviont made a goal right then of capturing and dissecting the next Terran ship they could cripple to find out what gave their ECM the advantage over the other races Naplia had conquered.

"We'll be at the battle site in a minute and a half, Admiral," Captain Kentondi said. "Missiles are prepped. Fighters holding for launch."

"Wait to fire until we assess the situation," Daviont said, "And cut us to sublight speeds in 50 seconds. Send to the fleet: stagger by threes."

"Yes, Admiral."

Daviont had brought the 1st and 3rd Colonial Squadrons with him—24 battlecruisers, including the reinforcements that had arrived in-system within the week. More than adequate.

Provided the Terrans didn't have any more surprises waiting for them.

***

The blue and brown ball of Baedecker Four exploded into view. Tag sucked in a breath. They'd dropped from ripwave 2 light-seconds out—risky, but it had worked without any of their ships overshooting. That was the warships, of course. The transports were dropping out twice the distance away, and proceeding by sublight to orbit. They simply could not maneuver with the precision of a warship.

And speaking of warships...

"Five contacts, bearing three three eight mark oh nine four," Princess said. "Naplian battlecruisers. They've still got the bombards and the transports hanging in far orbit, around the planet's rim."

Tag saw them, and so did Admiral Ergen. The Briddarri

ships unloaded salvos of missiles, heading straight in for their opponents at high sublight acceleration. His hands itched to drop some R-18s of his own, but Tag suppressed the reflex. "Stick to your positions. We hold for the mining complexes to catch up, and we follow them down. Watch for fighters."

TSS Confiance and the other three Terran ships took up long, arcing courses that brought them around the other side of the planet, right into the Naplians' backside. Their missiles rode the gravity well around Baedecker Four, acceleration screaming by the time they came up against the rear echelon of the Naplian ships. Two of the battlecruisers were caught between those salvos—one had its jump sails ripped off and its hull split in two, and the other came apart in the silent blinding fury of a reactor gone critical.

The other three battlecruisers fought ferociously, scoring hits on the combined Terran-Briddarri task force, but by the time they responded the Briddarri were close enough in the fight became a knife duel with particle cannon. Commodore Ram's heavy cruisers and destroyers added their railgun to the mix, exploiting weak points opened in Naplian shields by the Briddarri guns.

The transports and bombards lumbered away from the fight, but with their poor acceleration they couldn't get far enough fast enough. Briddarri fighters led by Wing Commander Happar cut across their escape route and through their flotilla. It wasn't long before a bombard vessel exploded.

A proximity alert chimed on Tag's display. *The transports are here.*

"All squadrons, find your escorts," Chok said. "Nova and Axe Squadrons have point. Let's go save our people."

Cheers erupted across the intra-comm. Tag lit up the sublights, and watched with pride as the rest of Bronze Squadron did the same. Their mining complex moved at a good clip with its holds nearly empty.

Nova Squadron's Warhawks and Axe Squadron's Raiders led the way, with freighters streaming in behind them. Their makeshift and mostly civilian armada dwarfed anything Tag had seen in his lifetime—and, he guessed, that went double for his pilots.

Baedecker Four loomed ahead, flashes from the warship battle behind its broad curve. Tag grinned. *We're coming, Marney, for you and Father.*

***

Sirens blared across Vossberg City. General Wood dropped his razor into an open bowl of water and hustled out of his tent, daubing shaving cream from his chin.

The camp around the power station was orderly these days, though there were far fewer supply crates of ammo, food—well, just about everything. But the men and women there had repelled every attempt by the one-eyes to dislodge them.

He grinned. Every novafired time.

"Sir!" One of his adjutants ran up, boots kicking up dust. His uniform was stained with sweat, like everyone else's in camp. "They're coming down! The Naplians are scrambling fighters."

"Outstanding. Get the comms gear up."

Wood followed the young man to the six-wheeled troop transport that housed the command communications gear. The view through the propped open hatch reminded him of a cave. Three women and one man were crammed inside a dark space lit up by the pale blue and green glow of their screens.

Naplian fighters screeched overhead. Wood counted at least three squadrons, and more sounded like they were taking off from the former Vossberg Terminal. He grimaced. Nothing like cutting this close.

"The message is coded private and sensitive, keyed to your decryption, sir," the lieutenant said.

Wood leaned over one woman's console and let the interface scan his retina. Then he input his nine-digit code. The scramble of letters, numbers and pictographs converted into readable text.

"'Bout time," Wood muttered. "Have you got Major Bond on the secure channel?"

"Yes, sir." The woman swiped a screen, tapped a panel, and gestured thumbs-up with her right hand.

"Frand, the show's started. Sobban is right on schedule. Take your battalion around to Castillo Fields. Looks like the landers are coming down on the plains just across Banner Canyon, so the bridge there is your objective."

"Quite right, General, though I pray we're not leaving you too short handed should the Naplians choose to strike the main base."

"You let me worry about that. Our job's to get the civilian

population to safety. I'm sure Sobban can spare some transports for us ground-pounders. Double time, Major."

"Yes, sir."

The comm clicked off. Wood brought up a tactical display. An entire wing of Terran starfighters were coming down through the atmosphere. Hundreds of other transports, every tramp and hauler imaginable, were right behind them, hanging at the fringe where air met space, along with two of the most massive vessels Wood had ever seen. The Naplians rose in waves to meet them.

"You got a good view for me of Major Bond's position?"

"One moment, sir. Drone eye view coming up."

Another screen showed a stream of hover-tanks sprinting out of four gullies to the south of Vossberg, plumes of dust trailing their wakes. Wood grunted. The only way he could get his tanks that close to Vossberg without trying to break the stalemate over the Santos bridge was to sneak a few at a time, under cover of darkness, into those gullies. And it had worked—somewhat to his surprise, because he figured the Naplians would have pounced on them at least once. But Major Bond's suggestion to move them at the slowest pace, allowing the hover engines to run nearly silent, paid off.

"Back trace the secure link to Commodore Ram," Wood said. "Tell him we're standing by to provide ground fire, should he need it."

"Yes, General."

More fighter engines screeched. Wood peered outside. There went another squadron rising high over the plains to the north.

Whoever was up there bringing the transports in, they'd better be good.

***

Six Naplian squadrons swept in, and Wing Commander Chok gave them permission to shoot every last one down.

Tag was ready. "Bronze Squadron, this is Lead. Break off in pairs and engage, but don't stray too far off the approach vectors of the transports. If they draw us out far enough that leaves them open to Naplian bombers."

"Roger, Lead."

The first Naplians didn't waste any time—missiles streaked in at the Terran fighters. Tag and Princess knocked down a handful with their point defense lasers, and the rest of Bronze Squadron did likewise. Tag pulled his Warhawk into a loop and dropped onto the tail of the nearest Naplian, with Princess hanging off his starboard wing.

"Incoming fire," she said.

Tag juked off course. The counter-fire from the Naplian missed. Tag returned the gesture with his railgun.

White-hot projectiles tore the fighter to shreds.

They swung back. A Naplian fighter-bomber, bigger and broader than its claw-winged cousins, was chasing down a pair of Raiders. Looked like he had a pair of frag missiles, big bulky suckers, strapped to his gut.

"Light him up," Tag said.

Together he and Princess launched an R-18 missile each. The weapons corkscrewed in and up toward the bomber. Whoever was manning the defensive guns aboard the thing was good—his shots took down both missiles before they could impact.

Didn't bother Tag all that much, because his railgun fire combined with Princess's ripped the bomber apart. Its payload detonated a half klick out. Tag flew through the ball of smoke and fire.

Below them, the Luran Plains spread out, brown and barren. Vossberg City poked up on the horizon. Even from this extreme distance, Tag could make out fewer towers than he remembered, and of the ones remaining, only a handful were spared damage. The city was more black and gray than shining silver.

Marney and Father had to be out there, somewhere. He couldn't think of them as being dead.

"Picked up a tail, Bronze Leader." That was Cage—Bronze Nine. "Could really use some help shaking him!"

Tag checked his sensors. He and Princess were closest. Where was Bronze Ten? "Cage, this is Lead. Any sign of Yammer?"

"Negative, Lead, and I've been way too busy to ask around!" Static flared across the open channel. "...firing on me!"

"C'mon, Princess." Tag banked hard to left. A Naplian fighter exploded nearby, showering him with debris, but Tag ignored the jostling. Cage was a kilometer out, and turning in a broad arc. His indicator on Tag's display twisted, but the red arrow following him couldn't be dissuaded.

"What's your play, sir?" Princess asked.

"Take lead. I'll line up on your six." Tag grinned. "One for

Two."

"Ah, good. I've been wanting to practice that one for some time now."

Princess accelerated ahead of Tag. He dipped into her wake, close enough that his Warhawk was hidden by her sensor profile but far back enough to receive no more than a moderate rocking from her engine wake.

They came at Cage and his pursuer as if they were crossing a T. Princess opened fire with her railgun, staying on steady course.

The Naplian veered off from Cage and dove head on to Princess, pounding at her shields with energy cannon. Green flashes rippled all around her. Tag targeted her with the reticle for his missiles. It flashed red and then went black, the computer balking at the prospect of lining up a shot on a friendly.

"Easy, I know what I'm doing." Though in all fairness, he knew Scrape would have protested far more loudly than the computer.

Princess's shields fell below 75 percent of their capacity, and she veered abruptly up and to starboard—which invited the Naplian to follow this new target that showed apparent fear. It turned accordingly.

And Tag launched a missile smack into its starboard wing.

The Naplian blew up with a flash so bright Tag's cockpit canopy dimmed by several orders of magnitude to prevent temporary blinding. He flew past and came up on Cage's wing. The Warhawk was singed black in several places, and by Tag's sensor estimate had its shields reduced to 21 percent. "How're you holding up, Nine?"

"Way better now that you're here, Captain!" Cage's voice shook, whether from adrenaline or anger or both, Tag couldn't guess. "Found Ten. He ran off after a one-eye bomber. Dumbass missed, too, but he commed me, said he's on his way back."

Princess settled onto Tag's wing, back a couple hundred meters to provide cover. Cage's shields began a steady uphill tick as they regenerated. Tag relaxed a bit. "I'll handle Yammer. Stick with us until he forms up. Meanwhile how's about we knock down a few more alien birds?"

"Affirmative, Lead," Princess said.

Cage chuckled. "I'm game!"

***

Wood strapped on his body armor and plucked his M36 from his tent. The Naplian rifle he'd taken from the fight at the governor's compound a month ago sat propped in the corner. It'd long since run out of power cells, and they didn't have any more Naplian tech to bring it back up. No loss. He preferred the flechette rifle with which he'd trained ever since he was a green private.

"What's the situation, Major?" He spoke into his communicator as he hustled to the front lines of the power station.

Major Bond's signal was shot through with static and weapons fire. "Making progress, General, but I daresay they're onto us. ...have a couple companies' worth of mechs and troops over here, holding fast to the other side of the bridge...use some fire support."

"Hang tight, Frand, I've got a couple things up my sleeve." Wood switched frequencies. "Comms? Get me the wing commander up there. Relay it through *TSS Confiance* if you have to."

"Yes, sir!"

The line clicked over. "This is Wing Commander Chok. I'm occupied at the moment, General."

"Yeah, well aren't we all? Look, I've got tanks skimming up to Banner canyon. They can hold the ground there for your landing but they've run into a one-eye armor group. That group would be a lot easier to get past if they were smoking craters, you follow?"

"I do indeed, and I have just the solution for you. I'll send a pair of squadrons down—might help us clear the skies of our infestation, too."

"Much obliged, Commander. Wood out."

Good. While it helped his armored spearhead out, that didn't mean Wood was going to sit on the sidelines. He reached the front of the power station, and the barricades atop the short switchback road leading to the upper end of the Santos ridge. "Ready, boys and girls?"

A dozen hover-tanks and piles of troops were gathered there, interspersed with mobile artillery and a handful of mechs. Wood patted the leg of one of the 4-meter tall colossi.

"Ready, General." One of his officers handed him a pair of binoculars. "Some of them are drawing off, see? Behind their barricades, a couple blocks to the rear. Must be headed over to see the ruckus Major Bond's kicking up."

"Not for long." Wood gestured. "Captain! Open up with the artillery!"

Booms rent the air and echoed across the plains as the mobile artillery fired mag-rail projectiles into the Naplian lines. A half-demolished office building, standing just beyond the enemy, crumbled in a wave of dust and smoke. Naplian tanks and transports were obliterated behind their barricades as the hypervelocity tungsten projectiles ripped through the front ranks.

"That'll do it! Open gaps in the shield and get in there!"

The shield shivered in four randomly spaced openings, wide enough to admit two hover-tanks side by side. They raced as fast as they could down the road, followed by troops on hover-sleds.

Wood grabbed the strap of a passing sled and hoisted himself aboard. Wind tugged at his fatigues. He'd be spaced if he was going to let the one-eyes keep the people of Vossberg trapped for one second longer.

***

Wing Commander Chok assigned Bronze Squadron and Halberd—a squadron of 12 Raiders—the task of air support for Major Brand's hover-tank assault. Tag was happy to fulfill the order.

The Warhawks swooped in low over the plains, shadows flitting across the 30-kilometer-long gash that was Banner Canyon. Ahead, the Terran hover-tanks were trading shots with Naplian mechs and tanks. The mechs Tag remembered well enough from that frenetic night spent fleeing the governor's compound, though from up here they looked about as dangerous as spiders under a boot. The tanks were of a similar shape, generally round and domed, with thick armor plating all around and four hover units, one perched on each corner. Green energy blasts pelted the Terran forces at a greater rate of fire than they could manage with their railgun cannon.

"Bronze pilots, go for that first line of one-eye tanks," Tag said. "Follow me in. Halberd, your crew can hammer the mechs behind them, wherever you've got the greatest concentration. All units, dig me some holes."

Tag grinned and lined up two of his missiles. The targeting computer gave him a pile of red marks to choose from.

He dove flat for the plains, and pulled up only a hundred meters from the ground. Dust billowed in his wake. Had to give Princess credit—she never left his wing, matching his every move.

The targeting computer beeped. Tag fired both missiles.

The first struck a pair of hover-tanks nearest the bridge, blasting them into a blackened crater. The second hit behind another trio that had just moved forward. The shockwave destroyed one and sent the other two tumbling to the lip of the canyon, where they disappeared over the edge.

Princess's missiles added to the destruction, and the two of them opened up with their railguns, taking out another pair of tanks as they zipped over the enemy formation. Tag's displays showed the rest of Bronze Squadron and the Halberd Raiders dropping their bombloads across the armored group, and for a few seconds Tag couldn't see anything below them but dust clouds and explosions.

"Come around for a second pass—assuming our Halberd buddies left us anything to chew on," Tag said.

"Affirmative, sir. It looks as though near half the targets have been eliminated."

"Half don't mean all!" Cage whooped through the intra-comm. "Sir, did you see that?"

"Cut the chatter, Nine." Despite chiding him, Tag couldn't erase his own grin. Nothing like giving the invaders a taste of their own medicine. "Keep Ten on your wing and form up for the next pass."

Sporadic fire reached up for them, but whoever was in charge down there split their targets between the Terran fighters and the hover-tanks. Tag saw the CDF commander on the ground had ordered his tanks across the bridge, and they skimmed the surface, in twos and fours, shooting into the confusion among the Naplian group.

The second pass was all that was needed. Tag stuck to his railgun and destroyed three more tanks; Princess, one. By the time the Raiders hit with the remainder of their bombs, the Naplians were reduced to a bare sixth of their force—and the CDF tanks tore into their ranks.

"This is Bronze Squadron to CDF units on the ground," Tag said. "Your path is clear."

"Bronze, this Major Frand Bond, Six-Five Armored Division Texans, Fourth Strike Team. Ta and thanks very much for a good show. We'll clean them up. Keep a weather eye for any Naplian droppings from their birds, will you?"

"Ten-four, Major." A coded message spooled in through his display: Wing Commander Chok. Stragglers from the aerial battle were headed toward Vossberg. "Look alive, Bronze pilots—we've got one-eyes inbound. Bring it around and keep them away from the canyon area."

Far above, hundreds of tiny streaks of fiery light burned through the sky. Tag started for a moment, thinking they were under some sort of bombardment, but calmed when he realized it was the orbital jumpers under Colonel Macken. Each streak was an individual jumper armored up just like the gorilla suits he'd seen pulling the Naplian prisoners around *Independence*'s hangar bay.

As they neared ground, the flames dissipated and pale gray wings blossomed from their backs. Tag's sensors zoomed in on one suit of armor, showing him a bruiser complete with an attached railgun, automatic rifle, and jetpack propelling it in a rough, fast flight down.

"And Major Bond? We invited some pals of ours to your party." Tag grinned. "Hope you approve."

CHAPTER TWENTY-ONE

lden stood on a ridge overlooking the Hessian, with Goetz at his right hand side and Rett at his left. The ground below them was scoured of sand by truck tracks and hover-vehicle paths. A fleet of 30, mostly comprised of sleds from Hessian's holds, were lined up in neat rows of eight outside open bay hatches. Truppen unloaded boxes from the sleds and from a handful of trucks, and carried them into the waiting transport.

"How soon until everything and everyone is evacuated?" Elden asked.

"An hour," Goetz said. "You're sure about this?"

"Absolutely. None of the monks can remain here. The Naplians haven't bothered the Iwa Valley, seeing as how desolate it is, but once we lift, they'll investigate the area. I won't leave the monks to be tortured and interrogated."

"The one-eyes excel at that," Rett grumbled. "Holo-image implantation—makes a man think he's walking inside a volcano when he's just sweating it out in a holo cell. But the burning feels real enough."

Rett, of the three of them, seemed to have adjusted the most congenially to becoming a Truppen. He paced the ridge, sheathing and unsheathing his retractable blades, as if eager to permanently plant one in a Naplian's abdomen. "Those transports approaching Baedecker Four's orbit. Word from Admiral Ergen is they'll engage the Naplian warships in orbit before they escort the ships down. If we want to slip out of here and link up with the Briddarri fleet, we have to be ready soon."

Elden nodded. "We'll meet up with them, yes, but slipping anywhere is not what I have in mind. Goetz, this transport—is she combat worthy?"

Goetz shrugged, a gesture done with the harsh sound of armor plate grinding. "Moderately. There's a handful of point defense lasers and a half dozen railguns. No missiles except for close range torpedoes in a couple batteries. But she does mount a pair of 32 cm particle cannon—so, destroyer-sized."

"That'll have to do."

"What's the play, Elden?" Rett asked.

"The play is, we're going to Vossberg City to assist in the civilian evacuation. Send word to your commanders—last thing I want to expose the Truppen to is friendly fire."

"All right, I can do that." Rett's voice rose a notch in volume and velocity. If he still had a human face, Elden suspected he'd be grinning ear to ear. "It's about time. You know how long it's been since I've fought the one-eyes hand to hand?"

"Two years," Goetz muttered.

"Two years! I'll go inform General Baesler, if that works, Elden. He's got a handle on the monastery evacuation but—"

"Yes, I agree. Tell him I want our troops ready to go as soon as the transports are full."

Rett bounded down the slope, kicking up dirt and leaping in long strides. Elden could see Erich Baesler's slight form among the robed monks and abbots by the trucks below.

Goetz shook his head.

"Problem?"

"He's nuts. Thinks being turned into these robot soldiers is some kind of VR party game."

"I think he's just bursting at the chance to finally do something his superiors will take pride in, given their dim view of espionage."

"Maybe."

"And you? How do you feel about this plan?"

Goetz faced him. Elden wasn't sure when he'd get used to his bodyguard and friend having glowing red optical ports instead of keen human eyes. "It's foolish—risking fifteen thousand Truppen for the enemy, but I get the enemy of my enemy is my friend thing. They're innocents. Of course, there's another reason we're doing this. Wester. And Marney."

"Yes. I won't argue that. They're the dearest of friends."

"Uh-huh."

Elden ignored him. His memories were clear, and Marney occupied a major portion of them. But he wasn't Elden Selva anymore—at least, not the young man she'd fallen in love with. He was Elden Selva the Truppen leader of the Northern Alliance's last military forces. He had no idea how she'd react if she knew, but it couldn't be good. What he did know was how to use the Truppen.

They needed a war, and he would give them one.

***

Jeopar heaved a box full of books from one of the monastery's trucks. His knees buckled. Before he could completely collapse and spill the contents, a Truppen plucked the box from his grasp.

"Please take care of those," Jeopar said. "There are books dating to the late 19th Century of Earth in there."

The Truppen carried the box away as if it were a ration pack, weighing next to nothing.

Jeopar couldn't bear to watch the contents of his monastery shoved inside the *Hessian* as if they were supplies for a military campaign. It was bad enough having to cram them all into boxes in the hasty withdrawal from the monastery. He could still see the cavernous, empty dome and the long, echoing hallways, devoid of prayer and preaching, of knowledge and service.

His house of God is empty.

"It's for the best," Erich said. "You know we can't leave the bunkers behind, not with all the tech hardwired in there."

"I would have thought wiping the computers would be enough."

"We have no idea what kind of info tech the Naplians possess, and from what Rett has told me they're pretty skilled at digging up secrets others think have been deleted. This is the only way to be sure."

"I understand. I wish no harm on my people. If I thought something could be gained by remaining behind and negotiating with the Naplians..." Jeopar couldn't think of anything to say.

Rett bounded over to them. "General? The consul says we're going to hit Vossberg and give the Naplians a bloody nose. Should help distract them so the rescue fleet can get the civilians out."

"All right. Saw that coming. I'll pass the word. Abbot, let me know the moment your people are finished unloading. *Hessian* needs her engines primed if we're going to lift off soon." Erich signaled to Colonel Diaz and other Truppen officers. "Excuse me."

Jeopar grabbed another box, this one more manageable, and handed it off to the nearest Truppen. Rett helped by heaving several heavy crates from the truck. "Sorry about all this, Abbot."

"Spare me any explanations of how this is militarily necessary," Jeopar said. "And pardon me for my tone. I'm weary with the contemplation of what this means for the faithful who have spent years seeking God's mysteries in our sanctuary."

"Yeah, I guess you would be." Rett moved in closer, a huge crate balanced in his hands. "Do you... that is, can I tell you something?"

"What do you mean?"

"I don't know much about your beliefs, but what I learned after being posted to Baedecker Four is that there's a part about confessing things. You know—things that load you with guilt."

"The old term for it is the Office of the Keys. As an ordained minister I can pronounce forgiveness for your sins in the stead of and by the command of God Almighty. He is the grantor of all forgiveness."

"Right. Okay. Well, with all the Truppen being networked I didn't want to tell Erich or any of them—especially not Goetz." Jeopar wondered if a Truppen could physically show signs of embarrassment, because when Rett dragged his right hand at the back of his neck it certainly seemed as if he were scratching. "The Naplians have this superstition about an alien outsider, someone who they have to keep from being killed, because when he dies, he's supposed to be brought back to life by people the one-eyes call Devastators."

Jeopar froze in mid-motion, a box halfway pulled from the sled. "I see."

"Yeah. We Briddarri know about that myth, and we've tried to plant suggestions at every turn to scare them off some of our operations. So then Elden's here—and I saw a chance to introduce more instability by bringing up the sacrificial tradition. I thought it would be a good way to save the people in Vossberg. But when Elden talked about the Truppen..."

"You realized a greater advantage was at hand," Jeopar said. "Because if Elden were killed there was a possibility he could be returned to life."

"And if he was brought back, as a Truppen, by the Truppen—" Rett pointed at the array of soldiers working around *Hessian*. "That would fulfill the Naplians' crazy prophecy about the

Devastators."

"Elden doesn't know this."

"No. I guess that's why I needed to confess. I misled him."

Jeopar nodded. "My son, it's good you recognized this. 'If we say we have no sin, we deceive ourselves, and the truth is not in us. If we confess our sins, he is faithful and just to forgive us our sins and to cleanse us from all unrighteousness.' So it remains true. I forgive you, and thus does God."

Rett's mechanical posture appeared to relax. "Thanks, Abbot. I know I'll have to tell Elden—but later, maybe, when this is over."

"Every man deserves the truth, no matter the pain it brings. And Elden chose the route of sacrifice, even without hope of returning. The fault is not entirely yours—though you did mislead him."

Behind them, a deep rumble emanated from *Hessian*. Heat waves rippled from the engines aft, and dust swirled out from underneath. "Listen up!" Erich's voice boomed across the terrain. "We're lifting for Vossberg at 1100. Every Truppen and every piece of equipment must be on board, double time! Make sure the monks are secure and given cabins!"

Jeopar's stomach clenched. There really was no going back.

Forty minutes later, he sat by a narrow view port on the observation deck of *Hessian*, just below the bridge. The room was a simple, rectangular compartment that ran the width of the hull, with jump seats and couches interspersed. The bulkheads and deck plates were a blue gray, the furnishings, chrome with brown upholstery. Rett was there, as was Erich and Abbot Sissok and the rest of the abbots and acolytes.

Jeopar rarely flew, so seeing the Luran Plains and Iwa Valley from this high up reminded him of a holo render. *Hessian* turned slowly back toward the Koth Mountains. White peaks glinted in the sun.

"Standby on the particle cannon," Erich said into his communicator. He glanced at Jeopar. "You might want to look away."

"No. It is—was my home, and my responsibility.

Erich waited a moment. "Fire."

Hessian's deck swayed. Blue-white flashes seared Jeopar's vision. He watched, hands pressed to the bulkheads, as the particle cannon annihilated the Iwa Valley floor, turning the verdant landscape to a charred hell. Explosions—from whatever was stored in the bunkers, Jeopar supposed—blew apart hills. The monastery's domes, towers, and walls vanished behind a curtain of fire.

Nothing remained but smoke and ruin.

Jeopar wept.

***

Sounds of battle echoed throughout Castillo Fields Stadium. Terran fighters raced back and forth across Vossberg's skies, clearing Naplian fighters away. Explosions shook the ground.

Antiny Wester smiled grimly. It was about time.

He and Marney were among hundreds of thousands of refugees packed into the stadium. More arrived hourly, as word of Wester's release made the rounds of the city. Wester had no idea how many people were left alive in the city, let alone in the rest of Baedecker Four's settlements. But once the shadows of the transport fleet passed overhead, ragged cheers arose from the throat of every able-bodied person in sight.

"The streets around the stadium are clear of soldiers, Father," Marney said. "We haven't seen a patrol for a couple of hours now."

"Good. They've been letting more refugees in but I had my doubts as to whether they'd leave us be."

"Well they certainly weren't going to leave us any supplies," Marney said. "How these people survived for so long I have no idea."

The tent city filled the entire field, wall to wall tarps and canvases and broken bits of Castillo's stadium walls. A few transport trucks had been dragged into place to serve as a makeshift infirmary. The stadium seats, slanting up in rows like the sides of an inverted pyramid, were stacked with more temporary shelters, so many drab and bright colors packed together it reminded Wester of an intricate, handwoven quilt.

And most everyone was busy packing what few belongings they had, grouping by families or by friends or by packs of survivors who'd banded together when neither friends nor families were left.

Marney issued instructions to several men from her group that had joined them from the demolished mag-rail station, and they in turn relayed those to the refugees. Wester knew it would be difficult to get everyone out, but if they started moving now, they could reach Banner Canyon. That was where lookouts had said the transports were landing, on the other side of the bridge.

"We're ready to go whenever you are, Father," Marney said.

"I need to address everyone. Where's Timothy?"

"He's at the main gate, keeping watch." Marney smiled. "I don't think he's slept well enough for days, but even I can't persuade him not to rest. He thinks of his time imprisoned as less of a hardship than the refugees endured, and so he feels he has to make up for that."

"He'll have the chance to rest soon enough. Here, give me a hand."

Marney clambered onto the hood of an eight-wheeled fire suppression truck, and helped Wester climb up. Together they stood on the roof.

"People of Vossberg City and Baedecker Four!" Wester's voice echoed across Castillo Fields, bouncing off the walls of the stadium. People everywhere stopped milling. Thousands of faces watched him. "Transports from our space forces are here. If all goes well, we will have you off the planet in a matter of hours. But I need you all to stay together, to remain orderly, and not fear what's outside these walls. I don't know what the Naplians will do when they see us leaving as one, but remember: this is our world, our home, and though we have to leave it behind, we will not be made fearful anymore."

Shouts and applause thundered throughout the stadium. Wester nodded. He raised his hands in a gesture of solidarity, but deep inside he was crushed. Baedecker *was* home. And here he was, leading his people away from it.

He hated surrender.

Timothy Ess hurried toward them, moving as quickly as his injured leg would allow. Since he'd gotten proper medical treatment upon their release, he didn't need a cane. "Sir! There's a Naplian unit headed this way—two companies, half a dozen mechs. I don't know their aim, but they're definitely on a direct path to the stadium."

Wester cursed. "Can we block the gates?"

"We can hold them." Ess had an M36 over his shoulder. "There's precious few weapons, but we can buy time if you take the refugees out the back gates. It'll mean a longer trek to the bridge but …"

"That will have to do," Wester said. "Marney, lead them out."

"No." Marney helped Wester down from the truck, and accepted a battered Naplian energy rifle from one of the men with Ess. "You lead them, Father—they know you and they'll hear you.

I'm not leaving Tim's side again."

Wester hesitated. He couldn't do that—leave his daughter there. "Marney, listen to me..."

Another set of engines rumbled overhead, of a different pitch and intensity than the civilian transports and Terran fighters Wester had seen. To the north, a huge, lumbering vessel with a dark gray hull loomed like a storm cloud.

Wester's eyes widened. "My stars."

"What is it? Whose ship is that?"

Wester stood there, staring. Ess filled in the silence. "It's a Northern Alliance troop transport. The kind they used to bring Truppen into battle."

Marney gasped.

"They've come back," Wester said.

***

Hessian reached the edge of Vossberg City in time for Elden to see the obliteration of the Naplian armored group.

"Set us down away from the battle," he said. "As near to the other transports as you can."

"Understood, General," Colonel Diaz said.

There were already dozens of freighters and haulers on the plains across the canyon bridge. CDF hover-tanks twisted their way through the wreckage of the Naplian force, sending the last few mechs, tanks and soldiers fleeing into the city. Squads of orbital jumpers landed in scattered rows nearby, folding up wings and ditching thruster packs. They weren't nearly as imposing as Truppen, but Elden knew enough not to discount the effectiveness of their armored exo-skeletons.

A flight of Terran fighters shot by, gray and white arrowheads on the blue sky.

"No, you listen! Send the code I transmitted to Admiral Ergen, and keep the fighters off our backs!" Rett growled. Whoever he was on the comm with seemed to be arguing his instruction. "The code will confirm my operative status. We are here to help secure the area as allies to the Terran and Briddarri forces against the Naplians!"

"Any luck?"

Rett nodded. Red optical ports dimmed and narrowed. "Briddarri are sticklers for protocol, I'd always thought, but you humans have them beat. Trying to offer help in the middle of a battle, and they're lining up an attack run on us!"

"I can hardly blame them. The last time many of these people saw a Truppen transport it was likely as an enemy vessel."

"I guess." Rett stiffened, and his eyes widened. "Hang on… Admiral Ergen? Yes, this is Operative Everett Lind. Thank the dead warriors it's you."

He paused. "Yes, sir, the reports on these Truppen are accurate. And yes, those bioscans I sent are, too. I'm…well, I'm one of them now."

Another pause. "Understood, Admiral. Rett out."

The Terran fighters abruptly banked away, presumably in search of other targets. "Report," Elden said.

"Admiral Ergen's got word to the Terran commander, so we're okay. Once we set down we're supposed to clean out any Naplians we encounter."

Elden nodded.

"Consul?" Diaz said. "We're scanning a column of Naplian troops and mechs headed toward Castillo Fields. There's at least 300,000 refugees packed in there."

"Whatever they're up to, it can't be good. Goetz, Rett, come with me. Colonel? Coordinate the landing with General Baesler. Have 800 men ready for me in the drop bays."

"Yes, sir."

Goetz, who'd stood by the main view ports like a statue, followed Elden and Rett off the bridge. "What's your plan?"

"To drop in on our Naplian friends, and prevent a slaughter."

"Sounds good to me. I recommend we spread out by octants, give each group independent operational status."

"I think they're well versed in said operations," Elden said, "But the three of us will take 160 men directly between that column and the stadium."

"Hope you know what you're doing, then," Goetz muttered.

Me too, Elden thought.

***

General Falloram was not a Ffawe given to fear. He'd taken the energy lash personally to dozens of soldiers who'd shown cowardice. There was no room for such shame in the heart of a Naplian warrior.

So he froze at the sensation of abject terror that cropped up when the huge armored soldiers leapt from the sky.

They landed in the middle of the street, and atop the nearest buildings, dozens of them blocking the way to the sporting arena. More dropped from the transport that rumbled overhead, hundreds, falling across several city blocks. They towered even over the most imposing Ffawe soldier, and were made every bit of sharp-edged armor. Blades protruded from clawed hands. Railguns bobbed on shoulder mounts.

Whispers traveled through the ranks. The men repeated one *Ffawe-aul* in particular. *Ziura.*

Devastators.

"Captain, remove those beings from our path," Falloram ordered.

The mechs trundled forward, showering the approaching enemy with rockets and energy blasts. But they moved from the line of fire with such speed Falloram was certain his eye was playing tricks on him. The enemy slashed through the front ranks of mechs, tearing them apart leg by leg and tearing their internal workings out.

Falloram and his soldiers took up defensive positions behind damaged hover-vehicles and broken buildings. He scored several hits, but the energy blasts didn't have near the effect on these machines as they did on *shirish* flesh. It took a fusillade from his rifle and the men around him to bring even one down. Whatever armor they had superseded Naplian shells.

One of the enemy warriors stepped onto the ruined form of a mech, and raised a railgun high. "These are the Devastators foretold!" His voice echoed off the buildings, amplified by speakers and translated into *Ffawe-aul.* How did the cybernetics know Naplian language? "These are led by the one who died and was harvested, Elden Selva, the Terran *maranat* who gave his life to free your prisoners!"

Falloram swapped out a spent power pack for a new one. That couldn't be true. The alien outside—slain—brought back by these machines? "Keep up the fire on their right wing!"

Some of the soldiers with him complied, regardless of the fear evident on their faces.

A handful, though, dropped their weapons. They made the ancient Ffawe gesture of warding against evil magic—the first two fingers of each hand entwined and pressed against the chest. Then they ran.

"Hold! Hold!" Falloram shouted.

He might as well have been yelling in competition with a whirlwind. Even as the bulk of his forces, a full third, took off down alleys and side streets. A pair of hover-tanks stopped dead in their tracks.

The machine men—the Devastators, for Falloram could think of no better way to describe them—overran their lines, and in an instant they were everywhere among the Naplians. Soldiers were cut apart and shot down.

Falloram cursed and fired and hurled pulse grenades. It was a fiasco. What was meant to be a simple extermination run had collapsed, between the fighters strafing and this second attack. Soon he was pressed into a corner between an alleyway and a half-destroyed tank. Screams, shouts, and weapons fire overwhelmed him.

A Devastator killed the two soldiers with Falloram, shooting one and stabbing the other. He fired point blank, melting its armor plating. A second later his gun was shredded like foil.

"Metal *shirish!*" Falloram spat on the clawed foot that dug into the quik-crete next to his boot.

"He was right, you know." The voice—no. It was impossible. "I am Elden Selva. Whatever your deranged prophecy says, consider it fulfilled."

Falloram's last thought was that he had failed on all fronts, right before a blade took his head off.

***

With a third of the Naplians running, mopping up the remainder became a much easier task.

Elden was sickened by the carnage, but more so by the fact that it had become easier for him to kill. He'd taken lives for the Northern Alliance—few, but necessary instances. He'd never celebrated them, and he took some solace from the honorable fashion in which he and opponents had faced each other.

This was no more honorable than hunting a fox for a refugee's meal. And simpler. He had not cared whether these aliens lived or died. They were his enemies. They took his best friend from him, threatened the only woman he'd ever really loved, and killed him.

He brought a halt to the slaughter when the last troops scurried away from the battle.

"Want to follow them?" Goetz's dark blue-gray armored

frame was slathered with yellow blood.

"No. Let them spread their panic to the others." Elden faced Rett. "You used me."

"Hey, don't say it like that. There was an opportunity to strike a crippling blow to the Naplian psyche. I had to take a chance —"

Elden grabbed him by the headpiece and slammed Rett up against a wall. Quik-crete pulverized and left a Truppen-sized outline. "Do not presume you can gamble with my afterlife. I was ready. I'd made my choice. And you forced me into this."

Goetz put a hand on his shoulder. "Sir, it wasn't right, what he did. But look at the result. This is what we'd wanted for the Northern Alliance. Power."

Elden focused his sensors on Rett, and perused the schematics the targeting systems gave him—detailed points he could exploit to quickly disassemble Rett and crush his headpiece. That would do him no good, though. He had no goal. None of them did. "The Northern Alliance is a fool's hope, Goetz. For now, there's just this mission. Then we will ponder the rest. Understood?"

"Yes, sir."

Elden released Rett. "Come on."

The three of them walked toward the stadium. Men and women were streaming into the now quiet streets. Diaz was right— so many people, crammed into one place. Elden fought the urge to jump to the nearest rooftop to escape the slow-moving flood.

Dozens of armed men and a few women led the crowd, among them, Timothy Ess and Marney. They had their guns, a motley mix of Terran and Naplian weapons, aimed.

Goetz aimed his shoulder-mounted railgun.

"No. Don't." Elden pushed it aside. He brought his speaker volume up. "You are safe now. Follow us. We're here to escort you to the Terran evacuation ships."

"Likely story from Truppen scum," Ess said.

"I don't expect you to trust us, Commander, only believe what you just saw."

Marney frowned. She lowered her gun. It was astonishing to see her here, beat up Naplian rifle in hand and clad in dirty fatigues, rather than resplendent in a white gown. "Tim, wait."

She walked out from the group.

"Marney!" Ess started after her.

She didn't look back, but held up a hand to dissuade pursuit. Marney stared intently at Elden.

Odd as it seemed, he shifted his stance. How could he be nervous in front of her, when he was a transplanted mind wrapped in a cybernetic battle suit of immense power?

"Your voice," she said. "It's familiar."

Elden watched her through his visual scans, matching the imagery with the memories of her as a teen girl, smiling, carefree, and suddenly she gasped.

He realized his head—his sloped, red-eyed Truppen helm—was tilting, chin down.

She stood toe to toe with him. Her fingers brushed the base of his neck.

"Elden?" She whispered.

"Is your father unhurt?"

"He's leading refugees out the back of the stadium. We thought we were going to die."

"You were. The Naplians would have seen to that."

"Is it… really you?"

He gingerly touched her hand with the claw tips of his. "I promised to keep you safe, and that promise isn't yet fulfilled."

Marney smiled, and once more Elden was ten years younger and unshackled from his worries. Tears glinted in her eyes.

She faced Ess and the refugees. "We're leaving. Follow them."

CHAPTER
TWENTY-TWO

T he cursed Briddarri were imparting their chaotic tactics on the humans from both nations. Daviont had to split and reform his fleet's squadrons several times during what had started as a raid and spread out over the Baedecker Two region to become a full-fledged melee.

Every time the III Corps' combined might had them boxed in, the ships of the Reittians—whom Daviont gathered were sometimes allies and sometimes enemies of the Baedecker humans —chose a single weak ship in Daviont's formation and threw their entire weight at it in a brute force assault. This resulted in heavy damage to a few Reittians and a lost Naplian ship, but also allowed the combined enemy fleet another chance to break out.

After the second instance, Daviont broke his fleet into squadrons again, giving them nominal operational independence, but as admiral it was his duty to keep them all on a leash. Their obedience to his command was of foremost importance. The emperors were not keen on vice-admirals and commodores running about sectors with a dozen or more warships at their command. Easier to keep one man—and his entire force—under wraps.

A Briddarri destroyer exploded, its marker winking out on *Narsa*'s tactical display. Captain Kentondi slapped his tactical officer on the back. "Exploit that gap! Put a squadron between that Terran cruiser and its Reittian friend."

More markers shifted position. The display was a huge mass of swirling indicators and curving lines as the computers not only kept track of every capital ship, fighter, and missile in play but also their projected courses. A Naplian heavy cruiser's main engines cut out, and it continued on its route, twisting without acceleration. A squadron of Briddarri fighters altered course at a hard angle and pounced on it, assisted by long-range missiles from a Terran cruiser. A moment later the Naplian ship was gone.

"They're finally moving off from Baedecker Two." Vice-Admiral Bouchtok's hologram wavered as the signal was interrupted by radiation from energy blasts. "*Catinal* has sustained drive damage, sir. We're not fit to chase."

"Send the rest of your squadron after them and form on *Narsa*," Daviont said. "I'm keeping the rest of the units back."

"Yes, Admiral. Any word from Gol?"

Admiral Hilder's squadron of 12 battlecruisers was out on patrol, deeper in the Baedecker system, when this fracas started. "Not yet. Rest assured, when he checks in, we'll put him to good use."

Bouchtok's squadron, the 15th Dragge, converged with the 19th Dragge and sent ten vessels in pursuit of the nine Briddarri ships. Daviont frowned. They were drawing them out beyond the gravitational pull of Baedecker Two, closer toward the twin stars. Meanwhile the remaining 16 ships—five Terran and 11 Reittians—split apart into twos and threes, with the Reittians close-in combat with their opponents while the Terrans stood off and lobbed long-range missiles into the fight.

"Third Squadron, cleave off six battlecruisers to run those Terrans off," Daviont said. "Keep the rest nearby and watch your vectors—those Reittian torpedoes tend to be fixed with shrapnel warhead."

The Naplian formations adjusted to his orders, and Daviont smiled as a Reittian destroyer exploded. The alliance arrayed against him was down by eight ships, leaving them with 24. Daviont's forces had lost seven ships, with a half dozen more damaged to near crippled, but his entire strength had been 60 at the outset.

Things would be cleaned up much more quickly if Hilder would get back.

"Sir, priority signal from *Dassa*," the tactical officer said.

Narsa shook, and Daviont held to the arm of Kentondi's chair for stability. "Confound it! Next one of you who lets Terran missiles get that close to our shields will be on the outer hull blocking them with armor plates!" Kentondi snapped.

Hilder's hologram sprang into existence next to Bouchtok. Compared with the serene stance of the latter, Hilder was rabid. "Tir! The two-eyes are at Baedecker Four! They've obliterated the patrol you left behind, and they're engaging in some kind of airlift."

Daviont stared. "That's not possible. We haven't heard anything from the planet, or from the patrol."

"Their signals are jammed, and it seems the Terrans and Briddarri slit their throats so fast there wasn't time for any resistance." Hilder sneered. "My word came from the last of our bombards and transports—half were destroyed, the rest managed to jump to the edge of the system onto our vector. When I checked with the ground forces, Colonel Jandiran confirmed the attack."

"Not the general?"

"Falloram's death. Jandiran rambled on about 'Devastators' but I shut him up long enough to ascertain the situation— someone's deployed cybernetic soldiers to Vossberg City."

At the word "Devastators," whispers rushed around the bridge. Daviont caught sight of at least one warding gesture before Kentondi shouted, "You dump that superstitious data from your heads right now! Concentrate on killing ships!"

"I'm heading to Four right now," Hilder said. "We'll scrape the scum off that planet once and for all—like we should have from the start."

"Admiral, I need your battlecruisers here. We've engaged the bulk of the Terrans, and the only..."

Hilder's signal cut out.

"*Siresh*," Daviont spat. "Tactical, watch that Reittian ship— it's lost its escort. Bring *Roya* and *Etincelle* around to cut her apart."

The ships shifted position, and in a few minutes, the Reittian was pincered. Fighter-bombers were shot down with rapid fire energy blasts. And the Reittian's hull bled from multiple impacts. The shields were down.

"Finish her."

Energy cannon broadsides from the two battlecruisers split the Reittian ship at the mid-axis. Ten seconds later the aft section exploded—core breach. The rest of the ship was left a lifeless hulk.

Suddenly something changed. The Reittian maneuvers became more erratic, and the Terrans didn't respond to what their compatriots were doing. The Briddarri turned around and dove back to the main fight, with Bouchtok's cruisers dogging them.

"What vessel was that?"

"Sir, ID was for *Wolverine*."

"The flagship." Daviont nodded. "They're leaderless. Good. Send to the fleet: concentrate on the Reittian forces. Without a rudder they're adrift. Take them down and then the rest."

A new sense of urgency seemed to permeate the bridge. Even Kentondi's mood buoyed—he berated less and complimented more.

They would have these attackers crippled. And then Daviont would end the chaos at Baedecker Four.

**

The communications alert drew Tag's attention away from the skies. There weren't any Naplian fighters left for him to watch for, it seemed—none had appeared for a long while. Down below, thousands of civilians were loading into transports that had settled onto the east side of the Banner Canyon bridge. Hover-tanks the size of insects ringed the area. More were kicking up dust around the city's edge, headed that way. He didn't see any activity at the Santos Bridge.

"All fighters, this is Wing Commander Chok. We're needed up space, on the double—Command is tracking Naplians jumping in from elsewhere in the system. Preliminary scans indicate a dozen warships."

"Blast," Tag muttered. "Bronze, this is Lead: form up on me and make for space. Looks like we've got more exercise scheduled up there."

"Sounds good to me, Lead," said Cage. "Winging circles over the civvies is putting me to sleep."

"I suggest you stay awake, Lieutenant," Princess said. "A Naplian cruiser is nothing but exciting."

"Yes, Ma'am!"

The Warhawks closed up into a diamond flight and boosted for the atmosphere's edge. The sky darkened until it went black, and jewel-studded with stars. And soon after, there was the Terran and Briddarri strike force. A stream of transports was visible in the far distance, white and gray specks vanishing in flashes of light as they jumped out of Baedecker to a predetermined rendezvous.

Tag flew through sparkling debris, the only remnants of the Naplian ships they'd struck on arrival.

"Tag, Mongoose here."

"Roger, Mongoose, I read. How's it look?"

"Not good from Baedecker Six. The scouts that went there

didn't find anyone left. None alive, anyway."

Tag scowled. There were only a few hundred people who'd settled on that harsh desert world, but for the Naplians to round up or eliminate even that many... "And here?"

"Fifty transports are away. It's going well. But we have to hold anyone off until the mining complexes get up. They'll be the heaviest loads."

"Yes, sir. Well, I think we've got it handled."

More flashes rippled space, this time from a different vector —and much larger. Tag's eyes widened. His targeting computer dutifully informed him he was staring at 12 battlecruisers. They looked like a squadron of fighters bearing down on him, only they were fighters a thousandfold bigger than his.

"Novafire," Chok whispered.

The strike force wasted no time. Admiral Ergen's *Winter Scourge* and the other five Briddarri ships launched salvos of missiles, with *Confiance* and the Terran ships joining them a second later.

Naplian missiles came toward them at equally frightening speed. And more shapes followed.

"Fighters! Six squadrons, repeat, *six* squadrons." That was Commander Vollan's voice, from aboard *Confiance*. "Keep them off our backs, Wing."

"Roger that, Command. All squadrons, break and attack!"

Tag sent Bronze Squadron into the midst, and more than 140 starfighters filled the sky with their energy blasts and missiles and railgun fire.

As his shields shuddered, Tag thought he'd better kill every last one of them if he was going to give Marney and Father their chance to escape.

"Picked up a tail," Princess said.

"I see him. You got him?"

"Of course."

Tag's Warhawk spun on its axis. He lined up a shot on the Naplian fighter behind him but it came apart with the impact of a missile. "Nicely done."

"Thank you, sir."

"Watch it, a flight coming from one oh five!" Cage said. "Yammer, back me up."

"Right on your tail, Cage."

Their fighters swung by Tag's field of view, hot in pursuit of the four Naplian fighters that had swept in from starboard.

And just like that, the battle was on again.

***

Elden expected to see CDF troops all around, such as the orbital jumpers assisting the civilians to the transports and the hover-tanks guarding the perimeter. There were plenty of ships around, and as he and his Truppen led Marney's huge column of refugees out of the city, another group of six left, dust whirling around their drives.

What he hadn't expected was the armored vehicles guarding the opposite end of the bridge. From the looks of it, they'd just arrived, and the soldiers at the lead were blocking crossing.

"We can plow through them in seconds," Goetz said. "Without killing them, if you want."

"No. That's General Wood. Let's speak with him."

"Doubt he'll negotiate with Truppen, sir. He's a veteran."

Marney squeezed past them. "Then let me do the speaking. Father and I."

Wester walked with her, glancing up at Elden as he did. He hadn't spoken a word since the two groups were reunited. Whatever the man was thinking, it couldn't be good. Even if he didn't have thermal scanners and life-sign readouts, he'd be able to tell Wester was angry. Why shouldn't he be? Not only had Elden admitted collusion with the former Northern Alliance, but he'd suddenly shown up with his mind plugged into the body of the very soldiers Wester had opposed.

"Halt! Do not advance any closer!" General Wood had a foot propped on the edge of a hover-sled that was angled across the bridge, and an M36 aimed their way.

"General! Don't shoot!" Marney spread his hands wide. "We have refugees for the transport."

Whatever the vessel was behind the armored units, it was bigger than any transport Elden had seen. It dwarfed *Hessian* by several orders of magnitude. And it was definitely not Terran or Northern Alliance design.

Wood lowered his weapon. "Marney? Governor? I'll be space. I'll be twice-spaced. We thought—we all thought you were dead."

"The good news is, General, that we're very much alive," Wester said. "We need to get these people off planet."

"Can't very well get you all aboard and keep the one-eyes

penned in," Wood said. "The Naplians back at Santos Bridge? They took off once the fireworks started over here. Soon as they get regrouped they're coming back."

"That's where these people can help." Marney touched Elden's arm. "This is Elden Selva, and Goetz."

Wood stared. He spat in the dust. "Bull."

"Hardly, General." Elden modulated his voice as close to his original as he could.

Wood shook his head. "This is crazy."

"Let us help. We will hold the Naplians back. I have a transport for my men. With our protection you can get this group gone."

Wood scowled. "This is insane."

"I won't disagree," Wester said. "But there isn't time. We have to do this."

"Fine." Wood slung the M36 from his shoulder. "You're the Governor, sir. Major! Get these people across, double time!"

CDF officers hurried amongst the refugees, and got them moving at a faster pace. Elden raised a hand toward Wester, offering to shake. "Good luck, sir."

Wester didn't acknowledge the gesture. "You didn't have to do this. There could have been another way. You should have walked from the NA when there was still a chance. And to think, I tried to protect you."

Wester joined the tide of refugees rushing across the bridge.

Elden turned, and took the Truppen with him back the other way, out of the path.

He didn't expect Marney to follow. "Where are you going?"

"I can help you." She still had her energy rifle.

"No. Go with your father. We will keep you all safe."

"Elden. You can't. Not again."

"Can't what?"

Her chin dipped. "Can't leave."

Elden looked over her head. Ess was shepherding people toward the giant transports. Ess, Marney's fiancé. "Marney. I will never forget you. But it's time for me to go. For good."

"You have to stop saying good-bye to me." She placed a hand on his arm. "It's hardly the mark of a good friend."

"Maybe. But it's better this way—that I should go my separate path from yours." He put his hand as gently on her shoulder as he could manage. "I'm not—I won't ever be who I was. That man, who loved you and was loved by you all those years past, is dead. This? This is not him, but think of me as a memory. That's all I can be."

Marney smiled up at him. Elden froze that image and stored it deep behind his operating memory. "I'll never forget you, even if you say you're not Elden. I know different."

She walked away.

Elden gripped his hands together so tightly the talons scraped at his palms. He hated having to lie to her.

"Sir," Goetz said. "The Naplians are headed to our position. Our scouts have engaged them, but they'll need support. They're two klicks away."

Elden glanced one more time at the transports lifting into the sky. Dozens more were leaving. Even the CDF troops had begun leaving their tanks, under Wood's orders, and loading up. There was no time to take every piece of equipment. His Truppen were the only people standing between them and the Naplians.

He would not let any of them down.

***

The *Confiance* reeled from a missile impact to its portside shields, and she veered off her course.

"Damage control to Section Six!" Commander Vollan shouted. "Watch those starboard scanner—close up the gap in the point defense!"

Ventilators hummed as they sucked away smoke. A pair of auxiliary tracking consoles had shorted out. Commodore Ram wafted the haze away from his face. "How did our missiles fare?"

"Multiple hits on the battlecruiser targeted, Captain. She's listing. Signs of atmosphere leakage and bulking hull plates."

"Route all power from aft batteries to the forward particle cannon and tear her apart," Ram said.

Lines lanced out from *Confiance*'s indicator on the tactical display, striking at the Naplian battlecruiser that had hit them unawares. Ram had no visual of the counterattack's effectiveness, but after 30 seconds of a lopsided exchange of blasts, the Naplian vanished.

"Target destroyed," Vollan said.

"Pick up the next one." Ram did not pause for celebration. He was down by two ships—one Briddarri light cruiser and the destroyer *TSS Kashin. Winter Scourge* was beset by three Naplian battlecruisers, but the amount of punishment she absorbed was phenomenal. Just as Ram was certain she would be destroyed, she managed to crack one of the three wide open, splitting its hull from the prow halfway down to the stern. Jump sails shredded, reflecting weapons fire and explosions like shards of a mirror.

Whoever the Naplian commander was fought mechanically, without guile or strategy. It was a bull-headed, front on attack, and it had cost him dearly: Four of the original 12 battlecruisers were gone, and two more critically damaged. Even odds.

Confiance shook under the impact of a hit. "Forward shields down to 35 percent," Vollan said.

"Hardly the place we can afford to lose them," Ram said. "Have you targeted our attacker?"

"Yes, sir."

"Two salvos."

"Aye, Captain."

Confiance's missiles met the attacking battlecruiser's in a swarm of red and blue lights in the holo display. Three-quarters of the Naplian missiles blinked out, while half of *Confiance*'s remained. A few made it through to the battlecruiser and struck home on the aft hull. Point defense lasers annihilated the Naplian weapons.

But a squadron of the alien fighters swept in across the interceding vector, firing off their own barrage. The combined blasts brought *Confiance*'s forward shields down for the barest second—and the missiles they launched at close range did the rest of the damage.

The impact shook the deck worse than the earthquake Ram remembered from his childhood, the one that had brought his skyrise tenement perilously close to collapse. The roof had crumbled, and the floor buckled, but the building held. Here, too, *Confiance* stood firm.

"Compartments Two-Eight and Two-Nine open to space," Vollan said. "Casualty reports coming in."

"Get that shield back up, Commander."

"Working on it, sir. That battlecruiser's launching another salvo, and the fighters are coming back for another pass."

Ram toggled the communications. "Wing Commander, if you're not too busy—"

"Mongoose has his teeth dug into some one-eyes," a voice cut in. "This is Captain Wester, Bronze Lead. "Need a hand?"

***

Tag raced into the midst of the Naplians, and blew two of the fighters apart before they even knew he was there. The rest of the squadron scattered.

Their attention was focused on *Confiance*, and the cruiser's mass had handily obscured Tag's approach. He wasn't alone, either.

Princess parked a missile into a third Naplian, and fired her railgun on a fourth that fled out of range.

"Chase those fighters off, kids," Tag said. "The commodore needs time for his shields to regenerate."

"Bet he'd be happier if a battlecruiser wasn't takin' potshots at him," Cage grumbled.

"That was my thought too."

"There is a spread of ten missiles inbound," Princess said.

"I see them. Nine and Ten, Four and Five—follow Princess and me. We'll cut across their approach and take 'em out. Watch their velocity, the acceleration makes us about as fast as Droma slugs."

"Roger that, Lead!"

Tag and five Warhawks separated from the rest of the squadron, which continued its pursuit of the remaining Naplian fighters that had gone for *Confiance*'s throat. Tag let the targeting computer pick the nearest missiles for jamming treatment. Soon as their vectors went loopy, and he knew their navigational aids were scrambled, Tag queued up the rock bags.

He flew at a T perpendicular to the missile's paths. Four bags launched from the underside of his Warhawk, each one a plastic container the size of a man's two fists combined. They were equipped with a timer and little else—after three seconds, compressed gases blew apart the containers. The so-called bags dumped their payload ahead of the missiles: thousands of grains of sand, in which dozens of pebbles were intermixed. Rock bags.

The missiles hit these expanding clouds of debris at thousands of kilometers per second and were destroyed.

"Captain Wester, this is Wing Commander Happar, Kazh squadron." The voice on the comm sounded as cheery as a guy out on a date with the prettiest woman around. "Our admiral would be grateful if we pooled our resources and struck that one-eye battlecruiser off the board. Seems the commander is a Naplian named Hilder, and *Dassa*'s his flagship."

Tag saw the squadron of green dots coalescing behind his six blue ones. "That sounds good to me, Commander. Let me gather the rest of my crew and we'll follow you in."

The six other Bronze starfighters whipped around onto his vector, having scattered the last of the Naplian squadron that had harassed *Confiance*. The lead heavy cruiser was still trading shots with *Dassa*, the Naplian flagship, and the Briddarri fighters banked sharply in front of Tag's Warhawks.

"We'll take port, and you starboard," Happar said.

"Right behind you." Tag lined up his last two missiles. He ran the sensors across *Dassa*, searching for something useful... There. "Princess, mark and pass the word: we're hitting that indentation just fore of the second jump sail. Check my data stream: it's shielded, but there's heavy damage underneath."

"Roger that, Tag. I'm transmitting to the rest of the squadron."

Tag grinned. He'd never have learned that trick, had it not been for the way he'd seen Scrape program the old Raider's sensors.

The combined two squadrons dove toward *Dassa* as a pyramid, first drawing some of her fire from *Confiance*, and then spreading it out as their formation burst apart into fights of four. Half spiraled to one vector and the other went "below."

Green flashes shook Tag's cockpit. "Watch the crossfire," he snapped. "Don't rely on the computer's evasion tactics, and keep an eye to your acceleration. Cage, your maneuvers are too predictable."

"I'm good, we can hold it."

But he wasn't following Tag's orders, that much was obvious from their wild—yet repetitive—flight path. "Cage, Yammer, change vectors!"

"They got us bracketed! I can't clear—"

Bronze Ten vanished from the display. A second later, Cage's fighter, Bronze nine, disappeared behind a tiny flash among the starry sky.

"Negative signals from either," Princess said.

Tag slapped his canopy. "Stay loose, Bronze. You get picked up by those cannon and you're particles."

They swung around to the other side of the Naplian's drive sails—and put the critical part of the ship between them and the guns. Tag's sensors flashed red at him: target acquired. "All fighters, lock and fire!"

The Warhawk cut acceleration and pivoted as it shot sidelong on its course. Tag launched both missiles, and fired a steady stream from his railguns.

Multiple strikes slammed into the shields, making them flicker wildly. There was a brilliant flare, then nothing—and finally, a bloom of red-orange light from the dark corner of the ship's hull.

"Direct hits," Princess said. "Three missiles."

"Concentrate your fire until we're out of range!" Tag's thumb went numb on the trigger.

A gout of flame shot out of the gap, and adjacent sections of shields collapsed. More flashes erupted from the opposite side of *Dassa*. Briddarri fighters scrambled away, splitting off in their fours again. Tag's sensors blinked; he was past effective range for his railgun, and his weapon shut down, even as it scanned for a new target.

Dassa bled air and debris from both flanks. Its weapons fire dropped off precipitously.

Tag signaled *Confiance*. "She's all yours, Commodore."

The heavy cruiser was near enough now that Ram didn't bother with missiles. Particle cannon blasts lanced out, slicing over and over into *Dassa*, as the Naplian spun slowly on its axis. The resulting explosion was as brilliant as the sun.

Cheers, scratchy with static, filled the intra-comm.

"Not bad for Terrans," Happar said.

"Thanks to you, too." Tag shook his head.

"The Naplian ships are pulling back, out of orbit." There was Commander Vollan again, on the main communications band. "We're waiting on the last few transports—and those mining complexes."

"This is Wing Commander Chok. Well done, Bronze Squadron."

"Thanks, Nova Lead," Tag said. "Need a new target?"

"Let's give some fire support to *Winter Scourge*, she's hard it..."

Suddenly the sky far beyond the Naplians wavered with light. Tag's heart sank. Really? More? "Never mind, Mongoose. I think we'll be plenty occupied."

"All fighters, prepare to disengage and emergency land on whichever ships can take you." No more Vollan—that was Commodore Ram speaking. "The main Naplian fleet has returned."

"Novafire," Tag said.

***

Elden and Goetz tore apart a Naplian hover-tank, cracking its shell open like cooked seafood, and watched as the occupants scrambled for safety.

To call it a rout was understating the defeat. The Naplians who did fight managed to put up a spirited defense, but they were only two-thirds of the aliens—the rest fled. Where they sought refuge wasn't any of Elden's concern. For all he cared, it could be in the dank confines of the same ruined mag-rail station where he spent the past three weeks with Marney prior to his temporary death.

The air throbbed with the pulse of ion engines. The two great landing ships were finally on their way, moving slowly over the city so near to the tops of the towers that everything, from the pinnacles to the pavement, vibrated.

"That's the last of them." Rett threw aside half of a mech. The other half was nothing but a black stain on the quik-crete. "All the refugees are out. The ones who chose to leave, that is."

"What of the rest of Baedecker Four?"

Rett shrugged. "Sparsely settled. You know that. Whomever the Naplians found in the outlying settlements were either killed or brought here. I doubt there's a Terran alive on the planet."

"Then we're done cleaning up." Goetz wiped his hands, claws scraping claws.

Elden was tired. Not in his body—that felt as if he could run for days and never be exhausted. But his mind, his soul, were run roughshod by the death and destruction. Even the time he spent hiding in the wreckage from the occupiers hadn't worn on him as badly.

This was his life now. He was a warrior, a consul of the last remnant of the Northern Alliance.

"Signal *Hessian*, and get our troops aboard. We're leaving."

"What about the rendezvous?" Rett asked.

"I haven't forgotten. We'll meet with them soon enough." Elden heard the *Hessian*'s engines roar as the transport lifted, and headed their way. "Your admiral and I can negotiate in due time."

***

"C'mon, c'mon, get yourselves aboard!" Tag snapped.

The last of Bronze Squadron made their mad dash to *Confiance*'s landing tunnels. Princess's starboard wing scraped sparks as she sped into the opening far faster than normal landing protocols designated. There were only a handful of fighters left, and most of the task force ships had fled.

Only *Confiance, Independence,* and *Winter Scourge* remained.

Tag burned in toward the tunnel as fast as he dared, focusing only on that yawning opening—though the sensors kept blaring the proximity of the approaching Naplian armada. More than 60 ships!

"The last transports are clearing atmo," Princess said, her voice ragged and the sounds of emergency klaxons screeching the background. "The mining complexes are coming out, with another transport on their heels. Not one I recognize..."

"Don't much care! Clear me a landing!"

He cut the engines and fired the braking thrusters the instant he crossed the threshold. The Warhawk's belly scraped along the tunnel, wings dipping and banging, sparks spraying from both sides. If the core couldn't handle the rough parking job, he had no idea how he'd ditch.

But she held. His fighter slowed drastically, caught in the grip of a catch-field deployed by the deck crew. Tag popped the seals and scrambled from the cockpit. A quartet of technicians sprayed the plane down in fire suppressant foam. Steam billowed from the wings.

Tag ripped off his helmet, gasping.

Wing Commander Chok was there. He clapped Tag on the shoulders. "You've done your people proud."

Tag grinned, and slumped against the floor. His butt hit the floor. He laughed, uncontrollably, until tears flowed.

Last thing he recalled was the sting of a subdermal injector and the bliss of the sedatives, before everything twisted and bent around him with the time-slowed stupor of a jump.

***

Too late.

Daviont closed his eye. The enemy was gone—those not destroyed. Thousands of Ffawe were dead, among them, Gol Hilder.

And for what?

"Shall...we lay in a pursuit course, Admiral?" Kentondi's voice was low.

"To what end? We have the planet, and we have the serjaum." Daviont was well aware he sounded bitter, and he couldn't care less. They had underestimated these Terrans—supposed primitives of a backwater world. Many had paid with their lives, on both sides.

And the Devastators were real. Daviont had no idea the reaction when word of their existence spread. Were any left on Baedecker Four? Could they find and exploit a weakness? Or would fear of the cybernetics paralyze his people? It couldn't. The Ffawe would have to overcome.

Meanwhile the war with the Briddarri would continue. The Naplians would defend their foothold. Only now, the Grand Alliance which the Briddarri had built would gain not one but two human nations.

More for Naplia to conquer, he hoped.

"All hail their Glories, Bonate and Benaltep," Daviont murmured.

EPILOGUE

Twenty-Two Days After The Invasion

Seventeen pilots.

That's how many Baedecker defenders among the fighters were lost. Tag had trouble thinking about the number, because two of them were his. Not just men who happened to fly in the same squadron, but his responsibility—his command.

There was some solace in the fact that they died protecting the innocent.

After the memorials, after the last flechette rounds were fired out of *Confiance*'s open hangar bay, and after the final vac-sealed casing was electromagnetically pushed into the depths of space, Tag finally felt he could rest. Cage and Yammer would never be bothered by the Naplians—their bodies were lost in the explosions of their fighters, and the empty casings would drift unharmed through interstellar space for eternity.

Chok took him aside. "I have some good news for you, Captain."

Tag leaned against a bulkhead, and loosened the fasteners of his dress whites. Far too tight and creased. Give him back his flight suit any day. "If it's another patrol, I'll take a pass."

"Not at all. We're all entitled to some R&R. *Confiance* and the rest of the fleet will remain here at the rendezvous for at least another day before we jump to Van Sutton Base."

"Glad to know the place wasn't overrun."

"They managed to hold off the Naplians who struck there. It seems Baedecker really was their primary target—the rest of their forces scattered throughout the sector and kept our patrols occupied while they locked down Baedecker System."

Tag didn't want to think about his home anymore. "What's the word, then?"

"The word is straight from Admiral Tatsura—all battlefield promotions and command appointments are hereby fixed. Congratulations, Captain Wester. Bronze Squadron is yours."

Chok saluted. Tag straightened and did likewise. His cheeks burned when he realized his dress jacket was flapping open like a Vossberg City awning in the desert winds.

"At ease, Tag. You've earned it. I wrote up a commendation for your acquittal in battle."

"Hardly needed. Two men died."

"Yes. And three men and women from Nova Squadron was lost." Chok shook his head. For the first time Tag noticed the lines around his eyes, and the shadows beneath. "Losing people under your command is part of the risk—they knew it was possible, too. But they were willing to sacrifice just as much as you were. They gave their all because they were led from the front, by a person who took the fight to the enemy and didn't flinch when the battle got heated."

Tag didn't say anything. He just wanted to sleep for a couple centuries.

"I also wanted to tell you there's a few visitors waiting for you in the observation cabin under the bridge."

"Really?" Tag's heart leapt.

"There's been transfers of personnel over to the mining complexes and vice versa. The risk is minimal—we're so far out in the middle of nowhere while the jump drives recharge it's safer than crossing a city park." Chok clapped him on the shoulders. "So get upstairs, and say hello to your sister and your father for me. That's an order."

***

Tag was out of breath by the time he sprinted through the open hatch into the observation cabin. Marney's cry and her hug crushed the rest of the wind out of him.

"Tag! You're okay! You're not hurt!" Marney's tears soaked his shoulder. "They told me you were alive but I never thought ... We'd never imagined..."

Tag patted her back, and grinned past his own tears. "Me? Dead? Did you really doubt the skills of the famed Captain Taggart

Wester?"

She slapped his arm, and laughed. "That's you, all right."

"It does a soul good to see you well, Marney, and ..." His throat closed up. "There were so many times I pictured you and Father as prisoners, or lost."

"The prisoner part was correct, for a while, Taggart." Father stood behind her, wearing a set of clean pressed fatigues. He'd lost weight—Tag could see it in the hollow of his cheeks. But the expression was still that familiar one of perpetual determination. Nothing could bowl over Antiny Wester.

"Father." Tag's chest ached. He held out his hand.

Wester clasped it in his own, and pulled Tag into an embrace. "Thank you for coming back to me, Son," he murmured.

"I thought you were lost," Tag said. "That I was the only one left."

"You've made me proud. A squadron commander, and a leader."

Tag shrugged. "Never knew I had it in me."

"No." Wester held him at arm's length. "I never doubted you did."

Tag could have thrown his Warhawk at the Naplians solo right then, and it was only then he realized they were not alone in the room. The cabin was a broad, square space with a set of floor to ceiling view ports on the back bulkhead, each one fitted with a retractable armored shutter. Tim Ess, Marney's fiancé, was there, but so were Commodore Sobban Ram, Commander Vollan, Speaker Zhatkowskii, General Wood, and Colonel Macken.

Tag saluted, all his bravado suddenly useless.

"Blast it, Tag, stand down." Wood saluted back. He handed over a cigar. "Here's to the victory."

"Ah, isn't there a danger in ..." Tag made a gesture to indicate an explosion.

"Pfft. Sobban's disabled the fire suppression scanners for the compartment, and got the ventilators chugging double time." Wood took a puff of his cigar. "I'd say we earned it."

"I agree," Ram said. "One and a half million civilians, all shepherded from Baedecker. Though the cost was steep. We have only a half dozen vessels left operational."

"We'll make sure the one-eyes pay for every life lost," Wood said. "This is just the start."

"What's the word, Commodore?" Tag asked.

"War, Captain. Admiral Tatsura was very clear in his

communique, when we finally broke through the Naplian interference: Terra is re-arming. I'm due aboard *Winter Scourge* within the hour to conduct negotiations."

"The Briddarri are more powerful than either of our governments, that much we and the Reittians agree on," Zhatkowskii said. "I don't like the idea of depending on these aliens any more than the next Terran, but there's little choice. The Naplians won't stop at Baedecker, not with all that serjaum in their hands."

"Sorry, General, but it feels like we failed our mission," Tag said. "We can't go home."

"No, we cannot, but it was no failure. We saved hundreds of thousands of lives. We dealt the Naplians a terrific blow—because not only did we weaken their forces at Baedecker, we killed one of their key admirals." Ram smiled. "More specifically, *Confiance* and Bronze Squadron did that, with Briddarri help."

"We'll make a new home for ourselves, Tag," Marney said. "Don't worry. Once we're settled in and rested, then we can continue."

"Continue?"

"With the fight," Marney said. "Father and I are going with Commodore Ram to speak with Admiral Ergen. Terra is going to enter the Grand Alliance."

Wood sucked on his cigar. "Amen to that."

"What about the Truppen?" Macken folded her arms. "You saw them at Vossberg, General, Governor. There have to be thousands, and a bird tells me there's a Northern Alliance consul running their show."

"I...we can talk to them." Wester indicated Marney. "The consul, Elden Selva—he led his men in defense of the refugees. I believe our negotiations will be fruitful, so that there's a permanent peace between us."

"Sure would be nice to have them in our ranks," Macken said.

"No. No cyborgs." Wood poked the air with the cigar. "I'll be spaced if we let those devils do our fighting—and you'll have my insignia on your desk, Speaker, if anyone thinks making more of them is a good idea."

Zhatkowskii frowned. "I'd never propose or approve such a plan. Leave the Truppen out of this. We can carry the fight without them."

Tag grinned. "All right. Let's make sure the only eye we leave the Naplians with is a black one."

***

Admiral Ergen walked the berths of *Hessian* at a leisurely pace. "Impressive. These boys of yours are just—breathtaking."

"Thank you, Admiral." Elden walked beside him, with Goetz flanking, and Rett trailing Ergen. Clanking Truppen feet drowned out the sound of Ergen's footfalls. "They are a fine force."

"Fine force? They're unstoppable. The honored dead warriors of Bridd Barra are lauding them from the depths of their lungs!" Ergen chuckled. "With divisions of Truppen, the Briddarri and the Grand Alliance could flatten the Naplians in five years or less."

"You really think it can be done, sir?" Rett asked.

"Son, with any luck, you can be the one leading your own strike team. You did much more than accomplish your mission; you brought me a new weapon, and from what I hear it's one that puts fear into the one-eyes better than anything we could manage." Ergen bounced a fist off Rett's armor. "You've done us all proud, Lind."

"Thank you, Admiral."

"Now, Mr. Selva—"

"His title is consul." Erich waited at the end of the catwalk, hands clasped behind his back. Elden didn't know what to make of the man. How could anyone give up the sensations, the sheer power, of inhabiting a Truppen body, to return to something akin to a weak human frame?

Mixed in with those emotions was the echo of the message that had been passed around the combined Terran-Reittian-Briddarri fleet, reaching every warship and freighter. Former Governor Antiny Wester celebrated the marriage of his daughter Marney Wester to Lt. Commander Timothy Ess, Terran Navy, that morning.

Elden would never go back.

"Consul, I'm the one who calls the shots out here, but just to make you feel more at ease, our battlefield command center back in Audrian space has authorized my offer: your Truppen, acting as a special division of the Grand Alliance. You'd be independent, answerable only to the battlefield command, which consists of all our allies. That means Terrans, too."

Elden tilted his head, and wished Marney were here. "Let

me discuss this with my men."

"Sounds like a plan. Meantime, Rett's coming with me.."
Ergen smiled. "Hope that isn't a problem, but if it is, well, remember we're escorting *Hessian*. For your safety, of course."

Goetz made a static-filled noise that could have been a man snorting.

Escorted? By a Briddarri battleship? "We appreciate the gesture."

Ergen saluted. "Gentlemen."

He brushed by Erich, with Rett following like a giant, cybernetic pet. Erich stared after them. "Are you certain that was wise, Consul? The Briddarri won't just talk to Rett—they'll scan every millimeter of his frame."

"I'm aware of that. We've chosen our side, General."

"Understood, sir."

Elden glanced up at his Truppen. Yes, they'd chosen their side. And with this chance at operational independence, there was the promise that someday, the Northern Alliance might be able to carve out a corner of the galaxy for their own.

If he had to destroy the Naplians to do it, all the better.

***

Abbot Jeopar was alone in the observation room. He knelt before a viewport. The stars burned in the deep black. Warships, some huge and nearby, others mere specks, filled his sight.

He prayed. Long into the shipboard night, until his knees quaked. He could not cease, because of what God had shown him.

All this time he'd sought to save the souls of the lost Truppen, to give them a modicum of humanity. Now, alone in the dark cabin, he marveled at his pride. Who was he to reverse death? Who was he to bring a soul back to this realm, after it had left?

Jeopar could not rid his mind of the nightmare—something terrible loomed, a great storm over the Luran Plains. He'd watched it from the Hirrenhausen Monastery walls, thick clouds of midnight blue rolling toward him. Rain hammered the desert. Thunder beat a drum that reverberated in his chest.

The cloud was filled with fiery red stars, thousands of them bunched in pairs.

Jeopar begged for courage. His had long fled.

What had they loosed on the galaxy?

My God, what had he done?

About The Author

Steve Rzasa is the author of three Takamo novels. He has several other science-fiction, steampunk, and fantasy novels, with a bunch more in progress. He was first published in 2009 by Marcher Lord Press (now Enclave Publishing). His third novel, Broken Sight, received the 2012 Award for Speculative Fiction from the American Christian Fiction Writers, and his debut novel, The Word Reclaimed, was nominated for the same. The Word Endangered was recently nominated for the Realm Award presented by Realm Makers.

Steve grew up in Atco, New Jersey, and started writing stories in grade school. He received his Bachelor's degree in journalism from Boston University, and worked for eight years at newspapers in Maine and Wyoming. He worked as a librarian for fifteen years, earning his Library Support Staff Certification from the American Library Association in 2014 —one of only 135 graduates nationwide and a handful in Wyoming. Steve now devotes all of his time to writing. He lives in Colorado with his wife and two boys. Steve's a fan of all things science-fiction and superhero, and is also a student of history.

Takamo Universe Books

The Emperor's War Series
Empire's Rift by Steve Rzasa
Strife's Cost by Steve Rzasa
Counterstrike's Ruin by Steve Rzasa
The Ice Cold Heart by KS Augustin

Aeon Project Series
Aphelion by AR DeClerck
An Enduring Sun by AR DeClerck (Aeon Project Book I)
Dark Star by AR DeClerck (Aeon Project Book II)
Decaying Orbit by AR DeClerck (Aeon Project Book III)
Resonance Factor by AR DeClerck (Aeon Project Book IV)
Escape Velocity by AR DeClerck (Aeon Project Book V)

Ammanian Origins Series
For God and Mars by Shona Husk
Last Run of the Ice Duchess by Shona Husk

Muto Chronicles Series
Rhats! by Kerry Nietz
Rhats Too! by Kerry Nietz
Rhataloo by Kerry Nietz
Rhats Free by Kerry Nietz

Omiata Chronicles Series
Degara's Mark by Amber Draeger
Degara's Bane by Amber Draeger

Also by Steve Rzasa
Mercury Hale Series
The Face of the Deep Series
Vincent Chen Series
Deception Fleet Series (with Daniel Gibbs)
Galaxy Bridge Series (with Daniel Gibbs)